The shining splendor of our Zebra Lovegram logo on the cover of this book reflects the glittering excellence of the story inside. Look for the Zebra Lovegram whenever you buy a historical romance. It's a trademark that guarantees the very best in quality and reading entertainment.

DESTINY'S EMBRACE

Suddenly, his warm lips were on hers. Maggie stopped struggling and lifted her arms to caress his muscular shoulders.

"Ah, Maggie, Maggie," Grayson murmured, showering her face with kisses, "Maggie, I need you."

I need you . . . The words pounded in Maggie's head as his kiss deepened. He needed her. She needed him. What was wrong in that?

He pressed his searing mouth to the soaked material of her bodice. Somewhere in the back of her mind, she heard the cotton cloth tear, but she didn't care. All she cared about was Grayson, and the wonderful things he was doing to her with his mouth and his hands.

"Grayson," she said, her voice breathy.

"Just tell me to stop," he whispered.

"No," she answered. "Don't stop. Not this time . . ."

SURRENDER TO THE PASSION

ZEBRA BOOKS
KENSINGTON PUBLISHING CORP.

For Donna and Ann . . .
the best friends a writer could have.

ZEBRA BOOKS

are published by

Kensington Publishing Corp.
475 Park Avenue South
New York, NY 10016

First printing: September, 1991

Printed in the United States of America

Prologue

Yorktown, Virginia
October 1780

Through the fringes of her lashes, Maggie Myers studied the handful of people that gathered around the open grave. Pot-bellied Father Rufus, the priest, dronned on with his eulogy. The hard, biting wind whipped off the Chesapeake Bay, blowing his black robes and twisting them about his feet.

It's going to snow, Maggie thought absently as her attention shifted to her sister, Alice, and her sister's husband, Manny. *I thought it was supposed to rain at funerals,* she thought.

Alice reached for Maggie's hand and gave it a squeeze. "Put up your hood," she whispered. "Or you'll catch your death."

Maggie tossed her head in defiance, letting the wind catch her mane of strawberry-blond hair and whip it across her face. She had no intention of lifting her hood. She needed to feel the chilling bite of the October air. After all, to feel was to live, wasn't it?

Father Rufus bowed his head, clasping his pudgy hands, and the mourners joined him . . . all but Maggie. She smiled sadly as the huddle of friends murmured in prayer, echoing the priest's words. It was for her sake they'd come, certainly not Noah's.

There was Pete, the blacksmith, his wife, Susanna, and their seven children who lived at the crossroad where Manny's tavern stood. Then there was Carter, the war hero, Mary, his wife, and even Carter's old grouch of a father, Harry. The Bennett boys stood to the rear the group. And, of course, there was Ezekial, the brother she'd never had.

Zeke lifted his head, gave a reassuring wink, then returned to prayer. Thank God she had Zeke or she'd never have survived the last two years, with Noah's illness and his inability . . . his *refusal* to work. It was Zeke who had encouraged her to pick up her father's tools and the soft leather and begin to make the boots herself. It was Zeke who had encouraged her to join the war effort.

Father Rufus made the sign of the cross and the mourners muttered a solemn, "amen." Maggie stood stock-still as they began to file past her on the way up to the old farmhouse where she and Noah had lived . . . the home where she'd grown up.

"So sorry for your loss," Mary Perkins soothed, clasping Maggie's hand.

"Let us know if there's anything we can do for you," Carter followed sympathetically.

When Harry passed her, he leaned and whipered in her ear, "Better off without him, I say," the wizened old man commented. "Just wish you'd married my boy Carter when you had the chance!"

Maggie gave Harry a pat on the arm. "Go on up to

the house and get yourself a cup of coffee. Be certain Alice adds a little nip, just to ward off the chill."

Harry's steel-gray eyes lit up with interest and he hobbled after his son and daughter-in-law, waving his silver-tipped cane and calling for them to wait up.

Maggie received kisses on the cheek and whispered condolences until finally the mourners had all passed and were headed up the hill to the house. Even Father Rufus agreed to have a cup of coffee and a slice of cake before he went on his way. Finally there was no one left but her and Zeke.

He picked up a shovel and dug into the soft mound of freshly turned soil. Maggie squeezed her eyes shut as the first shovelful of dirt hit the pine coffin. On the second shovelful, she ground her teeth. On the third, her eyes snapped open and she reached for the shovel, snatching it from Zeke's hands.

"You go on up to the house and see that everyone's fed. I'll finish here."

"Don't be a slow wit, Mags, a woman don't bury her man."

Maggie pushed back her cloak and stepped on the shovel, digging into the rich earth. "Just let me do it, Zeke. Let me alone. I need to be with him this one last time."

Zeke sighed. "You don't owe him a thing. You did more than most would have. You stayed at his side till the end. No man can ask more of his wife."

She threw the shovelful of dirt into the grave and dug for another. "I hear what you're saying. I know the truth of it. I just need a few minutes."

"I can finish it up later."

She lifted her head, her brown eyes meeting his worried gray ones. "I'm fine. I just feel like I ought to be the one to do this. Now go on with you."

Tugging his wool stocking cap over his head, Zeke muttered something beneath his breath and limped off, heading up the hill.

Maggie flung another mound of dirt onto the coffin. For several minutes she listened to the sound of the wind in the trees and the steady thud of earth hitting Noah's casket. She filled in the grave with shovelful after shovelful of rich red dirt. It felt good to use her hands, to work her muscles. Work always felt good. It cleared the mind, her da always said.

Finally her arms began to tire and she thrust the shovel into the ground, leaning on it to catch her breath. Despite the cold air, she was suddenly overly warm. She stared down into the hole. The white pine coffin was nearly covered. She rested her forehead on her hands.

"Ah, Noah. You finally did it. You drank yourself right into a grave."

She lifted her head and stared out over the bay in the distance. All was quiet on the water, but it was said the English fleet was on its way. A flock of Canadian geese flew overhead, crying mournfully.

Tears stung Maggie's eyes. She'd known all along that this was the way her life with Noah was going to end. So why did it hurt so much?

"I loved you in a funny kind of way, you know. I really did," she said aloud, barely recognizing her own voice. "But we just weren't meant for each other, were we? I was the fire, you were the cold dishwater always puttin' me out." She shook her head. "You never should have taken on as da's apprentice. You hated bootwork from day one. I never should have married you, knowing I could never love you the way a woman should love a man. I should have figured a way to take care of my mam on my own. I listened to you and da instead of myself. 'Course maybe it could have worked out if not for the war and all . . ."

She lifted the shovel and began to dig again. "Should have, shouldn't have, no point to it now, is there? What's in the kettle's cooked. I've got to go on from here."

In the back of her head she could hear Noah's irritating whine. *Where will you go? What will you do, wife, now that I'm gone, now that you're without a man?*

"Well, I'm not movin' in with Alice and Manny like they want me to, I can tell you that," she said, throwing another clump of dirt onto the coffin. "Guess I won't *do* anything. I'll just go on about my business, living here, making shoes, boots, and such. Doin' repairs. Hell, Noah, most of the county knew it was me and not you makin' those fine boots for our army."

With that said, Maggie felt better. She set down her shovel and walked to the edge of the grave. She bowed her head. "Guess it's 'bye to you, then, Noah. God bless your troubled soul. I just hope you find in heaven what you never found here on earth."

With that, Maggie turned away and headed up the hill to the farmhouse. With Noah at peace, maybe she'd finally find some of her own.

Chapter One

Yorktown, Virginia
June 1781

Maggie blew on the wooden dice in her palm and tossed them onto the scarred trestle table. They rolled to the edge, but fell short, right beneath her opponent's hooked nose. Maggie threw her booted foot onto the bench and slapped her knee gleefully. "Nicked! Blessed Mother Mary, Joey, I've trounced you again," she swore as she swept a handful of his coppers into her hand. "Best you go home whilst you've still got your boots!"

The men standing around the table broke into laughter, slapping Joey on the back as he pushed away from the table, taking his leather jack of ale with him. "God's bowels, but that girl's got an arm. I swear she cheats!"

Maggie reached across the bench, snatching Joey's ragged homespun at the collar. His jack fell from his hand sloshing ale onto his breeches and the floor. "What'd you say, friend?" she murmured, bringing his face inches from hers. "I know you didn't call me a cheat. There's only one thing I hate worse than a cheat, and that's a sore loser."

The little man trembled. "I—I . . ."

"Go on with you, Joey," Carter Perkins interceded, carefully loosening Maggie's iron grip. "You've had too much to drink when you start accusing Maggie of cheatin' you. Everybody in the county knows she can beat you at hazzard even with you cold-stone sober!"

Joey backed away from the table, wiping his mouth on his sleeve. "S-sorry to you M-Miss Maggie. D-didn't mean to insult you or nuthin' . . ."

Maggie jingled his coppers in her hand. "No offense taken then, but don't step up to play if you're going to be a babe about losin'. Never bet what you can't stand to lose is what my da always said."

"And damned good advice that was, still is!" Carter lifted his jack of ale in toast to the dead man as Joey disappeared into the crowd.

The five other men gathered around the gaming table, lifted their jacks in unison, and drank to Derek Lloyd, Maggie's deceased father.

"To a fine man," Pete said solemnly.

"May he rest in peace," added Les Bennett.

Several men crossed themselves before taking another gulp of the strongly brewed ale.

Maggie glanced away, wiping at her moist eyes with the back of her hand. *Just the smoke*, she told herself. But she knew better. Lately she was taken to tears, tears of loneliness, she supposed. Even her husband, Noah, had been some company before he died; now the house seemed so empty. Though Zeke had stayed on to help her with the farm, he refused to sleep in the farmhouse, saying it just wasn't fitting. Each morning he crossed the field from his mother's house to do the chores, and each evening he returned home.

Maggie dropped her winnings into her apron pocket and turned back to the group of men, busy refilling their jacks from a pewter pitcher on the table. She pushed back a handful of heavy strawberry-blond hair off her sweaty forehead, forcing a smile. *Life goes on,* echoed her father's words in her ear. *Life goes on, buttercup.*

"So," Maggie said, sweeping up the dice. "Who'll be next? Step right up, gentlemen. I'm not particular. I'm willin' to beat any of you . . ."

Grayson Thayer, a captain in the king's army, studied the tall, lusty-looking woman from the far side of the crowded public room. Christ, she was a beauty with that head full of firelit curls and those piercing dark eyes. Her breasts were full and rounded, forced to swell above the tight bodice of her common homespun gown. Her waist was small, but her hips flared womanly beneath her skirting. The wench had her leg thrown on a bench showing off an eyeful of her slender calf above her wrinkled red stocking.

Grayson smiled as he sipped his port. He'd never seen a woman like her in his life, all rough and harsh, filled with masculine subtleties, and at the same time so utterly feminine. He watched her moisten her lips with the tip of her tongue as she tossed the dice again. He wondered what she would taste like. Cheap ale? Or fireweed honey, all hot and sweet at the same time?

A familiar tightening in his loins made Grayson shift on the hard bench. He'd planned on turning in early tonight. He'd only walked a short distance from the camp to the tavern to have a drink and find some peace from the din of tent construction and general confusion associated with the setting up of a new camp.

The red-haired wench broke into laughter, clapping her hands as she was bested by a tall, blond farmer. The girl seemed to take as much pleasure from losing as she had from winning.

She had to be a whore. What other woman would behave so commonly among such rough men?

Grayson drained his cup and eased off the bench. A tumble with this trollop was just what he needed to forget his troubles. Slowly he approached her, circling several busy tables. Another red-coated officer called out to him, but Grayson ignored him, bent on his mission. Just the thought of the redhead made him warm at the collar.

As he was about to close in on her, Grayson saw the farmer she called Carter lean over and whisper in her ear. She filled the steamy June air with her husky laughter and brushed her thumb against her fingers. "I'll have to see your coin," she told him, smoothing his faded sleeve with her fingertips. "I'll not be short-changed, not even by a friend."

Carter took a step back in feigned injury. "Maggie! I'm surprised to hear you say such a thing. I always pay you . . . eventually."

"I'm not running a charity. Either you have the coin or you don't . . ." She dropped her hand to her hip, waiting.

Carter broke into a grin and looped his arm through hers, leading her off toward the staircase. "All right, but I hope you can sleep at night knowing you robbed a poor man of his last shilling."

Maggie rested her cheek on his arm and Grayson lost her reply in the sounds of the busy public room.

Silently, Grayson cursed as the redhead and the farmer climbed the steps leading to the private rooms above. Grayson wasn't certain he wanted to wait for the whore so he headed for the door.

Outside the tavern, he leaned against a knotty oak and fumbled in his scarlet coat for a cigar. Somehow the thought of the redhead rolling around in a bed with that plowboy bothered him, though he didn't know why. A whore was a whore . . .

He sighed, thrusting the cigar between his teeth but not bothering to light it. He stared up into the heavens above, wondering what his brother and sister-in-law were doing tonight.

A smile crossed his face. Now *there* was a woman. "Reagan," he whispered into the darkness, enjoying the sound of her name in the still, hot air. She was perfect, what with her intellect, beauty, her ability to deal with anything that came her way . . . A pity his twin brother had met and married Reagan first.

Grayson stared up at the dark sky listening to the rumble of thunder in the distance, toying with the cigar in his mouth. He knew he should get back to camp. He had documents to sign and matters to set in order before the morning drill. He thought of the redhead again. What had the farmer called her? Ah, Maggie. Maggie, wasn't it? "Maggie," he whispered.

As if his words had conjured her up, the redhead appeared in the doorway of the tavern. She swung around, waving farewell to someone behind her, the farmer Grayson supposed, then stepped out into the darkness.

Grayson hesitated in the shadows of the tree. Did

he want her? He broke into a smile as he took his cigar from his mouth and slipped it back inside his coat. Hell, yes, he wanted her! If she pleased him, he might well even keep her the night.

The instant Grayson moved, Maggie looked up. It was a moonless night. The sky was black and ominous. Dark rainclouds rumbled in the distance.

"Someone there?" Maggie called. The hair bristled on the back of her neck. She could his hear his breathing. She could smell his shaving soap. "I said, is someone there?" she repeated loudly.

Since the war had come to the South, the woods had become a dangerous place. There were passing soldiers from both sides, looking for trouble. There were deserters, privateers, Tory sympathizers, all out to reek havoc on the little crossroads that dotted the southern colonies. Cornwallis was said to moving his troops to Yorktown from Williamsburg any day.

Maggie squinted, staring into the darkness. If she went back into the tavern, she knew Carter would be more than happy to escort her home. But nearly a year ago when Noah died, she'd vowed never to depend on a man again. She'd made this walk from her brother-in-law's tavern to her farm a mile and a half away nearly a thousand times . . . alone. And tonight would be no different.

She dropped her hand to her hip in irritation. "What do you want? Coin? I haven't any? Food? See Manny in the kitchen for bread."

Suddenly a red-coated soldier stepped out of the shadows of a great oak tree. He was chuckling deep in his throat. "Brave soul you are, Maggie, to be out on a black night like this."

Her dark eyes followed his movement. He was

coming toward her . . . slowly. "How do you know my name?" She thought of the dagger she wore tucked in her stocking and wondered if she need reach for it.

He drew closer. "Overheard inside." He lifted his chin, indicating the tavern that loomed in the shadows behind her.

The soldier, an officer, was breathtakingly handsome with spun-gold hair and a lean, hard form. But what did that mean? Maggie knew a good-looking man could harm her as well as any. "Step aside, sir, and let me pass. I've a man to get home to." She never told strangers she lived alone. In times like these, it would be taken as an open invitation.

"Now, now, what's your hurry?" Grayson was close enough to make out the oval lines of her face, to detect the scent of her hair. She smelled like fresh-cut hay, sweet and pungent.

"I said, I've my man to attend to. I just came to bring my sister a loaf of—"

"You've got no man," Grayson interrupted. "I saw you inside with the farmers playing hazzard. You're a damned fine caster."

Maggie eyed the redcoat, unsure of what to make of him. He was still moving toward her, but her gut instinct told her he meant her no harm. "What, you having nothing better to do," she glanced at his insignia, *"Captain,* then spy on innocent women?"

Grayson reached for a lock of her wavy bright hair; she made move to back away. "Ah, a woman for certain, but for certain, no innocent."

She watched him lift the long lock of hair and bring it to his lips. "I beg of your pardon, sir. Now step aside, else I'll call for help."

Grayson watched her rosy lips move as she spoke. Christ, she made him hot! With one swift movement he grabbed her around the waist and pushed her against the rough-hewn cedar shakes of the tavern wall. He crushed his mouth against hers.

For an instant, Maggie was frozen in shock. This, this *soldier* was kissing her! She could feel his lips bruising hers. She could taste the sweet wine on his breath. Despite his force, his kiss was not unpleasant . . . He brought his hand up to cup her breast—

Mother Mary of God! What was she thinking! This man was a stinking redcoat! Maggie caught him by the shoulders and shoved him backward.

"What the hell!" Grayson muttered, stumbling to catch his balance.

Maggie slipped her hand down her bare thigh and grabbed her knife from her stocking. The dim light from the oil-cloth tavern windows struck the blade and reflected in the darkness.

Grayson caught sight of the knife and threw up his hands. "Easy, easy there, wench. I meant no harm. Just wanted to sample the goods. I've the coin. Whatever you ask." He could still taste her mouth on his. Her kiss had been even sweeter than he'd imagined.

Maggie panted in anger. She wiped her mouth with the back of her bare arm. "S-sample the goods! The coin! What the bloody hell are you talkin' about?"

"Your services, of course."

"My services?" She swallowed. Her head was in a muddle. She could still taste his mouth on hers. She was ashamed. She'd let a bloody redcoat kiss her and she'd nearly liked it! She looked down at his boots and then at him again. "You want your boots mended?"

"My boots? Are you addlepated, woman?" He ran his fingers through his golden hair. "What are you talking about boots? I want *you.*"

"Me?" She pointed at herself with the tip of the knife.

"I saw you go upstairs with the farmer. Surely if *he's* an acceptable customer, I am."

The realization that the redcoat thought she was a whore hit her in the face in an icy splash. "You son of a bitch!" she flared, brandishing the knife. "Get out of my path before I slit you end to end! How dare you accuse me of sluttin'!"

Grayson took a step back out of the wench's way. "By the king's cod! What are you ranting about, woman!"

"You! You thought I was a whore!"

Grayson dropped a hand to his sinewy thigh. He'd made a mistake. He could see it in her eyes. "M-my apologies. There's obviously been a mistake."

"Obviously," Maggie seethed.

"It's just that I saw you playing hazzard with the men . . ."

"I've a right to play a die same as you."

"One offered you money . . ."

"For my *services.*"

"You took him upstairs . . ."

"To measure his *feet.*"

Grayson frowned, suddenly wishing he hadn't downed that last tankard of port. "His *feet?*"

"Yes, to measure his feet, *Captain.* I'm no whore! I'm a bootmaker!"

Grayson looked away, a chuckle rising in his

throat. "A female bootmaker?"

"I fail to see the humor. I can sew a sole on faster and tighter than any man for three counties! I have to make a living the same as anyone."

So you don't have a man, Grayson thought. "No, I wasn't laughing at you. Only at myself."

"Get out of my way!"

He stepped aside. "I didn't mean to offend you."

"You didn't think calling me a drop-drawers would offend me!"

"Not if you were one!"

Maggie opened her mouth to reply and then snapped it shut. What ailed her, standing here arguing with this redcoat! "Get out of my path," she said in a low, threatening voice. "And you'd best not follow me home, else I'll sic my dogs on you!" Carefully, she eased past him, the knife still clutched in her hand.

"I'm not a man to follow women home." He turned to watch her disappear into the darkness. "It was an honest mistake," he called after her. "I said I'm sorry, what else do you want?"

"Nothin'!" she flung over her shoulder, hurrying down the road. "I don't want nothin' from you," she repeated under her breath, "you stinking redcoat . . ."

Grayson stood for a long moment staring into the darkness, listening to the sound of her footsteps as Maggie hurried down the road. Then, swearing softly beneath his breath, he ducked back into Commegys' Ordinary for one last tankard of port.

Once she was a safe distance from the tavern, and certain the redcoat wasn't following her, Maggie slowed her pace. She could still feel her heart pounding beneath her breast. She wiped her mouth with the back of her hand as if she could wipe away his memory.

"How could you have let a man kiss you like that?" she asked herself aloud. "You're lucky he didn't throw you on the ground and take you right there!"

An owl hooted in reply and Maggie grinned. "You agree with me, do you?" she called to the owl. She heard a flutter of wings and then silence.

She walked around the bend, through Devil's Woodyard, where a lonely man could hear the devil chopping his wood some nights, and up over the hill. In the distance she could see the glow of the lantern through Zeke's kitchen window. She had half a mind to stop and share a pint of cider with him. The thought of returning home to her empty farmhouse was none too appealing. But she kept walking.

She climbed over the fence at the apple tree and stepped foot on her father's land. On *her* land. In the far pasture she could see her old nag, Goldie, grazing. In a circle around her were several deer. Maggie smiled. The war had torn the little coastal town of Yorktown apart. Crops had been burned, wood cut, animals slaughtered, yet still, there was beauty to behold. You just had to look a little harder for it these days.

The sensible thing to do would have been to run and fetch her da's matchlock rifle and at least shoot the buck. It would be a long, hard winter with the British occupying the York Peninsula and no meat in her smokehouse. But she just couldn't bring herself to do it . . .

Slipping through the gate, Maggie walked up the

lane. She wished she hadn't locked her hounds in the barn. She always felt safer when they were here in the yard to greet her when she came home.

Maggie came to a sudden stop when she realized there was someone sitting on her front porch in her rocker. Her first thought was of the redcoat. But how could he have made it here before her? Her heart gave a little trip in her chest.

The figure stood. "Maggie," he said softly.

Relief flooded her at the recognition of the voice, and she hurried up the steps. "Mother Mary, Zeke, you scared the tar out of me!"

"Sorry. I didn't mean to."

"What are you doin' here?" She walked through the front door and down the hall to the kitchen in the back. Zeke followed.

He said nothing as she lit a candle by the embers of the banked coals in the fireplace. He turned a kitchen chair around and straddled it. "You in for a little moonlightin'?"

"There's no moon out tonight," she said dryly.

"There's a wagon train of Tories passin' through the crossroads tonight 'bout midnight."

"So . . ."

"Supplies, most of them stolen from us. They say there's leather aboard. I know you could use it with those orders coming in."

Maggie faced him with sudden interest. "Stolen, you say?"

"One of those damned Tory raidin' parties took it from a farmhouse over near Williamsburg. They burnt the man and his wife out and tarred and feathered 'em both."

"So why are you so willin' to have me along, to give

me a share? Whenever I've asked before, you said no. You said it was too dangerous."

"It is dangerous. These redcoats are going to be livin' in our backyards, drinking our water, eating our eggs!"

"So what makes tonight different?" She lit several more candles on the mantel, illuminating the cozy kitchen in soft light.

Zeke shrugged. "The plan calls for a woman. It was either get you in on it or put on a skirt myself."

Maggie laughed, clapping her hands. "Now that's a sight I'd like to see!"

"So are you with me or no?" He lifted a finger. "Now remember, this ain't just loosening a heel on a lieutenant's boot. You get caught and they'll hang you the same as the rest of us, female or not."

She crossed her arms over her chest. "Where's the shipment bound?"

"One of the Brit camps, I'd suppose."

"Flour, cornmeal, sugar?"

"Whiskey, calfskin, red cloth for uniform coats ordered especially. The goods were in Williamsburg waitin' for transport, but originally they were taken off a ship one of our men sank in the James. You know the game. We take theirs, they take it back, we take it again."

Maggie wondered if the shipment was bound for her redcoat captain's camp. She wondered if it was *his* new coat she'd be cheating him of. The thought was appealing. She lifted her lashes to stare into Zeke's ruddy face. "I'm in."

"You certain? No one will think any less of you if you pass. You do your part for our army already."

She gave a wave of her hand. "I fix their boots."

"Not only do you fix our men's boots, but you sabotage theirs!"

She joined in his laughter. "Sabotage! A hard word, friend."

"Only a woman would think of such a subtle way to make her mark."

Maggie suddenly grew serious. "I've no wish to make my mark, Zeke. Just to see this war end. To see these Colonies free."

Zeke stood and pushed in his chair, scraping it along the planed pine floor. "Then put out your lights, Maggie, and come along. Let's see what we can do for our men tonight."

Chapter Two

"Captain . . . Captain . . ." Private Michaels shook Grayson gently. "Sir, you have to wake up."

Grayson groaned as he rolled onto his back and shielded his eyes from the bright lanternlight. "God's teeth, Michaels, what is it?"

"Major Lawrence, sir. He just got information on some rebel activity at the crossroad up near Commegys' Ordinary." The towheaded young man, no more than a boy of fourteen, set the lantern on the campstool beside Grayson's cot and gathered up several empty sack bottles. "He wants you to take a few men and round up the troublemakers. He's got a shipment of cloth bolts coming in and a tailor scheduled for the end of the week. He doesn't want anything to come between him and his new coat. He wants to look good when General Cornwallis arrives. The major says the rebel bastards stole the last two shipments of cloth he had sent from Paris."

Grayson swung his legs over the bed and onto the canvas floor. He ran his fingers through his blond hair, trying to clear his head. "New coat? What coat? What the blast are you muttering about, Michaels?"

The young man offered Grayson his breeches. "I didn't ask questions. The major was in none-too-pleasant a mood, sir."

Grayson snatched his breeches from Michael's hand. "When is he ever?"

Major Roland Lawrence was a bastard of a commander. He gave no thought to the men below him, only to the task at hand. His ethics were questionable, but he was one of Cornwallis's favored few. He'd been promoted after several successful campaigns under the command of Colonel Banastre Tarleton, the butcher, and now held a comfortable position as one of the many aides to Cornwallis.

Major Lawrence was to be a liaison of sorts between the commander of the British forces in the south and the York Peninsula. His duty, once the entire British army under Cornwallis arrived, would be to procure houses and services, and see to it that shipments of goods made it through to the British army. It would be his duty to keep an eye on the local rebel scum. Their numbers were small, but the band was said to be active. Major Lawrence took their activities as a personal affront and was determined to see them hanged.

Grayson accepted the shirt Michaels offered him. He sighed as he stuffed his arms into the sleeves. "Sorry, son, I didn't mean to snap at you. It's just that this is the third time this week the major's gotten me out of bed to investigate some sort of rebel activity. I never see any rebels." He reached for his silk stockings hanging on the end of the cot. "Just cows and an occasional goat." He looked up at the private. "You think it's the goats after the major's coat cloth?"

down. There would only be one chance. When the first wagon rolled past Manny's tavern, she was to pull out of the cover of the woods and onto the road in front of them. She was then to turn in the road as if to head west, at which point she was to pull on the rope that would release the pin on the wagon wheel. The wheel would roll off and she would come to a halt in the center of the intersection, blocking the wagons' passage. At that point, Zeke and the other men would take over and she'd head out across the field on foot.

The first wagon approached the crossroad and Maggie lifted the reins with her trembling hands. This was her life she was risking for a cause she didn't know they could ever win. Was it worth it?

Hell, yes!

She clicked to the horse and her wagon rolled forward, out of the cover of the sycamore trees and thick honeysuckle vines. She bent her head, thankful for the dark night that would cloak her identity.

Carefully she guided her horse and wagon across the proscribed route. Purposely ignoring the approaching wagons, she jerked the rope attached to the wagon pin. Her wagon kept rolling, the horse clopping faithfully along.

Come on, she thought. *Why doesn't the wheel come off!*

She rolled another half a wagon length. Another moment and it would be too late . . .

Suddenly the rickety wagon lurched onto its side with such force that Maggie was catapulted off the bench seat and into the soft grass on the edge of the road.

"Son of a bitch!" a voice crowed. "You're blockin' the road!"

Maggie sat up, rubbing her forehead. The rifle she'd held in her lap had been flung from the wagon as well, and she struck her head on it coming down.

"Well, get up and get the wreck out of my way!" the man shouted from his wagon. The other two rolled in behind him and squeaked to a stop. "We got king's business here!"

Then, out of the black night came the dark figures.

"Step down off your wagons and no one'll get hurt," ordered one of the men in Zeke's group. To Maggie's surprise she saw that all of the men were hooded in white to conceal their identities. Clever, she thought as she watched from the tall grass.

The man in the first wagon put up his hands in surrender. "We want no trouble," he called out.

Without warning a man brandishing a rifle leaped from the canvas-covered rear of the first wagon.

The crossroad was suddenly a melée of confusion. Maggie didn't know who shot first, but suddenly the air was thick with smoke and bright with white light as shots sounded again and again in the still night air. Men hollered, the horses squealed in fright and leaped in their traces.

Then, it was over in a heartbeat. Two of the men in the transport wagons were dead, the other four were quickly tied up by two hooded figures. Maggie knew she was supposed to be high-tailing it out of here, but she was entranced by the entire operation. The hooded rebels moved quickly, working as one. They acted like players in a staged play Maggie had once seen in Williamsburg. Each knew his part; the timing was perfect.

Then from the east came a pounding of hoofbeats. Over the bluff appeared horses and riders.

"Redcoats!" one of the hooded rebels cried, sounding the alarm.

Maggie scrambled to her feet, picked up her rifle, and rushed toward the wagons. Hooded men were leaping up onto the wagon seats while others untangled the horses traces.

They mean to still take the wagons! she thought wildly.

One of the figures grasped her arm, his fingers biting sharply into her flesh. "Get the hell out of here," Zeke's familiar voice ordered.

"I'll go with you!" she cried. Automatically her fingers found the hammer of her rifle and she cocked it.

"The hell you will! Now run!" Zeke gave her a rough shove and raced for one of the wagons as it rolled away. All three horses and wagons were moving.

The wagon she had driven had been set aflame and left to burn in the center of the crossroad. The horse had been unhitched and led away.

Maggie looked up to see the redcoats coming straight down the middle of the road toward her. With a cry of fright, she ran. She raced through the tall grass that pulled at her hair and tangled in her skirts. Behind her she could hear the British soldiers shouting.

"You're letting them get away!" one of the captured Tories shouted. "They went that way!"

"Damnation!" Grayson shouted as he galloped into the crossroad. He hadn't expected there to be any real trouble. He'd just assumed this was another one of Major Lawrence's wild-goose chases. *Now* what was he supposed to do?

Luckily the dark night and the burning wagon in the center of the road provided enough confusion that his men rode in circles shouting, but not going after the stolen wagons. What the hell would he have done with them if he'd captured them?

A soldier slid off his horse and ran to the huddle of men tied near the road. "They say there's a woman," the private shouted to Grayson. "She went that way!" He pointed in the direction of the bay.

Grayson reeled his horse, Giipa, around and headed straight for the tall grass. Two soldiers followed. A woman among them! Damn, this bunch had balls! He rode through the grass and up a steep bank. Ahead he caught movement. A figure, running.

"Halt!" Grayson shouted. "Halt in the name of the king's army!"

The figure swung around and went down on one knee. In an instant he recognized the red-haired wench. It was Maggie! Maggie, for Christ's sake!

"Get down, Captain," one of the soldiers shouted from behind. "She's got a gun."

Grayson's eyes met hers; even in the darkness, he *knew* she recognized him.

Dear God! She was going to shoot him!

At the same instant that he flung himself from the saddle, he heard the echo of the rifle shot. His face hit the wet, boggy ground and for a instant he was stunned. The wench had shot at him! She'd tried to kill him!

"Captain! Captain!" one of the soldiers shouted, leaping off his horse.

Grayson swore beneath his breath as he pushed up off the muddy ground. There was a sudden crash of thunder followed by a bright streak of white lightning. The sky lit up for an instant and he saw Maggie sprinting across the open field. Rain began to fall.

The soldier crawled toward his commanding officer. "Captain?"

"Yes, yes, I'm all right." Grayson snatched his grenadier cap off the wet ground.

"Captain, she's getting away. You want us to get the others and go after her?"

Grayson wiped his white breeches, smearing the ill-smelling mud. He reeked like a London sewer in mid-July.

"Captain." The soldier slowly rose to his feet. "I asked if you wanted us to go after the woman."

Grayson looked up in the direction Maggie had run. With the next flash of lightning he saw that she was gone. He glanced down at the private peering into his face. "No," he said softly.

"Sir?"

"I said, no, boy. What do we want with a woman? She won't know anything. It's the stolen wagons that are important. Let's get back to the crossroad and see what the drivers can tell us. They'll be our best lead."

"Yes, sir."

Grayson whistled for his horse and the gelding came prancing over. Mounting, he spun around and headed back toward the crossroad, suppressing his desire to glance over his shoulder.

By the time Maggie reached her front porch she was shaking all over. She collapsed on the top step, wrapping her arms around her waist and gasping for breath. Her sides ached from the run. She'd nearly been caught!

She *had* been caught. The redcoat had seen her. He'd recognized her. She was sure of it.

A bright steak of lightning zigzagged the sky, illuminating the field that stretched in front of the farmhouse. The field was empty, no sign of horses and riders. So where was he? Why hadn't he and his mounted dogs followed her? Why weren't they here arresting her this very moment?

Maggie pushed back a lock of her wet hair, her breath finally coming easier. What was she supposed to do now? Zeke hadn't told her what to do if she got caught!

With the next streak of lightning she saw a figure running in an awkward gait through her field toward her. She jumped off the step. "Zeke!" The sound of the pounding rain and the booming thunder nearly drowned out her voice. "Zeke!"

"Maggie!"

She was so glad to see he was safe that she grasped his arms and spun him around. "Zeke! I was afraid you'd been caught!"

He pulled her out of the rain and onto the front porch and dropped a small bundle at his feet. "We're safe, all of us. The wagons, too. You were perfect, everyone said so. By daylight there'll be no trace of tracks, thanks to this." He motioned to the downpour.

Maggie's eyes suddenly grew wide. "Oh, God, Zeke, you can't be here!"

"Can't be here? What are you talking about?"

She wiped the rain from her full mouth. "He saw

me."

"Who?"

"The redcoat. The officer."

"What do you mean, he saw you? He saw a woman." Zeke laughed. "He could have seen me in skirts."

She shook her head. "You don't understand. He recognized me."

"You know Captain Thayer?"

"Yes. No, not really. I mean . . ." She looked away. "Zeke, you just need to get out of here. He's coming for me, I know he is."

He caught her shoulder, steadying her. "You're certain?"

"I knew the risk of joining you and your men, Zeke. I knew same as you."

He eyed her rifle that she'd left leaning against the step. "I could wait. Take care of him for you."

She grabbed the rifle and headed inside. "Don't be ridiculous," she flung over her shoulder. "What, you're going to shoot him and his men and bury them in a row beside my turnips?"

"It's been done, Maggie," he said gently as he grabbed the bundle of leather goods off the porch and followed her into the house. He found her lighting a candle in the kitchen.

She shook her head. "It's not been done on my farm. I won't kill like that. I won't be a a part of it."

"You were a part of it tonight. We killed two men." He dropped the bundle of leather that was to be her share in the raid on the table.

"It ain't the same thing and you know it." She lit a second candle, then a third.

"I can't just leave you here to wait for your own

hanging."

"Sure you can." She pulled her wet apron over her head and hung it on a peg on the back door. "You can and you will. He might just question me. He can't prove it was me."

"Maggie—"

She held up her hand. "Zeke, don't start with me. Just get on out of here while you can."

He flung a fist in the air. "You just going to give up that easy?"

"What do you want me to do? Run?" She poured some fresh water from a bucket into her coffeepot and reached for a tin of grounds. "Because I'm not. I'm not gonna do it. My whole life is here. My da's tools, my mam's roses . . ." She looked up. "Besides, who said I was givin' up?"

Zeke walked to the door. "You're sure you want me to go?"

"Yes, I want you to go and I don't want you to worry about me. I'll take care of the redcoat."

"How?"

"I don't know. I'll think of a way."

"Don't do anything you'll regret later."

Maggie swung around angrily. "If you mean sell myself, I wouldn't do it, and you know it!" Her hands fell to her hips. "You have no right to be thinkin' that way."

"More than one woman—"

"I said I wouldn't do it, not even to save my life! My body's *mine*. You know how I feel about that."

Zeke sighed, suddenly feeling so much older than his twenty-seven years. "I'm sorry." He rubbed the aching thigh of his crippled leg. "I feel like all of this is my fault. I should never have taken you along."

"It ain't your fault. I been askin' for two years to go along. It's my fault because I was seen and because I missed my mark."

Zeke tugged on his scraggly beard. "You shot at Captain Thayer?"

"What was I supposed to do?" She slammed the coffeepot down on the spider over the coals. "Him and that big horse of his was bearing down on me. It was shoot or be trampled!"

"Ah, God, Maggie. They say Thayer can be a real bastard when he wants to be. I can't let you face him alone."

"You know the rules," she answered quietly. "You ought to. You gave 'em to me yourself. No man gives himself up. Not for a friend. Not for his own mother. It's the only way you boys have held on this long." She paused for a moment. "Now go on with you. I imagine the captain'll be here afore long."

"You're just gonna wait?"

"No, I'm not gonna just wait. I'm gonna make myself some breakfast. Been collectin' Myra's eggs. Got a little bacon. Might even scare up a little peach marmalade. I'd offer you a plate, too, but seein' as I might have company . . ." She shrugged, a silly smile on her face.

Zeke hung his head. War, it made people do things they never thought they'd do. "If they take you in, you hold tight. Don't give 'em any information."

"Information? What could I tell him? His shoe size? I don't know who was wearin' those flour sacks over their heads." She smiled. "Though I got some ideas."

"Just the same, you take care. The best is not to say anything. We won't let 'em hang you."

"You better not." She pointed a finger. "Now get out of my kitchen, Ezekial Josiah Barnes, before I kick you out."

Maggie watched him until he disappeared down the dark hallway, dragging his bad leg behind him, and then went back to her coffee-making. She was amazed to realize she suddenly felt weak in the knees. *If they try to hang you . . .* Zeke's words scared her to her bones. Sure, she could talk tough when she had to, but inside she was trembling. She didn't want to have to die for this cause, for any cause, but then who did? What you want to do and what you got to do is sometimes two different things, that's what her da always said.

While the coffee was brewing, Maggie made herself busy in the kitchen. She brought up her precious eggs and bacon from the cellar. She cut slices of bread from a loaf and placed them in a toasting spider. She added wood to the fire and hunted down a cast-iron skillet. Dawn was just beginning to break as she poured herself a cup of coffee and slid into a kitchen chair to sip the strong, fragrant brew.

Resting her chin in her hands, she stared out the front window at the open field. The storm had passed; the dawning sunlight cast a golden halo over the wet field. Every stalk of grass seemed to glimmer.

Then she saw him. The redcoat. Captain Thayer. He'd come for her.

Chapter Three

Maggie's first instinct was to run . . . to slip out the back door and sprint across the field, past the cemetery and on toward the bay. But where would she run to?

Instead of running, she sat at the kitchen table and calmly drank her coffee. She watched the captain ride through her field, up to the front porch, and dismount. It was funny how in the early-morning sunlight he looked like a prince out of a fairy-tale book with his clean white breeches and gold-piped scarlet coat. His face was as handsome as any man's she'd ever set eyes on, and his hair was like gold spun from a spinning wheel.

"Anyone here?" he called as he threaded his horse's reins through the hitching ring off the front porch.

Maggie sipped her coffee, making no reply. Her heart pounded, but it wasn't quite fear she felt in her chest. What was it? she wondered. Anticipation?

The captain strode up her creaky porch steps, surveying the small farm. "I said, is anyone home?"

She lost sight of him, but she could hear him knock on the door. Finally it opened.

She listened, sipping her coffee as he walked into the parlor, called up the front steps, then cautiously came down the hall to the kitchen. His footsteps sounded hollowly in the rooms, seeming to echo their emptiness . . . her loneliness. When he reached the kitchen doorway, he stopped.

She turned until her eyes met his. For a moment their gazes locked. He had the most beautiful blue eyes she'd ever seen. They were the color of heaven.

"So you *are* here." He crossed his arms over his chest, taking a casual stance. "Why didn't you run while you had the chance?"

"How did you find out where I lived?" She pushed away from the table, wood scraping wood, but remained seated. *You're innocent until proven guilty,* she thought to herself.

"The tavern."

His distinctly masculine voice sounded odd in her kitchen. She nodded. *Lyla, the town whore, no doubt. The young girl was probably willing to provide information to turn a coin.* "So what do you want?"

"Want?" He lifted a blond eyebrow. "You tried to shoot me last night. You were caught involved in criminal activities."

"Criminal activities?" she mimicked. "I fear I don't know what you're talking about, Captain. I was here all night."

"You fear?" He grinned incredulously. "You

have any witnesses to say you were here all night?"

"No one but a single hen, a swayback horse, and a pack of hounds. I'm a widow." She drained her handleless china cup.

It was Grayson's turn to nod. "That's dangerous business you were a party to last night, Maggie. My superior officer is determined to catch that band of rebels. This is the third time they've stolen the bolts of cloth meant for his new coat."

"I didn't steal anything."

His gaze wandered to the stack of shoe leathers Zeke had left on her table. "Your haul?"

"My leather. I have to make a living."

"So you told me before."

"The last time the Hessians came through here they took my leather, my cow, and all of the chickens but for the one I hid under my bed." She got up and went to pour herself another cup of coffee. "They steal my leather and then they demand new boots. How am I supposed to sew boots with no leather?"

Grayson's easy smile fell from his face. "You make boots for us?" For some reason he was disappointed. Somehow he'd compared Maggie to his sister-in-law, who had been heavily involved in patriot activities in Philadelphia a few years back. He'd always admired her for her strength, her conviction.

"I make boots for whoever is willing to pay," Maggie responded cautiously.

He sighed. Of course she did. What else could he expect of a woman in her circumstances? Still he couldn't help thinking that everyone had to take a stand in their life . . . in this damned war. Either she was a loyal British citizen or one of the new breeds, an American. She couldn't be both. Selling boots to both sides made her a mercenary of sorts.

He watched her as she set a skillet over the coals. She dropped several strips of bacon into the pan and they sizzled, filling the cozy kitchen with a tantalizing aroma. His stomach growled with hunger.

He walked to the window and brushed his fingers over the filmy white curtains. "So what am I to do with you?"

"Do?" She dropped her apron over her head and tied the strings behind her back.

Grayson was mesmerized by her fiery waves of red curls and her haunting dark-brown eyes. Indian eyes, his grandmother always called them. "Yes, *do*. My duty is to seek out the rebels and bring them to justice."

"Rebels? What do the rebels have to do with a poor widow?" She turned her bacon. "I just don't understand what you're talking about."

He spun around, slamming his fist on the table. "Damn it, woman. This is no game! You could die for that stack of tanned leather."

Her face hardened. She didn't like being shouted at, and certainly not in her own kitchen! "So, are you going to arrest me or not?"

He jerked his hand off the table. What was it about this woman that irritated him and yet fascinated him at the same time? "Give me a reason not to."

"A reason?" Maggie's lower lip quivered involuntarily. She felt like a mouse cornered by a barn cat.

"Certainly. Just tell me why I shouldn't arrest you?"

She thought for a moment and then looked up at him through thick lashes. "Because I asked you not to," she dared softly.

"I want you to give me the names of the men who made you do it."

She laughed. "*Made* me? No one *makes* me do anything I don't want to do, Captain. I spent too many years playing that tune."

She was brave. Grayson had to give her that. Not many women would stand up to a man as imposing as he knew he could be. Slowly he came toward her.

She watched him.

"You'd have to give me your word you won't get involved again."

She shook her head. "If you're not going to arrest me, I want you to leave. Now." She didn't like him so close. He made her stomach flutter, her heart beat irregularly.

He stopped just in front of her and lifted a bit of hair off her shoulder, feeling its texture between his fingers. "I can't do this again. I get caught, I could be charged with treason. I find you involved with those rebels again, and you'll be turned in the same as anyone."

"Fair enough." She snatched her lock of hair from his hand. "Now if that's all you came to say, I want you to go."

His eyes narrowed as he studied her freckled face. There was something wholesome, something fresh and untamed about her simple ways. The girl was clever, too. She'd been quite careful to admit to nothing, though she knew full well she'd been caught red-handed.

"Oh, no, it's not as easy as that, Maggie mine. A bargain."

Her brow creased. "A bargain?"

"Yes. One kiss."

"I told you I'm no whore," she spit.

"All I ask of you is a kiss, a single kiss. It seems a fair request from a man willing to save you from the noose."

A kiss! I can't kiss him again, she thought wildly. "One kiss? Nothing more?" she heard herself ask.

"One kiss."

She nodded, remembering the feel of his lips on hers last night. "Then you go." She let her eyes drift shut as she waited for him to kiss her.

His chuckle made her snap her eyes open. "What?"

"I want you to kiss me."

"Me kiss you!"

"Yes. You were a married woman. Surely you must have kissed your husband. Now, give me a husbandly kiss and we'll consider this matter settled."

"Noah Myers never kissed nothing but a pint of ale!"

"Maggie, I have to be on my way before someone realizes I've left the camp."

She thought to refuse him, but how could she? The man was right. He held her life in the palm of his hand. He wasn't asking her to bed him. He wouldn't force her; somehow she knew he wasn't that kind of man. All he wanted was a kiss. With a groan she lifted up on her toes and brought her mouth to his. She was careful not to let any of her body touch his. Their lips met and she moved to withdraw, but he caught the back of her head with his palm and deepened the kiss.

Before Maggie knew what was happening, her tongue was touching his. His fingers threaded through her hair and her hands rose of their own accord to rest on his broad shoulders.

God, it felt good to be kissed like this. Like he cared.

Cared! Maggie stepped back abruptly. *Of course he didn't care! He didn't even know her!* Grayson smiled at her and she turned away, embarrassed by her wanton behavior.

"That was nice," he told her gently. "Now how about some of that bacon? Maybe you could fry up one of those eggs for me? I haven't had an egg in ages."

"You said you'd leave," she said angrily, her back still to him.

"And I will. After breakfast." He grabbed a chair and sat down at her table.

She turned back to him, the apples of her cheeks pinkening with rising anger. She opened her mouth to speak and then clamped it shut, whirling back around. Grabbing the eggs, she cracked them into the hot skillet the bacon fried in. She didn't want to make the blasted redcoat breakfast, but what was she to do?

Flipping the bacon onto a pewter plate, she slid the eggs next to the glistening strips and added a piece of toast. None too gently, she dropped the plate in front of him. "Eat and be gone!"

He glanced up, amused. "A fork?"

She crossed the room, retrieved one from a cup over the mantel, and slammed it on the table beside his plate.

"Won't you have some?" he asked, cutting the egg with his fork.

"Lost my appetite," she snapped, turning away.

He caught her apron string. "No, no, you come and sit with me." He indicated a chair with his fork and then took a mouthful of the egg. "Sit and talk with me."

She scowled. "I'd sooner sit and talk with the devil than you, Captain Thayer."

"Grayson."

"What?"

"No one ever calls me by my Christian name these days. I want you to call me Grayson. Now sit and talk with me while I enjoy my meal. I'll eat and then I'll go, I swear it. You'll never see me again."

With a sigh of resignation, Maggie took a seat across the table from the redcoat, wishing she could believe him. But somehow she knew that this wouldn't be the last she'd see of Grayson Thayer.

Maggie stepped into the public room of the tavern and surveyed the noisy crowd. A thick veil of smoke hung in the air. She squinted, adjusting her eyes to the dim light. Grayson wasn't there. Feeling foolish to have even been looking for him, she crossed the room and slipped into the back kitchen.

"Where you been?" Her brother-in-law Manny asked, as he dumped a sack of potatoes onto a wooden table. "We haven't seen you in three days."

She shrugged the leather pack containing several pairs of half-made boots off her back and set it aside. "Been around." After the close call earlier in the week with Captain Thayer, Zeke had suggested she lay low. She had told Zeke of the conversation she'd had with Grayson that morning in her kitchen. But she hadn't told him about the kiss.

"For once it was to your advantage to wear a skirt," Zeke had teased. "He let you go, hoping you'd show him a little favor."

Maggie had pitched a clod of dirt at Zeke, beaning him on the head and ending the conversation. But she'd still taken his advice and remained at the farm working her sparse garden, and starting on a boot order for several British soldiers camped near the tavern. It seemed it took her longer to make a bad pair of boots than it did a decent pair. She'd said nothing more of the redcoat captain who had spared her life, but she'd thought of him often. No matter how many times she pushed him from her mind, he reappeared. She saw his startling blue eyes, she heard his rich tenor voice, she tasted his lips on hers.

"Maggie! Have you gone daft, woman?" Manny broke her from her thoughts. "I asked if you could peel the taters. I got a crowd of hungry men out there."

Maggie took the knife he offered. "I can only stay a few minutes, then I got to head out to do some sizin' for boots. Where's Alice?"

He rolled his bulging eyes heavenward. "Upstairs, sleeping. Women's ailments. She said she couldn't lift another thing today."

Maggie grabbed a potato and began to peel. "You got to get some help here, Manny. You can't expect her to cook for the whole place, clean rooms, and watch your four children, with another on the way."

"We must work the works of him that sent me, said the Lord." Manny wiped his hands on his protruding stomach.

"Don't start that Bible quotin' with me. Work, yes, kill yourself doin' it, no!" She grabbed another potato. "Since the Brits started movin' in on us, it's been too much on her."

He shrugged his massive shoulders, unwrapping a quarter of beef he'd just brought up from the cellar. "You could move in, give her a hand."

"Ah, no. We're not startin' that again, Manny. I appreciate the offer, but I'm not movin' in with anyone. I'm gonna sit right there on my own porch and rock away the days."

"Not safe," he grunted. "A woman alone with these soldiers comin' and goin'."

She peeled faster. "I'm safe enough. Nobody's bothered me yet, have they? I got the farm, and with the few pennies I make fixin' boots, I'm doing as well as Noah ever did." *Better,* she thought to herself.

Manny took a meat cleaver and raised it to cut into the beef quarter. "It just ain't right, a woman doin' a man's work. Shoe-makin's men's work." The cleaver hit the wooden table with a thump and he raised it again.

"We've been through this before. I thank you for your concern, but mind your own knittin', Manny. Alice is your wife, not me."

"Thank the good Lord for that," he muttered.

Maggie grinned, still peeling potatoes. "What'd you say?"

"Nuthin'." He brought the great cleaver down and hacked off another hunk of meat.

She chuckled. "Well, I got a start on your potatoes, but I got to go."

"You're not leavin' me with twenty-five pounds to peel before supper!"

She handed him the knife. "That I am. It's not my place of business. It's yours." She grabbed her knapsack and waved as she went out the door. "Tell my sister I was askin' for her. And do yourself a favor, Manny. Hire yourself another cook!" With that, Maggie walked out of the kitchen and back into the public room.

Scanning the crowd of tavern patrons once more for her captain, she slipped out the door. Outside, she headed east toward the British encampment where several men who had ordered boots were residing. The men belonged to some sort of special detachment sent to keep an eye on the citizens of Yorktown no doubt. So far, Maggie hadn't seen them keep an eye on anything but their cards and Lyla. Maggie thought she'd fit the customers for their boots and then get home before dark.

As she walked along the road she contemplated her interest in Grayson.

She laughed aloud. Here she was thinking of him, calling him by name. She'd didn't know what ailed her, but she hoped she could cure it fast and simple. The man was dangerous. He was the enemy. Crossing the shallow creek that ran over the road, Maggie climbed the bluff to where she knew the men camped. On the crest of the hill, she could see that the encampment had been enlarged since the last time she'd been up here.

She couldn't help wondering what General Washington was up to these days. Did he realize Cornwallis intended to move his men from Wiliamsburg to Yorktown? Of course nothing was official yet, but Maggie and the others in the town knew it was only a matter of time.

Glancing up at the setting sun, she hurried along, wishing she hadn't stopped at the tavern. It was growing dark quickly and a soldiers' camp was not the place for a woman after dark.

Weaving her way through the maze of canvas tents, ignoring the occasional bawdy greeting, she located the men who'd placed the order with her.

"Here she is, the boot girl," Lieutenant Riker called from a camp stool, his speech slightly slurred. He was drinking.

She looked around, realizing that the area was secluded by trees. A small campfire provided light as darkness began to settle in. The group of lieutenants were gathered in a circle, a deck of cards resting on a barrel they were using for a table. A tapped keg of ale sat on a rock under a tree. "I could come back if this ain't a good time," Maggie said.

Lieutenant Riker, a man of no more than eighteen, raised off the stool and approached her. His dark hair was pulled back in a a queue, though several stands had escaped to fall across his cheek. His blue-green eyes were rimmed in red. "Don't be foolish, sweet. What we need here is a lady. A party's just not a party without a lady, is it, gentlemen?"

There were several chuckles and an occasional guffaw as the men murmured among themselves.

"Just the same. It's gettin' late. I got a cow to milk," she lied as she turned around. "I'll come back tomorrow."

Riker grasped her shoulder. "Now just wait a minute. You can't walk out on us like that. Not when we invited you to stay. It would be damned rude, wouldn't it, gentlemen?"

"Damned rude," echoed a burly man, appearing at her other side. "Join us."

She shook her head. "I'm going' home. Now let go of me."

Riker smiled. "Look at the way her eyes light up, Gordy. Damned if we don't have us a hot country wench here." He eyed her breasts, winking at his friend.

Gordy took her other arm. Maggie tried to twist away, but both men held her tightly. "Let me go," she cried, trying not to panic. "You can't do this. Someone will hear me if I scream."

"Nah. No one's going to hear you, sweet," Riker

answered. "Too busy with their own business. Besides, if they did hear, what would they care?" He twisted her arm. "Spoils of war is what we call baggage like you." He crushed his mouth against hers and Maggie's stomach heaved. All she could think of was Noah and his last fruitless attempts at making love to her. He had tasted of ale just like this man and it had made her sick to her stomach. She'd told Noah she wouldn't stand for any more and she wasn't going to stand it from this man, either.

With a cry of anguish, Maggie swung free of Gordy. She shoved Riker and clipped him hard in the jaw with her left fist.

"God damn, woman!" Riker cursed. "Mind your manners!" He cuffed her back, hitting her in the temple.

Maggie staggered backward, trying to catch her balance. *Dear Mother Mary, don't let this be happening to me,* she begged silently.

A man caught her from behind, steadying her. "A fine woman," he commented, grasping her tightly around the waist. "Sure wouldn't want to let her get away."

"Please. Let me go."

Riker walked up to her, nursing his jaw. "You ought have a little respect, missy. These gentlemen here are officers in the finest fighting army in the world."

"I think we ought to teach her a little lesson," the big one, Gordy, commented. He had tossed his coat aside and was pulling off his vest.

Maggie squeezed her eyes shut, twisting to get

away from her captor, knowing it was useless. He pulled her knapsack off her back and dragged her closer to the other men.

"Now wait a minute," Riker said, lifting a tankard of ale. "Who says you get first go, Gordy? I was the one that got her here!"

"You ordered boots! It was my idea to have a little futtering!" He stripped off his white shirt, baring a chest of black curly hair.

"What about me?" someone called.

"I was the one that caught her," her captor complained. "If it hadn't been for me, she'd have gotten away! I say I get her first!"

"Hold it! Hold it!" Riker raised his hands. "There's got to be a way to settle this in a civilized manner." After a moment of thought, he shrugged his shoulders. "We'll just play for her."

"Play for her?" questioned a red-haired man in the group. "What do you mean?"

"Are you dull-witted, Morrison?" Riker shot back. "I mean we'll play for her. A friendly game of laterloo."

"Loo . . . God's teeth," Gordy muttered, reaching for his shirt on the ground. "You know I'm lousy at the game."

"Play or don't play, girls," Ritcher offered. "Winner takes her first. The others can have their turns when the winner's worn out."

Listening to the men bargain over her like she was a side of beef made Maggie physically ill. All she could think was that she had to escape. Giving a scream, she rammed her elbow into her captor's stomach and dove for the ground.

But there were too many of them. Once on her feet, she barely made it out of the circle before someone caught her around the waist. There were hands everywhere, touching her, pulling at her clothing. She screamed again, and someone stuffed a handkerchief into her mouth. They forced her to sit on a campstool and quickly bound her feet together and her hands behind her back.

Maggie watched through hooded eyelids as the men gathered around the gaming table and one of them made the first deal. *I swear if I survive this,* she thought, *I'll get even with you. I'll get even with you all!*

Just then, another soldier entered the grove of trees. The campfire light flickered across his face and Maggie recognized him immediately.

Thank God! she thought. *It's Grayson! He won't let them do this to me, I know he won't!*

"Gentlemen . . ." Grayson greeted. His eyes met Maggie's, and for a moment she thought she saw compassion . . . even fear, but the expression vanished as quickly as it had appeared.

"What are you up to?" Grayson asked, trying to sound casual.

Riker stood. "Just a little, fun, sir." He threw a glance over his shoulder. "Got us a wench."

Grayson eyed the hands of cards. "Playing for her, are you?"

"We couldn't decide who'd take her first," Gordy volunteered. "It was Riker's idea!"

"Somehow that doesn't surprise me," Grayson responded dryly.

"You in?" Riker lit a thick cigar and inhaled.

Maggie's eyes locked with Grayson's; he looked away.

"Hell, yes!" Grayson pulled up a campstool, slapping one of the lieutenants on the back. "I'm in!" He took care not to meet Maggie's gaze again. "A wench like her? I'd be crazy to say no, wouldn't I, gentlemen?"

Chapter Four

The soldiers laughed as they shifted their campstools making room for Captain Thayer at the game table.

Riker offered him a cigar. "A friendly game of loo, sir. The winner takes her first." He winked at Gordy. "The rest of you will have to take the spoils."

There was more crude laughter as Grayson accepted the cigar and allowed a redheaded lieutenant to light it for him. "Loo, is it?" He took a puff. "Fair enough." His gaze flicked to Maggie and then back at Riker. "But it's winner take all."

"Winner take all! The bloody hell it is!" Gordy swore, leaping up. "We all mean to have a taste of her!"

Riker lowered his tankard, sloshing ale on the ground. "You can't just walk in here and change the rules on us. We're the ones who invited you to partake of our good luck!"

Grayson propped one booted foot on his knee. He didn't like Riker. He was a poor soldier, but because he was Major Lawrence's nephew he received special treatment in the camp. He disobeyed rules and regulations, then flaunted it in front of the other men. "You know, of course, that this is against regulations, Lieutenant."

Riker glanced across the barrel table at his superior officer. "What's written and what's enforced are two different things here, Captain." He smiled, but his voice was laced with barely controlled anger.

Gordy dropped onto his campstool. "You ain't got no right to come in here and tell us what to do with our woman."

Grayson tapped the ensignia on his shoulderboards. "You see this, Moore. This gives me the right."

Riker pushed back a stray lock of midnight hair. "So what you're saying here is that you're pulling rank on us."

"I'm saying, boys, that I've changed the rules. Winner takes her for the night. Losers bow out gracefully."

Gordy slapped the cards on the table. I bloody might as well go back to my tent. I'll not be dippin' my wick tonight!"

Several of the other men grumbled in agreement.

"Enough," Grayson interrupted. "Time's awasting. The sooner we get through this, the sooner I'll have the wench to warm my cot."

Riker's cold gaze met Grayson's. "We'll just see about that, *Captain,* won't we?"

With bitter anger, Maggie watched the entire exchange between the British officers. How dare he! How dare Grayson be a part to this! For an instant she had fooled herself into thinking he would stop them . . . he would save her. She nearly laughed at her own naivete. Captain Grayson Thayer was no better than the rest of the men in this camp. What had made her ever think differently?

The cards were shuffled and dealt and Maggie began to keep vigil on the game, all the while struggling to loosen the ties on her hands. No man would take her against her will. Too many times she had submitted to Noah. Husband or not, no man had a right to force himself upon a woman.

As the game progressed it quickly became evident to Maggie that either Riker or Grayson would win her. Both were superior cardplayers. She wondered who the winner would be. There was something about the dark, strikingly handsome Riker that made her skin crawl, but the thought of struggling with Grayson on a bed . . . that would be worse.

Ale flowed and the men grew louder and more boisterous as the game grew tighter. Several other men from the camp gathered around the gaming table, choosing sides and cheering the players on. Bets were placed and money exchanged hands as soldiers wagered as to who would sleep with the red-haired bootmaker tonight.

Once, Gordy brought Maggie his tankard of ale to sip from, but she knocked it from his hand with a twist of her shoulder. He moved to strike her, but Grayson interceded. He said he wanted her "unblemished."

As the game continued, Maggie watched with growing fear. She couldn't believe these men were playing cards for her! She couldn't believe she'd been dumb enough to put herself into this position.

She eyed the cards as they were laid on the table. It was down to Grayson and Riker; the others were nearly out of coin. She watched the players' faces. The game was quickly turning toward Grayson's favor and Riker was growing angrier by the moment.

Grayson laid a flush on the table and the other players groaned aloud as they lost the entire pool of coins to their superior officer. Two soldiers, out of money, dropped from the game.

The next hand was dealt and again Grayson looed the other players. Maggie swore softly beneath her breath. It had suddenly occurred to her that Grayson was cheating. No man's luck held out that well. The bloodyback redcoat was cheating! She nearly called out to the other men, but thought better of it and held her tongue. Reason told her she'd be safer if Grayson won her. Perhaps she could talk him out of the rape. Riker . . . he was a brutal man bent on vengeance. She could see it in his pitch-black eyes.

The players moved into the final hand and the last cards were played. Grayson took the pool, sweeping the coins from the barrel table, and Riker threw down his cards in disgust. Maggie closed her eyes, trying to calm her pounding heart.

Grayson stood, offering his hand to Riker. "I told you she'd be mine."

Riker made no move to accept his peace offering. "This won't be the last of this, Thayer."

Grayson moved toward Maggie, ignoring the lieutenant's obvious threat. All he wanted to do right now was get the girl out of here while he still had control of the situation. He grasped her shoulders and lifted her to her feet.

Maggie's eyes flew open. She mumbled something against the handkerchief stuffed in her mouth.

"I'll take it out," he said quietly. "But you have to keep your mouth shut, or we're both in trouble, you understand?"

She nodded slowly.

"Untie me," she rasped the moment he pulled the handkerchief from her mouth.

"I wouldn't be untying her if I was you, Captain," Gordy offered, coming to stand beside Grayson. "A wild wench this one is. She socked Riker right in the jaw."

"Let me loose," she repeated through clenched teeth.

"You won't run?"

"I won't run," she responded.

Grayson crouched in front of her and cut the ropes that bound her feet together. Just as he was about to stand, she brought her bound hands up under his chin, striking him hard and knocking him off balance. Jerking from his grasp, she dove left.

Gordy broke into a cackle as he went after her. "God damn, Captain. I told you she'd run off," he shouted as he caught Maggie around the waist and hauled her back toward Grayson.

Maggie kicked and bucked wildly. "Let me go!" she shouted. "Let me go, you sons of bitches, or you'll be sorry."

Riker leaped up and came toward her, but Grayson stepped in, putting out his arms. "Give her to me, Gordy," he said sharply.

Gordy glanced at Riker.

"Now!" Grayson ordered.

Gordy shoved her forward and Grayson took her into his arms, looping her bound hands over his neck so that she was unable to escape.

"Put me down, you bloody redcoat," Maggie threatened, her voice husky and low. "Put me down or you'll rue the day you ever touched me!"

The British soldiers were gathering around, laughing, elbowing each other, and calling out crude comments.

"Guess you'll have your hands full tonight, Captain."

"Damned if I'd want a she-cat to share my bed. I'll take little Lyla any day!"

Maggie lifted her lashes to stare into Grayson's blue eyes. "It's not too late," she warned between clenched teeth. "Ye might still save your balls if you free me now."

The soldiers howled with laughter.

"Damned if that sour mouth doesn't need a little sweetening!" someone called.

"A kiss!" another offered.

"Yea! Kiss her! That'll shut her up. Every woman needs a good kissing!"

Grayson took a step back, but the men had him surrounded. Riker's eyes were on him, watching . . . waiting . . . daring . . .

Grayson brought his mouth down hard against Maggie's, thrusting his tongue between her lips. She struggled but her strength was little to match his.

The men hooted and hollered with glee, pounding each other on the backs and dancing in circles.

Some well-wisher poured a mug of ale over their heads.

Maggie couldn't breathe. She could hear the men shouting. She could taste Grayson's mouth and feel the power of his assault.

When he pulled away, there were tears in her eyes. She pressed her face to his uniform, ashamed.

"Enough!" Grayson called. "Now let me through. I've business to attend to."

The crowd parted, allowing him to walk away. The minute they were out of the light of the fire Grayson leaned over to murmur in her ear, "Just keep quiet. We'll be in my tent in a moment."

"Let me go," she insisted, the fight nearly gone from her voice.

"I can't do that. You saw those men. I let you go and they all take turns at you. You want that?"

She didn't say anything. She knew he was telling her the cold hard truth of the matter, but she didn't care. What was he saying? That she should go along quietly just because he saved her from being raped by ten men . . . only to rape her himself? A sob escaped her lips.

Grayson hurried through the south sector of the camp, thankful his tent was a short distance from the others in his company. Private Michaels met him at the entrance to his tent.

"Captain Thayer?"

"Yes, Michaels, it's me. Just open the flap."

The boy stared at the woman in the captain's arms. It was quite obvious to him that she wasn't here of her own free will, unlike the others who frequented his captain's tent.

"Light a lamp," Grayson ordered.

"Yes, sir." The boy scrambled to do his bidding and in a moment the dark tent was filled with soft light.

Grayson walked to his cot and lowered Maggie onto it. As he raised her hands over his head he spoke, his voice harsh with authority. The teasing boy in him was gone. "Don't you move off that bed or I swear to God I'll tie you to it. You understand me?"

She swallowed hard, knowing he meant it.

"I said, do you understand?"

She lifted her head from his pillow, nodding.

"Good." He turned away. "That will be it for tonight, Michaels. You can go on to bed."

The boy lingered at the door, staring at the trembling woman. This wasn't like Captain Thayer to force a woman. The others . . . they always seemed to come so willingly.

"I said that will be it, Michaels!"

The boy snapped a salute and then ducked out of the tent, letting the flap fall behind him.

For a moment Grayson stood with his back to Maggie, deep in thought. What the hell was he going to do with her? What was he going to say? *Sorry, but I have to keep you here all night and make it look like I've raped you so nothing looks suspicious to Riker. You see, ma'am, I'm not actually a British soldier, I'm a patriot spy. A patriot spy in a hell of a lot of trouble . . .*

He shook his head ever so slightly. No, that wasn't going to work, was it? He spun around to face her.

Christ, she looked so scared. But why wouldn't she be? He walked over to the cot.

It was all Maggie could do to keep from cringing. "Please let me go," she whispered. "I won't tell anyone."

"I can't. Nothing happens in this camp that everyone doesn't know about. I can't let you go until morning."

She swallowed back the lump that rose in her throat. "Could . . . could you at least untie my hands?"

He took his knife from his belt and slit the hemp, letting the ropes fall to the cot.

Maggie sat up, rubbing her wrists, staring back at him.

"I won't hurt you," he said.

"Guess that depends on your definition of the word *hurt,* doesn't it?"

He ran his fingers through his golden hair, sighing as he looked away. He couldn't help wondering how the hell he got into these predicaments. Pushing up off the cot, he went to his field desk and grabbed a pewter cup. Uncorking a bottle he poured himself a healthy dose of claret.

Maggie sat on the cot, her legs drawn beneath her skirting as she watched him . . . waiting. *He'll not rape me,* she vowed bitterly. *I'll die first.*

Grayson took his time with his drink, then poured another and set the cup on the desk. Sitting on the edge of a campstool, he tugged at his knee-high boots. When they wouldn't budge, he swore. He'd sent Michaels to bed. Now how the hell was he going to get his boots off? The boy always did it for him. He glanced up at Maggie.

She shook her head ever so slightly. She knew exactly what he wanted before he spoke. Be damned if she was going to pull the man's boots off so he could throw her down and force himself on her!

"Maggie," Grayson said softly.

She shook her head harder.

"Maggie, come here. He pointed to his fine French boots. "Give them a pull."

She crossed her arms over her chest. "Boots on, boots off. I didn't know men were so particular!"

He loosened the holster around his waist in which he wore his pistol and laid it on the desk. "Maggie, I've got no patience tonight. Come over here. There's no need for me to call the boy when you can pull off my boots for me."

She thrust out her chin defiantly and Grayson nearly smiled. In the soft lamplight her face was as comely as the heavenly female forms painted in flowing colors on the ceiling of the Sistine Chapel. And her hair, God, it was beautiful, with its thousand shades ranging from brilliant red to honey blond.

"Don't look at me like this is my doing, Maggie. Who entered a camp full of soldiers after dark?"

When she made no response, his eyes met hers. "Either you get up," he said softly, "or I come over and get you up. You've caused me a damned lot of aggravation and I'm not in the mood for your games."

After a moment's hesitation he started to rise off the stool and Maggie jumped up. In bare feet she padded across the canvas floor of the tent. Biting down on her lower lip, she knelt on one knee and grasped his boot. It was the finest boot she'd ever laid eyes on. Sewn of dyed black calfskin, the pair were worth well over a year of captains' wages. The leather was soft and supple, well oiled and properly cared for. She always liked a man who took good care of his boots. It showed he was a man of sensibilities.

Grayson's gaze fell to the crown of her head as she tugged off one boot, set it aside, and reached for the other. He rested his hand on her shoulder keeping her from moving away as she removed the other boot.

Maggie didn't like being so close to Grayson. It muddled her thoughts. She could smell the starch of his pressed uniform, mixed with the scent of shaving soap. She could hear his light, easy breathing. How could a man sit so easily, knowing he was about to defile a woman?

Maggie pulled back, but he caught her arm.

"I said I wouldn't hurt you," he said. "Now stop acting like a scared rabbit."

"Scared!" She stood. "I'm not scared of anything!"

He rose off the stool and began to unbutton his scarlet uniform vest. "I don't guess you are, are you? But you should be. Those men wouldn't have just raped you, they'd have killed you. I've seen what men like that can do to a woman. It would make you sick."

"I've been in and out of camps a hundred times in the last two years," she challenged. "No one ever bothered me before."

"Times change, don't they?" He dropped his vest on a wooden peg rack strung between two tent poles. "This isn't the same army it was two years ago. The men are tired and they're afraid."

Her hands fell to her hips. Funny conversation for a man about to commit rape, she mused. "Are you afraid, Captain Thayer?"

"I said, call me Grayson." He drew his white shirt over his head, leaving Maggie to stare at the broad chest sprinkled with fine golden hair.

The sound of shouting and boisterous laughter made them both turn their heads in the direction of the noise. "Hell," he muttered, grasping her arm. "Strip off your dress and get onto the cot."

"What?"

"You heard me, now strip it and get onto the bed. There isn't much time!" He shoved her.

Already the rowdy voices were growing closer.

"Just come to check up on you, Thayer," called someone.

"Just want to be certain the hell-cat didn't slit your throat!"

Grayson peeled off his tight white breeches and grabbed his pistol off his desk. "Hurry!" he urged in a whisper. "They're coming."

Maggie had to force herself to look away from his nakedness. She was as shocked by the beauty of his flat muscular form as by the size of his male organ. Holy Mary! He was twice the size of Noah!

"Maggie, have you gone deaf?"

She glanced in the direction of the approaching crowd. "I'm no whore. I'll not do it."

"If they don't think *I* have, *they* will," he

snapped, grasping her arm and pulling her toward the bed. "Now step out of your skirt."

Knowing he was right didn't make it any easier. Tears stung Maggie's eyes as she fumbled with the button on her linsey-woolsey skirt.

"Quickly!"

She stepped out of it and handed it to him, knowing he could see her bare form beneath the filmy summer shift.

"The bodice, too. Keep your shift." He snapped his fingers "Hurry, girl."

"Hey, Thayer, old boy," someone called from just outside the tent. "You got her tied up or she got you?"

Grayson threw her clothing haphazardly to the floor and pushed her onto the cot, tumbling on top of her. Just as the tent flap lifted, he shoved his pistol under the pillow.

Maggie struggled beneath Grayson, trying to shove him off her. His face was buried in the crook of her neck. She could hear his uneasy breathing and practically feel his lips on her flesh. His nude male body was pressed against her curves, molding to her. In the fall to the cot, her shift had slid up and she knew she was baring her thigh and most of her hip to the men who were thrusting their heads through the flap in the tent.

A cheer rose from the soldiers and men clapped and whistled as they caught sight of their naked captain on top of the bootmaker.

"There you go, Captain Thayer," Gordy congratulated. "Looks to me like you tamed the wench well enough."

Grayson lifted up on one elbow, but kept Maggie pinned, his arm wrapped possessively around her. She pushed down her shift, eyeing the men at the door.

"Is there a reason why you're interrupting my pleasure?" Grayson asked good-naturedly.

"I told you, Captain," Gordy said drunkenly. "Riker thought we'd best be certain the hell-cat hadn't slit you end to end."

"Well, now that you've seen I fared well enough, I'll ask you to go."

"Right you are, Captain." Gordy saluted with his left hand and disappeared from sight. "Come on, boys, I don't believe the keg's dry yet!"

One by the one the men backed away and finally the tent flap fell and Grayson and Maggie were left alone.

"I should have known they'd come," Grayson said. "Where's my head these days? I should have been ready for them!"

Maggie held her body stiff beneath his as she stared up at him, frightened, not just of Grayson but of herself. Deep in the pit of her stomach she felt a warmth she knew he generated. Despite all that had happened tonight, a small part of her was excited by this man.

She held perfectly still as he traced the bridge of her nose with the tip of his finger.

"Pretty," he mused. "So pretty." He remembered the taste of her lips and the feel of the curve of her breast cupped in his hand. *It would be so easy to take her,* he thought. *Not by force, but by gentle wooing.* He lowered his mouth to hers letting his lips barely brush hers before he withdrew.

How long had it been since he'd made love to a woman? Lust he could remember . . . a blur of pretty faces and naked limbs. But love? Had he ever loved a woman? He thought of Maggie and the way she had looked that morning in her kitchen. He wondered what it would be like to wake up beside her at dawn and take her into his arms to kiss away her sleepy smile, to make her hot and damp with want of him.

To Maggie's surprise Grayson suddenly rose off the cot, taking his pistol with him. She watched in amazement as he walked across the tent, the muscles of his thighs and bare buttocks flexing as he went. He took a silk robe from one of the clothing pegs and, when he turned back around, he was decently covered.

Maggie sat up and reached for her skirt and bodice on the floor.

He poured himself another cup of claret and sat down in an upholstered wing chair that looked completely out of place among the other camp furnishings. "Get dressed," he said, gently, as it pained him. "Then you might as well sleep. I'll wake you at daybreak and then you can go."

Her dark eyes widened with surprise. "You . . . you mean you're not going to . . ." She let her words trail off into nothingness as she held her clothing crumpled in her hands.

He grimaced. "God's teeth, no," he said in his best arrogant-captain's voice. "I'm not going to rape you. Rape's not to my liking." He took a sip of his claret. "There're plenty of wenches in Yorktown willing, even if you aren't." With that he reached over and turned out the lamp, leaving Maggie in total darkness.

Chapter Five

Maggie ran through the weedy field, the early-morning dew wetting her bare feet and making the hem of her skirt damp. To the east the sun was just beginning to rise, painting the sky in a hazy rainbow of pinks and purples. Already the cool night air was burning off, lending to the heat of another June day.

Relief flooded Maggie as her rough clapboard farmhouse appeared in the distance. Her spotted coon hounds began to bellow at the sight of a human. The pitch of their howls changed as she drew near enough for them to recognize her. When she slipped through the gate the hunting dogs came bounding to her, circling her and licking her bare ankles.

"Honey! Roy!" She patted their heads, laughing as they leaped in the air, barking and nipping at her skirts. "How you doin', rotten three-legged dog?" She scratched the old male behind his ear and he plopped down on her bare foot, rolling with pleasure. Though she loved both of her father's hounds dearly, it was Roy that held a soft spot in her heart.

When he was just a pup he'd lost a rear leg in a muskrat trap, but it had never slowed him down a minute. In his younger days he'd been known as the best coon hound for three counties.

Jealous of the attention Roy was reaping, Honey pushed her head beneath Maggie's hand, and Maggie squatted to scratch the old bitch behind a ragged ear. "Now don't get yourself in a dither, old girl," she soothed.

"Where in God's green earth have you been?" Zeke called from the front porch.

Maggie straightened up, shading her eyes from the morning sun with her palm. "Zeke?"

His clothes were wrinkled and he looked like a man who'd gone without sleep all night. "When you never lit your kitchen lamp come dark, I came up looking for you. Where've you been?"

She took her time walking up to the porch, wondering what she was going to say. She wasn't ready to talk about what had happened last night or what Grayson had done. He'd saved her life again and she didn't know how she felt about that. The man didn't make any sense. Was he her enemy or her friend? An enemy didn't save your life . . . but a friend didn't wear the enemy's uniform. She didn't like gray areas like this. To her everything was black and white. He had to be friend or foe; there was nothing in between.

"I said, where've you been? I was worried to death about you."

She walked up the creaky steps and sat on the top one. "I've been at the camp," she said quietly.

"They brought you in for questioning?"

She stared out at the open meadow. "You could say that."

"Maggie, what's going on? Are you hurt? Did they hurt you?"

"I lost three pairs of half-made boots. They kept my sack."

Zeke stooped beside her, forcing her to look him straight in the eyes. "I said are you hurt?"

When she couldn't stand Zeke's scrutiny any longer, she looked away. "It was Thayer again. I got caught up with a bad bunch. He took care of it." She didn't say he saved her because she didn't like the idea of being so beholden to Grayson.

Zeke settled on the top step beside her. "Maggie, you know I've always kept my nose out of your business, but I got to tell you, girl. You got to stay away from Captain Thayer."

"He didn't do anything wrong. He was a gentleman." She thought of the glimpse of his nakedness she had caught and her cheeks colored. "At least more of a gentleman than the others."

"He knows you know us. He's just trying to get to us by way of—" Zeke stopped short.

"My bed?" she asked pointedly.

He looked away, embarrassed. "War's just as hard on woman as a man, maybe harder. I know you're lonely but—"

"I didn't let him bed me, Zeke. And I got no intentions to."

He sighed. "I know you don't. But things got a way of gettin' out of hand sometimes. They say he's a smooth talker. I just don't want to see you get hurt by some pretty boy in a red coat."

"If you're done with the lecturin', Papa Zeke, I think I'll go on inside and make myself some pancakes. You want some?"

"Uh . . . no. Thanks just the same, but I got to get into town." He stuffed his hands into his pockets. "Got some, uh . . . errands to take care of."

"Must be important if you're willing to give up my pancakes. You always did say I made pancakes that melted in your mouth."

Zeke's cheeks colored and he looked away. "Ah, well, I got that sickle to get sharpened and such."

"Go on with you then and stop worrying over me like a mother hen. I told you, I can take care of myself."

Zeke started down the steps and then turned back around. "By the way, I almost forgot, there's a meetin' tonight."

"You almost forgot?" Her dark eyes narrowed. "Where?"

"I don't know if it's such a good idea for you to come."

She came down the porch steps and stopped in front of him. "I'm too far in to bail out now. Where's the meeting, Zeke?"

"I don't want you to get hurt. I don't want this Captain Thayer to have anything on you."

"If you don't tell me, I'll find out myself. I'm as capable as any of you. What's more, I've got a way in and out of the Brit camp, and you and your men don't."

"I know, I know all of the reasons why you should have a part in it. I just have a hard time with you bein' a woman."

She bent down and picked up a handful of red soil and clenched it, letting granules sift to the ground. "You think I love Virginia any less than you do, Zeke Barnes? This land is my home. You think that because I'm a woman I don't hurt when I see our men die?" Her eyes met his, her jaw set with determination. "I got something to tell you. We women, we hurt more because you men try to save us from the pain by keepin' us out of it. Only you can't keep us out of it. We sit here and wait for you to bring home the bodies. We bury 'em and then we're told to go on with our lives. I don't want to sit, I want to be a part of the fight. I want to do what I can to help our men. God willing, we're going to win this war and then this is going to be mine, same as yours. Don't you think that makes it my duty to be a part of the fightin'?"

Zeke watched the red dirt fall from her hand until her palm was empty. "I guess you're right," he said finally.

Her voice carried softly on the wind. "Guess I am."

"John Logan's tobacco barn, ten o'clock tonight."

"I'll be there." She flashed him a smile. "Now get on with your errands and if you see that sister of mine, you tell her I'll be by after a while."

Zeke gave a wave and then started down the lane, leaving Maggie to watch him go.

"Captain Thayer reporting, sir," Grayson called from outside Major Lawrence's tent. "Permission to enter."

"Granted," came a gruff voice.

Grayson ducked inside, slipped off his grenadier cap, and saluted, holding his salute until it was returned. As he lowered his hand, his eyes went from his commanding officer seated at a camp desk to Riker, lounging comfortably on the far side of the tent.

Riker flashed a smug grin.

Grayson looked back at the major. He was a tall, bony man, his ashen face lined with wrinkles. Like most of the older officers, he wore an immense powdered wig, even in the heat. "You sent for me, Major Lawrence?"

"I did." The middle-aged man slapped down his quill. "I want to know what the hell is going on out there!"

"Going on, sir?"

"The damned rebels! They're annoying the hell out of me, Thayer! It's like being beat to death by a swarm of butterflies!"

Riker snickered.

"I don't know what you mean, sir." Grayson shifted his weight, his gaze wandering to the documents on the major's desk. On the corner rested a map of the York River and the Chesapeake Bay with ships sketched on it. There was a date scrawled across the top, but Grayson couldn't make it out.

"I mean I'm sick to death of it." His face began to turn purple as he half rose out of his seat. "They sneak in at night and pour water over kegs of powder. They let our horses loose. They steal uniforms off the clotheslines. They intercept shipments of foodstuffs. They keep stealing my uniform cloth sent by my wife!" He took a deep breath. "None of these childish pranks will hinder our superior army, but I'm sick to death of it. General Cornwallis expects me to get this area secured and keep it that way."

Grayson nodded. "Then our General Cornwallis is moving the entire army onto the York Peninsula?"

"You know I can't divulge that information, Thayer. Now pay attention to what I'm telling you. I've assured the general that these annoyances will come to an immediate halt. I want these troublemakers, Thayer! We'll hang a few of the cocky bastards and maybe then they'll learn their place!"

"But we don't know who they are, sir. They're very clever. So far I've not been able to—"

"I don't want excuses!" He slammed his fist so hard on the flimsy field desk that papers fluttered and an ink well fell to the ground splattering ink over the canvas floor. "I want results!"

Grayson glanced over at Riker who'd propped a booted foot on the major's cot and was calmly trimming his fingernails with a field knife. "I don't suppose Lieutenant Riker has any thoughts on this matter."

Major Lawrence sat down on his stool and wiped his damp forehead. "I've removed my nephew from that detail. No need for him to be traipsing about in this unbearable heat. He's to be my personal secretary from now on."

"I see." Grayson returned his attention back to the field desk. When the documents had shifted, the map of the placement of the British fleet had been covered.

"You'd better see, and see to it, Thayer. I don't know what your previous commanding officer let you get away with, though I've heard tales. But I'm telling you, there's no place in this king's army for philanderers! You find out the identities of those rebels and you bring them in. I intend to hold you personally responsible!"

"Yes, sir. Will that be all?"

The major began to fan himself with an Oriental silk fan. "Yes." He gave a nod and Grayson turned to go. "No. One more thing."

"Sir?"

"I am told you had a woman in your tent last night, Captain. A woman who did not come of her own free will."

Grayson glanced at Riker.

"I understand the occasional need for relief for you rutting bulls. But I must insist that you be more discreet." His steely gray eyes met Grayson's. "There are some of our fellow officers who do not look upon the term 'spoils of war' as we do."

"I understand that, sir."

"So just keep the young ladies quiet, will you, Thayer?"

Riker chuckled.

"Yes, sir," Grayson answered, disgusted by the major's attitude.

Major Lawrence sighed. "All right. That will be all." He held up a bony finger. "But I expect a full report by the end of the week. Things are heating up here on the peninsula, Thayer. No one knows what that bedlamite Colonial Washington is going to do. We haven't got time to dally."

"Yes, sir." Grayson saluted. "I'll have that report to you by the end of the week. Good day."

The major flipped a salute, excusing Grayson, and Grayson turned and walked out of the tent.

Outside, Private Michaels was waiting for him.

"What are you doing here?" Grayson checked his pocket watch. He had to meet his contact with the patriot army in half an hour. He was going to be late.

"I . . ." The boy fell into step behind Grayson. "I heard you'd been called in. I just wondered how you made out, sir. There wasn't much yelling, so I guess the major wasn't too angry."

"Not too angry." Grayson dropped a hand to the boy's shoulder, taking notice that he still had the physique of a gangly child. Then he remembered. The boy was only fourteen years old. Grayson couldn't help wondering how the hell the Army could justify sending children into battle. "Listen, do me a favor, Michaels."

"Yes, sir."

"Fetch my horse and saddle him."

"The major's given you some sort of duty?"

"He wants me to look into this band of rebels causing all of the trouble."

Michaels let out a low whistle, pushing back a lock of sandy hair. "Could . . . could I ride along?"

Grayson reached his tent and stopped. "Not today, son, but maybe another day, all right?"

The boy smiled. "All right, sir."

"Now go along. I'm in a hurry."

Inside the tent, Grayson disrobed, folded his clothing neatly, and then began to re-dress. He chose a pair of dark-blue broadcloth breeches and a white lawn shirt from the trunk at the end of his cot. Forgoing the stock, he slipped into a pair of calf-length boots and reached for his pistol. He didn't anticipate any trouble today; he was just going to meet with his contact to be certain there were no messages from his patriot commanding officer. But he wanted to be prepared just the same.

Since the British had made Williamsburg, Grayson had carried an uneasy feeling in his gut. The war was coming to an end, fast and furiously. What worried him was that he still didn't know who was going to win . . .

Zeke stood out on the front porch of Martin's Dry Goods, whistling to himself. Occasionally he dared a glance through the wavy glass window panes. He could see her inside, leaning over the counter, waiting as John Martin measured out her orders of flour and cornmeal and such. Finally she gathered her sacks, paid the proprietor, and started for the door.

Taking a ragged breath, Zeke walked straight up to the doorway, nearly bumping into her.

"Oh, excuse me," Lyla said softly.

When Zeke looked up at her, her eyes were focused on her bare feet. "Afternoon, ma'am," he said, whipping off his felt three-cornered hat.

"Afternoon," she answered, still keeping her eyes lowered.

She was so beautiful she took Zeke's breath away. She was a tiny little thing with thick blond hair that framed her delicate oval face. Without face paint he could see the porcelain shade of her skin and her blond eyelashes. "Um, could I help you with your things?" he asked awkwardly.

She smiled ever so slightly, lifting her chin until her eyes met his. They were a soft, grassy green. "You don't have to do this every week, Ezekial. What'll people think?"

He stuffed his hat on his head and reached for her sacks. "What'll I care what they think?" His hands brushed hers and a tremor of pleasure rumbled through him.

"It's just that . . . that a respectable man like you shouldn't been seen carryin' for a . . . a—"

"I don't want to hear that again from you, Lyla." He led her away from the store and through the crossroad where Commegys' Ordinary stood. She lived to the south through the pines, but Zeke didn't know where. She'd never let him escort her all the way home. "I told you. I don't care."

She walked beside him, a smile capturing her pretty face. "You know, I almost believe you, Ezekial."

Zeke smiled back, feeling his cheeks grow warm under his ragged beard. Then he caught sight of Maggie standing near her brother-in-law's tavern door, staring straight at him.

When he didn't speak, she called out to him. "Afternoon, Zeke."

"Afternoon, Maggie." He nodded and groaned at the same time. It wasn't that he cared if Maggie saw him with Lyla, it was just that he didn't want to have to hear her mouth later. He knew what she'd have to say about him toting packages for the town whore.

"Had that sickle sharpened for me like you said, Zeke?"

"Dropped it off at the blacksmith. Pick it up tomorrow." He walked past Maggie, with Lyla still at his side.

"I told you it wasn't a good idea," Lyla murmured the moment she was out of earshot of Maggie. "Now give me my sacks and go on." She opened her arms.

Zeke stopped and stared into Lyla's face. He could see her pain and it made him angry. "What do I care what the hell Maggie Myers thinks of me?"

"Don't tell me that." She snatched the bags from his arms one at a time. "Everybody in the town knows you're half in love with her."

"In love with Maggie! A man would have to be out of his tree to love that woman. Be like lovin' a copperhead snake!"

"You love her. I see it in your eyes, Ezekial."

Embarrassed by of this talk of love, Zeke ground his boot into the dirt. "It ain't that kind of love, Lyla," he said quietly.

She looked up at him. "It ain't?"

He hooked his thumbs into the waistband of his dusty breeches and focused on his boots. He could have sworn he detected a hint of hopefulness in her voice. "I can't say I don't love her," he said awkwardly. "I've known her all my life. But it ain't like a man loves a wife. She's got a fire in her, like she was meant for more than this little town. Me . . . I like it here."

Lyla reached out and brushed her fingertips across Zeke's cheek. "Thanks for carryin' my sacks."

"See you next week," he called after her as she walked away, her skirts fluttering in the hot breeze.

"See you next week," she answered.

Grayson rode his horse, Giipa, through a small field where wheat had grown before the patriots had burned it to keep it from the British. Then he sailed over a crooked fence and turned down a lane. Even with its burned fields, the Virginia countryside was breathtaking. Grayson hadn't realized how much he missed it those years he was in England going to school, or when he was up North with the Army, until he'd come home.

Raised on a sprawling plantation near Williamsburg, never in his wildest dreams had Grayson imagined he would be in the position he was in today. If he'd known what he knew now, he couldn't help wondering if he would have done differently.

Back in '74 while drinking in a tavern in London, he'd been approached by several Philadelphia merchants. They'd proposed a wild scheme, just wild enough to interest Grayson. They wanted to hire him as a spy. Concerned by the prospect of war, and the effect it would have on their businesses, they wanted Grayson to join the British army and keep them abreast of what was happening. When the war broke out and he was sent to the Colonies, he continued his mission, eventually working directly for the Colonial army under General Washington. For seven years he'd functioned under a false identity and he was beginning to tire of it. He felt like he was losing his grip on the man he'd once been. He'd played Captain Thayer for so long that he was afraid he was *becoming* him.

A dog barked, breaking Grayson from his thoughts. Realizing he had ridden into Billy Faulkner's barnyard, he dismounted and walked his horse to the hitching post. Several pairs of dark eyes peered from curtained windows as Grayson passed the farmhouse, but no one stepped outside. There were no sounds in the yard but the clucking and scratching of a few hens Grayson walked to the coral gate and leaned over. "Billy?"

Billy Faulkner gave a grunt in reply. "You're late. You're not supposed to come late."

Grayson leaned on the gate watching the small, powerful man lift straw with a pitchfork and toss it into a horse stall. "Got called in by Lawrence."

"Trouble?" Billy was a man of few words, but he was sharp. He was one of the best contacts Grayson had had in the last seven years.

"No. But we've got to watch our tails. I've been put in charge of rounding up the 'rebel scum' that's causing Lawrence all of the trouble. He's damned mad about those boys walking off with his coat cloth again."

Billy slapped his knee. "Fast bunch they are. Good sense of humor, too. I hear they got women cuttin' up the major's cloth to make us some of them stars an' stripes flags our army's totin' these days."

"You know who the men involved are?"

Billy shook his head. "Got some idea. But they're real careful." He grinned. "They wear flour sacks over their heads."

"I know," Grayson said dryly. "I've seen them in action."

"But as for who they are, I'd say it's better I didn't know. I got children to protect. The less I know, the better. I'm just a messenger."

"You're probably right. We're going to have to be very careful, more careful than we've been thus far. That pup Riker I was telling you about has been made Lawrence's private secretary. I think Riker's got it in for me. I had a little trouble with him over a woman the other night."

"Women!" Billy leaned on his pitchfork and spat on the ground. "More trouble than they're worth, I'll vow."

Grayson grinned as an image of a red-haired woman flashed through his mind. "Well, one good thing did come out of Lawrence calling me in. While I was in his tent I saw a map of the York River as well as the whole Chesapeake with ships drawn in. Ships that aren't there right now, Billy. There was a date, a proposed date for the engagement written across the top, but I couldn't read it."

"You think you can get a look at the map? Word is that that there bay may be how we can beat these bloodybacks. General Washington's workin' out a deal with the French. Seems like they may have a few ships to send our way. A Frenchy by the name of de Grass-y is in the West Indies but may be headed our way.

"Damn," Grayson breathed. "I'll be damned." He

looked up at Billy. I'll get the map and sketch a copy."

"It better be fast. We're sittin' on a keg of powder here, Thayer."

"And we don't know which way it's going to blow, do we," Grayson finished.

"That we don't."

"So you got anything for me? Where's Lafayette and Wayne. I haven't seen hide nor hair of one of our men in two weeks."

"Step inside." Billy swung open the gate. "And I'll fill you in. But it'll have to be fast. The wife's got goose on the table."

"Women are nothing but trouble, eh?" Grayson teased as he stepped inside the corral and closed the gate behind him.

Billy just grinned.

Chapter Six

"Evening to you, Carter," Maggie said as he stepped out of the pine trees and onto the road. "Where're you headed so late?"

The light of the moon reflected off his face illuminating his amusement. "No doubt the same place you're headed," he said with a chuckle.

"No doubt. Where's Mary think you've gone?" They walked along the road cut into the earth by years of passing footsteps and the roll of wagon wheels. In the distance Maggie could see the silhouette of a man headed in the same direction.

Carter shrugged. "She doesn't ask. I don't tell her." He looked at Maggie. "But she knows."

Maggie nodded. "I always liked Mary even if she did steal you away from me."

Carter laughed. "We were twelve that summer."

"I caught you kissin' her behind the schoolhouse," Maggie teased, brushing back a lock of hair. Though it was well after sundown, the heat of the day still rose up from the dry soil making her prickly with perspiration.

"You told me right there and then that you

weren't gonna marry me. 'Course I don't remember askin'."

Maggie gave him a punch in the shoulder. "You're shamin' me. My da always said I was too bold. He swore no one would ever marry me and I'd shrivel up and die a barren spinster!"

Maggie's laughter died away as she thought of how close to the truth her da had come. Here she was with Noah in his grave and no babe to cuddle at her breast and nurse with sweet milk. She couldn't help feeling saddened by the thought that she would never have children now. It left an ache inside her that kept her awake at night. But she'd been married once, she'd not make that mistake again. If dying childless was the price she had to pay, she'd just have to accept it.

Carter and Maggie overtook the figure ahead, moving more slowly.

"Papa!" Carter said with surprise. "What the hell are you doin' out here?"

The old man thrust his cane out and kept walking. "Same as you, I'd expect, Son."

"Papa, you don't belong out here."

The old man stopped short on the dirt road and swung around to face his son. "You tellin' me I'm too old to fight for my land, for my grandchildren?"

"Papa—"

"Don't you *Papa* me! I fought the French and them Iroquois back in '55 and '56. I might be too old to enlist now, but I sure as hell ain't ready to lay down and die." The old man started forward again. Carter could do nothing but follow.

"Papa, who told you about this meeting?"

"Don't matter," he grunted. "What matters is I got the invite. That's all it takes and you know it."

Maggie couldn't help but smile in the darkness. Harry Perkins was a tough old bird and she liked him.

Carter swore. "First a woman, now an old man!"

Maggie swung around. "I can't believe you of all people would say that! I'm as capable as you, Carter Perkins." She walked backward in front of him. "Mayhap a little more capable."

"Why would you say that?" he asked, his face taut with irritation.

"Because I got a way in and out of the Brits' camps. I'm free to come and go repairin' boots and takin' orders. What would happen if *you* walked into Lawrence's camp right now?"

"They'd likely fill his tail full of lead shot," Harry offered as he walked off the road to cut through the woods toward the river.

Carter scowled.

"I got a way in and out," Maggie went on, *"and* I've got a friendly captain who just might be of some help to us, though he don't know it yet."

"Whew! You're dangerous, girl," Harry said. "You just watch yourself. What these boys are doin' is babe games compared to what you're talkin' about."

She patted Harry's withered arm. "Don't you worry about me. I'll not take on more than I can bear."

Carter passed them as they reached the river. Ahead in the distance Maggie could see the outline of John Logan's tobacco house. Dim light filtered through the cracks in the walls that once allowed air to circulate around the drying tobacco. Since the war had begun, the barn had sat vacant.

A man with a flintlock stood in the shadows of the barn. "Name," the soldier demanded, his identity obscured by the darkness.

"Carter Perkins."

"Step inside."

"Name," the guard demanded of Harry.

Harry straightened to his full height, expanding his chest with pride. "Harry Perkins, Captain, Virginia militia, French and Indian fuss."

"It's an honor to meet ya, Capt'n Perkins. Go on in. They're waitin' on you."

When Maggie stepped up to be admitted, the soldier waved his rifle. "Evenin', ma'am. They're waitin' on you, too. Leave it to a Virginian to bring a woman into something like this."

Maggie only laughed. "Good even' to you," she said, bobbing her head as she slid open the door and stepped inside.

A dozen men had gathered in the dim lanternlight of John Logan's tobacco house. Built a hundred years earlier by his grandfather, the barn was a story and a half tall with rafters looming high above Maggie's head. She could hear the soft coos of birds roosting in the eaves. Though there'd been no tobacco in the barn for nigh on five years, the pungent smell of Roanoak was thick in the air.

All eyes turned to Maggie as she closed the door behind her. She suddenly felt self-conscious and found herself brushing out the wrinkles in her blue-tick skirting. *Why are they staring?* she wondered. *I got every right to be here!* And as she looked out at the men standing in a semicircle in front of her, as she began to make out the faces of friends and neighbors, she knew this *was* where she belonged more than anyplace in the world.

Zeke appeared at her side and cleared his throat, summoning the other men's attention. "Friends, for those of you that don't know her, this here's Maggie Myers. She was the one who helped us intercept those wagons last week."

When no one said anything, Maggie stepped forward, taking the initiative. "I know what a lot of you must think, me bein' a woman. You think you don't need me. You think it's dangerous for a woman to be doin' what you been doin'. But I want to tell you, it ain't no more dangerous for me than you. And me, I got no family, no husband, no babes. I'm probably a safer choice than most of you."

There were several nods of agreement.

"I think Maggie's right," said Pete Clendaniel, the blacksmith. "She did a damned fine job that night we took those wagons. There weren't no panic in that girl's eyes when the redcoats came bearing down on us. She drew that captain across the field, givin' us a chance to get away."

"I don't know." Carter spoke up, his gaze flicking from Maggie to the men. "She's a *woman,* for Christ's sake!"

Maggie turned to Carter. "I don't know what you're gettin' so fluffed up about, Carter. You never had a problem with me relayin' to you those things I heard in the camps."

Carter looked away. "Ain't the same thing."

John Logan patted Carter on the back. "Sure it is. Now, if no one's got any real objections, I say we accept Maggie Myers in as one of us. Agreed?"

"Agreed," echoed Les Bennett.

"Agreed," mumbled several more voices.

"Good. And now there's Harry Perkins. Any of you who know Harry know why he's here," Zeke said.

"Damned brave man," John said, offering Harry his hand. "Glad you can join us. Now if no one else's got anything to say on this matter, I say we move on to other business. We got exactly twenty-five minutes till the next bloodyback patrol rides by. I want you all scattered before then."

John took a suck on the pipe clenched between his teeth. When the rebel band had formed nearly a year ago, John had just naturally taken the lead. The owner of a sprawling tobacco plantation bordering the river, he had given everything he owned for the cause of freedom. Where rows of tobacco had once grown, he grew corn and wheat for the Colonial army. In the pastures where blue-blood horses had once roamed, he raised livestock to feed the hungry soldiers that passed by. "Now," John said, "let's have any business at hand."

Pete took a step forward. "I just wanted you all to know that I tried talkin' to Billy Faulkner and he just don't want any part of us."

"You were careful how you approached him, weren't you?" John questioned.

"Sure." Pete crossed his massive arms over his

round belly. "I didn't come out and say it, but he knew what I was talkin' about and he asked me not to come botherin' him again."

"Well enough." John nodded. "The best thing for us to do is to stay away from Billy Faulkner. He's never come right out and said he was a Tory, but you never know."

"More business?"

Maggie stood in silence, listening as the men discussed several subjects. She was amazed at how these poor country farmers and tradesmen like her da had so easily fallen into the role of aggressive, elusive fighters. They had contacts everywhere! They knew every ship that went up or down the York River. They kept careful track of overland shipments, escorting as many of their own as possible, always attempting to capture the Brits'.

In no time, the meeting was adjourned and the men hurried into the darkness, scattering like copper coins hitting the floor. Just as Maggie went out the door, John Logan caught her arm.

"Pleased to have you with us, Maggie.

She smiled at him, knowing his words were genuine. "Thanks. You won't be disappointed in me."

"I know I won't. Now you understand you'll not ride as one of the group, just as Harry won't. Your main job will to be keep your ears open in the British encampments and relay information to the group. You'll be called on occasion to join just as you joined us last week. Memorize the faces in the group you didn't know and remember that no one, and I mean no one, can be trusted but these men. Not uncles, not friends, not Jesus Christ himself."

Maggie nodded.

"Now what's this talk about Captain Thayer? Zeke says he's paying you some attention."

The sound of Grayson's name brought a pitter-patter to her heart. "Not much to tell. He was nice to me. Got me out of a spot of bad luck with a bunch of lieutenants the other night."

"You think this might be worth pursuing."

She lifted her head to meet John's gaze. "I think I got to pursue it."

John's eyes searched hers. "You be careful, Maggie. You take it slow. Spying is the quickest way I know to get hanged these days."

She flashed him a grin. "Don't worry about me. I can handle one bloody redcoat."

He patted her on the shoulder and leaned to blow out the lantern as he escorted her out the door "For some reason," he whispered in the darkness, "I've no doubt you can."

The following morning, Maggie rose early, refreshed by a full night's sleep. She hadn't realized how exhausted she been until she hit the goose-down mattress of her parents' four-poster bed. But then she'd remembered that she hadn't slept a wink the previous night.

She'd lain awake all night stretched out on Grayson's cot, listening to the sounds of the camp around her, listening to his soft breathing and later the sound of him sleeping. Through the darkness she'd studied the sleeping man, perplexed by him. What would make a man behave as Grayson had behaved? What kind of man wouldn't take advantage of a woman at his mercy. There was only one answer. A good man.

Maggie couldn't help smiling as she slipped naked from the linen sheets and pulled her shift over her head. Sweeping a faded cotton blouse and a tattered homespun skirt off a chair, she dressed quickly. She wanted to get into her vegetable garden and do some weeding before it got too hot. Downstairs in the kitchen, she let the hounds out the back door like she did every morning and then grabbed a bucket to fetch water for coffee. Just as she reached the back door, she heard the horrendous bellowing of Roy and Honey.

There was a stranger outside. The dogs never carried on like that when Zeke came. Picking up her rifle from the corner by the fireplace, Maggie backtracked, going out the front door.

The minute she stepped out on the front porch, her face lit up with amusement. There, perched precariously on her fence at six-thirty in the morning, was Captain Thayer!

Roy and Honey howled, racing in circles, snapping at Grayson's boots. "Down! Down!" he ordered, but the dogs just went wilder.

Maggie broke into laughter as she leaned the rifle against the side of the house.

"What the hell are you laughing about?" Grayson called, jerking his fancy French boot from Honey's jaws. "Call them off!"

"What are you doing here?" she asked, enjoying the sight of the uniformed captain perched on the top rail of her fence, trying to keep his feet off the ground.

"I brought you something," he shouted above Honey and Roy's bellows. "Now call off the dogs!"

Maggie's gaze fell to the leather knapsack lying on the top porch step. It was her knapsack! He'd brought back the precious half-made shoes the soldiers had stolen from her the other night! And lying on top of the worn leather sack was a single long-stemmed wildflower.

"Oh," she murmured, lifting the delicate blossom. In the heat of the summer, she didn't know where he'd found such a beautiful flower.

Absently she called to Honey and Roy, and the dogs immediately backed off. She slapped her knee and they turned and came running. She had just let them into the house when she heard Grayson's footsteps on the porch.

She turned to face him, the fragrant posy clutched in her hand. Suddenly she'd lost her voice. All she could do was look up at him with his meticulously pressed scarlet coat and his golden hair blowing in the warm morning breeze.

Grayson's gaze met hers as she stared at him with wide dark-brown eyes. She was a picture of loveliness this morning with her hair tumbled wildly over her shoulders and her face still wearing the mask of sleep. Grayson's first impulse was to reach out to her, to draw her into his arms, and kiss her rosy lips. He wanted to sweep her up and lay her in the dewy grass where he could caress her full, rounded breasts and taste of her womanhood. But all he could do was return her gaze, the electricity between them all too evident in the hot, still morning air.

Maggie was the first to look away. "Thank you," she whispered. "For my boots . . . and the flower." She lifted the blossom, inhaling its sweet fragrance.

"You're welcome," he said awkwardly. *Christ. I feel like a schoolboy at Eaton again,* he thought. "I hope everything is still there. I . . . I also came by to ask if you'd . . ." He laughed at his own foolishness and began again. "What I wanted to know, Maggie, was if you'd honor me by accompanying me to a bull roast at Mason Pickney's plantation on Saturday."

"Me?" She couldn't help smiling. Of course she couldn't go. Mason Pickney was a bloody Tory. She wouldn't be caught dead eating the man's roast, even if she hadn't had beef in nearly a year.

"Why not?" He smiled roguishly. "It might be fun."

"I . . . I don't think it's such a good idea." She twirled her flower by the stem.

"Why?" he asked, his rich tenor voice reverberating in the air.

"I don't know, I just . . ." She lifted her dark lashes. He made her warm in the pit of her stomach gazing at her like that. *Why not?* she asked herself. *What better way to keep tabs on the Tories and the Brits but to be right in the center of them?*

He caught her hand, turning it to study her palm. "There'll be the picnic, games, horse races. Like the old days before this damned war."

He brought her hand to his lips as Maggie watched, mesmerized. He kissed one knuckle and then the next, working down the row.

"All right," Maggie said, her voice sounding

breathy in her ears. "I'll do it. I'll go!"

"Grand!" Reluctantly, he released her hand. He knew he shouldn't be asking her. He knew there was no room in his life for a woman, especially a woman of Maggie's social class. The thought that she had no loyalties, that she was as willing to make a pair of English boots as American boots disturbed him greatly. But he just couldn't help himself. He'd lain awake half of last night thinking about her. Even when he closed his eyes, she was there, staring back at him with those immense brown eyes and that wild strawberry-blond hair.

"I'll come by to get you about noon," he said.

She watched him turn and go. "I'll be ready." She waved and then watched until he disappeared down the lane. Tucking the flower behind her ear, she picked up her bucket and headed for the well.

Just wait until I tell Zeke, she thought. *He's gonna be mad as fire!*

Zeke slammed his leather ale jack on the scarred tavern table. "You said you'd what!"

"I said I'd go with him," Maggie answered, using a cotton rag to wipe up the spilled ale. "Now lower your voice before someone hears you."

He grasped her arm, pulling her onto the bench beside him, "You can't go to Mason Pickney's bull roast! He's a damned Tory. Pickney's Folly will be swarming with British. As good as Pickney's been to the British army this past year, Cornwallis may be there himself!" Zeke hissed angrily.

"What better way," Maggie answered calmly, "to

watch the wasp than to be in the nest?"

"Hey, hey, what's the commotion?" John Logan slid onto the bench across the table from Maggie and Zeke.

She hooked her thumb in Zeke's direction. "He's being unreasonable."

Zeke leaned across the table, trying to control his anger. "Thayer's asked Maggie to that big bull roast at Pickney's Folly up on the bay."

John's gaze went to Maggie. "You're going to go?"

"Of course she ain't goin'," Zeke interrupted.

"Zeke, I know how you feel about this, but we've been trying for weeks to get someone into that party. It's places like that that we really get our information. A couple of bowls of punch and some officer is liable to spill anything."

Maggie covered her smile. She knew she'd won, and a thrill of anticipation ran up her spine. But still, she knew she had to take this seriously. This was business and she had to remember that. "I just think we'd be fools not to take advantage of this, John."

" 'Till he takes advantage of *you,*" Zeke muttered, lifting his jack of ale in defeat.

"He's been nothin' but a gentleman," Maggie corrected. "He's just lonely. I'm safe enough."

"It's up to you, Maggie," John said. "But if you're willing to go in, we're willing to back you."

"I can do it." She leaned across the table. "I know I can."

"First thing we've got to do then is to get you something to wear."

"Oh." She sat back with deflated sigh. "I hadn't thought of that. I don't have any fancy dresses." She pulled at her spotted bodice. "I'd look like the servants in this."

John covered her hand with his. "I can take care of that. You just come by my place tomorrow and my sister Liz will find you something appropriate."

Her face lit up. "You sure she won't mind?"

"Positive." John nodded at Zeke. "You with us, friend?"

"I'm with you," Zeke grunted. "Let's get something to eat and then we'd best start with a list of names of the important officers who might be at Pickney's. She's going to have to know who's who if anything they say is going to make any sense to her."

Maggie turned to Zeke. "I'll be all right," she assured him. "I'll make you proud of me."

He looked up at her, his face lined with emotion. "I don't want to be proud, Maggie girl, I just want to see you livin'."

Chapter Seven

"Holy Mother Mary," Maggie breathed, staring at her own reflection in Elizabeth's floor-length beveled mirror. "Is it really me?"

Elizabeth laughed, her voice as rich as her brother's, John Logan. "Of course it's you! Just a splash of paint, a twist of curls, and a bolt of silk for good measure."

Maggie turned sideways, her eyes still wide with amazement. The apple-green polonaise was the most beautiful gown she'd ever laid eyes on. Fashioned of brocaded silk, the boned bodice lifted her breasts: tightening at the waist until it flared seductively at her hips. More rich apple-green watered silk formed the skirting, looped up to reveal a soft yellow petticoat. On her feet she wore a pair of supple leather-heeled slippers with silver buckles, and covering her calves were a pair of sheer linen stocking clocked at the ankles and tied up with yellow satin garters.

Elizabeth had brushed her hair until it shone and then drew part of it back to fall in curly waves from beneath a tiny beribboned cap. Maggie's face had been subtly painted with rice powder and a touch of rouge on her lips and cheeks to bring out the natural glow of her beauty.

"God knows I wouldn't recognize myself on the road," Maggie protested. She was giddy with pleasure. She'd had a wonderful afternoon with Elizabeth and John in the garden, where they'd gone over the identities of all of the important British officers likely to be at the bull roast. They'd laughed and talked as if they'd been friends for years. Then Elizabeth had led Maggie upstairs, and with the help of two maids she had transformed her from a country wench to a cultured lady . . . at least in appearance.

"Ladies!" John called from outside the bedchamber door. "You'll have to hurry if we're to have Maggie back in time for Thayer to pick her up. I've already sent for the carriage."

"Oh, Elizabeth," Maggie breathed, taking the blond girl's slender hands. "I don't know if I can do this! You've sewn me in so tight I can barely take a breath and I'm all wobbly on these fancy shoes."

Elizabeth laughed, her clear blue eyes shining with merriment. "You'll do fine. Believe me. You'll be the most beautiful woman there!"

"But I don't know how to act—what to say. I can't talk like them. "I'm liable to make fools of us both."

Elizabeth brushed a hand over her protruding stomach. She was well into her sixth month of her first pregnancy and hadn't seen her husband in months. He didn't even know she was with child when he left for the northern campaign. Maggie's heart went out to her, yet at the same time she made her proud. Elizabeth Logan Campbell was a true woman of the revolution. "Do as little talking as possible; men like those don't like a talkative woman.

And when you must speak, just try to imitate the other women, like you've imitated me today."

"But I've never been to a fancy party like this before. I won't know what's proper."

"You do as Captain Thayer does. If he rests his napkin on his knee, you rest your napkin on your knee. If he laughs at one of Lawrence's inane jokes about the Germans," she shrugged, "you laugh. It's simple enough."

"Simple enough for you! You weren't born in a dirt-floor cabin!" Maggie ran her hands down her waist, amazed by the womanly figure she never knew she had.

"You'd be surprised what you can do when you have to." Elizabeth lowered her gaze to the polished wood floor, suddenly lost in her thoughts.

"Ah, Liz, I'm sorry." Maggie squeezed her arm. "I didn't mean to make you feel bad."

Elizabeth lifted her chin determinedly. "I was just thinking of those soldiers in Williamsburg we cared for last year. I never thought I could hold a man down while another sawed off his leg." She shook her head. "I never thought I could do it, but I did."

"It was a brave thing to do. Everyone in the tavern was talking about you."

Elizabeth exhaled softly. "I think about that poor man in Williamsburg and then . . . then, I can't help wondering if there's a woman somewhere holding down my Rob this very moment—" Her voice caught in her throat and she turned away, ashamed by the hot tears that filled her clear blue eyes.

Impulsively, Maggie wrapped her arms around Elizabeth's trembling shoulders. "It's gonna be all right," she soothed. "One of these days Rob Campbell's going to come walkin'—walking through that door." She grasped Elizabeth by the shoulders, peering into her tear-streaked face. "He's going to walk in that door and lift you into his arms and he's going kiss you long and hard."

"Do you think so, Maggie?"

Maggie smiled. "I know so."

"Liz!" John called from the hallway. "She's got to go! I don't want to be there when Thayer arrives to pick Maggie up at her house."

"Oh, dear . . ." Elizabeth pulled an embroidered handkerchief from her sleeve and dabbed her eyes. "I apologize for my behavior. I didn't mean to keep you."

"Pshaw!" Maggie gave a wave. "What good's a friend if you can't cry on her shoulder once in a while? Now I gotta—" Maggie broke into a smile. "I must," she imitated Elizabeth's clear, precise speech, "go. But I'll speak with you on the morrow."

Elizabeth laughed at Maggie's antics, waving as she swept out of the bedchamber and accepted John's arm, allowing him to escort her downstairs.

"By the king's cod," Grayson swore softly as Maggie came onto the front porch of her farmhouse.

She laughed, throwing back her head, her rich, husky voice filling the hot afternoon air. "Hell of a sight I am, don't you think?" She spun on her toes for him, her cheeks rosy with excitement. It felt so good to be admired by a man, even if he was the enemy.

Grayson offered his hand to help her down the steps. His voice caught in a lump in his throat, and for a moment he found himself speechless. The country wench had shed her patched homespun for an apple-green satin gown, befitting of any society lady. She was the most beautiful woman Grayson had laid eyes on . . . even more beautiful than his brother's wife, Reagan. The sight of her standing on the porch steps, her dark brown eyes riveted to his, made his heart pound, his knees weak. But how could that be? She was an uneducated, poorly spoken, rough-and-tumble farmgirl. Her parents had been bond servants for God's sake!

Maggie accepted his hand and bounded lightly down the steps. "Close your mouth, Grayson. You'll let the flies in," she teased.

Embarrassed by his own reaction, Grayson found himself speaking in his captain's arrogant tone. "Well, God's bowels, Maggie, you startled me. Where the hell did you get that gown?"

"What did you think I was going to wear to Mason Pickney's, a flour sack?"

"I . . . I didn't think about it, actually."

They came to the open carriage Grayson had arrived in. "Neither did I till you were gone. But a friend loaned it to me."

He arched an eyebrow. "A friend." What friend would Maggie have who could afford such trappings?

She gave a nod. "A friend. Now are you going to help me into this contraption, or am I to run behind?"

Grayson chuckled as he swung open the half-door to the carriage and took Maggie's hand, assisting her up. "In you go." He stepped in behind her and snapped the door shut. "Onward, Michaels."

The private driving the carriage tipped his cap and

gave a slap of the reins and the vehicle lunged forward.

Maggie gasped, sinking into the soft leather bench seat. Her second carriage ride in one day!

Grayson eased into the seat across from her as the carriage rolled down the dirt drive. The urge to kiss that sweet neck, to nuzzle her breasts where they swelled from the green silk was so overwhelming that he didn't trust himself to sit beside her. From here, he could at least admire her fresh, striking beauty without doing something foolish he was sure to regret later.

Maggie settled herself on the seat and spread her silk skirts as Elizabeth had instructed. Then, striking her Spanish lace fan on her knee, she spread the fan wide and fluttered it. This was all a game: she'd seen that soon enough. Even if she wasn't a real lady, she could certainly *act* the part.

Grayson rested his arm across the the back of the leather seat and stretched out, crossing his legs at the calves. As he did so, Maggie couldn't help noticing how well the breeches fit his sinewy form. By the holy virgin he was a fit man! From the tip of his polished shoes, to the top of his grenadier cap, he was all hard and muscular. Her thoughts went back to the glimpse of his nakedness she'd caught that night in his tent and she looked away.

Sure, Maggie girl, she told herself. *He's a fine form of a man who makes your heart flutter and your belly go hot, but that there's a red coat he wears and he's the enemy. Plain and simple. So mind why you're here and quit simpering like a lovestruck schoolgirl on May Day!*

Maggie lifted her lashes. "Tell me, Captain, what's

a man like yourself doin' asking a girl who sews boots for a living to a party like this?"

Grayson watched the way the hot July air rippled through Maggie's waves of red hair as the carriage sped down a winding road to the northeast, "Good question," he answered honestly. "I don't know myself."

"Fair enough," she conceded, "because I couldn't tell you why I said yes." She was lying, of course; she *did* know why. She'd said yes because she thought there might be some information to be gleaned from conversations at a Tory gathering where redcoats oozed at the seams. But deep inside she agreed to go because she wanted to be with Grayson. She wanted to hear his rich tenor voice. She wanted to feel her hand in his. God help her, she wanted to taste his lips again.

Grayson forced his gaze to wander to the passing countryside. How could a woman like Maggie, a woman born of the Colonies, not feel the call of freedom? How could she sit across from him, an English soldier in her eyes, and feel no resentment? Didn't she understand what Washington's men fought for? Didn't she realize what was at risk? He wished he could tell her. He wished he could make her understand what those men were willing to die for . . . what *he* was willing to die for.

But that wasn't up to him, was it? He couldn't afford to get involved with this woman, not emotionally. This was just a dalliance like all the others and he had to keep that in mind. *Play the part of Captain Thayer and you'll be safe,* he told himself. *Play the part.*

Grayson turned back to Maggie. "So, sweet, tell

me, what does a country girl usually do on a Saturday afternoon when she's not attending bull roasts on the Chesapeake . . ."

Maggie and Grayson spent the hour-and-half-long carriage trip to Pickney's Folly talking about their childhoods, about horses, about foolish things like when the tinkers came to town. They laughed and teased, their gazes locking again and again. By the time they rode up the long semicircle, tree-lined drive of the Virginia plantation, they were warm with the sun of the day and the heat of their merriment.

More than once Grayson thought of how glad he was that he had finagled his own carriage sent by the Tory, Pickney, rather than sharing carriages with the other lower ranking officers. He selfishly wanted Maggie all to himself, to savor every heartwarmingly honest word she spoke, every unrehearsed gesture she made. Grayson had spent so long living a lie that it thrilled him to be with someone who had the freedom to be so honest in every word and deed.

Maggie leaned over the edge of the carriage, her eyes lighting up with excitement as she spotted the carriages ahead filled with arriving guests. There were beautifully dressed women everywhere. And the lawn crawled with red-coated soldiers looking to Maggie like red ants on an anthill. Ahead, the manor house sprawled across the hill above the bay, its brick exterior climbing three stories into the bright blue sky.

"Holy Mary! The house is so big it could hold every man, woman, and child in Yorktown!"

Grayson looked up at the house that loomed above them. "New money. Pickney only built it a few years back. I wish you could see the house at Thayer's

Folly. You'd love it. It's not as impressive in size, but it gives off an aura of, oh . . . I don't know, regal stability. Someday when I get home my brother and I are . . ." He let his sentence run incomplete when he realized she was staring at him with those dark eyes, an odd smile on her face. "What?" he asked, suddenly uncomfortable.

She shook her head. "Nothing. Go on. It's just the way you said that. The way you talked about your home. You sounded different. You didn't tell me you had a brother. Is he in the Army, too?"

Grayson made a point of brushing an imaginary bit of lint from his coat. He was going to have to be more careful of what he said or he was liable to slip up with this woman. She made him too comfortable and he couldn't afford to be comfortable. "Yes. I've a brother—a twin brother, Sterling. Bastard Colonial scum."

His words caught her attention and she looked up, unable to resist a smile. "A twin brother? Another man like you? Holy Mother Mary! And he's a rebel?"

The carriage came to a halt and Grayson shot up. "Ah, we're here. Come, dear," he fell into his role, "let's greet our host."

Maggie stood, taking the hint that the conversation about his brother was over. Smoothing her skirts, she waited for Grayson to leap down and then offer her his assistance. But instead of offering his hand, he caught her around the waist and lifted her from the carriage. All too naturally, her hands fell to his broad shoulders. He held her just a second too long after her feet hit the grassy ground and then suddenly he was whisking her toward a line of chattering gentleman.

"Mason! Mason!" Grayson gave a wave to a short, rather plump gentleman in a lavender satin coat and breeches.

"Thayer! Good to see you could make it!" Mason Pickney turned his eyes to Maggie and clutched his chest in a rather dramatic sweep of his hands. "Heaven on earth, who *is* this paragon? Surely you haven't had a wife shipped in from a Turkish harem?"

Grayson flashed his host a devil-may-care grin. "God rot your greedy bowels, Mason! You know I'm not a marrying man!" He took Maggie's hand in his, forcing her to come forward. "This is the Widow Myers of Yorktown, Maggie to her friends."

Mason's soft, pudgy hand took hers and it was an effort not to grimace at the feel of his sweaty palm as he made a great show of kissing her knuckles. "So pleased you could come and grace my lawn with your beauty, Maggie."

She didn't like him. Not from the first sight of his bulging eyes and ruddy face. "Pleased to be here," she answered. She looked up at Grayson. "It was kind of Captain Thayer to invite me."

Mason gave Grayson a slap on the shoulder. "Horses won't be racing for another hour, so feel free to show the lady around. I've just purchased another Reni. The painting arrived from France only yesterday." He brought a chubby hand to his cheek. "It's so exquisite it will bring tears to your eyes, Thayer."

"I'm certain it will," Grayson answered politely.

"Well, you know where my art gallery is. First floor, just through the solarium. If you find yourself thirsting, have one of my niggers fetch you a glass of port or a tankard of Madeira from down by the water. The food will be out directly."

Grayson grasped Maggie's hand, steering her away from their host. "Thanks to you, Mason." He waved. "I'll let you know what I think of the Reni."

"I've got ten pounds riding on Riker's bay," Mason called after Grayson. "You interested in a wager?"

"Not when it comes to that black devil. I'll keep my coin, thank you."

"Riker's here?" Maggie whispered the moment they were out of earshot of Pickney.

"Don't worry. We'll stay clear of him. He's not likely to cause any trouble here."

He dropped a hand casually on her bare shoulder and Maggie's mood lightened. What was wrong with her? What did she care if Riker was here or not? She wasn't afraid of him or any other man!

Grayson led Maggie down a brick path around the enormous house and down the sloped back lawn. From the crest of the hill she sees the enormous Chesapeake Bay spread before her in all of its wonder. Bright sunlight reflected off the blue-green water like a thousand twinkling skies in the heavens.

Everywhere Maggie looked there were new sights and sounds to behold. Tables and chairs shaded with colorful awnings were casually placed across the manicured lawn. There were fiddlers playing a merry tune seated beneath a white-and-red striped canopy. White-garbed Negro servants, as many in number as guests, walked from group to group offering an assortment of refreshments from fresh lemonade to a fine French wine.

As Grayson led her from table to table, introducing her, Maggie relaxed, beginning to enjoy herself. It was like a dream come true to walk on Grayson's arm and have men bow to her and ladies curtsy. Heeding Elizabeth's words she remained silent for the most part, speaking only when spoken to. To her amazement, she found herself catching tidbits of potentially beneficial information here and there.

According to the drunken Major Marlboro, an error had been made. Clinton and Cornwallis were arguing over troops. Cornwallis insisted he needed more men before marching onto the peninsula. Clinton, still in New York, saw no need for so many troops in the South when the war was still being waged in the North. A lovestruck Lieutenant Ladkin explained to her which rebel armory near Williamsburg he was about to destroy just before asking her to marry him. And then of course there was Captain Perkery, who, while escorting her to her chair, had explained his theory of how the Yorktown rebels causing all of the fuss were not Yorktown locals, but actually Mohawk savages shipped in from the New York colony.

The hours slipped by like minutes as Maggie sopped up information like a crust of bread in a plate of milk. But she actually had fun doing it! When Grayson left her side, instead of being fearful, she found herself asking bold questions, plying answers from smitten, drunken redcoats. Men ushered her from table to table of delicacies like jellied calve's feet and pickled eel pie. And when the musicians' instruments were tuned and the music struck up, she danced country dances until she was breathless. There was so much to see, so much to absorb!

The guest of honor, a thousand-pound bull, was roasted in a huge pit lined with brick and then skewered and toted around the lawn by twenty young Negro men before it was finally sliced to be consumed by Pickney's guests. There were horse races, tennis, gaming tables, and even a dancing girl to entertain the redcoats.

Sights and sounds whirled Maggie into a state of confusion until finally, well after dark, she told Grayson she was ready to go home.

"Home?" Grayson moaned, aghast. "But the night is young. I'm not ready to let you go."

He brushed his lips against hers and she laughed, as intoxicated by the soft waltz drifting up from the bay as by the nearness of Grayson. "Holy Mary. I've got to get home. Father Rufus will have my head if I'm not in church come tomorrow morning bright and early."

"Father Rufus!" He backed her into the shadows of a great oak tree. "What about me? Father Rufus never took you to a bull roast!"

She felt the rough bark of the tree against her bare back. "What about you? I've been here with you for hours."

"Ha!" he challenged. "I've barely seen you. Every man on this lawn has danced with you at least once."

"Every man but Riker. I never saw him after the race."

"Too busy whoring upstairs I should suspect." Grayson caught her around the waist, his fingers aching to caress her soft curves. "Now tell me, you don't really want to go home."

She smiled, lifting her hands to rest on his shoulders. "I fear you've had too much to drink, Captain."

He grinned boyishly. "Unlike my fellow officers?"

She had to laugh. By nightfall there were already several handsomely dressed redcoats sprawled unconscious on the lawn. "It's been a night I'll never forget, but I tell you the truth when I say I have to get home."

He caught a handful of her bright-red hair and brought it to his lips, inhaling the sweet, fresh scent. "Ah, Maggie mine. What am I to do with you?"

"Do with me?" Her dark eyes met his as she felt him draw her closer. "I don't know," she said softly. "Kiss me, I'd suppose."

"Kiss you?" he echoed huskily "Like this?" His lips met hers, gently.

"Yes . . ."

But he didn't stop with one kiss. His lips met hers again and again. "Like this?"

"Yes."

"And this?"

"Yes, yes," she whispered. Her flesh tingled with response as she met his mouth again and again. His tongue met hers and the kisses deepened. She couldn't get enough of him. It had been so long since she'd felt a man's touch, and even then, Noah had never stirred her like this man stirred her. There was heat deep in the pit of her stomach that rose, fanning out to light her limbs on fire. Grayson brought his hand up under her breast and she moaned softly. With his fingertips he stroked her breast through the satin of the gown teasing her, sending thrilling sensations through her until she felt her nipple grow hard against her shift. She knew she shouldn't be doing this. She knew she couldn't be get involved, but she couldn't help herself.

"Oh, Maggie, Maggie," he whispered, his tongue teasing the lobe of her ear as he thrust his hips against hers, making her feel the hardness of him against the mound of her womanhood. "I could take you here, now on the grass."

She laughed, his words bringing her back to reality. "No," she murmured, "No more, Grayson." She covered his hand with hers, resting her head on his shoulder as she tried to catch her breath. "I can't."

As Grayson stood holding her in his arms, his thoughts began to clear. *What the hell do I think I'm doing here?* he chastised himself. *Maggie's no whore to roll in the hay with and then walk away. Don't get yourself involved with her. You'll be sorry. You'll regret it till your dying day.* The word "love" hovered in the recesses of his mind, but he pushed it aside, knowing how utterly ridiculous the thought was. Grayson Thayer in love with a bootmaker? Hah!

Another minute passed and Maggie lifted her head from Grayson's shoulder. "Let's go," she said softly. "I want to go home." She was shaken to the bone by her response to Grayson. The idea was to use him to aid her patriot friends, but she feared the plan was crumbling. Her job was to use him, not fall in love with him.

Chapter Eight

Maggie meandered down the dirt road, dragging a stick behind her with one hand. She'd promised her sister and Manny that she'd come by the tavern and help at the supper hour, but she wasn't anxious to get there. She was afraid she would see Grayson . . . she was afraid she wouldn't.

It had been nearly two weeks since the bull roast, and in that two weeks, so much had changed. July had come and Cornwallis had taken Hampton Roads, then Yorktown, and finally Gloucester Point on the opposite shore of the York River. Though Yorktown would not due for a naval base for Clinton, Cornwallis chose the old tobacco port and proceeded to move his entire force of men onto the peninsula.

The bull roast had turned out to be profitable for the rebel band led by John Logan. He and the others had been thrilled with the information she'd brought back to them, so thrilled that they urged her to see Captain Thayer again soon. But she didn't know that she wanted to see him. It was too dangerous; he'd somehow dug into a place very close to her heart and she was scared.

Holy Saints! It was hard to believe she'd only met Grayson a few weeks ago. It seemed like an eternity. Only a few short weeks ago her life had been orderly, if not a little dull, but suddenly everything had changed—her life seemed out of control! She wanted to see Grayson so badly that she felt a physical hurt inside her, but she knew she'd be better off without him. What could come of it but ill? There was no denying their attraction to each other. How long could she resist his charms? The real question was, did she want to?

She'd vowed never to become involved with another man. Noah had nearly ruined her life. He'd treated her like a possession, no better than the hounds. He'd belittled her until she had doubted her own judgment, her own abilities. No man was ever going to do that to her again.

Maggie hurled the stick she'd been carrying into the air and watched it glance off a tree before falling into the thick grass. Heavens, but it was hot tonight! She wiped her brow with her forearm thinking of the fall and winter to come. She couldn't wait for those cool breezes to begin blowing off the bay. The thought of cuddling up beneath a soft, worn quilt . . . Ah, to sleep. It had been nights since she'd slept. It was just too hot. Her mind was too filled with thought of Grayson, of the war, of Grayson . . .

Maggie approached the crossroad where Commegys' Ordinary stood, and as she crossed over she spotted Zeke walking in the opposite direction lost in conversation with a petite blond woman. Maggie scowled, thinking to call out to him, but then decided against it. She didn't know what the hell Zeke was doing with the town whore, but tonight was not the night to discuss it. Tomorrow. She made a mental note to be certain to speak with him about it tomorrow when he came to help with the chores. She'd been telling Zeke for two years that it was high time he found himself a wife, but he certainly wasn't going to find a decent girl being seen with the likes of Lyla!

Maggie walked past several townsfolk drinking ale under one of the big elms outside the door. "Even' to you," she murmured as she passed.

"Evening, Maggie," Peter, the blacksmith, greeted.

"Hey, Mags, how about rolling a keg out here?" Carter teased as she passed him.

"You'll have to talk to Manny about that!" she answered as she slipped through the tavern door and the heat hit her like the opening of an oven door. She cut across the public room, forcing herself not to look for Grayson.

"Manny!" she called as she walked into the kitchen. "It's hotter than a summer day in hell in there! How do you think you're going to sell food and drink if you boil all of your customers?"

Manny looked up from where he was slicing a huge apple pie. Sweat ran in rivulets off his temples and down onto his shoulders. "Makes 'em drink plenty of ale."

"Makes 'em ornery." She pulled an apron off a peg on the wall and slipped it over her head. "You best try and get some of those windows open."

"Can't," Alice said, coming in the back door with two empty slop buckets. "Manny painted 'em shut."

"I did not, Alice. And the Lord said, 'Let the lying

lips be put to silence, which speak grievous things proudly and contemptuously against the righteous.' "

Maggie rolled her eyes. "You'll be righteous enough if those soldiers bust out your precious new glass windows, Manny."

"You tend to the serving, Maggie, I'll tend to the state of my building."

Maggie shook her head, sweeping up a tray of filled plates. "Who's this for?"

"Table under the south window. Lieutenant Riker and his crew."

Maggie paled. Other than spotting Riker from across the lawn at Pickney's bull roast, she hadn't seen or spoken to Riker since the night Grayson had saved her from him.

Alice grasped Maggie's arm. "You all right, Sister? You look as if you've seen a ghost." She shifted a pot of turnips onto her hip and crossed herself superstitiously.

"No, no, I'm fine." Maggie smiled down at her sister, noticing for the hundredth time how tired she looked. She wasn't carrying this pregnancy as well as the others. Her face and hands were puffy and there were big dark circles beneath her eyes. Five children in seven years was just too many for a woman trying to help her husband run a successful tavern. "You sit down whilst you mash those turnips. I'll be right back."

Maggie pushed through the kitchen door and headed straight for Riker's table. She'd be damned if any man would make her tremble! It was high time she met up with Lieutenant Riker and demanded her money for the boots he'd taken without payment. When Grayson had returned, her knapsack, one pair of boots had been missing from it—Riker's. She hadn't said anything to Grayson about it because it was her business and hers alone, but the more she thought about it, the angrier it made her. Riker had no right to steal from her!

"Maggie! Get us some ale here!" a patron called as she passed his table.

"Be right back, Jonas," she threw over her shoulder.

"Hotter than blue blazes in here," a soldier told her, catching her skirt. "Can't you do anything about it? Open some windows? Something?"

"You can prop open the door is all I can tell you, soldier." She snatched her skirt from his hand and moved on. "You're not any hotter than I am!"

Spotting Riker's table ahead, Maggie stiffened her spine. He was there all right, there with the same bunch he'd played cards with that night. "Even' to you," she said, sliding her tray onto the table.

Riker glanced up, his mouth slipping into a smile. "Look who it is, gentlemen. Our Maggie. Woman of many talents, aren't you? Sewing boots, serving ale . . . slutting."

The men at the table broke into ribald laughter, but she ignored Riker's comment. She'd not betray Grayson with the truth of what had really happened that night, not after he could have well saved her life.

She grabbed a pewter plate and slid it across the table to the far end. "Speaking of boots," she said, sliding another plate heaped with mashed turnips, fried bacon, and sweet peas, "I believe you and I have a bit of business to discuss, Lieutenant Riker."

"Business?" He pushed back a long lock of sleek midnight hair. "Business, you say?"

The men elbowed each other, snickering and murmuring among themselves.

"Business. Would you care to speak to me in private?" She used the same voice she'd used at the bull roast.

"There's nothing you can't say in front of my friends, lover."

Maggie lifted the last of the plates and slammed it down in front of Riker. Several string beans popped up and fell onto his lap. "All right. You owe me for the boots." She was fast losing her temper. What made this man so arrogant? It was obvious he needed taking down a notch and maybe she was the one to do it.

"What boots?"

"You know what boots." She tried to keep her voice low and even. "The boots you stole out of my knapsack."

"I don't know what you're talking about." He glanced up at the other men. "You know anything about boots, boys?"

"Don't know a thing about boots," Gordy answered innocently. "Pass the salt cellar, Carl."

Maggie swept up her tray. "Either you pay me the agreed-upon sum, or you return the boots. You can't wear them like that anyway. They're not done."

"And what are you going to do if I don't pay?" He looked up, his face covered in a sheen of perspiration.

"Guess I'll speak to that uncle of yours, Major Lawrence, is it? I understand he wants his men to keep in line, no thieving, no *kidnapping.*"

"You threatening me, Maggie?" Riker rose up, pressing his arms on the trestle table. "Because I don't like being threatened—not by a woman, not by anyone."

"Riker, let her be."

Maggie felt someone touch the small of her back and she swung around. Grayson! She took a deep breath. "Stay out of this," she warned. For some reason it infuriated her to see Grayson standing there at her side, coming to her rescue again. Who the hell did he think she was, her guardian angel! She didn't need him to settle her affairs!

Her gaze locked with Grayson's. "I said I don't need your help. Just go on, I can take care of this on my own."

"Just come on, Maggie, let him be." Grayson grasped her arm, but she yanked it from his grip.

Riker flashed that stupid grin of his. "You sure took a shine to the bitch, didn't you, Thayer? One tumble and you're strutting at Pickney's like some peacock with your peahen on your arm? One tumble, or is she your regular now?"

With Riker's last word, Grayson lunged forward, punching Riker in the jaw.

"Son of a bitch!" Riker shouted, stumbling away from the table.

Maggie ducked as Riker swung back.

"Grayson!" She tried to catch his arm and break up the fight, but it was too late. Riker's men leapt up from the table as other patrons gathered around, shouting threats. A soldier shoved Gordy, Gordy shoved him back, and suddenly there were two more men swinging fists. Like a chain reaction, one soldier joined in after another until a full-blown brawl erupted in the public room.

Maggie dove for the cover of the trestle table as a

chair went hurling through the air. Fists flew and pine furniture crashed. Someone was gathering pewter plates and sailing them through the air one after the other. With the first sound of shattering window glass, Maggie cringed, holding her hands over her ears. *Oh, God, Manny's windows! He's gonna be hot with me!* she thought in consternation.

Peering up between the bench and the table she spotted Grayson and Riker still locked in a fist-to-fist struggle. At some point Grayson had peeled off his uniform coat, freeing his arms to swing more easily. He was bleeding from a cut on his right cheek, but Riker's face was covered with blood, his nose cocked at an odd angle. Fueled by blind fury, Riker shouted obscenities, swinging wildly. Grayson ducked and dodged with the grace of a dancer, his muscles rippling beneath his torn muslin shirt. The men went round and round, neither gaining much ground until Grayson sunk a fist into Riker's stomach and the dark-haired man spun around, stunned, and slumped onto the table above Maggie's head.

"Son of a bitch!" she shouted, grabbing a pewter tankard as it rolled by. Lifting the tankard she brought it down sharply on Riker's foot, and the semiconscious man bellowed with pain. Leaping up, he spun around and tripped over a prone body. "Where are you, Thayer?" he shouted, stumbling, blinded by the blood running down his face. "Where the hell are you?"

Maggie watched as he disappeared into the crowd of angry soldiers.

Just then two men came up behind Grayson, and Maggie gave a scream as they both bore down on him at the same time. Somehow Grayson managed to dodge them both, and came up swinging. Lifting one arm into the air, he heaved him forward, knocking the man's accomplice to the ale-drenched floor.

Maggie couldn't resist a yelp of approval.

The sound of her voice caught Grayson's attention. "Maggie?" He wiped his face with his sleeve, and in the process spotted Maggie beneath the table. "Maggie?"

"Don't you Maggie me," she snapped, suddenly recalling that this whole fight was his fault in the first place. If he'd just minded his own business and not insisted upon coming to her rescue, Manny's windows would still be intact!

"Maggie, you all right. Not hurt, are you?" He bent over.

"I don't need you to tend my business, Grayson Thayer," she shouted from beneath the table. "I did fine before you came along, I'll be fine when you go!"

"I just wanted to help." He ducked as half a table flew by, hit the rough-hewn wall and splintered into pieces.

"Help, indeed! You call this help?" she fumed, opening his arms in protest.

"Look, Maggie." Grayson eased down on his knees, trying not to wrinkle his pressed breeches any worse than they already were.

"Get away from me, Grayson." She crawled backward. "You wanted a fight? You got one! Go ahead! See if you can bust some more heads!"

"Maggie!" He ducked his head, and crawled under the table. "Damn, it's wet under here!" He pushed a glob of congealing potatoes and gravy aside and moved closer to her.

"Yes, it's wet under here!" she shouted backing up against the wall. "It'll take a week to clean this place up. You know how much business Manny will lose in a week's time?"

"I didn't mean to start a fight, but Riker, he's been asking for it since the day he stepped foot in camp."

She crossed her arms over her chest, her legs drawn up beneath her. "So did it have to be in my brother-in-law's tavern?"

"We'll pay for it."

"Damned straight you'll pay for it!"

Something crashed on the table above and both of them ducked, covering their heads with their hands. When Maggie looked up, Grayson was grinning.

"What?" she demanded. "What's so funny?" She couldn't help smiling back; his grin was infectious.

"Us." He began to chuckle.

"Us?"

"We started the fight, and here were are safe and sound while they're up there getting their heads cracked!"

Maggie suppressed a chuckle, though she was still angry with Grayson. It really *was* funny. The sounds were deafening. Furniture was splintering, men were groaning and shouting, and Manny was hollering above it all, trying to get the men out of the tavern and onto the lawn before the walls caved in.

"So now what?" Grayson asked, still lost in laughter.

Maggie clutched her stomach. "We get out of here, don't we?"

"Out of here?" Grayson peered out at the commotion. "You're kidding."

She shook her head. "Just follow me, Captain."

She gave a wink, and then dropped onto all fours and crawled over his legs and out from under the table.

Unable to control the urge, Grayson stroked her bottom as she crawled past him. Maggie swatted at his hand, but kept moving.

"Come on!" she called over her shoulder. "Hurry! Manny's gone for his rifle. He's hoppin' mad! He finds out we were part of this and both our tails'll be in a sling!"

Still laughing, Grayson gave up on staying clean and crawled out from under the table after Maggie.

She led him along the wall, under a table, over a bench. Pewter plates and forks flew over their heads, but Grayson kept crawling. Once she stopped short as a man fell to the floor in front of her. Grayson caught her bare foot and tickled her as she crawled around the prone body.

"Cut it out!" she giggled. "Cut it out or I'll clobber you with something!" She threw, an empty salt cellar over her shoulder and Grayson had to duck to keep from getting hit.

Just as they reached the open door, Grayson heard someone shout his name from behind.

It was Riker. Out of the corner of his eye, Grayson saw him coming at him from across the room.

Maggie leaped up and grabbed Grayson's hand. "Come on!" she shouted. "Hurry!"

They slipped out the door, and hand and hand they sprinted across the road. Instead of taking the road to the east, Maggie led him straight into a greenbriar thicket.

"How the hell are we going to get through that?"

Grayson protested, still allowing her to drag him along.

She jerked his hand. "Trust me!"

Following her into the thicket, he watched with amazement as Maggie drew back what looked like a wall of greenbriars and slipped through. "Hurry!" she urged.

Grayson ducked through the hedgerow and she eased back the wall of spiny vines.

"Ouch!" she muttered, holding up a finger. A single drip of crimson blood oozed from the tip.

Without thinking, Grayson grasped her hand and closed his mouth over her finger.

Maggie gave a little gasp and then looked up, her dark gaze meeting his. This man, he was like a fever that just wouldn't let up. "We have to hurry," she whispered, feeling the heat of his mouth and the wet of his tongue on her finger. "He's liable to come after you."

"Where're we going?"

"My place." She looked down at the ground and then back up at him. "Your cheek's bleedin'. I'll clean you up and then you can go back to the camp."

Grayson slipped her finger from his mouth and then took a firm hold on her hand. "Lead the way; I'm at your mercy."

Maggie dashed off, and hand and hand they ran through the thicket of trees, through Carter's west bean patch, across the road, over a dry streambed, and through Devil's Woodyard. Both panted in the heat of the humid night, but it felt good to run. Their lungs were filled with air and their hearts beat with adrenaline.

Maggie led Grayson over her back fence and onto

her own land before she finally slowed to a walk. She released his hand and clutched her stomach, panting for breath.

Side by side they walked through the weedy field and down her dusty drive. "Holy Mary, I've got to have a drink before I pitch over," Maggie declared, heading for the well.

Grayson followed her to the brick well and watched as she drew up a bucket of water. What a sight to behold. Maggie was in the twilight, with her hair strewn down her back, her sleeves pushed up to her elbows, her sunburned face dotted with perspiration.

She lifted the wooden bucket onto the side of the well and took a dipper to scoop out some water. She drank greedily, letting droplets dribble off the dipper to dampen the bodice of her simple cotton gown.

"Ah, that's good," she murmured as she handed him the ladle.

As Grayson drank, she dipped her hands into the bucket and splashed water onto her face and bare neck. When she spied him watching her, she flicked the water off her fingertips into his face, laughing.

Grayson took the dipper and flung the remainder of its water onto her. "Oh!" She squeezed her eyes shut at the shock of the icy water in her face.

Grayson snickered.

She grabbed a pewter cup off the well wall and dipped into the bucket. "Two can play that game, Captain!" She threw the water at him and then screamed with laughter, dodging as he reached for another dipper of water.

Grayson ran after her, and when he drew close enough, he threw the dipper of water at her, splashing it down her dress. Maggie squealed and ran for the bucket.

Her next cup of water hit Grayson square in the chest, soaking his white muslin shirt and plastering it to his chest.

As Grayson wiped his shirt, she lifted the bucket and threw the contents.

"Damn!" Grayson shouted. "That's cold, woman!"

She dropped the bucket down the well and hauled it up as fast as she could.

"Don't you dare, don't you dare," he threatened, wiggling a finger, "or you'll be sorry." He wiped his face wet from the dousing she'd already given him.

She only laughed harder. But when he made a move toward her, she dropped the bucket full of water and ran. A moment later Grayson tackled her and they fell to the grassy ground.

"Let go! Let go of me," she screamed, tears of laughter running down her face as she tried to crawl away. "You're wet!"

He rolled her onto her belly and caught her wrists, pressing her into the sweet, pungent grass. "I've got news for you, sweetness, you're wet, too, but you're going to get even wetter!"

Maggie screamed and tried to scramble out from under him, but he held her tight, dragging her toward the well. Reaching the well, with Maggie still trapped beneath him, Grayson lifted the bucket and poured the entire thing over her head.

Maggie spit and sputtered as Grayson laughed, the two of them now soaked to the bone. "You don't play fair!" she protested, kicking. "You don't—"

Then suddenly, his warm lips were on hers. She

stopped struggling, and lifted her arms to caress his muscular shoulders.

"Ah, Maggie, Maggie," he murmured, showering her dewy face with kisses. "Maggie, I need you."

I need you . . . The words pounded in Maggie's head as his kiss deepened. He needed her. She needed him, what was the wrong in that?

He pressed his searing mouth to the soaked material of her bodice. Somewhere in the back of her mind she heard the cotton cloth tear, but she didn't care. All she cared about was Grayson and the wonderful things he was doing to her with his mouth and his hands.

She felt the warm night air caress her bare breasts, but she only laughed, flinging back her head. She threaded her fingers through his golden hair and guided his mouth down to her ripening nipple.

"Grayson," she said, her voice breathy.

"Just tell me to stop," he whispered as he took her nipple into his mouth and sucked gently.

"No," she answered. "Don't stop. Not this time . . ."

Chapter Nine

Maggie lay still in the fragrant, damp grass as she allowed Grayson to remove her wet skirt and the tattered bodice he'd torn. His fingertips caressed her quivering flesh through the clingy, transparent cotton of her shift and she sighed. She'd had no idea sins of the flesh could be so wondrous!

With Noah she'd never felt more than a stir of sensation as if the fulfillment had been there lurking behind some great wall inside her but was unattainable. From the first night they shared a bed as man and wife, her husband had made no attempt to please her, only himself. His lovemaking had been rough and fast, as if he found her distasteful.

Those first nights Maggie had lain awake and cried long after Noah snored beside her. But she'd grown used to what her mother had called *"wifely penance"* and soon it was nothing more to her than a nightly ritual like cleaning her teeth. Still, when Noah had returned from the war and moved to his own room, Maggie had been grateful; her only regret was knowing that she would never conceive and give birth to a child of her flesh.

Grayson's mouth twisted hungrily against Maggie's, pressing her into the grass. "Maggie, Maggie mine," he whispered.

She lifted up to meet him halfway, savoring the taste of him. She knew she shouldn't be letting him touch her like this. It was wrong. Grayson Thayer was the enemy. But this was what she had wanted from the first moment she'd met him outside Manny's tavern. This man filled a void in her that no one had ever filled before, that she feared no one would ever fill again. He excited her; he made her feel strong and bold, as if she could conquer the world, or at least Mother England. What harm could there be in that?

She knew this could only be a passing fancy. She knew Grayson wouldn't stay long, wouldn't need her long. A day, a week, a month and then he would move on to another war, another camp, another woman. But right now was what mattered to Maggie, not tomorrow, not next week. She didn't even know for certain that there would be a tomorrow. Right now Grayson made her feel alive in a way she'd never felt alive before. How could she deny herself even the briefest moment of happiness, a happiness she would savor the rest of her life?

Grayson sat up, his body straddling hers, and began to pull off his clothing. Maggie's fingers ran over his, helping him, laughing as she threw his white vest into the air. Yes, this man wanted her and she wanted him. Tomorrow she would worry over the consequences.

The three-legged coon hound, Roy, caught Grayson's uniform vest in his teeth and ran with it,

Honey following after him. The crippled Roy ran so awkwardly that Honey quickly caught up and a tug-of-war ensued. Grayson and Maggie laughed at the sight of the dogs fighting over the bit of clothing. The sound of rending cloth filled the hot night air and suddenly each of the two dogs had their own bit of the vest. Maggie's gaze traveled back to Grayson's, her dark eyes still laughing, as the hounds disappeared under the front porch with their booty.

"Those filthy dogs owe me a new vest," Grayson protested as he peeled off his wet white shirt.

"This is war, Captain. I can't be held responsible for their actions."

Grayson stole a kiss and she reached out tentatively to touch his nipple. It was a tiny nub, soft and pliable, but to her surprise it hardened beneath her fingertips. "The feeling is the same for you as for me?" she murmured in awe, watching Grayson's face as his eyes drifted shut.

"Nice," he answered.

She lifted up and touched her tongue to his nipple curiously.

"Better," he groaned.

She flung herself back on the grass, smiling up at him as he lowered his head to nuzzle her aching breasts. "I didn't know it could be like this," she said softly, already adrift in the sensations his tongue created.

"You said you were married," he answered, kissing his way to the soft spot at the base of her neck. "Surely—"

"What Noah did to me was nothing like this. It never felt good." She ran her hands over his broad, sinewy shoulders exploring every inch of his muscular back. "He made me feel dirty, like it was wrong for him to touch me."

"Wrong?" Grayson stretched over her, brushing a firelit tendril off her forehead. "How could it be wrong? This is what God made man and woman for."

This and to make babes, Maggie thought. *Wouldn't it be a wonderful thing if this man gave me a child tonight? Then I would have a piece of Grayson, of the happiness we share here tonight to keep with me the rest of my life.*

"This is what I was made for?" she asked him, holding his blue-eyed gaze.

He kissed her softly on the mouth, his tongue darting out to test her lower lip. "Yes, Maggie. You were made for love like no woman I've ever known."

"Then show me." She looped her arms around his neck, pulling him down onto her so that she could feel his bare chest against hers, flesh to flesh. "Show me, Grayson. Love me, if only for tonight."

A lump rose in Grayson's throat as he buried his face in her thick strawberry-blond hair. *Love you? I'll love you for tonight, and for always, Maggie mine,* he thought. But he couldn't bring himself to say the words. It wasn't right. It wouldn't be fair to her to draw her into his lies. Yet he knew he couldn't tell her who he really was; he would be risking her life as well as his own. Maggie was right. This was for tonight. Only for tonight and then he would never touch her again, he vowed.

Bringing his mouth down hard against hers, Grayson pushed all conscious thought from his mind. Just for a few moments he wanted to forget who he was, who she was . . . He wanted to feel loved, to feel needed. He wanted to make Maggie happy.

Their tongues intertwined in a dance of love and he swept his hand over her soft curves, reveling in the moans of pleasure that escaped her lips. God, she felt good beneath him, her body all damp and sweet-smelling like the grass.

Rolling off her so that he could lie at her side, he propped himself on his elbow. "So beautiful," he murmured as she looked up at him, drowsy with sensation.

"Brazen, maybe," she answered, enjoying the feel of his hot gaze on her naked flesh, "but never beautiful."

Grayson leaned to touch his mouth to hers as he began to tentatively stroke her through the wet cotton of her shift. Then, pulling the damp material over her head, his fingers found the hollow of her belly. He traced intricate patterns, his fingertips sweeping her creamy thighs. When he brushed the bright triangle of down between her legs, her eyelids fluttered.

"Oh," Maggie whispered, stroking the banded muscles of his arm. " 'Tis wonderful."

Grayson smiled in the semidarkness. *So honest . . . she was so breathtakingly honest.* He leaned to suckle one breast and then the other, and then he moved lower.

"Grayson," she moaned, threading her fingers through his hair. Her entire body was aflame with desire. Oh, what he was doing to her with his tongue? "Grayson, please . . ."

"Please what?" he asked, a husky catch in his voice.

"Please don't torture me like this." She put her arms out to him. "I need to feel you . . . to feel you inside me," she whispered. A curious, hot excitement filled her as she watched him sit up and remove the remainder of his clothing. When he unhooked his breeches she shamelessly lowered her gaze to his engorged shaft.

Grayson laughed softly, intimately. He'd never had a woman so refreshingly bold, so willing to admit to her own sensuality.

Maggie lifted her hips as he stretched out over her, savoring the feel of his hard, tight body pressed against hers. As their lips met her thighs parted of their own accord accepting him.

She moaned in his ear as he slipped into her, and for a moment he was still, allowing her to adjust to the feel of him. Then he began to move.

His kisses seared her mouth as he moved inside her, stirring a heat so hot that she thought she would die of it. She could hear her own heart pounding, the blood rushing to her head, making her dizzy and faint. Her own labored, breathing mingled with the sound of his. Her entire body pulsed with aching passion as he thrust into her again and again. Biting down on her lower lip, Maggie arched her back, struggling, searching for something unknown.

Then she heard herself cry out with sudden pleasure. She felt as if her entire body was splitting into a thousand shards of bright light to fill the night sky. The intense pleasure ebbed, and Grayson began to move again. Ripples of sensation radiated through her body as he gave one final thrust and found his own fulfillment.

When he withdrew from her and rolled onto his side, Maggie curled up beside him in the grass, resting her head on his broad shoulder. Tears slipped from her eyes.

"What is it?" Grayson asked softly, his voice still husky. "What's the matter, Maggie mine? Did I hurt you?"

She lifted her head from his shoulder to take in his heavenly blue eyes. "No," she whispered. "Ye didn't hurt me. It was . . . it was wonderful. The most . . ." She laughed at her own foolishness and brushed the tears from her eyes. "I don't know why I'm crying."

He smiled up at her as he drew her into his arms. He couldn't help wondering if she was crying for the same reason he felt like crying. Because there was no hope in this. What they had just shared couldn't happen again. He couldn't let it.

For a long time Maggie lay in Grayson's arms, content to listen to the night sounds of chirping crickets and rustling trees. Then finally she sat up and pushed back a handful of hair. "Stay tonight," she told him impulsively.

"I can't."

"Just tonight."

He started to speak, but she pressed her fingers to his lips. "Listen to me." She whispered as if there was someone nearby to hear them. "We both know no good can come of this. It's better that we end it before there's bad feelings, but," she took his hand in hers, "we've got the rest of tonight. I think we're both in need of a little comfort. What harm can there be in that, friend to friend?"

His gaze locked with hers and for a long moment there was silence. "Just tonight?" he asked finally, wishing he could offer her a lifetime.

"After tonight I don't want to see you knockin' on my door and you won't see me at your tent. It'll be a deal, fair and square."

Don't do it, an inner voice warned Grayson. He smiled a bittersweet smile. "Just for tonight, then."

She pressed her mouth to his and bobbed up before he could catch her. Gathering her clothes by the rising moonlight, she called to him. "Come on inside, where the bugs won't bite your bare arse."

He stood and began to pick up his own clothing, folding it neatly as he watched her race across the grass calling good night to her hounds. She was so beautiful, unclothed with her long, lithe legs and curvaceous hips and breasts. While Grayson felt a little foolish standing naked in the yard, it looked so natural for Maggie. It seemed as if this was where she belonged, here in the moonlight, her clothes thrown over her shoulder, her hair blowing in the hot night breeze.

"Are you coming?" She ran up the porch steps and the front door banged behind her as she slipped inside.

Grayson found her on her hands and knees in the kitchen digging through a jelly cabinet. "I got just the thing here." She rose, a dusty bottle of wine in her hand. "I was saving it for something special, but—"

Grayson wrapped his arms around her waist, planting a kiss on the tip of her freckled nose. *"You* are something special."

She made a face and broke from his embrace. "I'll just get two cups and then we'll go upstairs."

She retrieved the cups and started out of the kitchen, but Grayson came up behind her and swept her into his arms. She threw back her head and filled the dark, empty house with husky, sensuous laughter.

Grayson carried her easily up the steps. "Which way?" he murmured, nuzzling her neck.

Maggie paused for a moment. The room where she slept now? No, that was her parents' bedroom, the bedroom she and Noah had shared after they'd been wed. She didn't want to sleep in the same bed with Grayson; it somehow seemed sacrilegious, not to Noah, but to herself, to what she and Grayson shared.

"Down the hall!" She pointed with the dusty bottle of claret.

"Glad you made up your mind before I dropped you, wench." He pushed open the last door on the right with his bare foot and stepped inside. He lowered her to the floor. She slipped into his arms and kissed him.

"Lift the windows," she whispered, "whilst I get fresh sheets." Setting down the cups and bottle, she disappeared into the hallway, coming back with a pile of linens. They were thin from years of wear, but smelled of sunshine.

Grayson propped open all of the windows and then helped her with the sheets. Together they made the bed and then flopped down on it to sip from the simple handleless pewter cups.

For a long time they were quiet, lost in their own thoughts as they watched the curtains blow lightly in the night breeze and the moon slowly rise in the sky. In the distance thunder rumbled and there was an occasional streak of lightning. Ahead of the approaching storm came a refreshing breath of cool air.

Finally Maggie set down her cup and crawled across the bed to where Grayson lay, his arms tucked beneath his head. "I won't forget tonight, not as long as I live," she murmured, stroking a lock of his blond hair.

Grayson reached out to take her in his arms and pull her down to him. "I won't, either," he whispered, nearly choking on his words. "So come, Maggie mine. Let me love you. Let me love you tonight."

Just after dawn Maggie slipped from beneath the sheet and padded barefoot across the floor to retrieve her shift. Dropping it over her head, she turned back to the bed and smiled.

Grayson slept soundly in the tangle of cotton sheets, one hand flung over his head, his magical hair spread across the pillow. Maggie hugged herself. It had been a glorious night! Grayson had made love to her as she knew no man would ever make love to her again. He'd made her laugh; he'd made her cry. He had made her want to love him . . .

At that thought, Maggie turned away. Love? What ailed her? This man was an officer in the king's army. He was the enemy! But how could that be? In the past she had always felt a hatred in her heart for the redcoats. It disgusted her to walk through their camps and smile and laugh as if she wanted to be friends with them. So where was her hatred for this man?

Catching a last glimpse of Grayson's sleeping form over her shoulder, Maggie hurried out of the room. She needed fresh air. She needed to think.

As she started down the stairs, Maggie heard her hounds baying. There was someone outside. She took the steps two at time. Zeke! How could she have forgotten? He had promised to come by early with his wagon and take her blueberry picking. She couldn't let him know Grayson was here!

By the time Maggie reached the downstairs front hall the dogs were barking viciously. It couldn't be Zeke—Honey and Roy never carried on like that with someone they knew. It had to be a stranger. At the sound of a harsh male voice, Maggie threw open the door. She immediately regretted not going first for her flintlock rifle.

It was Riker.

"Back! Back!" he shouted as Roy and Honey circled him, their teeth bared.

"Honey! Roy!" Maggie shouted from the porch.

The dogs whipped around to look at their master.

Maggie slapped her leg, suddenly aware that she

was standing in the morning sun wearing nothing but her shift.

The dogs came running.

"Honey . . . Roy, sit," she commanded, pointing to a patch of grass near the well as she came down the steps.

They did as they were told but rested nervously on their haunches watching the stranger.

Riker came toward Maggie. "I'm looking for Thayer," he said, his wicked dark eyes raking over her.

Maggie stopped short, taking notice of his immensely swollen nose and blackened eye—the result of last night's fight, no doubt. "Good for you."

"Where is he?" he demanded angrily.

She rested her hands on her hips, refusing to cower. Grayson wasn't supposed to be here. The English didn't want him here; the patriots didn't want him here. But he had protected her once; she'd protect him. "Do I look like the captain's keeper to you?"

"Look," he grabbed her arm, yanking her forward. "Don't get uppity with me! I'm just trying to save Thayer's ass. The major's looking for him."

Maggie heard Roy and Honey growl. Out of the corner of her eye she spotted their slight movement.

"Let go of me," she murmured through clenched teeth, feeling that hatred bubble up inside her. "Let go of me or—"

"Or what?" Riker snapped. "What? It's your fault I'm in trouble with my uncle. You're the one that started the brawl in the tavern last night. You're the one that ought to pay for the damages!"

The instant he drew back his hand to slap her, the dogs leaped. By the time his palm made contact with her cheekbone, Honey and Roy were on him, snarling and snapping at his legs.

Maggie broke free of Riker's grip and stumbled backward.

"Call them off," he shouted, shaking his leg as Honey sunk her teeth into his stocking-clad leg, drawing blood. Riker kicked the hound in the stomach and she howled with pain, rolling across the grass. With a snarl, Roy leaped into the air and bit him in the arm, tearing his sleeve.

"Honey! Roy!" Maggie shouted, clapping her hands. "Come! Come!"

But the dogs were frenzied by the man's attack. It was their instinct to protect Maggie, to protect each other.

Maggie grasped Honey by the rear legs and began to drag her backward. She didn't see Riker draw his pistol until it was too late. "No!" she cried, cringing as Riker pulled the trigger.

Roy gave a yelp of pain as his body was thrown backward with the impact of the musket ball.

Maggie turned and ran for the house. She could hear Riker's laughter ringing in her ears. *Go ahead and laugh,* her mind screamed. *Have a good laugh, because it's going to be your last!*

"Tough, are you?" he called after her. "Why are you running, then? Can't stand up to a man, after all, can you, Maggie the bootmaker?" he sneered.

Riker was still chuckling when Maggie burst through the front door a moment later, her flintlock in hand. She pulled back the hammer and Riker's laughter died away. His pistol hung in his hand, unloaded. His horse was a good twenty-five paces away.

Maggie lifted her rifle onto her shoulder.

"You wouldn't dare," Riker shouted nervously.

"No?"

"I'm an officer. Someone will come looking for me."

She shrugged. "There've been deserters before."

"The body." His voice shook ever so slightly.

"I got a new plot dug up for greens." She smiled. "Who'd think to look for you in the garden? No one'd ever know but me and the turnips."

Riker dove to the ground as she pulled the trigger. The shot missed him by no more than a hairbreadth.

She cursed her bad aim as she began to reload. First the powder, then the shot, then tamp lightly. Riker was crawling toward his horse near the fence.

"You're not going to make it," Maggie shouted. "Face it, coward. You're about to die!"

"Maggie!" Grayson burst through the door and onto the porch. "What the hell are you doing?"

"Thayer! Thank God!" Riker shouted. "The bitch is trying to kill me!"

Grayson reached for her rifle, but she held fast, tears beginning to slip down her cheeks. "Let go. The bastard killed my dog."

Grayson glanced across the grass to the bloodied body of the three-legged dog she called Roy. The female was huddled over him, licking his wounds.

"Maggie, love, that's not enough reason to shoot a man."

"The hell it isn't!" She wiped her teary eyes on her shoulders. "You come here, you take our homes, kill our men, rape our women, steal our food . . ." *Steal our hearts!* she screamed inside. "You deserve to die!"

Grayson grasped the flintlock, his hands covering hers. Out of the corner of his eye, he saw Riker mounting his horse and riding away. "I thought you didn't care what we did, Maggie, as long as you could turn a coin off it." His eyes narrowed as he studied her tear-streaked face. Those were not the words of a mercenary Maggie had just spoken. They were the words of a woman who cared—a woman who had chosen a side.

"I don't care!" she shouted, suddenly turning her anger on Grayson, suddenly remembering that she had made love with the enemy. It was her fault Roy was dead. It was her punishment.

"I don't care," Maggie repeated. "Not about him, not about you! Now just get off my place, you hear me! You get the hell out of here before I shoot you, too!"

He slowly relaxed his grip on the rifle. "You want me to go?" he said softly. *But what about last night?* he wondered. *What about last night when you said you thought you could love me? God, Maggie mine. I could use some love.*

She thrust out her jaw, ignoring the way his golden hair fell across his shoulders making her want to reach out and touch him. "You deaf? I said go."

His blue eyes met hers for a brief moment and then he walked inside the house.

When Grayson came down the farmhouse steps fully dressed a few minutes later, she ignored him. She sat in the grass cradling Roy's shuddering body, the tears falling on his soft belly.

"He's still breathing," Grayson offered over her shoulder. "You could get him to someone—a surgeon."

"Go!" she muttered. "Can't you see you've done enough? Just go."

Grayson glanced out over the fields that reminded him so much of home. He wanted to tell her that this wasn't his fault. He wanted to defend himself, to tell her that he wasn't the man she thought he was. Instead, he tossed his scarlet coat over his shoulder and walked away, headed east toward the British camps.

That night Grayson sat at his camp desk, his goose quill poised. "Dear Sterling," he'd scrawled across the page.

He reached for the bottle of claret, forgoing the glass, and took a long pull on the bottle. His bloodshot eyes went back to the letter.

"Dear Sterling . . ."

But what did he say next? *Dear Sterling, I'm in trouble. Dear Sterling,. I'm losing my grip. I want out. I want to be the Grayson Thayer I was before the war. I'm sick of the deception. I'm tired of living a lie.*

And what of Maggie? What could he tell his brother of her? *Dear Sterling, I'm in love with a bootmaker . . . a woman I can never have. A woman who says she's taken no side in this war, yet I suspect she lies.*

He thought of Maggie sitting in the light of the morning sun cradling her dying dog's body, her white shift splattered in crimson blood. His gaze went to the uniform coat now pressed and hanging neatly from a peg. Blood. That was what the red coat meant to him these days. Blood. The blood of too many men. God, but he was sick to death of this war!

He took another pull of wine and looked down at the letter on the desk in front of him. "Dear Sterling," He dipped the quill into the ink and began to write . . .

Chapter Ten

Maggie lay on the bank of the creek staring down into the clear blue running water. Strips of green-and-brown grass jutted up from the rocky creekbed swaying with the flow of the water. A catfish slithered by and Maggie made a futile attempt to catch it by the tail. Her hands wet, she splashed her face and bare neckline, sighing at the feel of the cool water against her skin. Holy Mary! It wasn't but ten in the morning and already the August heat was unbearable!

Maggie rolled onto her back, cradling her head with her arm and stared up into the tree above. Absently she brushed her flat belly with her other hand.

Then that thought washed over her as it had a hundred times in the last few days. A babe! She was going to have a baby! Grayson's baby! She'd known it almost from the moment of conception. Even before she had missed her flow, she *knew* in her heart of hearts that finally she was carrying a child.

"Grayson," she murmured aloud. God, she missed him. It been more than a month since he'd spent the night with her, a month since she'd caught more than a glimpse of him across the British camp or in Manny's tavern. The only other contact she'd had with him was when he'd sent his fancy boots to be repaired, and that had been by way of a young private. But then Grayson *had* promised her he'd not bother her again after that night, hadn't he?

So why was she angry with him? Why was she angry that he hadn't come back? How many nights had she lain awake in that bed in the back bedroom smelling his masculine scent on the sheets and wishing he would walk through the door?

It didn't make any sense to Maggie, especially now that she knew she carried his child, a child she had to protect, even in her womb. How could she still want Grayson, knowing he was the enemy? Knowing it was Grayson she silently fought as she delivered her shoddy boots to the British and picked up information to be passed on to the patriot camps forming near Williamsburg?

Even now, as she told herself Grayson was the enemy, she wanted him here beside her. Not to tell him of the baby . . . she was not a fool. It was her own doing that got her into this situation. She needed no man's help, especially not Grayson's. She would deal with her pregnancy on her own.

But she wanted to hear his voice, to feel his lips on hers just once more. She wanted him so badly that she ached for him.

She hugged herself, feeling the warmth of her

middle. *It's just lust,* she told herself. *Lust pure and simple. You can't betray your country, your babe, yourself, for lust. Fight it,* she told herself. *Fight the urge that makes you want to get up and run to him. Fight the urge to give yourself to him, knowing nothing can come of it but ill luck and sorrow.*

A twig snapped and Maggie sat upright, reaching for the flintlock rifle resting on the grass beside her. These days she didn't stray far from her farmhouse without carrying a weapon.

With each day that passed, it looked more and more as if Virginia would be the final battleground of the war between King George and his American colonies. So much had happened that the politics of it made Maggie's head spin! Word was that a Frenchman was headed for the Chesapeake Bay with nearly thirty ships sent by France to give aid to General Washington. Even more important, the scuttlebutt was that the great commander Rochambeau had offered the patriot general half of all that was left in his war chest. With those monies, God willing and the creek didn't rise, John Logan told her, they could win the war.

Grasping her rifle, Maggie sat up on her knees and took aim at the tall grass in the direction the sound had come. She heard footsteps, and after a moment of contemplation, she lowered her rifle. Zeke. It was Zeke. She could hear him dragging his bad leg through the brittle August grass. More twigs snapped and tree branches swayed and suddenly he appeared.

"Maggie?"

She laid aside the flintlock. "You're gonna have

to start chirpin' like a bird or something to warn me it's you. The way you're always sneaking up on me, I'm gonna blow a hole through your head one of these days, Zeke."

He scratched his scrawny beard. "I've gotten right fond of this head. I wish you wouldn't."

"Then stop sneakin' up on me like some redskin." She spun around in the grass and faced the stream.

Zeke took a seat beside her. "You been quiet lately." He picked up a smooth stone and pitched it into the water. "Somethin' up?"

"How would you know if I've been quiet or not? Seems to me you've been pretty scarce around these parts."

He tossed another stone into the water. "Don't start with me on Lyla again, Mags. I ain't up for it today."

"Nothing but ill can come of it, Zeke. She's a whore, for God's sake!"

Zeke whipped around, his jaw clenched in anger. "Don't say that. I don't want you sayin' that about Lyla."

Maggie drew her legs up beneath her cotton dress, hugging her knees. "It's the truth, isn't it?"

He glanced away. "It don't matter."

"The hell it doesn't!" She rested her hand on his shoulder. "Zeke, she's not one of us."

He turned back, his cool gray eyes fixed on hers. "And you ain't one of them, Maggie."

Her eyes immediately teared up. She knew what he was talking about . . . Grayson. Somehow he had known she had been with him, slept in his arms. Zeke said he had seen it in her eyes the very next morning when he'd come to help with Roy.

"It's not just the redcoat, though that sure ought to be enough. Dressin' up in one of Elizabeth Logan's fancy dresses or talkin' like you're better than us don't make you one of them. Your papa was a bondman same as mine. He come to this country to make a better life for his wife and his children. It's men like Thayer that bought the bonds."

Maggie covered her ears with her hands in a childish attempt to escape Zeke's words. *You're not one of them,* echoed in her head. *You're not good enough to be one of them* . . . echoed louder. "Just hush your mouth, Ezekial. Who said I wanted to be one of them? You've got no right to judge me!"

He caught her hands and pulled them away from her head. "But you got a right to judge Lyla?"

"It's not the same! She's a whore!"

"And what am I that makes me better, Maggie girl? Tell me that. I'm a poor dirt farmer that lives with his mama," he said, his voice growing louder. "I'm a cripple!"

Maggie's face immediately softened. What was wrong with her, fighting with Zeke like this? He was her friend. She draped her arm over his shoulder and gave him a squeeze. "And fought well you did, at Long Island. You should be *proud* of what you did for the cause of freedom."

He pushed back a handful of sleek hair off his forehead. "Speakin' of that . . . that's what I came down here to tell you. I didn't mean to get into a shoutin' match with you, Maggie."

Her eyes met his and she smiled. "I know you didn't."

He stood, hooking his thumbs into the waistband of his patched kersey breeches. "We got a problem and John sent me to ask if you'd bail us out."

"Problem? What kind of problem?" She stood and brushed the grass off her skirting. She had to get into town. She'd promised her sister she'd help her with the noon meal at the Ordinary.

"We got a job to do tonight and Harry's gout's actin' up. He can't hardly walk. He said he wanted you to go in his place."

"Me?" She couldn't resist a grin of pride. "Really?"

"Of course, right away Carter says no." His brow furrowed. "What is it with you two lately? He's awful worried about your comin' and goin'."

She shrugged. "You know how Carter is. Women are supposed to be in the kitchen, a babe in arms and another—" She went silent, suddenly thinking of the baby she now carried. Her cheeks colored and she looked away. "Anyway, who cares what Carter Perkins thinks? If John Logan says I'm in, I'm in."

"Now wait a minute. Don't you want to know what we're doin' first?"

She picked up her flintlock and headed for the farmhouse, leaving Zeke no choice but to follow her. "I don't care. All I want to know is if I get to wear one of them flour sacks on my head!"

Grayson dismounted beneath an elm tree on the bank of the York River. Tying Giipa to the tree, he walked down to the water's edge to look out at the river. He wiped his brow. He'd forgotten how hot Virginia was in mid-August. God, what he wouldn't give to strip naked and dive into the cool water. So why didn't he?

Maggie would, wouldn't she? he chided himself. *Maggie* . . . It had been a month since he'd seen her. It had been a month since he'd held her in his arms and made love to her. He tried to tell himself that it was just the sex he missed, but it was more. He missed *her*. He missed her husky laughter, her simple, honest talk.

How many times had he dressed in the darkness of his tent, intending to go to her, only to change his mind again? He had promised Maggie he'd not be back. He'd promised himself. They'd both agreed that there was no future in the relationship, that neither was interested in continuing it. It was too dangerous for Grayson to become involved with any woman as long as he remained a spy among he Brits. A woman with no loyalties to either side could be more dangerous than the enemy.

But after what Maggie had said about Riker, Grayson had to take into serious consideration that Maggie might well be a patriot. After all, if she was, she certainly wouldn't tell a British officer, would she?

Grayson exhaled slowly, watching a gull swoop and dive out over the water. When he had thought she had chosen no side it was easier for him to tell himself she wasn't the woman for him. This fledgling country was too important to him to have a wife who didn't believe in the same freedoms he believed in.

Wife? What the hell was he thinking of? Maggie, his wife? He laughed aloud. Maggie was a bootmaker. Thayers didn't marry bootmakers! A woman like Reagan, his brother's wife, that was who he would marry. Although Reagan was not from a well-connected family like the Thayers, at least she was well educated. She was a lady. Maggie was barely a step above a barmaid. He couldn't take her home after the war!

That thought brought more laughter. What made him think she'd have any interest in going anywhere with him anyway? She'd kicked him off her farm, making it quite evident that she had no desire to ever see him again. She'd threatened to shoot him! Of course that was because she thought he was a redcoat.

Grayson cursed foully. How had his life become so complicated? There had been a time when he'd been so certain of himself and what he wanted from the world, what he was willing to give. Today, standing here on this riverbank, he wasn't certain of anything—not one damned thing.

The sound of an approaching horseman caught Grayson's attention and he turned, his hand automatically slipping to the pistol he wore at his waist. The rider appeared through the trees and Grayson broke into a grin. The man who rode up to the edge of the river was a mirror image of himself. *Sterling.* God, it was good to see him!

Grayson stood back watching his brother dismount, and for a moment the two regarded each other. Even after all of these years it amazed them that they were so identical in appearance. They had precisely the same golden-blond hair, the same sky-blue eyes.

Grayson smiled and offered his hand. "By the king's cod, it's good to see you, Brother."

Sterling laughed at his brother's curse. He sounded so English, Sterling had to remind himself who Grayson really was. He ignored his brother's formal greeting and wrapped his arms around him, squeezing him tightly. "Don't put your airs on with me, little brother. I'll not be impressed."

The men laughed together, holding each other for just a moment before Grayson backed awkwardly away, feeling foolish over the emotion that welled up in his chest. Sterling was the only person in the world he knew he could count on these days. Of course there had been a time when their relationship had been strained—back in the early years of the war when Sterling had thought Grayson to be an Englishman rather than a Colonial.

In the midst of the Brits, the winter they occupied Philadelphia, Sterling had even gone so far as to have his brother kidnapped and had taken his place. Grayson had spent months sitting in a cold jail cell somewhere in the New York wilderness going over and over in his head what he would do to his brother when he caught him.

But once they were reunited and the matter rectified, Grayson had realized he'd been wrong not to tell his brother what he'd been about since the beginning of the war. He realized he'd had no right to spare Sterling the worry of the true danger Grayson was in. They were brothers, and just as they had shared the same womb in their mother, they had to share in each other's lives. In the years since Philadelphia, it had often been Sterling's letters smuggled into Grayson that had kept Grayson going.

Grayson turned away to look back over the river, swallowing the lump in his throat. "You took a great chance coming, Sterling."

Sterling shrugged, coming to stand beside his brother. "I've taken worse. I wanted to see you. Your last letter . . ." He paused. "I've been worried about you, Grayson. I think it's time to come in."

"No."

"For Christ's sake, it's been seven years! You've done more than your duty. It's time to let someone else take your place."

"We're too close to the end, Sterling," Grayson answered. "I can't back out now."

"It wouldn't be backing out! No man can stay undercover seven years and not—"

Grayson turned. "Not what?"

"Not get shaky."

"What are you talking about? I've made no mistakes."

"No big mistakes. Not yet. But I've seen it happen, Grayson. You spend seven lonely years pretending to be a man you're not and you start to lose focus. You start to let down all of those barriers you've built to protect yourself and the ones who work for you." He took his brother's arm. "You let down those barriers and you're going to make a mistake. People are going to die. *You're* going to die."

"You don't know what you're talking about," Grayson scoffed.

"I damned well do! You forget, I spent a few years playing this game of spying. I *know* what it's like. Just that winter I spent in Philadelphia pretending I was you, I could feel myself slipping. It was like being a madman having two people inside me."

Grayson rested his hands on his narrow hips. "It's too close, Sterling. I can feel the end coming. I can feel it in the air like a thunderstorm about to break." He turned to look his brother in the eyes. "It's like being in the eye of a hurricane. You know that electric calm just before the wind shifts."

Sterling sighed. "You and my wife would have made quite a pair, both of you loving danger the way you do. I swear, the two of you feed on it."

"Speaking of your wife, how is she and the boy. 'Trees' is it?"

"Reagan is fine, as pretty as a picture and as feisty as a caged cat with these redcoats running wild. As for my son, his name is Forrest and you damned well know it!" He punched Grayson gingerly in the arm.

"Ah, that's right!" Grayson tapped himself in the forehead with his knuckles. "Trees . . . Forrest. Close wasn't I?"

"Very funny." Sterling picked up a stick and hurled it over the edge of the bank. "So tell me about this woman, this Maggie."

Grayson frowned. "Not much to tell you other than at this moment she detests me. Last I saw her she wanted to blow a hole through my chest. She shot at me once. I don't think she'll miss next time."

Sterling couldn't suppress a grin. Grayson could well have been talking about Reagan and how she'd been early in the winter of '77 when Sterling had met her. "Sounds like a hell of a woman. You going to let her slip through your fingers?"

Grayson turned to face his brother, his face stricken with uncertainty. "She's a bootmaker."

Sterling chuckled, lifting a blond eyebrow. "A bootmaker?"

"She makes boots for our men," he took a breath, "but for the Brits as well."

Sterling's smile fell. "I see."

"The worse thing is, I don't know that I care. When I'm with her, she makes me feel—" He brushed back his hair. "Christ, listen to me! I sound like a boy at Eaton again."

"I can't tell you what to do, but as far as choosing sides, it's hard for some people. Look at this from her point of view. In an area like this, the bootmakers and farmers were probably barely affected by the king and his tariffs, by any of the politics that led to all of this. All she sees is her land torn apart, brothers, uncles, cousins killed—and for what? To some Colonists, one side is as bad as the other. To some, war just isn't the answer."

"She's a bootmaker, Sterling. She lives in a house not much larger than our dairy. She sews boots with her father's tools. She never went to school. I doubt she can read or write."

"Ah hah." Sterling nodded. "Wrong social class."

"You can't say it doesn't make a difference."

Sterling's blue-eyed gaze met Grayson's. "No. No, I can't. But I can tell you that if this girl is the *one,* it doesn't matter who she is, or what she's done. I firmly believe that we only get one chance at real love in a lifetime, and I just don't want you to miss out. I want you to be as happy as I've been since Reagan Llewellyn stormed into my life."

"We have nothing in common. Her father was a bond servant, for Christ's sake!"

Sterling made a fist and swung it in the air with enthusiasm. "But isn't that what this new country of ours is fighting for? The right to make our own choices? The right to break down the social classes we've lived with in England for a thousand years! We win this war," he went on, "and marriages between classes will be seen more and more. We'll be marrying who we wish, not who our parents betrothed us to when we were fourteen."

Grayson stared out over the York River, watching a small British transport ship sail up the river. "Why is nothing clear in my head anymore?" He pushed back a lock of hair that had come loose from his queue. "Why is it all a jumble?"

"I told you why, Brother." Sterling took him by the shoulder. "Because you've been at this too long. It's time you turned in that red coat of yours and came home to Thayer's Folly. Maybe even home with a bride."

When Grayson made no reply, Sterling reached into his pocket and pulled out his watch. "Listen, I've got to go. I have some business to attend to for Colonel Hastings in Williamsburg. I wish I could stay and talk, but—"

"I know. But it's not safe anyway. Too many eyes, too many ears. I'll not get into that game of having people take you for me again." He laughed. "I had nightmares for years about that after Philadelphia."

"Yes, well, I had nightmares for years about being caught in whorehouses by my wife, so I'd say we're even."

Their laughter died away and Sterling threw his arms around his brother. "Come home, Grayson. The arrangement for your death and the end of Captain Thayer of the king's army can be made in a day or two."

"I can't," Grayson murmured, squeezing his eyes shut. "I just can't. Not yet."

Sterling stepped back. "I haven't got time to argue with you now, but I swear this won't be the last you hear of it."

"Your being six minutes older than I doesn't give you a right to tell me what to do." Grayson untied Sterling's horse's reins from the tree branch. "Now go on with you," he teased, "before you really make me angry and I have to blacken one of your eyes."

Sterling grasped his saddle, ready to mount. "Tell me at least that you'll think about coming home."

The sudden sound of hoofbeats made Grayson whip around and Sterling mount.

"Go on with you," Grayson told his brother. "I'll talk to you soon." He slapped the horse's hindquarter and Sterling rode off.

Private Michaels rode into the clearing, twisting to see who barreled past him on horseback. He was still looking behind him as he dismounted. "I almost thought that was you, Captain."

Grayson laughed. "That knave? He's an informant, and a poor one at that." He smoothed his vest, falling into his role. "So what is it, Michaels? What do you want and how the hell did you find me?"

"I just guessed you might be here."

As the boy rattled on, Grayson made a mental note to remember to no longer use this spot as a meeting place. He *knew* not to use the same place more than once or twice. Where was his head?

"I know you like your quiet," Michaels went on, "and I wouldn't have bothered you, but Major Lawrence wants you right away. Something about the rebels. He wants you on it this minute. You and Lieutenant Riker."

"Riker?" Grayson strode toward his horse. "Since when is Riker back on this?"

"I don't know, sir. But the word is that the major is mad with Lieutenant Riker so the lieutenant's trying to make it up to him. They say he told the major he could have the identities of the rebels in a matter of days." The boy paused, obviously wanting to say something more.

"And?"

Michaels swallowed. "And they say Riker's got it in for you, Captain. He wants to see you court-martialed. Worse . . ."

"Worse? What the hell are you talking about Michaels? I've done nothing to deserve a court-martial. It will be a fine day in hell when a man is court-martialed for having a lady in his tent!"

"It's not that, sir." The boy reached for the reins of his borrowed pony, purposefully avoiding looking into his eyes.

"Not that? Then what is it?" Grayson bellowed. "And look at me when you address a superior."

"Word is, Lieutenant Riker is saying," the boy's lower lip trembled as he forced himself to look his beloved captain in the eyes, "he's saying . . . you're a traitor . . ."

Chapter Eleven

Maggie waited in the darkness, listening to the sounds of the rustling trees and the even give and take of Zeke's breath. In her hand she carried her papa's old matchlock rifle; tucked into the waistband of Zeke's spare breeches was a pistol.

The breeches felt odd to Maggie, as if she was somehow more exposed without the billow of her skirts. But John had insisted she wear men's breeches and pin her hair up on her head so that it couldn't be seen beneath the flour-sack mask she would wear.

Maggie ground her boot into the damp leaves and Zeke rested his hand on her shoulder. "Easy, Mags," he murmured, his voice barely a whisper on the wind. "You got to learn patience."

"Where are the others? John said the timing here was vital. He said the dispatches would arrive with an evening patrol and be picked up by the eleven-thirty patrol. We've got to be in and long gone by the time the Brits realize the dispatches are missing."

In the hopes of gaining information concerning

British fleet movement, General Washington had put out a request to the patriots in the Yorktown area to concentrate on obtaining information. He wanted dispatches intercepted and spies in the British encampments to be listening with both ears. With half of Rochambeau's war chest and DeGrasse and his French fleet headed for the Chesapeake, the Americans were turning toward the offensive.

It was just by dumb luck that John had overheard a conversation in Commegys' Ordinary pertaining to the dispatches being passed in a mailbag by way of a farmhouse northwest of Yorktown tonight. Because of General Washington's request, John felt it was the band's duty to try to intercept them.

Far in the distance the sound of a whippoorwill rose in the hot night air. Maggie smiled to herself. Whippoorwills didn't call after dark. She repeated the sound, signaling to the approaching men that all was safe.

Zeke grinned. "You catch on fast."

"If I'm gonna do this, I need to do it right," she answered.

A moment later she heard footsteps and the slight scrape of tree branches. The silhouettes of several men appeared in the light of the half moon.

"Mags." There was an edge to Carter's voice. "What are you doin' here?"

She grinned. "Takin' your papa's place. Didn't he tell you he's down with the gout?"

Carter frowned. "Guess he did, but he didn't say nothin' about you comin' in his place."

Maggie stepped up to him, agitated by the tone in

his voice. "Why is it that all of a sudden you don't want me around, Carter? You think I can't be trusted?"

"Somebody saw you the other day comin' out of Thayer's tent. I thought you said you wasn't seein' him anymore."

"For your information, Carter," Maggie said, steppping up to him, "I was doing some bootwork for him, not that it's any of your business what I do—"

"Carter . . . Maggie," John interrupted. "That's enough. This is neither the time nor the place to discuss this issue. You know better. You have concerns, you bring them up at a meeting." He turned to the other men. "Let's concentrate on the task at hand. Do you have the masks, Pete?"

The blacksmith stepped forward, dropping a pack to the ground. "Got 'em, John." He immediately began to pass out the flour-sack masks. "Be sure you give 'em back, boys. We don't want 'em hangin' out to dry on clothes-washin' day."

The men chuckled.

John squinted in the moonlight and read the face of his gold pocket watch. "Is everyone certain of his . . . or her job? Zeke?"

"I take the front door—"

"I thought I was taking the lead," Carter interrupted.

John glanced at Carter. "We discussed this. We all take turns. First man in takes the greatest risk of being shot. "You cover him going in, Carter, and then guard the front door. Les?"

"I go in through the back, and stand guard at the

back door once Zeke, you, and Maggie are inside safe and sound."

John gave a nod, turning to Edwin, Les's brother. "Ed?"

"I guard the drive and keep an eye out for red-coats."

"You see, hear, or even *smell* anything out of the ordinary and you let us know," John instructed. "You understand?"

Edwin grinned, swinging a flintlock rifle over each shoulder. "Got it."

"All right then, let's go. We have just enough time to get in after the eleven o'clock patrol passes and get out before the eleven-thirty finds we've been there." The group split and headed for their horses hidden in the trees a quarter of a mile north.

John stopped Maggie. "You understand the operation?"

She smiled up at him. "I'm not addlepated. It's simple enough. Go in, pick up the dispatches, and get out." She slipped her arm through his and together they started through the woods. "So stop worrying about me."

"I'm concerned about this unrest between you and Carter. It could get in the way of what we're trying to accomplish here." He held back a pine bough, letting Maggie through.

"I don't understand it, John. It's like he's turned on me. I guess he can't accept a woman in the group."

"Well, I'll speak with him."

"Why not just let it simmer a while?" Maggie countered. "If I show him I can do as good a job as any man, if I show him I can be trusted, then maybe he'll back off. He's just concerned for everyone's safety, that's all it is."

John let out a sigh. "You're right. I swear, you're more level-headed than I am, Maggie. You ought to be leading these men, not me."

They both laughed at the thought. "Nah, I couldn't take your place, John. Nobody could."

He reached his horse. The others were already mounted and waiting. "I appreciate your confidence." He turned to the other men as he swung easily into his saddle. "All right, men, let's move. I need not remind you that we travel in silence."

Maggie mounted the horse Zeke had brought her this afternoon and then reined in behind the other men. When she'd asked Zeke where the horse had come from, he'd been very mysterious in his reply. "Let's just say he was 'liberated' from oppression and leave it at that, Maggie girl," he'd answered.

Maggie stroked the horse's sleek neck as the band rode out of the woods and onto a narrow path. Liberated? What had Zeke meant? Had he stolen the horse from the British encampment? She found it hard to believe he would bring her a stolen horse that could be so easily traced. Well, whatever the case, she was grateful. That old nag of Noah's had been able to pull a wagon, but she hadn't been worth two pence when it came to a hard ride. Zeke had led her away, saying he would get what coin for her he could.

Maggie rode in silence in the midst of the men, feeling important. She was afraid, but it was a good kind of fear, the kind that made you cautious. It felt so good to be doing something worthwhile. It took her mind off Grayson and the child of his she carried.

A mile from the farmhouse where the dispatches were said to be waiting, John led the patriots off the road and into a streambed. They rode a half a mile before he suddenly called them to a halt. A minute later the sound of hoofbeats hammered on the road.

The British patrol. And right on time.

The men sat astride in utter silence listening to the hoofbeats approach, pass, and then die away. Even the patriots' own horses seemed to sense the need for invisibility. When John motioned all was safe, the men and Maggie filed one by one through the trees and back onto the road.

It was only a minute before they turned off the road into a drive and Maggie spotted the bright yellow lights of a farmhouse. She immediately detected the sound of laughter and a stringed instrument.

Maggie glanced at the others. They were dismounting and pulling their masks over their heads. Sliding off her gelding, she tied him to a tree with the other horses and pulled the flour-sack mask out of the waistband of Zeke's breeches. Slowly she pulled it over her head, concealing her face. The coarse spun material was rough against her skin and the remaining powdery flour irritated her nose, but she could see, and that was all that mattered.

John, recognizable only by his pale-blue breeches, gave a nod and the men fanned out. Maggie fell in behind John. Edwin remained behind to guard the horses and watch for an unscheduled patrol. The laugher grew louder as Maggie approached the whitewashed, clapboard farmhouse. The windows were thrown up and the door left wide open, to battle the heat, no doubt.

"Where's the guard?" Maggie whispered.

John put a finger to the place on the flour-sack mask where his lips would be and shrugged. Twenty paces from the farmhouse he stopped her with his arm and pointed.

In the darkness Maggie could make out Zeke's limping silhouette as he neared the door. Pete walked beside him, easily spotted, despite his mask, by his immense size. The others ran toward the back to prevent any of the redcoats from utilizing the rear door.

Inside the farmhouse the Brits began to clap and whistle. Maggie could detect separate voices. One man was teasing another about something. For God's sake, they were drunk! What a stroke of luck!

Zeke flattened against the outer wall of the house and eased toward the front door.

Out of the candlelit windows rose a soft, feminine voice. A woman . . . singing. The Brits inside grew louder with each passing moment, but still Maggie heard the woman's voice, so strangely soft and delicate despite the bawdy laughter.

Zeke stepped forward, his rifle on his shoulder as if he were about to burst in, and then suddenly he halted.

"What is it?" John whispered in a hushed voice. "Does he see something?"

Maggie's heart rose in her throat. The woman

. . . it had to be Lyla.

Then suddenly from behind Maggie there was a gunshot. She and John whirled around into a crouch, rifles aimed. To their horror they saw Carter standing, his flintlock limp in his hands.

"It just went off," he swore desperately.

John had an instant to make a decision. Surely the men inside the farmhouse had heard the gunshot. Did he and his men hightail it out of there and hope they could outrun the English soldiers or did they proceed hoping the warning wouldn't prove fatal?

Zeke faced John, waiting for the order to proceed or run.

John gave a wave of his fist. *Go,* he signaled. *Go!*

Zeke leaped into action. He threw himself through the open doorway to the farmhouse with Pete directly behind him. John sprinted across the grass and Maggie followed.

An instant after Zeke stepped through the door, the remaining patriots broke in through the back. By the time Maggie slipped inside, there were redcoats all over the floor, their face pressed into the plank floorboards. Even from the back of their heads, she could recognize several officers. She thanked God she was wearing the flour-sack mask.

In spite of Carter's bungle, the patriots had managed to take the British officers utterly by surprise. They had been so occupied with their merrymaking that they'd never heard Carter's misfire. Maggie imagined there'd be hell to pay tomorrow over the Brits not posting a watch outside.

The main room of the simple farmhouse was littered with ale and wine bottles and scraps of food. The furniture had been pushed aside to make a dance floor. Off to one side was a table heaped with trays of sweets. They were celebrating some officer's birthday!

Maggie heard a whimper and looked up to see the town whore, Lyla, standing half naked in the shadows of the fireplace. Maggie was ashamed by her presence, and frightened for her at the same time. Maggie glanced at Zeke, but he seemed not to have noticed Lyla. He was shouting orders to the British officers lying on the floor, swearing he would kill them all if they moved an inch.

"The dispatches," Zeke ordered in a gruff voice. "Where are they?"

Already John was searching the room. On impulse Maggie snatched up a scarlet uniform coat and tossed it to Lyla so that the thin woman could cover her nakedness.

Zeke pressed the barrel of his rifle to the nearest redcoat's head. "I asked where the dispatches were," he repeated threateningly.

The officer shook his head. "No dispatches."

"Liar!"

Maggie began to search the room, digging into cupboards and overturning furniture.

"I . . . I swear," the officer repeated with a hiccup.

"That's not what I heard," Zeke said through clenched teeth. "Now tell me where the blasted messages are and we'll be on our way. We got no taste for blood, only information."

The drunken officer Zeke had singled out trembled with fear as the man above him cocked his flintlock. "Please don't shoot," the redcoat pleaded. "I swear on my mother's grave there were no dispatches tonight. We were taken off the mail route."

"When?"

"To-today."

"Who got the dispatches? Where are they?"

"I . . . I don't know, I swear I don't know. They don't tell us. No one tells us anything."

Maggie kept an eye on Zeke as she continued her hunt for the mailbag. In the kitchen and upstairs she could hear the other patriots ransacking the house. Minutes later they all returned to the main room.

"Nothing," Les declared.

"Nothing," John echoed, disguising his voice.

Pete shook his head.

Zeke cursed beneath his breath.

Maggie couldn't believe their ill luck. They'd gotten in so easily, with not a shot fired, only to find that it had been a waste of time. *They've got to be here somewhere,* she said to herself. *Think! Where would you hide something precious?* She thought of her da's mother back in Ireland. He'd said she had a secret hiding place. Where?

The fireplace, of course! The only object left standing after a fire. There'd been a hollowed-out place behind a brick in the little cottage, her da had said. It was where Grandma Maggie Anne had hidden her golden crucifix. Maggie dropped to her knees and began to push one brick and then another looking for one that was loose.

Pete and Les had tied up the British officers and prepared to go. Zeke waved to her to come, seeming to look straight through Lyla's quivering form. One of the men had led Lyla to a chair and made her sit, but no one had tied her up. They all knew her. They all knew she was no threat.

Maggie shook her head wildly, not daring to speak, when Zeke waved again, beckoning her. *They're here. They've got to be here,* she told herself. She pounded on the brick with one hand, steadying herself with her rifle with the other. Nothing moved, not a brick.

In frustration she scooted across the wide hearth and thrust her free hand up into the chimney. She smiled behind her flour-sack mask when her fingers touched something hard dangling inside. She heard one of the British officers swear as she crawled into the cold fireplace. This was no mailbag! Too heavy. Far too heavy! She ran her fingers along the inner brick wall of the fireplace trying to unhook the bag from the rusty nail it hung from. Suddenly the strap broke and the bag came crashing down, some of its contents spilling onto the hearth.

Les gave a hoot of delight.

Maggie could do nothing but stare at the shimmering gold coins. There was more money lying at her feet than she'd ever seen in her lifetime!

A payroll. It had to be payroll money. What it was doing here, she didn't know.

Zeke hustled to Maggie's side, a small wooden crate he'd found on the floor in his hands. Stooping beside her, he carfully lifted the torn canvas bag of gold coins into the crate and helped Maggie to pick up what had spilled. Then, handing Maggie his rifle, he lifted the crate into his arms and hurried for the door. He brushed past Lyla, giving no indication he knew her.

Outside, the patriots ran toward their horses hooting and hollering in glee. Zeke handed the crate up to Les who was already astride, and then Zeke turned back to Maggie. He gave her a boost into her saddle. "Go home," he told her sharply. "Go home and go to bed."

"It's gold coin. Did you see it all?" she bubbled with excitement. "What are we going to do with all of that money?"

John slipped handed Maggie the reins to her horse. "Meeting two nights from now, Les and Ed's duck blind. "We'll talk then."

With that, Zeke slapped Maggie's horse on the rump and the horse bolted. Maggie rode off into the moonlit night still wearing her mask.

"Captain? Captain . . ." Private Michaels shook Grayson gently. "Captain, wake up."

Grayson rolled in his cot and attempted to pull the light cotton sheet that covered his nude body up over his head.

Michaels carefully swept back the sheet. "Sir, you have to wake up."

With a groan Grayson rolled onto his back and opened his eyes, shielding them from the lanternlight with a cupped palm. "Michaels?"

"Yes, sir." The boy eyed the empty claret bottle lying beside Grayson's bed. "Major Lawrence wants you."

"Now?"

"Now." Michaels picked up the claret bottle and set it on a clothing trunk.

Grayson swung his feet over the side of the bed and cradled his head in his hands. His skull was pounding, his tongue thick and cottony. "What's happened?"

"I don't know exactly, but it has something to do with payroll for one of the Hessian regiments."

"Payroll? Why are were concerned with payroll in the middle of the night and what the hell do I care if the Hessians get paid?"

"Sir . . ." Michaels began to lay out Grayson's pressed uniform, "I think the rebels stole the payroll."

Grayson swore foully beneath his breath and then glanced up, trying to focus. "Tell me something, Michaels, how the hell is it that you say you don't know what's going on, but you always know exactly what's going on and before I do?"

The young private shrugged. "I don't know, sir."

Grayson laughed without humor, wishing he hadn't brought home that last bottle of claret from Commegys' Ordinary last night. He'd sat there all evening waiting, watching, as he had so many nights in the last weeks, hoping to catch just a glimpse of Maggie. It felt good to just see her even if they didn't speak. But last night the tavern had been unusually quiet. Maggie had never appeared.

"Captain . . ." Michaels urged gently. "The major's waiting. Riker, too."

Sweeping back the hair that fell across his forehead, Grayson pushed up off his cot and reached for the creased breeches Michaels offered.

An hour later Grayson headed back toward his own tent, but instead of going inside, he circumnavigated it and headed for the stabling area where the horses for his company were kept. The British encampment, shrouded in that half darkness of dawn, was quiet. The only men visible were those standing watch.

In a matter of minutes Grayson had Giipa saddled and he was on his way. Damn those men, they were getting bold. Stealing a payroll! They were going to get themselves hanged if they didn't back off. Grayson didn't know who the men were who formed the Yorktown band, but he had to find out and warn them Riker was on to them. Standing in Lawrence's tent, Riker had sworn to his uncle that he would find the Colonial traitors and make an example of them. He'd hang them right in front of Commegys' Ordinary as a warning to all who thought to cross him.

Grayson's first instinct told him to go to Maggie. She knew everything that went on in Yorktown. She would know who the men were. He knew her well enough to know she wouldn't give him names, but if he warned her, he knew she'd pass on the message.

The thought of seeing Maggie again, of hearing her husky voice, made him urge Giipa into a run. God, he missed her. Nothing seemed to be going right these days. Grayson found himself in one tight spot after another. He was finding it more and more difficult to move freely about the British camp. Riker watched him constantly, daring him to make a mistake. For weeks Grayson had been trying to get a second look at that map with the ship movement he'd seen in Major Lawrence's tent, but so far he'd had no luck.

Grayson rode into Maggie's yard, and the hound she called Honey came running from beneath the front porch. The sight of the lone dog reminded him of why he was no longer welcome in Maggie's house. Christ, what was wrong with Riker? What kind of man was he that he chose women and helpless beasts to prey upon? He was a bully, that's what he was.

Honey barked, circling Grayson as he dismounted, but she didn't seem to be a threat. Slowly he made his way to the farmhouse, speaking in a soothing voice to the dog. "Good girl, good Honey," he cajoled. "Where's Maggie? Can you tell me where Maggie is?"

Maggie stood in the kitchen, watching Grayson through the rippled-glass window. She knew she should grab her flintlock and run him off, but she couldn't do it. She needed to see him, to talk to him if only for a moment. Rubbing the sleep from her eyes, she went through the motions of making a pot of coffee. After the raid last night she'd come home and gone directly to bed as Zeke had instructed, but she'd slept poorly, finally rising a few minutes ago.

Placing the pot of water on an iron spider, she listened to the front door creak open. "Maggie?" Grayson called from the front hall. "Don't shoot. I know you're in there. I just want to talk to you."

She heard his footsteps in the hall and then he

was there, standing in her kitchen doorway. "Maggie," he said softly.

It was all she could do to keep from flinging herself into his arms. She turned her back to him, stooping to scratch old Roy behind his ear. Miraculously, the dog had survived Riker's gunshot and was slowly recuperating thanks to Maggie's crude surgeon's skills.

"He's alive," Grayson said with relief. "I wouldn't have believed it, as bad as he looked."

She ignored his remark. Who was he to pretend he cared about her old hound? "You're out early, Captain. Your men run low on ale? Or is it food they be needing? My last chicken's been gone two weeks. Maybe it's dogs you're lookin' to shoot."

God, he'd missed the sharp bite of her tongue . . . her perceptive cynicism. "Maggie, I have to talk to you."

"So talk." She kept her back to him, afraid that if their eyes met, she'd be in his arms, touching him, brushing her lips against his.

"I need your help." He paused, wondering what he could say that wouldn't put his true identity in jeopardy. "Something . . . something happened last night and I was wondering if you knew anything of it."

"No, I can't help you, Captain. I slept sound all night."

Stroking his chin, Grayson scanned the cozy kitchen. It was obvious she wasn't going to make this easy for him. "Mag—" He stopped short as his attention came to rest on the object tossed thoughtlessly on the kitchen table.

At the sound of his strangled voice, Maggie spun around, following the direction of his gaze. She froze for a moment in horror, then dove for the table. But Grayson was closer. He grabbed the bit of cloth in his hand and she latched on to its corner.

"Maggie . . ." He ground his teeth in fury.

"Give it to me," she demanded.

His blue eyes locked with hers in a battle of wills. With sudden force he released the flour-sack mask and Maggie fell back clutching the damning evidence in her hands.

Chapter Twelve

The moment seemed to stretch into a lifetime as Maggie stood with the flour-sack mask in her hands not knowing what to say, what to do. What was the sense in denying her involvement with the patriot band when the evidence was clutched in her hands. Grayson wasn't stupid.

Standing with his fists clenched at his sides, Grayson could feel his anger rising until he feared he would lose control. He wanted to take Maggie by the shoulders and shake some sense into her. How could she be so foolish as to risk her life in such a dangerous escapade! Didn't she understand that one mistake could prove fatal?

Despite his ire, Grayson couldn't fight the pride that welled in his chest making his throat constrict. She was on his side! The side for freedom! What she was doing in the British encampments peddling her wares, he didn't know. But he did know that no man or woman would take the risk she had taken last night unless they were fully committed to the patriot cause.

So now what did he say? How did he react?

Grayson's heart twisted in his chest. He couldn't tell her who he was! To Maggie he had to remain Captain Grayson Thayer of the king's army. To her, he had to remain the enemy. It was the only way he could protect her.

"How could you be such a fool?" he snapped, his blue eyes fixed on hers. "You stole a payroll, for Christ's sake!"

Maggie held the mask behind her back as if she could hide the truth of her actions. "Payroll? I don't know what you're talking about."

Her tone was so surprisingly even that Grayson almost felt compelled to believe her. *What a fine spy she'd make,* he thought. *Better than me.* He laughed, but his voice was without humor. He used his best captain's tone, dripping with sarcasm. "Let's skip your protests, Maggie, shall we? I haven't time for your games. I have to decide what's to be done."

"Done?" she echoed. Would he turn her in, despite what they'd shared? Would she turn him in if their positions were reversed? Just how deep did her loyalties to these United States run? She honestly didn't know, and that thought frightened her more deeply than the threat of hanging from a noose.

"Yes, done," Grayson went on angrily. "What the hell am I supposed to do with this information?" He turned away from her so he could collect his thoughts. She looked so damned beautiful this morning with her hair a mass of tangled fiery tresses and her face an innocent mask of sleepiness.

He took a slow, deep breath, trying to push the images of her rosy lips, her full breasts, from his mind. "That bit of moldy sack is sufficient evidence to hang you, Maggie! To have me court-martialed if I don't turn you in!"

Maggie swallowed against the lump in her throat. Even now, as Grayson stood before her in his fancy pressed scarlet uniform and his meticulously combed hair, she wanted to make love to him. *Why, I'm no better than Lyla,* she thought as she forced herself to look at his broad shoulders instead of the floor. "I'm sorry," she whispered. "I didn't mean for you to ever know."

"Of course you didn't," he shouted, trying to ignore the tremor in her voice. "But what difference does that make now?" He spun back around to face her. "Maggie, we're in a hell of a fix here."

"I didn't mean for this to happen. I didn't mean to get you involved." She lowered her voice a notch. "I didn't mean to care about you."

"And you think *I* did?"

The harsh truth of his words stung her like a slap in the face. "I can't tell you who the others are," she stated flatly, "no matter what. So don't ask."

"Did you mean to use me as a way to get information?"

"No," she retorted miserably. It was only a half lie. "You were the one who came to me—that first night at the tavern, the card game." Her gaze riveted to his. "I don't whore," she spit, "not for money, not for anything."

Oh, God, he'd hurt her, he could see it in her eyes. "Maggie, it's got to stop—here, now," he said quietly. "Before it's too late."

"I can't make any promises," she answered boldly. "I don't make the decisions."

Grayson took two long strides toward her and

grabbed her arms. The flour sack fell to the planked floor. Suddenly his anger was there again. but it was fueled by his fear for her safety. "Don't you understand the danger, not just to you but to everyone in Yorktown? Major Lawrence could sweep the entire town and throw you all onto a prison ship. He could send you away from your homes without a stitch of clothing or a bite of bread at the very least."

He held her wrists so tightly that the pressure brought tears to her eyes. "Don't you understand what it's like to have no control over your own life," Maggie murmured. "Over who you marry? What you grow? We Virginians can no longer accept the oppression of King George."

If only you knew, Maggie mine, he voiced silently. *If only I could tell you just how well I know what it's like to have no control!* He thought of the uniform he wore and the sights he had witnessed these past years, having no choice but to remain silent because of the role he played. It made him sick to his stomach.

Grayson stared into Maggie's Indian-brown eyes. She was so frightened. And yet somehow she stood strong against him. She stood strong for the patriot cause.

Suddenly he pulled her roughly toward him, crushing his mouth to hers. It was a kiss of desperation, of deep-seated fear for them both.

"Maggie, Maggie mine," he murmured against her lips. He thrust his tongue into her mouth, needing her as he had never needed any woman.

For a moment, she struggled to push him away. She beat him with her fists as he propelled her backward onto the kitchen table. But then she was kissing him back, her own need as intense as his.

Grayson brought his knee up between her thighs and she twisted against it. He cupped her breast in a rough caress and she cried in—pleasure, in pain, he didn't know.

"Maggie, Maggie, what are we to do?" he whispered urgently as he lifted her skirts to touch the soft curls at the apex of her thighs.

Maggie was caught in a whirling tidepool of indecision. A part of her, her heart, wanted to make love to Grayson, here, now on the kitchen table with the light of early morning pouring through her windows, knowing he might see her hang by nightfall.

Yet the sensible part inside her told her it was wrong. It would only worsen matters. What would he think of her after he'd had his way? Would he think she had given her body to him in the hopes that he would spare her? The thought that he would think her a whore was worse than the thought of dying.

With a sudden burst of anger Maggie shoved Grayson backward. "Nooo!" she cried, leaping to her feet and shoving her skirts down over her bare hips. "Get out," she shouted. "Get out of my house!"

"Maggie. Please, I need you."

"Well, I don't need you," she lied. "And if you think I'll lay with you so that you won't turn me in, you're wrong!"

Lay with him so that he wouldn't turn her in? What the hell was she talking about? "Maggie, I didn't think—Maggie, I love you. I wouldn't—" He reached for her, but she slapped at his hands.

"Get out," she ordered, refusing to listen to him. She picked up the flour-sack mask from the floor and threw it at him. "Take your bloody evidence and get out!" She knew she wasn't thinking clearly. She knew she wasn't making sense. But she was tearing up inside. All she could think of was the baby, her love for Virginia, and the way of life her da had known. All she could think of was her love for Grayson. She loved the enemy. She *was* his whore.

"Get out!" she screamed. "Get out of my house! Out of my life, you stinking bloodyback!"

Grayson felt tears sting his eyes and he turned away, refusing to let her see his weakness. Last year, two years ago, he'd have faced her and fought for her love. Where had his strength gone? Was it being sapped by all of those bottles of claret he was consuming? Or was it being sapped by the burdens of his duties? Both, he supposed.

Slowly he bent to retrieve his grenadier cap. He could hear Maggie sobbing behind him. All he wanted to do was to take her into his arms and kiss away the fear, the hurt. But he couldn't. She had spurned him and his love. She hadn't been able to look through the red coat to see the man beyond. Not that he blamed her. But that was simply the reality of the matter, as real as the fact that he couldn't disclose his true identity to her, not even to win her love.

Without turning back to look at her, Grayson walked out of the kitchen, down the hall, and out the front door toward his waiting horse, the mask still in his hand.

Maggie slumped into a hard kitchen chair and dropped her face into her hands. She cried as she had never cried before. Nothing was ever going to be right again. If he didn't turn her in, if he walked away right now, she knew she would never be the woman she had been before Captain Thayer forced himself into her life.

Would Grayson turn her in? She couldn't blame him if he did. His life could be at stake as well. Couldn't he be charged with treason for aiding and abetting the enemy? Couldn't he be tortured and hanged at her side?

A sob wracked Maggie's body. How could she have been so stupid as to have left the flour sack on her table? It was just that no one ever came into her house but Zeke. Never in a lifetime had she expected Grayson to walk through that door, this morning of all mornings.

It wasn't herself she was worried about—if he turned her in, he turned her in—but what of the others in the band? And what of the babe she carried in her womb? Didn't that child have the right to see the sunshine, to taste fresh water from a well, to touch the soft down of a newly hatched chick? Didn't that child have a right to live?

Maggie was so lost in the depths of her despair that she never heard Zeke come in the front door.

"Maggie? Maggie girl, is that you?" Zeke hurried down the hall toward the sounds of her wracking sobs. "Maggie, what is it?" He stopped short in the doorway to stare at her slender form slumped over the table. How long had it been since he'd seen Maggie cry? Years. "Maggie," he repeated softly.

"Zeke?" She sniffed and wiped her face with the

back of her hand. She couldn't bear to look up at him.

"What is it?" He sat in the chair beside her, and reached for her hand.

Maggie pulled away as if not wanting to soil him with her touch. "Oh, Holy Mother Mary, Zeke. I've done it this time."

"What, Maggie, what have you done?"

She took a shuddering breath, forcing herself to look her old friend straight in the eye. "Captain Thayer. He found the mask. He knows I was in on the payroll theft."

Zeke tried to keep his voice even. "You told him about us?"

She shook her head. "No, of course not."

"Maggie, how did this happen? I thought you said you weren't going to see the captain anymore."

"I wasn't," she murmured, fighting back a fresh wave of tears. "He just came. The mask was on the table." She gestured limply. "It just happened, Zeke."

"Oh, Maggie," Zeke breathed. Awkwardly he wrapped his arms around her shoulders and drew her against his slightly hollowed chest. "Maggie, we've got to get you out of Virginia."

"No." She rested her head on Zeke's shoulder, comforted by the smell of sweet hay that clung to his worn broadcloth shirt. "I can't do that. Maybe if Major Lawrence gets one of us, he'll be satisfied. I go, and he may not give up until you're all caught and hanged."

"You hear what you're sayin', girl?" He squeezed her tightly and then pushed her back so that he could see her face. "So tell me, why didn't Thayer take you prisoner? Why'd he leave you here knowin' you'd have time to warn us?"

"I don't know," she whispered. "I don't understand him. He doesn't think like any man I ever knew."

"Bottom of the barrel. You think he'll turn you in or not?"

"I don't know."

Zeke glanced out the window and then back at Maggie. "You think he's in love with you, Maggie girl?"

She looked up through teary eyes. "What do you mean?"

"If he loves you," he said gently, "then just maybe he can't bring himself to turn you in."

Maggie's eyes met his. "If you was in his place, would you turn in a woman you loved?"

Zeke's cheeks colored beneath his scraggly beard. An image of Lyla came into his mind. Sweet Lyla. "I can't tell you that, because I don't know," he answered honestly. "Love's a strong thing in a man's heart."

"In a woman's, too," Maggie whispered.

For a moment they were both lost in their own thoughts; then Maggie pushed away from the table and went to get Zeke and herself a cup of coffee. "So, what do we do now, friend?"

"Do?" He rocked his chair back at an angle, the wood scraping wood. "We don't do a thing. We wait."

"Wait for the soldiers to come get me?"

"I don't think they'll be comin'. Just the same, I want you to lay low for a few days at my house. Mama could use the company. This way, if the redcoats do come for you, we'll see 'em comin'."

Maggie brought him a cup of coffee. "I guess this means I can't ride with you anymore, not even if this wind blows over, doesn't it?"

He nodded, slurping his coffee. "Sorry, Maggie. It wouldn't be safe. You shouldn't know our comings and goings anymore, either. We can't risk other people's lives. Can't risk the operations, either."

Maggie slipped back into her chair, cradling her coffee cup. She couldn't remember a time when she'd felt this miserable. Even if she managed to scrape through this with her life, what would she have? In the last year the cause for freedom had become everything to her. The men she worked with were her friends. Would they be afraid to speak with her on the street? Would she be turned away from their homes? What reason would she have to get out of bed in the morning?

The babe. It came to her like a streak of lightning. She had the baby. Grayson's baby. Of course she had a reason to live, a cause to fight for. A bare smile formed over the rim of her cup.

Zeke was right. Grayson wasn't going to turn her in. He stood right there in the kitchen and said he loved her. Once she thought it was safe, Maggie would pack a bag and go north to New York where her cousin Trudy lived. Trudy would take her in. There Maggie could build a new life for her and her baby. She'd say her husband was dead. With so many war casualties, no one would question her pregnancy. No one but Trudy would ever have to know the baby wasn't Noah's.

Maggie looked up from her coffee cup, feeling much better. Her da had always said a man felt better when he had a plan. "All right, Zeke," she said. "I'll come stay with you and Mildred."

Zeke stood. "Good. Now run get your things and we'll go before the good captain has a chance to come back for you."

"I'll have her kidnapped," Grayson told Private Michaels. "That's what I'll do." He took a gulp of the sweet Madeira the barmaid had brought him. "I'll have her kidnapped and taken home where she'll be safe. Then when this bloody war's over, I'll marry her, that's what I'll do."

"Yes, sir," Michaels agreed from across the trestle table in the rear of the Commegys' Ordinary's public room. For the last hour the boy had been trying unsuccessfully to lure his captain away from the tavern and back to camp.

Michaels didn't know what had happened to Captain Thayer this morning, but he knew it was something terrible. He'd come back to his tent in a foul mood, ranting and raving. By noon he had been headed for the tavern where he'd sat all afternoon consuming too much wine and not enough food. An hour ago Michaels had come to check on Captain Thayer and found him talking crazy. Michaels didn't understand half of what his commanding officer said, but he knew they were things that could be misconstrued by men like Riker. Michaels knew he had to get Captain Thayer out of the tavern before it filled with the evening crowd of redcoats.

"Kidnap her and make her my rebel wife, that's what I'll do. The hell with the British army, the hell with General Washington, I'll marry her now!"

"Captain," Michaels said gently. "We should go, sir."

"Go? Go where? I'm tryin' to tell you, Michaels, I don't care what she's done, whose side she's on, whose side *I'm* on, for that matter. I just don't bloody care."

Whose side? What in the good Lord's name was the captain talking about? Then Michaels remembered the rumors stirring in the camp. Hadn't Riker practically come out and accused Captain Thayer of being a traitor to the Crown? A shiver of fear crept up his spine. The boy lowered his voice. "You've had too much to drink, sir. You need to go back to your tent."

Grayson wiped his mouth with the back of his hand. Yes, he'd had too much to drink, but it still wasn't enough. He still hadn't washed Maggie's memory from his mind.

His Maggie, his brave, strong-willed Maggie was a rebel for God's sake! Probably a spy. Why else would she be in and out of the British encampment the way she was? Well, she might be a hell of a spy, but she certainly wasn't much of a bootmaker! He reached beneath the table and fumbled with the sole of his French boots. Hell, they were looser now than they'd been *before* he had her repair them!

He let go of his boot, letting his foot hit the floor, and reached for the tankard of Madeira. It was empty. He banged the tankard on the table. "Another, Michaels!"

"We really should go, sir."

"I said another! One for the road."

Reluctantly, Michaels took the tankard and slid off the bench to find the barmaid. Coffee, that was what his captain needed. Perhaps a cup of coffee would straighten him out. It wasn't that Michaels could say Captain Thayer was drunk. He'd never seen the man drunk, not like the other officers at least; he never slurred his words or tripped over his own two feet. No, Captain Thayer was never drunk like that. But how could it be good for any man to consume that much wine? And what of all those strange things the captain was saying? Yes, it was better to get him out of the tavern before he got into trouble.

Michaels retrieved the cup of coffee and headed back toward the table in the rear of the tavern where Captain Thayer sat. The captain hadn't moved, except that he had something in his hand now. A piece of cloth . . . like a sack one could buy sugar or flour in.

"Sir. A cup of coffee for you." Michaels eyed the sack in his captain's hand, wondering why were there holes cut in it?

"I didn't ask for coffee."

"I know you didn't, sir, but I thought you could use some."

Grayson eyed Michaels standing behind him. Why did the boy look so frightened? Grayson stuffed the flour-sack mask back into his coat. "All right," he conceded. "We'll go."

"I think that's a good idea, sir. Maybe a nap would do you some good."

Grayson pitched several coins onto the table and then swept up his cap. From there he headed for the door with Michaels trailing directly behind him.

"Son of a bitch," Zeke murmured under his breath as Grayson brushed past him. Zeke waited until the captain was out of earshot and then he leaned across the table to speak to Les and Edwin. Carter, seated beside him, turned an ear.

"That's it, boys," Zeke said. "It's got to be Maggie's mask."

"I thought you said you thought she was safe."

"I said I didn't think he'd turn her in," Zeke snapped. "How was I supposed to know he'd be drownin' his sorrows in a bottle and flashin' the mask for all the world to ogle?"

"How long do you think it will take before somebody notices he got it?" Les asked.

"Not long," Ed offered. "Not long a tall."

"So what do we do?" Carter asked, his face flushed. "There's nothin' we can do but hope he keeps his mouth shut."

Zeke stared Carter straight in the eye. "Damned if there isn't something we *can* do. This is Maggie we're talking about here. We take him out, that's what we do!"

"Kill him?" Carter mopped his brow with a tobacco-stained handkerchief. "I knew we shouldn't 'ave brought a woman in! I knew it!" He glanced up at Zeke beside him. "Thayer's an officer. We can't just kill 'em for no reason can we?"

Les drained his leather jack of ale. "Seems to me we got plenty of reason. That mask could get us all kilt."

"I say we just do it," Zeke said shakily. "As much as he's had to drink, I don' think he ought to ever make it back to the camp."

"Don't we need to talk to John?" Edwin asked.

"No time." Zeke leaned closer. "Let's just get it over with. We can catch him in Devils Woodyard, do it, and be done." He took a deep breath. "You with me, friends?"

Les slapped his hand on the table. "I'm in. I got no problem killin' the bastard. Me and Ed, we'll do it ourselves if you like. Might even have a bit of fun with it."

"For Maggie," Ed agreed. "We got to do it for Maggie's sake. For us all."

All eyes turned to Carter, and the man glanced up, sweating profusely.

"We'll not force you," Zeke offered.

"No. I'm in. I'm in," Carter stammered. "Just scares the livin' daylights outta me, killin' an officer, that's all."

Zeke gave a nod. "Now you boys listen and listen well, because we'll only have one chance at this . . ."

A few moments later, single file, the men left Manny's ordinary. They fanned out, appearing to all go their separate ways. Minutes later they met in a grove of pines.

"Darn if you ain't got it right," Les whispered. "The captain's comin' this way. He'll pass here any minute."

Pete, who had met Les just outside the ordinary, handed out flour-sack masks.

"What about the boy?" Ed asked, taking a practice aim with his primed flintlock. "Do we kill him, too?"

Zeke pulled his mask over his head. "I don't see why we have to. He wouldn't know nothing. But let's take him prisoner, at least for the time bein'. John'll know what's to be done with 'im."

"All right, boys, here comes our captain," Carter

whispered.

The patriots waited until Zeke gave the signal and then they charged the British officer and the young boy. Captain Thayer reached for his pistol, but Les brought his rifle down hard against the captain's head and the Brit crumbled to ground. "We take him alive," Zeke had said. "We find out what he knows of us, and then we kill him."

At the moment the other men surrounded Captain Thayer, Carter went for the private. But the boy was a fierce fighter for his size. He kicked and bucked, pummeling Carter in the face.

Carter swore, swinging his fist and knocking the boy to the ground. When the patriot fell on top of him, the boy reached for his attackers' mask. Carter released his weapon in the attempt to keep his face hidden. The boy took that instant to slip from beneath Carter's bulk. The young private was on his feet in an instant . . . running.

"Stop the boy," Carter shouted.

The men looked to Zeke for approval.

"We don't have time," Zeke responded roughly. "He didn't see us. By the time he makes it back to the Brit camp we'll be long gone."

Zeke turned and gave a nod to Les and Edwin, and the two brothers lifted the tied and gagged the captain and then the band of rebels hurried into the woods.

Chapter Thirteen

Private Paul Michaels raced through the dense Virginia forest ignoring the branches that slapped him in the face and the greenbriars that ripped at his breeches until his legs bled. He ran as hard and as fast as he could, petrified by the masked men. Were they chasing him? He didn't know; he was too terrified to look back.

Finally, when he thought his lungs would burst, he forced himself to sneak a peek over his shoulder. There was no one there. He slowed to a trot and then a walk, clutching his chest as he struggled to fill his lungs with air. Paul's entire body shook with fear; he'd wet his breeches.

He dropped onto a fallen log and cradled his head in his hands. They'd taken Captain Thayer! Who? The bloody rebels, of course—the bloody masked rebels who the captain had been assigned to track down. Paul knew he had to get back to camp.

He had to tell Major Lawrence.

But as his breath came easier, a strange thought entered his mind. What if . . . what if what Lieutenant Riker had said was true? What if his captain really *was* one of the rebels? The thought was absurd. His captain, a traitor? And yet . . .

Paul went over in his mind the things Captain Thayer had said in the tavern, strange things about not caring which side the woman, Maggie, was on, not caring which side *he* was on. Something about lies.

What if this was the way rebels were bringing Captain Thayer back into their fold? What if it had all been planned? The boy laughed at the absurdity of the idea and his voice echoed in the treetops. The masked rebels scared him so badly, he was thinking crazy! Of course Captain Thayer wasn't a traitor. He'd gone to Eaton and Oxford, hadn't he? He'd joined the military even before the war against the Colonies began!

Paul pushed himself up off the log. He had to get back to the camp and tell Major Lawrence what had happened. The major would send men to rescue the captain . . .

Unless, of course, the captain *was* one of the rebels. Then Paul would be signing his death warrant.

Paul pushed back a lock of his white-blond hair, fighting the tears that stung his eyes. What was the matter with him? He was a man of nearly fifteen. Why couldn't he think straight? Why didn't he know what to do?

Because he was afraid, afraid for Captain Thayer.

As remote as the possibility was, the truth was that Captain Thayer might be a rebel spy. They said there were spies everywhere in the camps—washwomen, whores, soldiers you'd never suspect.

Paul knew it was his duty to go to Major Lawrence and tell him everything. Not just about the captain being captured, but about what the captain had said in the tavern, about the mask he'd put in his coat, the same mask the rebels had worn when they'd kidnapped him. Paul knew he had to tell the major all of it, else he could be charged with treason as well. So why wasn't he on his way?

Because he loved Captain Thayer.

Paul wiped at his teary eyes with the back of his blood-encrusted, briar-scratched hand. No matter who Captain Thayer was, traitor or Englishman, he loved him. No one had ever been as nice to him as Captain Thayer, certainly not his father, who'd sent him off to war at twelve years old. Captain Thayer had nursed him himself when Paul had come down with the pox in the South. Captain Thayer had defended him when Lieutenant Riker had falsely accused him of stealing from his tent. Captain Thayer had brought him sweets from Williamsburg.

So what did Paul do? He didn't know. Who should he tell? He didn't know. He dropped back onto the log in utter, frightened bewilderment, knowing that as the minutes ticked by, the remaining minutes of Captain Thayer's life might be ticking away as well.

Then it came to him as suddenly as a revelation from God. The red-haired woman who had been so nice to him. The bootmaker. The other soldiers in the camp said she was one of those neutrals—she wasn't for any side but her own. Surely she would help him. Only last week she'd let him play with her dogs while she mended the captain's boots in her shed. Maggie was her name. Maggie. It had to be the Maggie the captain said he loved. She was the only woman he'd been with in two months.

Maggie would know what to do, wouldn't she? Of course Paul knew there was a chance the woman was in on the kidnapping, but he weighed the idea in his mind and decided he'd just have to take a chance.

Leaping up off the log, Paul changed directions and headed for the little farm just outside the town of York.

"So why didn't you marry my son when that worthless piece o' filth you called husband died?" Mildred Barnes asked in her usual straightforward manner. "You and Zeke could have had a fine passel o' boys by now. I'd have a grandchild to rock on my poor knee, 'stead of goin' to my grave with achin' arms."

Maggie turned away from the window. She'd only been here at Zeke's for a few hours and already she was getting restless. It just wasn't like her to be indoors in the midst of the day. She mopped her perspiring chest with the sprigged kerchief she wore around her neck. "I told you, Miss Mildred. The only reason I didn't marry your son was because he wouldn't have me."

The ivory-haired woman slapped her knee. "Horsedung! Ezekial's loved you since the two of you was wrestlin' over fishin' poles down by the river."

"Yeah, he loved me so much, he gave me a black eye over that fishin' pole." At the memory of the shiner Zeke had given her, Maggie covered her eye with her palm. She'd been a hell of a sight at that Sunday morning Mass.

"Well, you've ruined it now, Maggie Myers! Near broke his heart. He's done taken up with another from what I hear."

The elderly woman's words tapped Maggie's attention. She had wondered if Miss Mildred knew of Lyla. "You don't say," she said innocently. "And which one might that be?"

Mildred gave a snort of derision and plucked her corncob pipe from the pocket that hung inside a slit in her dress. "Don't be playin' games with me, Maggie Myers. I powdered your bottom when you was a babe."

Maggie smiled, wondering what unstated right that seemed to give women. "So you've heard he's keepin' company with Lyla?"

"Strangest keepin' company I ever heard of—walkin' a whore home from the store oncst a week, and now walkin' her to Sunday meetin'!"

Maggie's brown eyes widened. "He's taking her to church?"

"No, he don't *take* her!" Mildred shifted in her chair and reached for her leather tobacco pouch resting on a footstool. "He don't pick her up in his wagon. He don't invite her to his mother's house for Sunday dinner. Near as I can see, he don't even talk to her! He just walks beside her, and when they get inside the Good Lord's house, she sits in the back, same as every Sunday, while he moseys on up to sit with Harry and me."

Maggie went to light a broom straw from the smoldering coals in the kitchen fireplace. "Harry Carter sittin' on your pew with you these days, is he?" she teased, coming back into the front room. Maggie had always been interested in what was happening in the local Episcopal church most of the citizens of Yorktown attended. As a child she'd sworn to her parents that when she grew up, she was going to convert, but as the years passed, she grew comfortable with her Catholic religion, or at least with her relationship with God, so she'd never bothered.

Mildred sucked on her pipe as Maggie held the glowing broom straw to the bowl. In a moment the elderly woman was rewarded by a puff of sweet-smelling smoke. "Now Harry Carter, there's a fine man."

"Sweet on you, is he?" Maggie teased.

"Oh, pshaw!" Mildred leaned back to enjoy her smoke. "Folks like us, we're too old for such." She winked. "Not that we don't think 'bout it oncst in a while!"

Maggie laughed, turning back toward the window. Across the rolling field she could just make out the outline of her farmhouse. Heavens, but she'd missed that house when she left Yorktown. So many memories, good and bad. But she couldn't think about herself, she had to think about her baby. If her child was going to have a fair chance at life, it would have to be far from here where no one would know of the babe's illegitimacy.

Movement in the field caught Maggie's attention and she immediately stepped closer to the window, sweeping back the loomed-lace curtains Mildred was so proud of.

"What is it?" Mildred asked. "Redcoats? Fetch me my papa's wheellock. Won't no redcoat take my Maggie long as I'm breathin'."

"No," she said. "A boy. Not comin' here, though. He's headed for my place." Maggie watched as he climbed the fence and went straight for the farmhouse. Who was it?

"A boy?" Mildred slowly rose from her chair. "A boy you know?" When she reached the window, she gave a snort. "Looks like a redcoat to me."

"Paul," Maggie murmured. It was the boy, Paul Michaels, who had brought her Grayson's boots. The same boy who had been at his tent that night Grayson saved him from Riker and his men.

Mildred's steely gray eyes narrowed as she studied Maggie's face. "You're not thinkin' 'bout goin' up there to see what he wants, are you?"

"He works for Captain Thayer," Maggie answered, lost in her own thoughts. Grayson must have sent the boy with a message. Was Grayson in trouble? A spine-tingling shiver of fear rose up her backbone.

"Captain Thayer? Seems to me, Maggie Myers, that he's the man Zeke's hidin' you from."

Maggie shook her head. She made her decision in an instant. "I won't be gone long."

The old woman grabbed Maggie's arm. "Think what you're doin', girl. This ain't no game you been playin'. Didn't you see them bodies hung out to dry by nooses around their necks, down by the corner oak? Birds picked their bones clean on account of the Brits wouldn't let us cut 'em down and give 'em a decent burial. You want birds pickin' your flesh after they hang you as a traitor to King Georgie?"

Maggie gently loosened Mildred's grip. "I'll be all right. But I have to go." She went for the door and picked up her own rifle and cartridge box. "Grayson might need me." On impulse she thrust one of Zeke's old three-cornered hats on her head and reached for the saddlebag he always left by the door in case he ever had to flee Yorktown quickly.

"You're throwin' away your heart on that man," Mildred warned. "And it's not the red coat that's the worst of it! He'd never marry a woman like you. It's the family name, the fancy schools. You'll never be one of 'em, Maggie Myers, not as long as you live! You'll never be nothin' to him but his whore." The old woman hobbled after her as she went out the door. "You should stay where you belong. With the people you belong with. You should have married my Zeke. That's what you should have done!"

But Mildred's words fell on deaf ears. Maggie was already running across the field toward her own house. Minutes later, as she hopped the fence, she saw Paul coming down her front steps. When he spotted her, he came racing across the yard.

"Miss Maggie! Miss Maggie!" He waved as he ran.

"What is it, Paul? What are you doin' here?"

He struggled to catch his breath. "Captain

Thayer, ma'am."

"What's wrong?"

"Kidnapped. They hit him over the head and carried him away. They tried to take me, too, but I ran."

Fear made the hair on the back of Maggie's neck bristle. She grabbed the boy by the shoulders. "Who? Who took him?"

"The rebels! Wearin' masks!"

Maggie looked away, swearing beneath her breath. Zeke! How could he! He'd walked away from her house knowing he was going after Grayson, but not having the guts to tell her! She whipped back around. "Where, Paul? You have to tell me where this happened."

"The woods between the tavern and our camp. You know, the road through that Devil's Wood." He looked up at her, twisting his hands with anxiety. "You have to help him. I don't know why they took him."

Maggie's face hardened. Take care, she told herself. Make sure this isn't a trap. Make certain he's telling the truth. "Did you already go to your camp and tell someone there that Captain Thayer's been kidnapped?"

He hung his head. "No, ma'am."

"Why not?"

"The captain, he's been acting so strange lately. And Lieutenant Riker, he's been calling the captain a traitor." The towheaded boy went on even faster than before. "None of it makes any sense. In the tavern Captain Thayer had one of those flour-sack masks. He was talking crazy. Too much drink. The captain he hasn't been sleeping right lately. He was talking about loving you," Paul's cheeks colored, "about not caring which side anybody was on." He looked up at Maggie. "I was afraid to go to the camp. Afraid what the lieutenant said might be true."

Maggie laughed humorlessly. Grayson a spy! That was absurd. Still, the boy's fear seemed real enough, as did his story. Why hadn't she thought of it before. Of course Zeke would try to kill Grayson!

Maggie grabbed Paul by the collar of his red coat and began to pull him along toward the barn to fetch her saddle and bridle. She'd catch her horse on her way across the field. "I want you to take me right to the place where the masked men attacked you. Can you do that, Paul?"

He nodded, following her into the barn. "Yes, ma'am."

"Good." From there, Maggie would just have to guess as to where they'd taken Grayson. Surely they wouldn't have just shot or hanged him. They would have tried to get information out of him first. Maggie winced at that thought. She was no innocent. She knew both sides tortured prisoners before they killed them. It was the way of war, Zeke had once reminded her.

She pushed the thought of Grayson dying at Zeke's hands out of her mind as she shoved the heavy saddle into Paul's arms and grabbed her bridle. She'd just have to find the men, wouldn't she? She'd have to find the patriot band and pray they hadn't yet killed the father of her unborn child.

* * *

Grayson slipped in and out of the depths of consciousness. He heard muffled voices around him. He felt the bite of the rough hempen ropes that bound his wrists above his head, the weight of his entire body pulling down on them. He was in the woods, but near the river, he surmised. He could smell the water.

Slowly he became aware of the excruciating pain radiating from his wrist through his arms. Strung up from a tree. He was hanging a good foot off the ground. Who'd done this to him? What had happened? The numbing veil of the alcohol he'd tried to immerse himself in was gone, leaving him with bitter reality.

The rebels. Damn! The rebel band had him. What a fix this was! A flood of memories washed over him: the terrible fight with Maggie this morning, the warning from Major Lawrence, and then the tavern. Grayson remembered drinking in the tavern and then starting bask to camp with Michaels.

Michaels! It was all Grayson could do to keep from opening his eyes to see if the boy was here. But if he opened his eyes, if he moved an inch, the rebels would know he had come to, and he would lose the advantage of time to think.

Pushing aside the pain that threatened to slow his thinking, Grayson forced his mind to function. *Think!* he told himself. *Think!* He'd been close to death more than once in the last few years, but never this close. He'd never been able to smell its stench before. *And how ironic,* he thought. *To be tortured and killed by men on my own side!*

So how are you going to get yourself out of this mess? he asked himself cockily. Reason. It was his only chance. Reason with them. Stall them until he could get someone to verify his identity.

Against his will, a groan of pain escaped his lips and he heard a man turn toward him. Grayson opened his eyes to see two dark eyes staring through holes in a mask.

"He's comin' to," the dark eyes murmured.

Grayson bit down on his lower lip, fighting the pain in his wrists and arms. "The boy," he said, surprised by the agony he heard in his own voice. It was if he was somehow detached from himself, as if another man spoke. "Where's the boy?"

"Believe I'd be worried about myself," another masked man stated.

Grayson glanced at the trees around him. He saw no sign of Paul Michaels' body. He prayed the boy had escaped. "The boy knows nothing. He's of no good to you."

"No." The second masked man gave Grayson's body a slight push and Grayson swung from the rope. "But *you* are, *Captain.*"

The pain was suddenly so great that Grayson thought he would black out. "You've made a mistake," he ground out. "I'm not who you think I am."

A third man called from a few feet away. "We ain't got time for this talk," he offered. "Just see what he knows and kill him. The boy's made it back to the camp by now. These woods are gonna be crawlin' with bloodybacks in a matter of minutes!"

The first man scrutinized Grayson. "What do you mean you ain't who we think you are?"

"Zeke!"

"Hush, Carter!" Zeke pulled off his mask and thrust it into his belt.

It's Zeke, Maggie's friend, Grayson thought. *They do intend to kill me, here and now, else he wouldn't reveal his identity.*

Zeke's eyes met Grayson's. "You were sayin'?"

"I was saying . . ." Grayson swallowed the bile that rose in his throat. "I was saying that I'm one of you. Major Grayson Thayer detached from the First Legionary Corps. I'm . . . I'm a spy."

The man called Carter laughed aloud. The other men chuckled . . . all but Zeke. Zeke prodded Grayson in the belly with the tip of his bayoneted rifle. "A spy, you say? Well, you're liar, Captain Thayer, same as you're a drunken sot, a cheat, and a womanizer."

Grayson detected some emotion in Zeke's voice—anger, resentment, maybe even a hint of jealousy. Certain that it was concern for Maggie in Zeke's voice that made him speak with such bitter resentment, Grayson grabbed at straws. "I love her, if you're talking about Maggie Myers. I want to make her my wife."

Zeke gave a belligerent laugh and hawked and spit on the mossy ground. "It's too late to save yourself, redcoat, now tell me what you know about us. You tell us what we need to know and you'll die quick and easy. You go stubborn on us and," he exhaled, "I can't be held for my men's actions." He took a step closer to Grayson. "Now, who else knows?"

"Please. Just cut me down. I can prove to you who I am."

"Kill him," Carter insisted. "Just kill the bastard and let's get the hell out of here."

"What do you mean you can prove it?" Zeke asked.

Grayson took a deep, ragged breath. The pain in his wrists and armpits had numbed to a dull, lifeless throb. Did he dare reveal his contact? The man and his entire family would most likely have to be moved.

"I said, what do you mean? Come out with it, we ain't got all day, *Captain.*"

"Billy, Billy Faulkner," Grayson replied in a rush of air."

Zeke glanced over his shoulder, a strange look on his face. "Billy Faulkner?" he repeated, turning his gaze back to Grayson. "Billy Faulkner's dead. Him and his whole family burned up in a fire somebody set two nights ago."

"Dear God," Grayson muttered. "Who did it?"

"Good question," Zeke answered. "Maybe you did."

"Somebody's comin'," Carter shouted in a hushed voice. "Shoot the bastard and let's go!"

"It's clear," the lookout called from beyond Grayson's view. "It's just Maggie."

"Maggie!" Grayson called hoarsely. "Maggie!"

"Shut him up," Carter insisted.

With a sweep of his rifle butt, Ed hit Grayson in

the temple. Grayson felt the strike, a flash of pain, and then he went limp, dissolving into the relief of unconsciousness.

An instant later Maggie came riding into the small clearing, her horse's hooves throwing up dry leaves as she rode around in a tight circle, a flintlock rifle in her hand. "What the hell is going on here?" she asked, eyeing Grayson's still form hanging from the tree. At least he was still alive; she could see the rise and fall of his bare chest. Her gaze met Zeke's, cold and demanding. "Zeke?"

"He knows too much, Mags," Zeke answered carefully. "It's not just your life we're talking about. Not just ours. There're more people involved than you realize, people we have to protect. You know the word is Billy Faulkner was a messenger for us. They say he was murdered by the Brits because someone slipped with their tongue."

"We're not talkin' about Billy Faulkner here. We're talkin' about you, we're talkin' about me, we're talkin' about that man hangin' from that tree." She tried not to look at Grayson strung up from the poplar branch, the blood drained from his face. "Now tell me the truth, Zeke. Did you leave my house this morning meaning to do this to him?"

"No." Zeke stared at her, the hurt plain on his face. "Of course not! But we caught him in the tavern waving your mask." He took a step closer. "Don't you see, Maggie. He has to die. I was just tryin' to spare you. I knew how you felt about him, or at least how you thought you felt . . ."

She swallowed the lump in her throat. So this was what it was to come down to, was it? Did she cut

Grayson loose, thus turning against her friends—her country. Or did she let Zeke see justice done and witness the murder of the man she loved?

"Zeke. You don't have the right to make this kind of a decision. Where's John? We don't do hangings here! This prisoner"—her eyes grew cloudy as she stared at his boots hanging well above the ground—"should be transported to Williamsburg. There are men there who know how to deal with this. They'll get to the bottom of it. They'll know if he has to die for what he knows."

"Damned if we don't know how to deal with it, Maggie," Ed said, whipping off his mask. "What's wrong with you? You gone soft? We kill the bloody redcoat. You can't expect us to let him go because you have bedded with him!"

Zeke whipped around. "Hush your mouth, Edwin, before I hush it for you."

Maggie stared down at Zeke from beneath the brim of her cocked hat. "Cut him down, Zeke." *There.* She'd done it. She'd made the decision. She loved Grayson Thayer. She loved him beyond words. She loved him more than she loved Virginia, more than she loved these United States.

"You know I can't do that, Mags," Zeke answered carefully.

Her dark eyes pierced his. "Cut him down or I'll do it."

"Don't let her do it!" Carter warned. "Don't let her sway you. He makes it back to his camp and we all die. I told you we shouldn't have let a woman in! I told you she'd be trouble."

Maggie turned in her saddle and took aim at

Carter's middle. "Drop your weapon and shut your mouth, Carter. I've had enough of you."

Carter looked up wild-eyed at Zeke. Zeke glanced at Maggie's careful aim, then gave a nod. Carter was too hotheaded anyway. He might well shoot Maggie rather than Thayer in a fit of anger.

But instead of dropping his rifle, Carter turned and ran through the woods. Maggie let him go. All she wanted was Grayson. "Just cut him down, Zeke. He'll do you no harm. I can promise you that." She took a deep breath. "I'd slit his throat myself before I let him harm one of you."

"Think what you're doin' here, Mags," Zeke tried to reason with her. "You take this redcoat and you can never come home again. You'll be a traitor the rest of your born days."

Maggie sighed, taking care not to look up at Grayson's still body. "It's like this, Zeke. Either I'm a traitor to this new country of ours, or I'm a traitor to my heart."

"He's not one of us. Men like him don't marry women like you. You don't even know that this man wants you. You willing to give up your whole life hopin' he does?"

"Who said I wanted him?" she snapped. "I just can't see him die like this."

It wasn't that she was fool enough to think she was going to save his arse and he was going to declare his undying love for her and carry her off and marry her. She wasn't that stupid. She knew there were too many differences between their stations in life to ever make it work. And the truth was that she didn't know what she was going to do with him, once she freed him. She'd cross that bridge when she came to it. All she knew right now was that she couldn't let Zeke and these men murder him.

"Maggie—"

"No more talk, Zeke. I can't make you understand. You never loved someone. You don't know what it feels like."

"I know better than you think," he answered stoically, putting himself between her horse and Grayson's hanging form.

Maggie turned her horse and walked him between Zeke and Grayson, swinging Grayson's body to make way as carefully as she could. Gently, she touched his face. "Grayson. Grayson, can you hear me? We're in a tight spot here. I've got to have your help."

"Don't do it, Mags," Zeke said, knowing he should lift his rifle to her but not having the heart. All he could think of was Lyla and what he would do if put in the same position. What if it was Lyla hanging from that tree branch?

"Maggie?" Grayson answered, in a fog of pain and confusion.

"I'm gonna cut you down," she murmured, taking Zeke's own knife from his saddlebag that she carried on the back of her horse. "You ready?"

Grayson's eyes flew open upon the realization that Maggie was really there. "Maggie!"

"Don't do it, Maggie," Zeke pleaded, his eyes filled with pain. "Please—"

With one sweep of the knife she clutched, Maggie reached behind her and cut the rope that held Grayson above the soft humus ground. He fell across her horse's back and Maggie sunk her heels into the gelding's side, riding past Zeke and into the cover of the forest.

Chapter Fourteen

"Can you pull yourself up?" Maggie asked, her voice tight in her throat. She reined around a shaggly black cedar tree and turned onto a narrow, overgrown game path she and Zeke had traveled a thousand times as children.

Grayson gripped her waist and threw one leg over the moving horse's rump. "I can manage. Keep riding," he answered hoarsely. "They'll be right behind us."

Maggie nodded, too wrought with emotion to speak. *Holy Mother Mary! What have I done?* she asked herself. *I've gone against everything I believe in for this man. I've aided the enemy. I'm a traitor to my own friends, to Virginia, to the country I vowed to stand beside. And for what?*

Maggie rode in silence through the forest, keeping a steady pace. To her surprise, Zeke and the others didn't follow them. She could hear nothing but the pounding of her own horse's hooves and the sound of Grayson's breathing as it came more easily. Slowly his grip around her waist tightened. She could feel him regaining his strength as he recovered from the shock of his ordeal.

"We've got to find a place to hide until I decide a plan of action," Grayson said finally, sounding more like himself. "Can you think of somewhere safe, Maggie?"

His arms around her waist suddenly felt more like a caress. She shifted uncomfortably in her saddle, wishing she had brought along a second horse. She didn't like him so close, his warm hands tight around her. His touch made it too hard to think straight. "You think I'm stupid?" she snapped in revenge for her mixed emotions toward him. "Of course I've got somewhere safe." She was angry with him, angry because he'd forced her to make a decision that would change the path of her life forever.

"What's the matter?" he asked, massaging his wrists. "Why are you angry?"

She gritted her teeth, urging the gelding faster. "You know what this means, me saving you from the noose? It means I can never go home again. It means I betrayed my friends, my country," she spat.

"Betrayed?" He took a deep breath. The time had come. It was time he told her the truth. "Maggie," he said gently, "you didn't betray the United States. You rescued me—granted from our own men, but that's beside the point."

"I don't want to hear your nonsense just now, else I'm liable to kick you off the back of this horse and leave you for Ed and Les. They'll take no pity on you, I can guarantee you that!"

"Maggie." He leaned forward and to one side so that he could see her face. Her skin was flushed, her eyes too wide. She had the look of a soldier who'd been through one hell of a battle. "Don't you hear what I'm saying, sweet? Don't you understand? We're on the same side, you and I."

She laughed bitterly, her voice echoing in the trees above. "Save your lies, Captain, for the likes of Lyla. You've done me enough harm for one day." She took a fork off the game path that led down toward the York River.

Cut into a steep, tree-lined bank was a "fort" she, Zeke, and Carter had dug as children. It was as good a place as any to hide out for the night. Come morning she'd have a better idea as to how she was going to get out of here and what she was going to do with Grayson.

"Maggie!" he said, exasperated. "Here I am, declaring my deepest, darkest secret and you're laughing. Don't you see, I'm a spy. I've been one for years."

"I got no doubt you're a spy, but a stinking bloodyback spy."

He stroked his stubbled chin. He should have known this wasn't going to be easy. Nothing was with Maggie. "I can prove it to you."

"I'm not interested in your proof. I'm not interested in anything you got to say, Captain." She ducked as she rode under a tree branch, and the branch struck Grayson in the face. "Duck," she said, knowing her warning was too late.

Grayson cursed foully. "Maggie," he gripped her

waist in building anger, "you're not being reasonable."

She reined in her gelding and slid down. "Not interested in being reasonable. Get off, and get the saddlebag." She began to remove the horse's bridle.

"What are you doing?"

"I can't hide the horse. He's gotta go. He'll go back to the house most likely. Zeke'll find him."

"I need this horse. I've got to get to Williamsburg. My contact, Billy Faulkner's been murdered. I have to get to my commanding officer."

Maggie whipped off the saddlebag, and before Grayson realized what she was doing, she whacked the horse on the rump and it bolted off.

"God's bowels, woman! Have you lost your mind?"

She thrust the saddlebag into his open arms and strutted past him. "We got to get inside. A Brit patrol passes in a few minutes. I'd imagine every redcoat and rebel in the county's gonna be lookin' for you tonight, Captain." She swung around. "And you call to anyone red or blue coat, and I'll shoot you, I swear to God on my da's grave I will!"

"Maggie! Aren't you listening to me!" He followed her down a narrow cut path in the bank. "I said I'm not a goddamned redcoat!"

She pushed back a curtain of greenbriars and morning glory vines to reveal a hole in the earthen wall of the bank. "Inside. Hurry. The patrol'll be by any minute. I sent Paul on to tell Major Lawrence what happened. Figured it was the best way."

Grayson stooped and followed Maggie through

the invisible opening in the bank. "Paul?"

"Paul Michaels. You know, the private you were with."

"Paul," he murmured, remembering that that was Michaels' first name. "Is he all right?"

"Scared half out of his head, but safe enough, no thanks to you. I guess Carter really walloped him. Somehow he got away." She crawled to the rear of the dugout fort she and the others had built so many years ago. Through the ceiling motes of sunlight filtered through carefully constructed air holes covered by underbrush. Slowly her eyes adjusted to the dim light.

Grayson sat on the hard dirt floor just inside the door. "I understand. You sent him on? Start from the beginning, Maggie, and tell me what happened. I take it you weren't in on my capture."

She set aside the saddlebag and bridle and brought up her knees beneath her quilted green petticoat. "No, I wasn't in on it. I don't know if it was planned or not," she went on miserably. "Zeke said something about you being in the tavern wavin' my mask."

"Dear God, what have I done?" Grayson muttered as his brother's words came back to haunt him. *Sooner or later you're going to make a mistake,* Sterling had warned. *Then people are going to die. You're going to die . . .*

Grayson lifted his head to look at Maggie, his beautiful Maggie. "I've got no excuse, except too much drink and that's no excuse."

"Drink! Is that every man's downfall?" she asked

bitterly. "My husband, Noah, was a drinker, drank himself right to death. I hate a man who drinks."

"You don't understand, Maggie. I've been under a great deal of—"

"Save your story, Captain, because I don't want to hear it. I don't want to hear anything you got to say." She peered at him from beneath the brim of her three-cornered hat. "I hate you."

"Maggie!" He tried to take her hand, but she shrank back against the earthen wall. He exhaled slowly, his eyes trying to search hers through the dim light of the shelter. "Maggie, what have I done to make you say such a thing? I'm in love with you, girl."

She thrust out her lower lip, vowing to ignore his wooing words. "What do you mean, what did you do? Don't you understand? I can never go home again! I'll be a traitor in my friends' eyes the rest of my livin' days."

"Jesus Christ! What do I have to say to make you believe me? I said, I'm not a redcoat. I've never been a redcoat and I can prove it to you once we make it to Williamsburg."

"I'm not going to Williamsburg."

"Yes, you are." He crossed his arms over his chest, stretching out his long legs. "If you're going to be stubborn about this, I can be stubborn, too, Maggie Myers. You're going to go to Williamsburg, and I'm going to prove to you that I'm not the enemy. If you want to leave me then, it's your option."

"It's your option," she mimicked, swaying her

head. "You and your fancy words; you're trying to trick me."

He chuckled. "I'm not trying to trick you. I'm just trying to prove my innocence."

"You, innocent? Hah! As innocent as that whore Zeke's courtin'!"

Grayson couldn't help but smile as he stared across the little earthen fort at Maggie, who'd drawn herself up against the rear wall to get as far away from him as possible. Her pretty pouting mouth was turned down, her jaw tight with resignation. She was bound and determined not to believe him!

"All right," he said, deciding to humor her, "let's just say for a moment that I *am* a redcoat." He held up a finger. "Which I'm not. But if I was a redcoat," he narrowed his eyes, trying to appear sinister, "what were *you,* a rebel if there ever was one, going to do with me?"

He was making fun of her. She *knew* he was making fun of her! "I don't know," she answered, refusing to meet his gaze. "I don't know what I'm going to do with you. Shoot you between the eyes, mayhap."

He chuckled, his voice growing so warm that it began to penetrate the cold shell Maggie had so carefully constructed, a shell that she'd hoped would protect her from Grayson and the feelings she had for him.

"Why'd you do it, Maggie mine? Why'd you ride in and risk your own life to save me, the enemy, from hanging?"

She thought of the baby nestled in her womb and she had to control the urge to brush her fingertips over her belly. She hung her head. "Because I couldn't let them kill you," she whispered. She vowed she wouldn't tell him of his child and would hold true to her promise. "I just couldn't . . ."

"Oh, Maggie," Grayson crawled to her and took her into his arms.

She tried to pull away, to ward off his gentle touch with blows, but he trapped her hands and pressed his lips against hers. "Maggie, I'll prove it to you, I swear to God I will," he murmured against her lips. "I'm not the enemy. I'm not *your* enemy. I love you, Maggie mine."

His mouth pressing hers made it hard for Maggie to think. Her mind told her it was lies, all lies, Captain Thayer spoke, but her *heart,* her heart hoped Grayson told the truth. Her da had always said the truth was sometimes stranger than a lie.

"Ah, Grayson, I've missed you so much," she whispered, throwing caution to the wind if only for a brief time. "I wanted you so bad. I wanted to come to you. But we said—We made a deal."

He kissed the length of her slender neck, feeling her pulse quicken. "Yes, yes, I know what we said, what *I* said. But I was a fool to think I could stay away from you. Somehow you dug your way beneath my skin, straight to my heart, Maggie. I can't tell you how many times I dressed to come to you in the night."

She laughed, as the dirt fort and the desperation of her situation melted from her mind. All she

could think of was Grayson and the way he made her feel. The way he touched her, the way he whispered those sweet words of love in her ear. "I waited for you," she breathed as she slipped her hand beneath his torn white shirt and stroked the corded muscles of his broad chest. "I wanted you . . ."

"Pride," he said with a laugh as he nibbled her lower lip, sending chills of excitement through her, "damned pride that kept us apart."

She nodded her head in agreement, reveling in the feel of his hand cupping her breast through the material of her bodice. "Being sensible's what kept us apart. It was the *sensible* thing to do."

"To hell with being sensible." Grayson tightened his arms around her, tracing her lips with the tip of his warm tongue in a slow, sensuous dance.

Maggie's tongue darted out to meet his and she melted into his arms, her breath quickening as she explored the cool cavern of his mouth.

Withdrawing from his kiss, Maggie pulled out of his arms and reached for her saddlebag. Removing a wool blanket, she spread it on the dirt floor and then opened her arms to him again. Grayson lowered her gently onto the rough blanket and pulled away the kerchief that covered the swell of her breasts. His mouth touched the soft curve of her flesh and she let out an audible sigh, feeling a heat rise within her as his gaze raked over her, devouring her. She could feel him wanting her, needing her . . .

"Grayson," she sighed, reaching behind his head to loosen the bit of ribbon that kept his hair tied back in a queue. "Grayson, I've wanted you since the moment you left my bed." His thick golden hair came loose from the queue and fell like a curtain around his face, tickling her breasts.

"I've wanted you, waited for you my whole life, Maggie," he whispered. "I was beginning to think you'd never come." He kissed his way to the nubs of her nipples as she unhooked the clasps of her bodice and pushed the material back over her shoulders. She urged him softly, her voice barely more than a sigh as he brushed his thumb in a circular motion around the pink aureola of her breast.

Maggie traced the line of his jaw and his high cheekbones and then clasped his face with both hands and guided his mouth to the peaks of her breasts. He cupped her left breast and lowered his mouth, teasing her nipple with the tip of his tongue with tantalizing slowness.

Somewhere in the distance, Maggie heard the sound of hoofbeats and the rumble of male voices as the British patrol rode by their hideaway. But knowing they were safe, deep in the mound of the riverbank, she ignored the soldiers, pushing all conscious thought from her mind. All she wanted now was to feel Grayson inside her, to hear the soft caress of his voice, to see his eyes on her as they grew dark and stormy with desire.

Moaning softly with pleasure, Maggie slipped her hand over his flat stomach and down the the waistband of his uniform breeches. Boldly she ran her fingers over the hot bulge beneath the straining cloth, the heat of her own ardor building with each stroke.

Groaning, Grayson sat up, his hair brushing the roof of the earthen fort. Keeping his eyes fixed on hers, he drank in the passion that illuminated her dark brown eyes as he stripped naked and leaned to slip off her remaining clothes.

When they were free of the confines of their clothing, he stretched out over her and they kissed again, mouth against mouth as he pressed his hard, muscular body against the soft curves of hers. "Maggie, Maggie," he whispered. "Promise you'll be mine, promise me you'll always be mine."

But she made no such promise. She only threaded her fingers through his and parted her thighs, lifting to feel his swollen manhood against her. "No talk," she whispered as the sweet aching in her loins spread like the heat of a flame. "No promises. Please."

The husky catch in her voice and the throb of insistence in his groin made Grayson push aside all thought of the future. What mattered now to Maggie was this moment. Later there would be time to talk, to reason, to make plans.

At her urging he slipped into her with one thrust and she moaned, falling back onto the dirt floor. She wrapped her legs around his waist and together they moved as one, both reaching for the stars in the heavens, both needing the satisfaction of fulfillment.

And when it was over, when Maggie had touched the stars and fell back gently to earth, Grayson took her into his arms and showered her face with damp kisses. "I love you, Maggie," he whispered. "I love you and I want to make you my wife."

Maggie sighed, already drifting off to sleep in the security of his strong embrace. "Marry," she murmured, settling her cheek on his bare chest. "Damned if I'll marry a redcoat . . ."

With the first golden rays of daylight, Grayson was up and out of the safety of the fort. Barefoot, he walked down to the river and knelt to bathe his face. Throwing Maggie's flintlock rifle onto his shoulder, he stood and stretched, staring out at the sparkling blue water of the York River. He watched as a gray-and-white sea gull dove out of the sky and skimmed the surface of the water in search of food.

Grayson had to get to Williamsburg. There this true identity business could be all straightened out, at least with the Yorktown rebels. With proper documentation from his patriot commanding officer, he would be able to prove to Ezekial Barnes and his men that he was indeed on their side, thus absolving Maggie of any wrongdoing. But as for his position amidst the British, Grayson wasn't certain where he stood. How the hell was he going to get back in now?

Of course there was no question in his mind as to whether or not he was *going* back in, it was simply a matter of how. He'd made a mistake, a grievous error back at that tavern, but that was all the more reason why he had to get back in among the Brits. He had to prove to his commanding officer, to Sterling, to himself that he could still do his job.

But what of Maggie? She was so damned hard-headed that even after all he'd said last night, she still refused to believe he wasn't the enemy. The proof, of course, lay in Williamsburg. But she said she wasn't going to Williamsburg. She said something about going north, far from Yorktown where no one would ever find her. Of course Grayson knew he couldn't let her go. She was the best thing that ever happened to him!

Well, Maggie would just have to go to Williamsburg, wouldn't she?

"Grayson?"

He turned from the river to see Maggie standing naked in the early-morning light. She held up her skirt to cover her lithe form, but the bit of wrinkled green quilting did nothing but make her appear even more desirable.

"Grayson, what are you doing out there? This beach is patroled!"

"Just went by," he answered, pointing south.

Maggie's gaze went to her flintlock pistol tucked into the waistband of his breeches and to her rifle he carried over his shoulder, attached by a shoulder strap. "You took my weapons," she pointed out. "I want them back."

He lifted a blond eyebrow. "So you can shoot me in the back?"

"I'm not going to shoot you. At least not unless you try to do something foolish."

"Like flag down the Brit patrol?" he asked, using Captain Thayer's arrogant tone.

She crossed her bare arms over her chest, pinning the green skirting tight around her waist. "Somethin' like that."

"Maggie . . ." He looked away and then straight back at her. "What do I have to say to convince you I'm not Captain Thayer of the king's army?"

"You're not Grayson Thayer?" Her jaw tightened as the memories of last night's lovemaking slipped away. This morning the cold reality of life was slapping her in the face again.

"Yes, of course I'm Grayson Thayer, but I'm not really a captain in the Army. I mean I am, but that's not who I work for."

"I know," she nodded, the sarcasm thick in her voice. "You're a spy. You've always been a spy."

"Exactly, since before the war even."

"What kind of fool do you take me for? We didn't *have* spies before the war!"

"It's very complicated, Maggie, but I can explain it all if you'll just allow me."

She dropped a hand to her hip. "Tell me something. If you're one of us, how come we don't know it? John, our leader, has contacts in Williamsburg. *They* know what we're doing."

Grayson wiped his brow. "Spies like me . . ." He exhaled, and began again. "It's such a dangerous job that as few people who know about it, the better. The deeper my cover, the safer I—and the contacts who work for me—are." Recognizing a flash in her eyes that hinted she believed him, he went on. "You know the man, Billy Faulkner?"

She nodded.

"Billy was my contact here in Yorktown."

Her eyes narrowed suspiciously. "But he said he wasn't interested in helping us. He said he wanted no part of the war."

"He had to say that. He's been a contact for years—for other men before me. He was protecting his family."

She came further out into the sunshine and sat down, covering herself as best she could with the petticoat of her dress. "They burned him out, you know."

"Who?"

She shrugged. "We don't know. But we got word a few days ago that he was a contact. They say someone let it slip. They say they tortured and killed him, then burned the house around him and his family when he wouldn't talk."

Grayson rested his hands on his thighs and grimaced. "They were looking for me."

"Paul said Riker was accusing you of being a traitor."

He looked up. "There, you see. It all makes sense, doesn't it? I *could* be one of you."

"Redcoats are always accusing people of being traitors. They'd rather do that than drink ale."

"Look, Maggie, just come with me to Williamsburg and I'll prove to you who I am. You can meet my brother and see Thayer's Folly."

"I'm not going to Williamsburg. I don't want to see your fancy house and I don't want to meet your brother. I just want you to swear to me on your mortal soul that whoever you are, no harm will come to my friends."

He came toward her. "You have to come."

She leaped up. "I don't have to come. I'm goin' to New York."

He took another step toward her and she took one back. "You're going with me if I have to tie you and carry you all the way."

She let the green petticoat drop to the ground in sudden, blind fury. "You wouldn't dare."

His arm shot out and he caught her wrist. "Try me!"

Chapter Fifteen

"I hate you, Captain Grayson Thayer!"

"Major. I told you, I'm actually a major. I worked hard for that promotion."

"I despise the ground you walk on. When Zeke finds out you've kidnapped me, he's going to hang you by your toes and let the ground squirrels chew your flesh," Maggie vowed as Grayson dragged her through the forest by a rope that bound her wrists. "Zeke's gonna chop you up in pieces and pickle your liver in a pickle barrel. Then he's gonna put it in a glass and set it right out on the counter at Manny's tavern so everyone can walk by and say, 'Yes, indeed, that there's Captain Thayer's liver. May the bloody redcoat never rest in peace.' "

"Enough, sweet." Grayson wiped his brow with his dusty sleeve. "You've been going on like this for two hours. Let's talk about something other than my demise, shall we?" He stepped over a fallen log, and the rope tied around his waist that stretched to her wrists went taut. He stopped and waited for her to catch up. He hated to tie Maggie like this, but it seemed the only way he was going to get her to Williamsburg.

"I don't want to talk about anything else." She stepped over the log and he moved on. "I like thinking about how those men are going to torture you when they find out you took me against my will. You can't carry a woman off tied like a calf and expect to get away with it in these parts."

He groaned aloud. Between the heat of the day and Maggie's nonstop talk, he thought he was going to go mad. Maybe he should have left her behind when he'd had the chance. "If you'd been sensible about the matter, I wouldn't have to tie you like a calf!"

"Being sensible? Who's the one that's not being sensible? We've got every man in the county, red coat and blue, looking for you, and you're traipsing through the woods right in the thick of them!"

"I told you. I *have* to get to Williamsburg. I have to let my commanding officer know I'm alive. I have to find out what happened to Billy Faulkner."

She gave a snort and came to a halt. You don't need me, then. Just let me go on my way."

Impatiently, he snapped the rope between them. "Keep moving. It's near noon. If we can stick to these game paths and we don't run into any trouble, we'll make it to Thayer's Folly by dusk."

"I told you, I ain't goin'."

"I'm *not* going," he corrected. "If you're going to be my wife, you're going to have to speak properly." He glanced over his shoulder. "That night we went to the bull roast I didn't hear any 'ain'ts' or 'gonnas'."

"That's because I was under cover," she sniffed. "A lady doesn't talk like that, but I *ain't* a lady. My da was a bootmaker, bound himself out to come to the Colonies. He never learned to read or write, but he could add a bill for an order of shoes quicker than any man I ever knew."

"You don't read or write, either?" Grayson asked hesitantly. Not that it mattered. It was too late for those considerations. Far too late. He loved Maggie and he was going to make her his wife. It was as simple as that.

Maggie walked up beside him, suddenly indignant. "Of course I can read and write! My da worked many an extra night to pay for a tutor for my sister and me. Neighbors laughed at the idea of a woman needing to be able to read and write, but da wanted a better life for his children than what he had."

"Wise man." He glanced back at her. "There's a wonderful library at Thayer's Folly. You're welcome to borrow anything you like to read."

She gave a sigh, finally falling silent. She was mad as hell with Grayson for forcing her to come with him to Williamsburg, but a small part of her, the tiniest sliver, was excited at the prospect. As the hours passed and they continued their trek northwest, the more curious she became. What would Thayer's Folly be like? Would it be like that Tory Mason Pickney's grand house? Would there be fine-kept lawns and scrubbed-faced Negros serving lemonade? And foremost in her mind, was Grayson really a spy for the United States? The thought was just too good to be true.

"You can untie me," Maggie told Grayson when they stopped at a stream that in the summer heat had dried up to nothing more than a slow trickle. She raised her bound wrists to him.

His blue eyes met hers. "You won't run?"

"I should. It's not right to make someone go where they don't want to go."

"It's important to me, Maggie, that you know who I really am. I've been playing the part of Captain Thayer so long that I need you to believe I'm Grayson Thayer, Major in the American army, Virginian planter." He laughed as the words slipped from his mouth. Ten years ago he'd sworn to Sterling that he could never be a planter like their father and his father before him. The land had meant nothing to him ten years ago—now suddenly it meant everything.

"If you knew how your story sounds," she still held up her hands, "you would see how hard it is for me to believe. You got such a reputation—"

"Captain Thayer has a reputation." He clasped her hands. "I'm telling you, that man isn't me. At least I don't want him to be. This war, it's changed me, Maggie."

"I'll go with you to Williamsburg and I'll let you show me your proof, but you have to swear you'll let me go." She looked away as he loosened the knot on the rope and untied her. "I have to go then, Grayson."

"But I want you to be my wife."

She laughed, but not in a hurtful way. "I can't be your wife."

He rubbed her wrists where the rope had left ugly red marks. "Why?"

"A hundred reasons, a thousand reasons."

"That's absurd. You can't deny you care for me."

"It's more than care." She stroked his whiskered cheek. "I probably love ye, but it's not enough."

"Not enough! Maggie—"

The sound of hoofbeats drew Grayson's attention. "Soldiers . . ."

"Redcoats or bluecoats?" she asked, reaching for her pistol he wore tucked in the waistband of his breeches.

His eyes met hers for a moment and then he let her slide the pistol from his waistband. "You're not going to shoot me, are you?"

"Not unless you make me mad."

He glanced at her, realizing she probably meant it, then reached for her hand. "I don't know who's coming, but I say we don't wait around to find out. Either side, we'd be better not to tangle with them. Come on."

Together they raced through the forest, dodging prickly holly trees and ducking beneath branches. Discovering a game path barely wide enough to walk even single file, they went east, away from the threat of soldiers, then northwest again, in the direction of Williamsburg.

Late in the afternoon when the shadows finally lengthened and the relentless heat of the day eased, Grayson pointed ahead to a pile of stones neatly stacked. "There," he murmured, indicating with his hand. "That marks the southeastern corner of Thayer's Folly." He dropped the saddlebag to the ground and lowered his hands to rest on his hips as he stared out at the rolling acres of field and forest.

Maggie whipped off her three-cornered hat, in reverence. Home. She could understand that. Grayson was coming home, she was leaving.

He took her hand, his blue eyes twinkling with pleasure and lighting up his entire suntanned face. "I don't want to go in until nightfall because I don't want anyone seeing me until I talk to Sterling. But we could sneak up and watch."

"Spy on your brother?" She dropped her hands to her hips. He sounded like a child about to play a prank. "You wouldn't!"

He took her in his arms, spinning her around. "You have to understand the relationship Sterling and I have. This is the man who poisoned me, had me captured and put in a prison, and took my place."

"And well he should have if you were a redcoat!"

"But I wasn't!"

In the long hours it had taken Grayson and Maggie to make the trek from Yorktown to Williamsburg, he had explained to her how he'd gone to work spying on the British for Philadelphia merchants before the war, and then for General Washington after the Philadelphia occupation. He told her of the years he'd spent as a British officer while reporting to his own patriot commanding officers. It was a wild tale of military secrets and close brushes with death, such a wild tale that Maggie thought it all just might be true.

Her brown eyes narrowed as she considered Grayson. "From what you say, Sterling didn't know you weren't a redcoat."

He stole a kiss. "Details. Minor, unimportant details."

She rested her hands on his broad shoulders and lifted her chin to be kissed again. Soon she'd be leaving for New York, never to see Grayson again. In the meantime, she was going to savor every moment, every word, every touch of his hand. She was going to save every memory in her head to be cherished in the years to come. "I still don't think it's right, spying on your brother and his wife."

He kissed her again, this time running his tongue along her lower lip. "Where's that sense of adventure, Maggie?"

She stepped out of his arms and picked up the saddlebag from the ground and tossed it to him. "You'll be lucky if you're not shot for trespassing!"

He laughed at the thought of how close Maggie came to the truth. "Actually we better lay low," he agreed as he started across the field. "Our gamekeeper, Lucius, must be near ninety by now. Even before I left ten years ago he was crazy as a loon and as good a shot as one. He's liable to lift both of our caps if we're not careful."

Maggie's hand went to the battered three-cornered hat she'd taken from Zeke's house. "Gamekeeper, is it? The Thayers have a gamekeeper? My da's grandfather was a gamekeeper for some lord in England."

Grayson waited for her to catch up, and hand in hand, they waded through the waist-high weeds. "Most plantations don't have gamekeepers anymore, but Lucius was my grandfather's gamekeeper, then my papa's. Sterling couldn't very well send him off, a man in his late seventies." He shrugged. "So Lucius just stayed on. From what Sterling says, he doesn't do much hunting for the table anymore, but he keeps himself busy spying on redcoats and visiting old Mable Lukins across the river at Fortune's Find."

Maggie smiled. That told a lot about a man, the way he cared for his father's servants. Perhaps meeting Grayson's brother wouldn't be so bad after all. "How big is this Thayer's Folly?" she asked, gazing out at the overgrown field that seemed to stretch on forever.

"Big."

"Big?" Maggie moistened her lips with the tip of her tongue. Seeing all of this reminded her that Grayson was probably rich, very rich. "How big is big?"

"Couple of thousand acres. And don't look so frightened." He grabbed her by the shoulder and kissed the top of her head. "A woman who's willing to go up against a band of spooked rebels certainly couldn't be intimidated by a few thousand acres of Virginia soil. Now, Sterling's older by a couple of minutes, so he inherited, but he always said if I ever wanted to come back to Thayer's Folly, we'd be partners. He always told me he'd be willing to split the plantation in half if I'd come work at his side."

"That's what you mean to do then?"

"After the war, if Sterling's still willing. Of course he always offered when I was busy saying no. I never thought I would want to come back here. I was always a city man. Taverns, cards—"

"Loose women," Maggie injected.

He led her along a hedgerow between the field and the woods. "Women, granted, but that was before I met you, Maggie mine. I never loved any of those women."

She squeezed his hand, jealous at the thought of the other women who had touched him the way she'd so intimately touched him, women who would touch him when she was gone. "Did any of them love you?"

He looked away guiltily. "To tell you the truth, I don't know. They said so, but I never stayed with anyone long enough to find out." He kept his eyes on the deer path that ran along the hedgerow, uncomfortable thinking about all of those women he'd bedded . . . women whose names he could no longer remember. He stopped and turned Maggie to face him. "It doesn't matter. What matters is you and me. After this damned war is over, and I know it will be soon, I want to come home to Thayer's Folly and learn how to run this plantation like my papa wanted me to. That's why I need you, Maggie. I want to share this with you."

She swept back a lock of his golden hair, wanting to believe he meant what he said, wanting to think it really could work, but knowing better. 'If it sounds too good to be true,' her da always said, 'then it probably is.' "And what if we lose, Grayson, what then?"

"That's one of the reasons why it's important that I keep my British identity. If we lose, which we won't, but if we did, Thayer's Folly would be granted to me as reward for fighting for Georgie. God forbid we should lose the war, at least Sterling won't lose the land."

Maggie walked away. "You got it all bundled up in such a neat package. But life isn't that way, Grayson. It's never neat the way you fold your clothes. It's messy. Nobody follows the rules like they're supposed to. Nothing ever works out the way you want it to."

"You're such a pessimist, Maggie." He took her hand, swinging it. "Quit worrying. We're going to be all right, you and I, we're going to be fine. Now come on. Let's go see what that brother of mine is doing tonight!"

A few minutes later, Grayson crept through a maze of trimmed boxwood, pulling Maggie behind him. "I can hear them. They must be playing cricket on the lawn. Sterling always was a better cricketer than I was, the hellhound!"

Maggie crept behind Grayson listening to the sound of husky female laughter, mingled with a man's voice . . . a voice that sounded much like Grayson's. Again and again she heard the thwack of a wooden paddle making contact with a wooden ball.

Pressing a finger to his lips, Grayson parted a thick hedge of Queen Anne's lace at the edge of the boxwood garden and peered through. Her curiosity getting the best of her, Maggie wriggled up beside him.

Out on the finely trimmed lawn were a man and a woman, each hitting a ball with a long wooden paddle. They laughed and teased as they attempted to hit the ball between a series of posts in the ground. Maggie watched with fascination, having heard of cricket, but never actually having seen the game played. The woman, who had quite a good aim, was tall and elegant with a head of rich auburn hair she wore tied back in a thick green ribbon.

Maggie's eyes went wide as her gaze settled on the man. He was an exact duplicate of Grayson from the tip of his golden-haired queue right to his shiny black boots. Dressed in a pair of fawn breeches and a white linen shirt left open at the neckline, he took Maggie's breath away. Grayson had warned Maggie he and his brother were twins, and yet she hadn't expected them to be so similar that she wasn't certain she would know the difference if Sterling were in her bed!

"Holy Mother Mary," she whispered. "My grandmother'd say you two were devil-spawned to be so alike."

Grayson glanced at her, and then back at Sterling and Reagan who played their game of cricket, unaware they had spectators. "Eerie, isn't it. We had a grand time of it as boys. Never had a schoolmaster who could tell us apart."

"And your mama and da?" Maggie continued to stare at Sterling in utter awe.

"Oh, they could tell from the moment we were born they said."

"How? He even laughs like you do."

Grayson grinned boyishly. "Personality they say. Sterling was a good young man, a son our father could be proud of. Learned his letters, said his prayers, and he never whistled in church. Me—"

"I can guess," Maggie murmured. "Caught

kissin' the dairy maids at thirteen, no doubt."

His smile went sheepish. "Worse. And it was Mama's handmaid."

Maggie rolled her eyes heavenward and turned her attention back to Reagan and Sterling. Grayson's brother hit the ball hard and long, knocking his wife's ball out of line of her posts and far from the gaming area. Reagan called him a pettifogging cheat and tossed her knifelike paddle at him, nearly striking him in the head.

Sterling laughed, throwing down his own paddle and running after his wife, who tried to make a quick getaway. Maggie couldn't resist a smile as the mirror image of her own Grayson swept his wife into his arms and buried his face in her breasts that swelled above the flowered chintz bodice of her obviously expensive gown.

Maggie grasped Grayson's arm and turned away. "Shame on you! You've got no right to spy on them!"

Grayson kissed her full on the mouth and parted the lacy white flowers again. "They won't strip off their clothes—too many servants." He glanced up at the darkening sky. "Of course the sun is going down—"

Maggie gave a snort and grasped his hand, jerking his head out of the bushes. "I'll not be a part of the likes of that! How would you like it if he was starin' through the bushes at you and I rollin' in the grass!"

Grayson's eyes sparkled with mischief as he wrapped his arm around Maggie's waist and lifted her, kissing the damp skin of her neckline. "Is that an offer?"

"Indeed not. Now hush your mouth," she warned, covering his mouth with her hand, "before they hear you. I'm a decent woman, and I want you to remember that, Grayson Thayer, or whoever you are. I never laid with a man before or after my husband until you come struttin' along and tricked me—"

"Tricked you, hah!" He laughed deep in his throat as he covered her protesting mouth with his. "You seduced me, woman. You take me to your house on the pretext of cleaning my wounds and the next thing I know you've got me stretched out on the grass beneath you."

"Oh! You!" Maggie struggled to escape his embrace. "Let me down this minute. I'm headed for New York, I am. I'll not be accused of being a common drop-drawers!"

He smoothed her bright-red untended hair. "I'm just teasing you, Maggie. "I'm just teasing, sweet." He pulled her against him, and she lowered her chin to his shoulder, giving up the struggle.

"I don't want to be here, Grayson," she whispered. "I'm afraid."

"Of what?" He pulled her back so that he could gaze at her face, the face he'd come to love.

She looked away, unable to bear his scrutiny. "Oh, I don't know. This place, your brother, your sister-in-law. They're going to think I'm a strumpet."

"No, no. I'll tell them we're to be married. Better yet, I'll tell them we're already wed."

"You'll tell them no such thing. It's a lie. Father Rufus'll be having me say Hail Marys till I'm hoarse if I tell such lies."

"Oh, Maggie, Maggie. What am I going to do with you?" He pushed back a lock of her hair and brushed a kiss across her cheek. "I'm telling you it's all going to be all right. Reagan and Sterling will love you. You'll see."

"I don't care if they like me or not," she lied. "I just don't want anyone calling me your whore when my back is turned."

"Sweet, in this family we call people names to their faces. Now let's go. I've got a mind to share a palm toddie with that my brother of mine." He released Maggie and parted the flowers again. "All safe," he told her. "Look, they're gathering up their balls to go in."

"So what do you do now that you've sneaked up on them like a thievin' redskin?" she asked, lowering her voice as Reagan and Sterling came toward the hedge.

Grayson pressed his finger to his lips. "Shhhh."

With a groan, she crossed her arms over her chest, wishing she'd never come along, wishing she'd never met Grayson Thayer.

A moment later Maggie heard Sterling and Reagan's voices as they approached the Queen Anne's lace hedge. Then suddenly Grayson let out a horrendous, bloodcurdling shriek and hurled himself over the hedge at Sterling.

Reagan screamed and Sterling dropped the game pieces he carried and raised his arms in defense. Grayson knocked him head-over-heels and the two rolled over and over, wrestling to gain the upper hand.

"You son of a bitch! You scared me half out of my wits," Sterling protested as he fought to pin Grayson's arms to the ground. "You're lucky I didn't shoot your sorry ass."

"Me? You're lucky I wasn't some vengeful red-coat, else I'd have shot you and carried that beautiful wife of yours off."

Unsure of herself, Maggie climbed through the bushes, stepping into Reagan's view.

"Oh." The auburn-haired woman put her hand to her chest. "You scared me nearly as badly as Grayson. You must be Maggie." She offered her hand.

Maggie swallowed hard against the lump of fear in her throat. "Um, yeah. How'd you know?" She wiped her filthy hand on her torn petticoat and accepted Reagan's hand giving it a squeeze.

"Grayson," she nodded to the two men still grunting and rolling in the grass, "told Sterling about you in a letter. I knew you had to be special to hold my brother-in-law's eye."

Maggie withdrew her hand, feeling deathly inadequate compared to the beautifully dressed woman who spoke so properly. "Not so special," she mumbled.

Reagan dropped her hands to her hips, turning her attention to the two brothers. "Enough! Enough. If the two of you don't break it up, I'll set my hounds on you!"

Grayson twisted Sterling's hand behind his head and groaned as he tried to force him flat on the ground. "Just trying to teach him a lesson, Reagie. I'm gone too long and he gets soft."

Reagan walked to the two men still wrestling and

grasped her husband's neat blond queue, giving it a harsh tug. "I said enough, Sterling Thayer! You two've got no better manners than barn cats!" She prodded Grayson none too gently with the toe of her dyed green calfskin slipper. "You hear me, Grayson? Get off my husband. You injure him and it'll be me you have to pay your debt to!"

Reluctantly, Grayson rolled off his brother and dropped onto the grass, panting heavily. "Strong man for being so old," he teased.

Sterling laughed, sitting up as he struggled to catch his breath. "Spare me any jokes pertaining to my age, please. I'm feeling feeble enough as it is with that son of mine to run after all day." He glanced up, noticing Maggie for the first time. A smile came to his lips as he hopped up and came to kiss Maggie on the cheek. "I don't have to ask who this is. She's as beautiful as you said."

Maggie blushed. "Pleased to meet you."

Grayson rose to his feet and came to link his arm through Maggie's. "We're going to be married, Maggie and I."

Reagan smiled. "Congratulations."

"We are not," Maggie corrected, elbowing Grayson in the side.

Reagan pursed her lips. "Oh." Her gaze went to her husband, then Grayson.

"She's just shy," Grayson explained. "It's really all settled."

Maggie turned to Grayson. "I tell you, you're going to go straight to hell and going to burn in eternal flames for lying! I said I wasn't marrying you. Now take it back."

Grayson glanced sheepishly at Reagan and Sterling. "Well, actually, it's not completely settled. Maggie here is having a little problem with my identity."

"That's certainly not surprising," Reagan offered. "Seems to me Sterling and I had problems with that a few years back."

"Speaking of identities, *Brother,* what the hell are you doing here?" He looked around. "Who knows you're here? It's not that I'm not glad to see him," Sterling explained to Maggie, "but word is, this little brother of mine is in the hot seat. Half of Virginia's looking for him."

Grayson seized his brother's arm. "It's a long story, and one I'd prefer to relate over a palm toddie."

Sterling waved a hand. "Well, come on in with you and let's at least get Maggie some refreshment. The two of you look like you've had one hell of a trip. It's a wonder you ever made it with Clinton's redcoats running amuck the way they are."

Grayson retrieved the saddlebag from behind the hedge and took Maggie's arm, escorting her toward the house. "Just like two rabbits in a briar patch we were." He winked at Maggie. "We slipped directly beneath their noses, safe and sound."

Chapter Sixteen

Maggie tried not to gape as she walked up the winding brick walkway toward the immense Georgian redbrick house that loomed ahead. Stretching two and a half stories into the sky, the L-shaped country house was styled with elaborate rows of header bricks, and whitewashed shutters on every window. Beds of flowers grew along the inside walls of the bricked courtyard between the two wings of the house. A mother cat and her kittens played in a bed of herbs near a back door.

"Quite something, isn't it, sweetheart?" Grayson asked, grinning like a schoolboy. "Reagan keeps it as well as my mother ever did."

Maggie gave a gulp. Overwhelming was what it was. Holy Mother Mary! The detached summer kitchen, the aroma of fresh-baked bread seeping from its walls, was nearly as large as Maggie's entire house back in Yorktown! The yard around the great brick house was sprinkled with dependencies—a smokehouse, a dairy, an icehouse—and in the distance Maggie could see huge barns for livestock and crop storage. From what she could see,

Thayer's Folly was much like the great manor in which Maggie's da had lived as a boy back in England when his grandfather had been a gamekeeper. Her grandfather had been a servant to a man who owned a home like this!

Maggie twisted her perspiring hand in Grayson's, feeling as if she ought to be walking in through the servants' entrance instead of weaving around toward the front door. *Oh, heavens,* she thought. *I don't belong here! What Zeke said, what Mildred said . . . they were right, they were all right. Grayson Thayer wasn't for the likes of her! She was a bootmaker's daughter for heaven's sake!*

But it was too late to back out now. Here she was, walking beside one of the masters of this great plantation, listening to him chat with his brother and sister-in-law. Catching a quick glimpse of Grayson's startlingly handsome face, Maggie lifted her chin a notch. *He* didn't seem to realize she didn't belong here. Perhaps no one else would, either. Besides, it was just for a few days, wasn't it? She promised Grayson she'd stay a few days and then she'd be gone. She'd already sent a letter to her cousin in New York saying she was coming, so it was settled. A few short days with Grayson and she'd be gone from his fancy life of rich clothing and manor houses.

Sterling went up the steps of the front stoop and pushed open a great carved door, decorated by a scrolled doorknocker with the letters "C" and "S" carved in the center. When he realized the doorknocker had caught Maggie's attention, he ran his fingers over the polished silver. "Beautiful, isn't it? A gift to my great grandfather, William Thayer, from King Charles the Second himself."

Grayson leaned against the doorframe, already feeling more relaxed than he had in months. "The official word is that King Charles gave it to grandfather with the deed to this land out of thanks for the part the Thayers played in restoring the Crown to him, but our father always said it was a bribe to get William out of England. It seems he was beating the king too often at the gaming table."

"Not only did he get the land and the knocker, but our great-grandmother in the bargain," Sterling finished. "They say she was the most beautiful woman in London and she was apparently none too pleased to be married off to a man headed for the god forsaken American Colonies."

Maggie looked up, a smile on her face. "Your great-grandfather played cards with a king?" she asked, her voice breathy with disbelief.

"That he did," Grayson took her arm and led her into the front hall. "Now come along. My brother's promised me a palm toddie and I intend to get one. I haven't seen a bottle of arrack in six months."

Maggie walked beside Grayson through the front hall and into a paneled parlor to the left. She tried to keep her mouth closed and not gasp at the beauty of the home in which Grayson had grown up. The house was simply but elegantly furnished, with various pieces constructed in the last one hundred years, but there was an air of dignity about the house that Maggie hadn't felt in the pretentious home of Mason Pickney.

"I'll show you around later," Grayson murmured

in her ear as he offered her a seat on an upholstered settle. He brushed a kiss across the top of her head. "Don't worry," he whispered, "you're going to be fine."

Reagan called to a servant and then entered the room behind her husband, coming to sit beside Maggie. She patted Maggie's knee through her dusty, torn green petticoat. "Grayson dragged you here on foot from Yorktown? What a brave woman."

Maggie gave a gulp, wondering if Reagan realized how close to the truth she'd come. "Ah, yes," she answered, concentrating on her speech. "Grayson ran into a bit of trouble, so we had to keep our heads low."

"Ran into a bit of trouble! God's bowels, she's not jesting." Grayson perched himself on the arm of a winged-back chair. "You're not going to believe what I've done, Sterling."

Sterling poured a dose of arrack from a decanter into a handleless pewter cup and accepted a pitcher of water from a young blond girl in a starched mobcap. Maggie couldn't help noticing the way she cut her eyes toward Grayson as she set down her tray on a sideboard before sidling away.

"Actually, I probably will have no trouble believing it," Sterling answered, adding water to the arrack before handing the cup to Grayson. "But go ahead and try me anyway."

Grayson took a sip from the cup and gave a sigh. "Damnation, but that's good." He lifted his cup in salute to Maggie and then continued his conversation with his brother. "It is a long story, and I'll give you the details later, but the gist of the matter is that I've futtered things up royally!"

Sterling turned to Maggie. "Port, claret, some Madeira? What can I offer you, Maggie?"

She smiled hesitantly. "Just water . . . please."

"Water then." He poured water from the pitcher and brought it to Maggie along with a goblet of claret for Reagan. "Go on, little brother, I'm waiting."

"It seems my dear Maggie, here, who led me to believe that she was neutral, is actually one of the Yorktown rebels everyone has been talking about."

All eyes in the room turned to Maggie, making her feel as if she owed them some sort of explanation. "I . . . it was by accident. I guess. I mean, I didn't start out meaning to join the band. It's just that I sell my boots and make repairs in the camps, the British camps." She shrugged. "After a while, I started hearing things, so I started reporting them. Later, my friend, Zeke, asked me to join the group."

Grayson stood, stretching his lean legs. "She's riding with the masked men, for Christ's sake!"

Reagan sat back against the settle, a smug smile on her face. "And you thought she didn't care." She waggled a finger at her brother-in-law. "I told you. Grayson, you should have let women start fighting this war five years ago and we'd have sent the redcoats running for Mother England with their coattails between their legs."

"So what's Maggie got to do with your . . . error, Brother?"

Grayson sighed, swirling his palm toddie in his

pewter cup. "I discovered what Maggie was doing when I found a mask at her house after a Hessian payroll was taken."

"We were lookin' for mail bags with dispatches in them," Maggie injected.

"Anyway, we sort of had a disagreement. I was angry with Maggie because she'd taken a risk like that. And of course I was trying to figure out a way to get a warning back to the other men in her band that Riker and Major Lawrence were on to them, without actually telling Maggie who I was."

Sterling lifted an eyebrow. "Or who you weren't, as the case may be."

"Right. Well, I left angry and ended up in her brother-in-law's tavern having a few."

"Oh, Jesus, Grayson," Sterling's face went hard. "You didn't."

Grayson lowered his gaze to the polished hardwood floor. "I don't know exactly what I did or said, but apparently men in her group saw me with Maggie's mask. Anyway, they ambushed me on the road and meant to kill me to keep Maggie's secret."

"They didn't know who you really were?" Sterling offered.

"Hell, no. You know how Colonel Hastings feels about not disclosing identities. If a man doesn't absolutely need to know who I am, he's not going to know. Billy Faulkner was the only man in Yorktown who could identify me, and he was already dead, except I didn't know it."

Sterling turned away, slamming his fist into his palm. "I knew this was going to happen! I *knew* it, Grayson. You should have come the hell home when I told you to!" He paused, and a deafening silence hung in the air.

Maggie's heart went out to Grayson as she suddenly came to the realization of what a grave error he had committed when he'd allowed Zeke and the others to know he knew she had played a part in the payroll theft. The sound of his strained voice, the tone of his brother's, made it obvious to her that Grayson had told her the truth when he said he was a patriot spy. No one could fake the pain and fear she heard in the voices of the two brothers.

"So how did you get free? You convince them of who you were?"

Grayson laughed humorously and went to make himself a second palm toddie. "Not hardly. They were all Maggie's friends and already had it in for me, seeing as how," his gaze went to Maggie, "well, let's just say they didn't like my association with their friend. Anyway, the only way I escaped a lead ball through my chest or a noose around my neck was because of Miss Bootmaker over there."

Maggie stared at the scuffed toes of her work boots.

"The private who was with me when I was ambushed, Michaels, managed to escape. For some reason he went to Maggie instead of back to the camp to tell Lawrence. The next thing I know, Maggie's riding in, all hell and fire and cutting my sorry, drunken ass down out of a tree. I rode off a free man." He took a deep breath and then his words came more slowly. "She saved my life, Sterling. I've cheated the grim reaper more than once in the last couple of years, but this time I wouldn't have gotten out of it, Brother. I dropped my guard. I lost my edge."

Before Maggie realized what she was doing, she was up and crossing the room. She linked her arm through Grayson's and kissed the hard biceps of one of his arms. What could she say? He'd failed miserably. Not only had he risked his own life but probably those of men who worked for him. She couldn't help wondering if he was inadvertently responsible for Billy Faulkner's death. Yet she still loved him. All she wanted to do now was comfort him.

Sterling turned to face his brother. "Well, what's done is done. You're not the first man to make a mistake, and I fear you won't be the last. I suppose all we can do is cover your tracks and sweep up now."

Maggie felt Grayson's muscles tense. "I can't just leave it, Sterling," he said gruffly. "I have to go back in."

Sterling laughed. "You've got to be joking! I've got news for you, Brother, this is the end of your career. I'd imagine your commission will be retired in a matter of days."

"I'll talk to Colonel Hastings. Surely he'll—"

"He'll realize it's time you came in. Look, Grayson, you did your duty, more than your duty. It's been seven long years and it's time to come home."

Grayson's sky-blue eyes lighted with anger. "You've been in since the beginning. I don't see you 'retiring.' "

"Not under cover. I haven't been undercover except for an occasional mission since Philadelphia and you know it."

"It was your choice. Look, Sterling, just because you couldn't take the pressure—"

"It's pretty obvious *you* couldn't stand the pressure, little brother, else you wouldn't have been drowning your sorrows in your cups."

Reagan suddenly stood, clearing her throat. "Gentlemen, gentlemen, you want the entire household to hear you?" She eyed them both. "Now please lower your voices and excuse us." She lifted her chin regally and turned to Maggie. "Would you care to see your room. Maggie? I've had a bath sent up."

Maggie was caught between wanting to remain at Grayson's side and wanting to feel clean again. She was grimy, and she was tired and achy to the bone from her long trip. She looked up at Grayson, hating to see the etched lines of anguish on his face.

"Go ahead, sweet," he told her, covering her hand with his. "I'll be up shortly." He looked at Reagan. "My room."

Reagan's gaze met Maggie's with uncertainty. "I gave her the blue room, but whatever you like—"

"The blue room will be fine," Maggie interrupted, embarrassed that Grayson would want her to share his room in his brother's house. Did he want her to just wear a sign across her chest declaring she was his whore? She followed Reagan out of the parlor, not knowing what else to say that wouldn't make matters worse.

But Reagan graciously breezed right over the incident, chatting pleasantly as she closed the sliding doors that led into the parlor. "I know you must be hot and tired after your journey. I saw you didn't have a chance to bring clothing so I took the liberty of having some garments sent to your room," she said above the din of Sterling and Grayson's shouting behind the paneled doors. "I would guess you and I are about the same size, though my hips haven't been the same since Forrest was born." Her light laughter filtered up to the high ceiling, echoing off the walls.

"Th-thank you." Maggie self-consciously smoothed her tattered skirting and looked back toward the parlor. "With the doors closed I can't tell the difference between them; their voices are so alike."

Reagan smiled down at her. "Odd, isn't it. Let me tell you, it took a long time for me to grow used to the fact that there was always a man walking around out there who looked exactly like my husband." She lifted both eyebrows. "It could have made for some interesting situations if I didn't watch myself."

Maggie laughed at Reagan's sense of humor, her tension easing a little as she followed her up the wide grand staircase to the second floor. *Maybe this isn't going to be so bad after all,* Maggie thought. Both Sterling and Reagan were going out of their way to make her comfortable. They seemed to understand her ill-ease.

"Now don't pay attention to their arguments," Reagan assured her as she lifted her chintz skirts and turned on the first landing. "They always fight. But they love each other fiercely and that's what matters, don't you think?"

"I . . . guess so." Maggie studied the family portraits as she and Reagan went down a long, candle-lit hallway flanked with closed paneled doors. "Reagan, could I ask you something?"

"Of course. Heavens, but it's nice to have another woman in the house to talk to. I miss my sister so much."

"What I wanted to know was, how long have you known Grayson?"

"Since the winter of Valley Forge. I met Sterling when he was lodged in my family's home during the occupation of Philadelphia."

"Only you thought he was Grayson?"

Reagan laughed, smoothing her auburn hair. "So you've heard that crazy story."

"I have, but I really didn't believe Grayson when he told me. I thought he was spinning tales. I guess I've gotten so used to men and their lying that I can't tell when they're telling the truth."

Reagan stopped at a door and rested her hand on the knob. "Well, I can certainly understand that." She reached for a silver candlestick on the wall. "Sterling and I had our share of lies, justified or not. But we worked it out, and this is what we've got to show for the perseverance."

She pushed open the door and a little boy bobbed up from a bed. "Mama?"

"Just came to give my best boy some love before he went to sleep," Reagan said, crossing the room and setting the candlestick down on a small stool.

He let out an exasperated sigh. "But you already gave me love when you tucked me in, Mama."

Reagan laughed as she settled on the edge of the bed. "Well, that's a mama's prerogative, isn't it? Besides, I wanted you to meet someone."

The little blond-haired boy, a miniature replica of Grayson and Sterling, looked up at Maggie with bright-blue eyes.

"This is the Widow Maggie Myers, Forrest. She's a friend of Uncle Grayson's."

"Uncle Grayson! Uncle Grayson's here?" The little boy struggled to escape the confines of the cotton sheet his mother had tucked beneath his chin.

"Lie down, young man. Where's your manners? You're not going downstairs again tonight. Now say good evening to the Widow Myers and then it's time you went to sleep."

The boy eyed his mother and then looked back at Maggie. "Good evening to you, Widow Myers," he said politely. But then, no longer able to constrain himself, he bounced up again. "You came with my Uncle Grayson? Do you know if he brought me a present? He can't come very much because he's a busy man, but he always sends me presents. Do you know if he brought me one this time?"

"Forrest! Forrest," Reagan chided. "What a rude child to ask for gifts!" She lifted the sheet and her mouth dropped open. "And what a rude child to be sleeping without his nightshirt!"

The blond boy dropped back onto the pillow again. "It's just too stinkin' hot for nightshirts, Mama. You and papa don't wear a nightshirt, not even when it's cold, so why do I have to wear one?"

Maggie couldn't resist a giggle.

Reagan tried to hide a smile behind her hand. "You'll have to discuss that issue with your father in the morning. Now, go to sleep." She pulled the sheet over his bare chest and then kissed her fingertip and planted the kiss on the end of his nose. "Good night, Forrest."

"Good night, Mama. Good night, Widow Myers." He bobbed back up again. "If Uncle Grayson can, could you tell him to come say good night. I'll wait up," he finished hopefully.

Maggie grinned as Reagan passed her with the candle. "I'll tell Grayson to be sure and say good night, but I don't know how late it will be." She paused, then spoke again. "And if it's all right with your mama, you could call me Miss Maggie." She wrinkled her nose. "Widow Myers makes me feel too old."

The little boy laughed and settled back on his bed. "Mama?"

Both Maggie and Reagan stepped out into the hallway and Reagan stuck her head back in the child's room. "I suppose Miss Maggie would be appropriate. Now say your prayers and go to sleep."

Reagan pulled the door closed and leaned against it for a moment. "Heavens, but that boy tries me."

"He's beautiful." Maggie sighed, thinking of the child that lay nestled in her womb, the child Grayson would never know. "And such a big boy for what . . . three? He speaks so well."

"He does, and I swear we're not going to teach the next one to speak until it's time he went to university." Reagan waved a hand and ushered Maggie down the hall.

"You have another?"

Reagan tossed a wry grin over her shoulder. "Finally." She patted her stomach. "Sterling's beside himself. He's hoping for a dozen boys. Myself, I think it's time we had a girl around this house to balance things out." She stopped at a door and pushed it open. "Go ahead in. This is the blue room. I always thought it was so cozy. My sister loves to stay here when she comes to visit."

Maggie stepped inside the room that glowed softly with candlelight and she gave a little sigh of approval. "It's beautiful." The walls were papered in sprigged blue flowers with green leaves, the four-poster bed lined with light cottony bedcurtains sprigged in the same pattern. The room was tastefully furnished with several small tables, a clothing trunk, and two upholstered chairs in the same blue-flowered pattern. Soft, filmy drapes blew in the slight breeze that came through the two large windows that opened above the bricked courtyard. A painted Chinese screen had been set up near the door and behind it waited a huge bathing tub.

"I've left you towels and a sleeping gown on the bed. Also a tray of tea and some biscuits. I apologize, but the tea is homemade. I refuse to allow English tea into my house."

Maggie nodded, running a finger along the edge of a smooth cherry tabletop. "My mama always made our tea; she hated to pay the tax."

"Well then, I'll say good night. I'm exhausted. I can having a morning meal sent up, or would you prefer to join us in the courtyard?"

Maggie smiled. "I . . . I'd like to eat with Grayson—with all of you, I mean." She lowered her gaze. "See, I'll be going in a few days and I want to spend as much time as I can with him."

Reagan nodded, making no attempt to pry. "Please make yourself at home then. There're no pretensions here. Feel free to come and go and, honestly, let me know if there's anything you need. There's a gown in the chest that should fit you quite nicely."

Maggie lifted her lashes, hesitating but wanting to say something. "I . . . I want to thank you for bein' . . . for *being* so nice to me."

"For heaven's sake, don't be silly. When Grayson wrote us about you, I knew you were special. We're glad you came."

"I thank you, anyway." Maggie smiled back.

"Good night," Reagan murmured, and then backed out of the bedchamber and closed the door quietly behind her.

For a moment, Maggie stood frozen in disbelief gazing at the room around her. It was like a dream that had come to life! With a squeal of delight she raced for the high four-poster bed and leaped onto it, face first, laughing into the goose-down pillows. As a child she'd imagined what it would be like to sleep in a room like this! She rolled over and kicked off her boots before lying back on the soft tick to stare at the canopy of the massive bed, a pillow hugged in her arms.

It wouldn't be too hard to get used to this, she mused. *Servants, candles on every wall, thick-bed linens, and pretty wallpaper.* Realizing what she was thinking, Maggie groaned and pushed off the bed, throwing the pillow. "Don't be a goose," she chastised herself aloud. "You're not staying here. You can't," she whispered to the reflection in a wavy mirror that hung on a wall near the door.

It would never work, she reminded herself, staring at the wild-haired woman in the mirror. *The two of you are as mismatched as a German boot and a French calfskin slipper. He's too rich for you, Maggie Myers, too smart, too worldly. He'd tire of you in a year and find himself another woman to warm his bed, and it would kill you.*

She wiped at the dark smudge of dirt on the end of her nose and turned away from the telltale mirror. She didn't like that sadness she saw in her dark eyes. Life was too short for sadness and regrets. She'd made her plan and now she had to stick to it. She'd stay here with Grayson two days, maybe three, and then she'd head for New York. New York was where her baby would have a fair chance at life.

Suddenly tired beyond reason, Maggie began to strip away her dirty clothing. Leaving them in a pile beside the door, she walked behind the screen and slipped into the heavenly water. Relaxing in the tub with the water nearly to her chin, she soaped up a washing cloth with fragrant soap left on a stool and began to lather her dusty skin. She washed her entire body and then her hair and then, tying it up in a thick towel, she leaned back in the tub and closed her eyes.

Rest. That was what she needed. A good night's rest and she'd feel better in the morning. She'd be able to see everything more in perspective. Of course Grayson didn't *really* want to marry her. He didn't *really* love her. He was attracted to her, perhaps he was even infatuated with her—but *love?* A man who grew up in a house like this just didn't fall in love with a bootmaker's daughter. Maggie sighed, made drowsy by the warm water. Yes, she had to get to New York while she still had a little sense, else she feared Grayson would break her heart.

When the bedchamber door opened sometime later, the sound made Maggie jump. Had she been asleep? She didn't know.

"Maggie?"

"Grayson?" She relaxed again, resting her back on the rear of the tub again. "I'm taking a bath." She yawned and stretched in the water. "I didn't know a body could get so dirty in one night."

He chuckled. She could hear him moving in the room, but he didn't come behind the screen.

"I'll be out in a minute." She smiled to herself. "You could come in and soap my back if you wanted."

"Take your time, sweet."

She frowned and began to rinse her body one last time. "A terrible fight that was with your brother. Did you settle it?" she called, a little hurt that he hadn't come around the silk screen.

"Not really. There'll be a meeting with our commander, Colonel Hastings, tomorrow. I won't know anything until I've talked to him. I've gotten myself into a damned bit of trouble here, Maggie. If only I'd listened to Sterling."

"You're tellin' me!" She paused, gathering a towel and wrapping it around her breasts as she stepped out of the cool water. "I wanted to tell you, Grayson, that . . . well, that I'm sorry I didn't believe you when you said you weren't a redcoat." She folded back the Chinese screen so she could see him.

And what a sight he was, with his classic good looks and cocky grin, standing there with his thumbs hooked in the waistband of his breeches. He, too, had bathed and re-dressed in simple fawn-colored breeches and a open-necked muslin shirt.

She turned her attention to combing out her wet hair with a silver-handled brush left beside the bathtub. "It's just that it was such a mad story, and soldiers," she shrugged, "they're all liars. They all deceive. I just thought you were one more passin' through, wantin' a piece of tail before you moved on."

Grayson broke into an odd grin and turned his back toward her to glance out the open window into the darkness of fallen night. "I take it it's to be separate beds with us here?"

She sighed, feeling that familiar ache deep in the pit of her belly. She wanted Grayson, as she knew he must want her, but somehow it just didn't seem right. Not here in the Thayer home, not under these circumstances. "I think it better, don't you?" she asked. "You know . . . with me leavin' and all."

He came toward her, and Maggie heard a sigh escape her lips. She was cool and drowsy from her bath and the thought of snuggling in Grayson's arms on that big bed was almost more than she could bear.

He leaned carefully, almost gentlemanly to kiss

her and Maggie let her eyelids flutter shut. *Just one kiss,* she told herself. *Just one.*

But the moment his lips touched hers, something clicked in her head. Something wasn't right. Her eyes flew open to stare into Grayson's bemused blue eyes. "Grayson?"

"Maggie." He had a silly grin on his face.

Her eyes narrowed. "Why, you . . . you son of a low-bellied rotter!" She gave him a shove as she clutched the towel she'd nearly let drop. "You're not Grayson."

Sterling broke into laughter. "I wondered how long—"

"That was a stinking thing to do to me, Grayson!" Maggie shouted at the top of her lungs. "Grayson! Come in here! I know you're out there!" She riveted her eyes on Sterling. "And it was a stinking thing for *you* to do as well!" With that she gave Sterling another hard shove backward toward the tub. He lost his balance and fell bottomfirst into the tepid bathwater, splashing buckets over the sides and onto the floor.

The door burst open and the real Grayson appeared in duplicate clothing as his brother, clapping his hands and laughing. "It took you longer than I thought, Maggie girl!" He offered his hand to his brother who was sputtering soapy water. "A hand, Brother."

But when Sterling accepted his hand and Grayson began to pull him up and out of the tub, Grayson let go and Sterling fell back again into the tub. "Son of a low-bellied rotter, indeed! You kissed her, for Christ's sake! I didn't say you could kiss her, Brother!

It took Maggie a numbing moment to collect her thoughts, but then she spun around in fury to face Grayson. "You! How could you do that to me?" she demanded, clutching her towel to her damp, nude body with one hand while prodding him with the other. "You're lucky I didn't take a roll on that bed with him! It would serve you right!"

He put up his hands in defense. "Easy, easy, it was just a joke, Maggie. No harm done."

"No harm done!" she stammered. "You embarrassed me! The both of you ought to be ashamed of yourselves."

Having climbed out of the bathtub, Sterling reached for a towel off the stool and dried his face. "It was just a joke, but it was all *his* idea," he accused as he backed his way out of the bedchamber. "Well, good night."

The moment he was gone, Maggie turned on Grayson again, this time dropping her towel and grasping him by the arms to propel him backward toward the tub.

"No, no, Maggie, I just got out of the bath," he protested, staggering. "Can't you take a joke, sweet?"

"Not when I'm the butt of it," she answered, giving him a final shove.

But when Grayson fell back, he pulled Maggie with him and the two fell into the bathtub, wrapped limb in limb. Grayson burst into laughter as she fought to escape his embrace and pulled her into his arms to kiss her. "Ah, Maggie. We'd have such a fine life together, you and I. Think about it, will you?"

Maggie's anger spent, she pressed her hands onto his chest and brought her mouth to his again. "Hush your mouth and kiss me again," she murmured.

"Kiss you? Kiss you?" he teased, lifting her in his arms and out of the tub, a husky catch to his voice. "I can kiss you. I can kiss you on your mouth." He kissed her mouth as he crossed the floor to the bed. "I can kiss your neck." He kissed her neck. "I can kiss your breast."

Maggie arched her back as he laid her across the bed and stretched out over her, his mouth catching her swelling nipple gently between his teeth.

"Yes," she whispered, giggling, "and where else can you kiss me?"

He gave an animal-like growl as he drew his mouth down over her flat belly toward her woman's mound, his tongue carving a hot, wet trail of desire. "Ah, where else, you ask?" he bedeviled. "It's much easier if I show you, my sassy rebel."

Maggie wove her fingers through Grayson's golden hair and settled back on the goose-down tick. "Show me, then," she whispered, her laughter mingling with his. "Show me."

Chapter Seventeen

Grayson exhaled slowly as he smoothed the green lapels of his dark-brown uniform coat, noting the green hearts sewn at the elbows. "By the king's cod," he swore in Sterling's direction, "is this what you Colonial clods call a uniform?"

"Colonial clod? Do you hear yourself?" Sterling paced the tiny sitting room outside Colonel Hastings' office dressed identically to Grayson in the uniform of an officer of the First Legionary Corps of Virginia. "You best remember who you are and not put on any of Captain Grayson Thayer's airs or you're likely to wind up in the brig instead of receiving an honorable discharge."

"I'm not looking for an honorable discharge," Grayson commented, snatching off his borrowed black leather cap, which, trimmed as it was with a green turban about the crown and knotted in the back with yellow tassels, seemed foppish to him. "I have to go back in, and I well expect your support, Brother."

At that moment a young sergeant who acted as

Colonel Hastings' secretary appeared at the door. He stared at the remarkable likeness in the Thayer brothers for a moment before remembering why he was there. He cleared his throat. "The . . . the colonel will see you now, sirs." He gave a quick salute and sidestepped both men.

Taking a deep, cleansing breath, Grayson threw back his shoulders and walked through the colonel's door. Inside, he lifted a smart salute and waited for John Hastings, a man in his midforties, to return the salute.

"At ease, gentlemen," the colonel said, looking up from a pile of scattered papers and giving a sweep of his knotty-fingered hand as he completed his salute. "Close the door and have a seat."

Grayson and Sterling removed their caps and accepted the two straight-backed chairs placed in front of their commanding officer's desk. In silence they waited for him to complete the paperwork he was engrossed in. After a minute or more, the colonel set aside the stack of papers and removed his spectacles, massaging the bridge of his nose.

"Damnation, but the two of you are a sight! Uncanny it is!" He leaned back in his chair, crossing his arms over his broad chest. "Straight off, who's who? I can never tell the two of you apart." He raised a finger, narrowing his gaze. "And I'm not up for your games, Grayson. You're in enough trouble as it is."

"I'm Grayson, Colonel," Grayson said, breaking into a easy smile as he offered his hand. "And it's good to see you, sir. It been more than a year."

Colonel Hastings accepted his hand with a squeeze. "Good to see you in one piece, son. More than once we thought we'd lost you down South."

Grayson grinned, leaning back easily in his chair. "No, sir. You'd not be so fortunate."

Colonel Hastings turned to Sterling on the left. "Fortunate, hell! You boys are two of the best men I've worked with since this cursed war began. I just wish I had more men like you."

"Well, thank you, sir." Sterling responded graciously.

"We're pleased we have your confidence, sir." Grayson slid forward in his chair. "Now I've already got a plan as to how I can get back into Major Lawrence's camp *and* make a gain at the very same time."

The handsomely graying colonel gave a dry chuckle. "Bold as ever, aren't you, son? Seems to me I ought to hear a little groveling. You gave us a hell of a scare, Thayer. You screwed up royally and you ought to be strung up for it."

Grayson lowered his gaze to the colonel's scarred desk for a moment and then lifted his eyes to look directly at his commanding officer. "All I can say now, sir, is that I'm sorry. I erred. I have no excuse. But I can tell you it will never happen again."

"At least and not live to tell about it," Sterling murmured.

Colonel Hastings glanced at Sterling and then back at Grayson again. "It's your brother's opinion that you've been out too long. That you bungled because you lost your edge."

"I repeat, sir. It will never happen again."

"It's no crime to admit the pressure has gotten to you. It's not General Washington's policy to keep men in the field, like you've been, for more than a year or two at a time. Just too damned risky."

"I realize that, sir. But my case is different."

"Yes, yes. I have your records here and I've read them over thoroughly." He nodded at Sterling. "The records of *both* of you. I know about the escapade in Philadelphia. You two must have angels sitting on your shoulders to have scraped out of that in one piece."

Grayson's face was solemn. "I'd like to go back in immediately, sir. We'd be fools not to have a man on the inside at Yorktown. There's no telling what Cornwallis is going to do. He and Clinton seem to be having some sort of tug-of-war with troops."

"That's all fine and good, Grayson, but back to the problem at hand. I need to decide if it's a good idea if you go back in. I need to decide if it's good for you, good for all of us. You know your father and I were good friends. I feel responsible for you boys. You get yourself killed and—"

"I'm not going to get killed."

Colonel Hastings leaned over his desk, wrapping his knuckles on the wooden surface. "I understand from your brother that the only thing that came between you and a musket ball between your eyes was a hellfire young lady by the name of Maggie Myers."

Grayson glanced down at the black boots Maggie had polished only this morning. "That's true, sir."

He looked up. "What I'm asking for is another chance."

Colonel Hastings exhaled, leaning back in his chair. "All right, for the sake of argument, let's say I do agree to let you go back in." Sterling gave a groan, but the colonel ignored him, going on. "How the hell do we manage it without raising suspicions as to your true identity?"

Grayson stood, feeling more comfortable on his feet. "I've put a great deal of thought into it, sir, and I think my idea would prove to be very serviceable."

"I'm listening."

"The rebels captured me and that's all the redcoats know, correct?"

"So we gather."

Grayson broke into a boyish grin as he walked behind his chair and leaned forward on its back. "So send a message to Major Lawrence and offer me in a prisoner exchange."

Sterling swore beneath his breath.

Colonel Hastings cocked an ear. "A prisoner exchange?"

"Certainly. This way I'm successfully replanted in the pits of Babylon *and* we get one of our officers back in return."

"Too simple," Sterling commented.

Colonel Hastings lifted a graying eyebrow to Grayson. "And what is your comment to that observation?"

"God's bowels! Don't you see, Sterling," Grayson said with excitement as he came around the chair.

"That's the glory of it. It's so simple, it would never occur to the bloody fools that they're being duped!"

"What makes you think they'd be willing to trade to get you back?" Colonel Hastings stroked his chin. "Your military records with the British are not exactly exemplary. You've been demoted more times than you've been promoted and you seem to aggravate the hell out of every commanding officer you work for."

Grayson shrugged. "It's the part I play."

Sterling leaned forward in his chair. "Colonel, I can't believe you're seriously considering this."

"I've made no decision, and I can tell you I don't intend to make one today. I just want to know what it is Grayson here has up his sleeve. He's a clever boy."

"And his cleverness is going to get him killed!"

Grayson turned to Sterling. "I made one mistake, do you intend to punish me the rest of my life for it, Brother? Where's your loyalty? I can do this and do it right." He raised a fist. "Damn it! Don't you see? I deserve another chance."

Colonel Hastings looked from one brother to the other and then leaned back in his chair, crossing his arms over his chest again. "All right, Grayson, you've said your piece. I'll need a day or two to think about it."

Grayson retrieved his cap. "Thank you, sir."

Sterling raised out of his chair and reached for his cap as well, assuming he, too, was being dismissed.

"Not you, Sterling. I want you to stay."

Grayson lifted a blond eyebrow. "Sir?"

"You heard me. I want to talk to Sterling . . . alone. With our Lafayette on his way to Williamsburg, we've got other business to attend to that's not of your concern."

Grayson glanced down at Sterling, who was taking his seat again. "Very well, then," he said, trying not to be angry with his brother. "You want me to wait for you, Sterling."

"No. You and Maggie take the carriage and go home. I've my horse. Reagan'll be furious if we're all late to supper."

Sterling gave a nod and then turned to Colonel Hastings, snapping a salute. "Sir."

"Dismissed." Colonel Hastings returned the salute and Grayson had no choice but to walk out the door.

Outside the redbrick house that had been made into offices for the Army, Grayson leaped into the carriage where Maggie waited and tossed his hat onto the leather seat. He called to the driver to head for home and then settled back on the carriage bench across from Maggie.

Unlike any woman he had ever known, Maggie said nothing. She only looked at him . . . waiting. Grayson could tell by the anxious look in her dark eyes that she wanted to know what had happened in Colonel Hastings' office, but somehow he knew that if he didn't offer any information, she wouldn't ask. At least not now.

He smiled at her and she smiled back. "Heavens, but you're a sight for sore eyes," he murmured.

Her cheeks colored as she glanced down at the beautiful apple-green caraco jacket and matching petticoat Reagan had loaned her. This all seemed so unreal. The beautiful home at Thayer's Folly, the kindness of Sterling and Reagan. Maggie brought her hand to her throat and stroked the soft cotton of the modesty piece she wore tucked in her neckline. She felt so much like a queen today dressed in stylish clothes and riding with her dashingly handsome soldier in a carriage that she didn't even mind tight-fitting heeled slippers that hurt her feet.

"You want to see more of Williamsburg?" he asked, unable to take his eyes from her.

She shook her head. "No."

"More shopping?"

She laughed. "Holy Mary, no. You've bought me far too many gifts already." She thought of the boxes of items to be delivered later to Thayer's Folly. Why, Grayson had even bought her a trunk to transport her belongings to New York when she left.

"Because I love you." He reached for her gloved hands and took them in his. "I just want to make you happy, Maggie mine. It's all I want."

Her dark gaze held his for a moment. "Noah used to say the very same thing."

"I'm not Noah," he countered. "You married *him* out of necessity, marry *me* for love."

She looked away, but didn't withdraw her hands from his. Williamsburg was alive with the hustle and bustle of late afternoon. Children ran in the streets laughing and chasing one another. Patriot soldiers seemed to burst from the very seams of the town now that the British had evacuated it. The streets brimmed with venders calling out their wares.

"Fresh fish! Fresh fish! Buy my fish!" called a short little woman in a drooping mobcap.

"Cool milk! Last of the day!" cried a young girl carrying a yoke with a bucket balanced on each end. "Cool milk!"

Maggie glanced back at Grayson. "I should think it will be good to be home. It's a wonderful place, Williamsburg. I like the people."

He brought her gloved hand to his lips. "Colonel Hastings made no decision. He wanted to talk to Sterling, but he still said it would be a few days."

"You mean he's even considering letting you go back!" She snatched her hand from his grasp. " 'Twould be lunacy."

Grayson leaned back, resting his back on the smooth leather of the seat and stretching out his booted feet. "I have a plan." He tapped his temple. "A damned good one and the colonel knows it."

"I thought we agreed it was time you hung up your red coat and replaced it with a blue one."

"No. You and my brother agreed, not me. I agreed to nothing of the sort."

"You'll lose your head. You'll be hung out at the crossroad for the crows to feed on your gullet."

He grimaced. "God's teeth, woman, but you've got a way with words. Must you be so gruesome?"

She slipped off her seat and sat next to him. "How many friends have you seen die, Grayson?"

He blinked. "I've seen many men die. Killed too many."

"But *friends*. Do you know what it's like to cut down their bodies and then have to scoop 'em with a shovel to bury them because the redcoats wouldn't let you cut 'em down any sooner."

He draped his arm around her shoulder and kissed a curl of her sleek, combed hair that had escaped her straw bonnet. "I'm not going to die. Marry me and give me something to come home to."

She sat back in the seat to watch the countryside roll by as they wound their way out of town. "I thought we agreed we weren't going to talk about that. It'll do nothin' but ruin the time we've got left."

"Nothing." He took her chin and forced her to turn her head so that he could kiss her.

"What?"

"Nothing. It will do *nothing* but ruin . . ."

She bit down lightly on his lower lip. "What? You're my schoolmaster now?"

"It could work, Maggie. If only you could have seen yourself come down the grand staircase this morning. You looked as if you belonged, like none of us will ever belong."

"You've been too long in the sun Grayson. What do I have to say to make you realize you and I aren't cut from the same cloth? I sew boots to feed and clothe myself, for heaven's sake!"

He frowned. "You may sew them, but I'll not say how well."

She raised any eyebrow, fighting the urge to smile. "What do you mean?"

"These boots I had you resole back in Yorktown. They rubbed a damned blister on my heels walking yesterday." He lifted a foot. "They never rubbed before."

She patted his thigh. "I can always take another look at them."

"And well you should. I paid a king's ransom for them."

"Serves you right. Better places that money could have been spent," she lectured. "Do you know how often our soldiers go to sleep at night with empty bellies?"

"I had to look the part, didn't I, Maggie?"

"I think you like the fancy boots and starched matching uniforms."

"I think—" Grayson suddenly looked up. "What the hell?" Maggie followed the direction of his gaze to the dusty road ahead where a rickety, two-wheeled cart had turned over. A crowd of men and women had surrounded the vehicle in the center of the road and they were shouting angrily.

"Casey, stop here," Grayson ordered the driver.

Before Maggie could speak, Grayson was out of the carriage and sprinting toward the commotion. After a moment's hesitation, Maggie jumped out of the carriage with the help of the driver and made her way toward the crowd of irate men and women.

"See here!" Grayson said, pushing his way through the throng of farmers and farmers' wives. "What's this all about?"

As he forced his way to the center of the circle, he could see an elderly man with a raised pitchfork holding back a burly red-faced farmer. Someone had unhitched the old man's oxen from the cart and then tipped the cart over, its contents of turnips spilling onto the roadway. A dark-haired woman in a striped tick petticoat was leading the oxen away.

"Get back," the wizened man threatened. "Get back or I'll poke you full of holes!"

"Try it, Tory scum, and I'll snap your neck with my bare hands!"

"You got no right to take my oxen!"

"I say, what's this about!" Grayson repeated, coming to stand as close to the two men as he dared. "Whose oxen are those, and why's that wench leading them off?"

The old man turned to Grayson with hate in his eyes. "They're mine, and this bastard, he's got no right to take 'em."

The red-faced man turned to Grayson. "This here's Reynold Hogg, Tory scum from over to Coon's Corner, Major Thayer," the man said, thinking it was Sterling he spoke to. "He thinks to come into town and sell his turnips, but I say he don't belong. He wouldn't sell when we needed food for our men."

"You took my vegetables anyway, didn't you, Skeeter Townsend?" Reynold spit a brown stream of tobacco onto the red-faced man's boot.

"Why you!"

But before Skeeter could raise his fist, Grayson caught it. "Now easy, easy there." He looked behind him at the angry sea of faces. Everyone was talking at once, shouting obscenities and tossing an occasional turnip at the Tory. "Back up, will you, and give us some air?"

Maggie climbed on top of an overturned wooden crate and watched with curiosity as Grayson spoke to the incensed crowd of commoners.

"You've got no right to take this man's property," he told them sternly.

"He's Tory trash, Major Thayer," a woman hollered.

"Tar and feather him, I say," offered a blond-haired young man with a cowlick.

"Don't belong on roads with decent folk," said another.

Grayson held up a finger and the men and women began to lower their voices. "How old are you, Reynold Hogg?" he asked the old man.

Reynold screwed up his face. "Nigh on eighty. But what the hell's that go to do with my turnips, soldier." He spoke the last word as if it pained him.

"Eighty years old," Grayson told the crowd, giving particular attention to the burly Skeeter Townsend. "For four score of years this man was an English subject. For eighty years he obeyed his king in word and deed." Grayson looked at the men and women who surrounded the overturned ox cart. "If you'd followed one way of thinking for eighty years, wouldn't it be hard for you to change? Think from this man's point of view for a moment." Grayson lifted off his uniform cap and tucked it beneath his arm. "Can you blame him for not being willing to go against all he's ever believed in for the utterly unknown? What we seek in this fight for independence is something no one in the world has ever known. Equality and inalienable rights are ideas that are hard to swallow."

"Don't make any difference," Skeeter insisted. "He don't like our way of thinking, he can go the hell home to Mother England's bosom!"

Maggie watched the crowd as several people nodded their heads in agreement, but still, Grayson had caught their attention. He had them thinking, she could see it in their sunburned faces.

"No, no, you're wrong, Skeeter," Grayson said. "This man has a right to this road, the same as you. Because when we win this war we'll be united as one people. All who agree to the freedoms laid out in our Declaration of Independence will be welcome."

"But he's for the bloody British." Skeeter protested.

Grayson shook his head. "It doesn't matter. As long as he does our Army no harm, when this war is over, and the end is coming . . . Reynold Hogg will be a man equal to you, Skeeter Thompson. For those who remain in these United States after the war, there will be no sides. We will stand strong as one in the Commonwealth of Virginia, one nation under God."

Skeeter lowered his head, shuffling his big feet. "Guess maybe I got a little carried away, Major Thayer."

Grayson dropped his hand to the red-faced man's

shoulder. "Everyone's blood is boiling these days. It's the heat. Now go on with you."

The crowd parted as Skeeter made his way to the woman who had been leading the oxen away. "Let 'em go, Martha. Anything like their owner, they're probably too stupid to pull a plow anyway."

Maggie watched as Grayson organized several other men to upright the two-wheeled cart, while women began to toss the turnips back onto the bed. The boy with the cowlick backed the oxen back into their traces and in a matter of minutes, the farmers and their wives had scattered. Grayson stood tall alongside the road, watching the old man, Reynold, climb back onto the seat of his cart.

"If you're expectin' thanks," Reynold spat a long stream of tobacco onto the ground, "you ain't gettin' any," he told Grayson.

But Grayson only smiled. "You'd be best not to take those turnips in tonight else you may lose your oxen for good the next time."

Reynold frowned and lifted his reins. "Damned rebels and your speeches," he muttered as he plodded off. "United as one, bloody hell! We ain't lost yet."

Maggie covered her mouth, trying not to laugh aloud as the old man in his cart rolled away.

Grayson spun around to face her. "So what are you laughing about?" he asked, smiling at her standing on the dusty road, her bonnet thrown back across her shoulders, her red hair blowing in the late-afternoon breeze.

"You," she told him. "So much for heroism. He

didn't even appreciate what you did for him."

Grayson shrugged his broad shoulders as he took her arm and led her back to their waiting carriage. "It doesn't matter, Maggie. What matters is what's right." He lifted her up into the carriage and she rested her hands on his shoulders staring into his blue eyes.

"You honestly mean that, don't you?" she asked softly.

He jumped up into the carriage and settled beside her, his arm draped over her shoulder. "That I do, Maggie mine. And that's why I have to go back to Yorktown."

Chapter Eighteen

Maggie sat under an apple tree, her back against the rough bark of the trunk, her legs drawn up beneath the skirt of her pale-blue sack gown. She watched a bee buzz lazily above a bed of clover before finally settling on a lavender blossom in search of nectar. She smiled and took another bite of the apple she'd picked from the tree.

It was midafternoon, a perfect time at Thayer's Folly to slip away and be alone for a little while. Grayson and Sterling had gone down to the southern fields to inspect a barn being built to store and dry wheat, and Reagan had gone into town to oversee her printers as they printed her weekly newspaper. The idea of a woman writing and printing a newspaper had seemed beyond belief to Maggie a few days ago, but after getting to know Reagan better, it seemed perfectly acceptable.

Yes, life here at Thayer's Folly had been full of surprises. These people who were the grandchildren of lords, and the children of statesmen were not what she had expected at all. They were just like her friends back in Yorktown, only they spoke with fancier words and slept in larger beds. Certainly, they had servants, fine carriages and meat on the table each evening, but *inside* they were the same people. They wanted the same things for their children, for the country they were forging, and Maggie felt a closeness to them she'd never have thought possible.

Instead of ridicule for her working-class lineage, Maggie received nothing but consideration. Even Reagan's friends had been pleasantly welcoming at the tea Reagan had hosted yesterday. No one seemed to care that she was a bootmaker; all they wanted to hear about was the war news from Yorktown and tales of her involvement with the masked rebels. She was a heroine of sorts to these richly dressed women and she had to admit she enjoyed their attention.

The thing was, the longer Maggie stayed, the more she liked it here at Thayer's Folly. She did miss Zeke and the others, but this life was so exciting. There was something new to see and do every hour of the day. Life at a big plantation was filled with duties in the bake house and the dairy. There were sheets to be inventoried and ill servants to look in on. And even though Grayson couldn't appear in public with his brother because of his undetermined status, the Thayers still managed to entertain with small dinner parties and picnics by the river.

Maggie rubbed her achy wrist absentmindly. Was she being foolish not to consider Grayson's proposal of marriage? The more she thought on the idea, the more confused she became. The baby she carried made everything so much more difficult. On one hand, she wondered if she was doing the unborn babe a disservice to take him or her from all that was possible here on Thayer's Folly. Couldn't she just marry Grayson, have his child, and live happily the rest of her days here on this beautiful plantation?

Or was she fooling herself in thinking she could make their relationship work? Could she ever *really* fit in? Would Grayson become bored with her simple ways? Would he resent the child Maggie carried who wouldn't be born of the bloodlines he had been born of? And most important, would Grayson expect her to be a woman she could never be? Would he ask too much?

Maggie got up and brushed the grass from the soft blue material of the sack gown Grayson had purchased for her in town a few days ago. Though simple in lines and comfortable, the gown was still one of the most beautiful pieces of clothing Maggie had ever owned. She walked across the grassy field toward the house. Of course the bedchamber she slept in was filled with beautiful things Grayson had bought her: bonnets, gloves, silk and cotton stockings. Why, there was even a silver-handled toothbrush!

She couldn't resist a smile. Grayson really did love her, didn't he? Else why would he spend his money on her so freely? At the sound of his voice, she looked up. Across the yard she saw Grayson and the same maid who had made eyes at him the first evening they'd come to Thayer's Folly. Inga was her name. Reagan said she was a worthless, lazy chit, and that she only kept her on because her ill mother had been such a loyal servant.

Inga was hanging out sheets on the line to dry, laughing in high-pitched squeal. The flaxen-haired girl sounded like a rutting piglet to Maggie.

Maggie stopped to watch Grayson. He was talking to her as he helped her hang the wet, cumbersome sheets over the line. A pang of jealousy rose in Maggie's throat. Everywhere he went, people seemed to like him. Women flirted shamelessly with him in the shops where he had bought Maggie her clothing, pretending she was his cousin and he was Sterling. The servants all made a fuss over him, saying Major Grayson this and Major Grayson that. Cook made his favorite meals. The laundress changed his bedsheets daily and ironed his shirts herself. From infant to elderly, the women seemed to find him irresistible.

Just then, Grayson glanced up. He waved. "Maggie! Where've you been? I've been looking for you."

She walked toward him, unable to resist a smile. In the last few days she had learned to tell her lover and his brother apart. At first it had seemed impossible because they appeared so identical at first glance. But as the days passed, she noticed the slight nuances that distinguished one from the other. Grayson strode rather than walked. Sterling had an annoying habit of cracking his knuckles when lost in thought. Of the two men, Grayson was bolder. He flirted with Reagan, he teased the serving maids, he played practical jokes on visitors.

"I just took a walk," she answered. "I thought you'd be gone longer."

He grinned. "I missed you."

The grimace Inga made at Grayson's comment didn't go unnoticed by Maggie. "There're apples all over the ground," she went on, ignoring the maid. "They need to be picked up before they rot."

"I'll send someone this afternoon."

Maggie stopped at the corner of the clothesline and watched for a moment as Inga hung a pair of her new lace-trimmed drawers out to dry. Never in her life had Maggie had someone hang out her clothes. Since she was five she'd hung out her own clothing or they would not have gotten dry.

Ducking beneath the clothesline Grayson plucked a bleached mobcap out of Inga's basket and pulled it over his head. The maid squealed into the palm of her hand. Maggie lifted an eyebrow.

"Your new cover?" she asked. "You going to sneak into the redcoat camp wearing a cap and skirt? Let me guess, you're the washwoman." She crossed her arms over her chest, taking in the new look with a nod. "Mayhap this identity will be more successful."

He curtsied, lifting an imaginary petticoat. "At your service, Miss Maggie. Washin's done, cows is milked, and I's picked four baskets of apples. Can't I *please* take a little rest, Miss Maggie? You just workin' this poor girl to death!"

She couldn't help laughing. He looked so utterly ridiculous in his handsome burgundy breeches, white shirt, and that silly mobcap perched on the top of his head. Maggie tried to grab it, but he dove under a string of billowing wet pillowcases and disappeared from sight. "You'll have to catch me,

Miss Maggie," He said in a high-pitched falsetto voice.

Maggie bounded after him, ignoring Inga's frown. "No need to run," Maggie called, turning the corner at the smokehouse. You know I can run as fast as you . . . faster."

"Ha!" Grayson protested, disappearing behind another outbuilding. "Haven't caught me yet!"

Maggie ran after him, but when she came around the next clabbard dependency, Grayson was nowhere to be seen. She came to halt, and dropped her hands to her hips. Now where had he gone? she wondered. He couldn't have gotten far. She crept up to the corner of the next building and peeked around the corner. Still no Grayson.

Passing one small dependency building after another, Maggie searched for him, but he was nowhere to be seen. She tried calling his name, but he didn't answer.

"Grayson!" she finally said. "You win! I give, now come on! It's time we started getting ready for Reagie's dinner party. You know she hates it when you're late!" Walking along the perimeter of dependencies, Maggie turned in between two buildings and dropped her hands to her hips in exasperation. "Grayson!"

Suddenly a door swung open and he popped out, still wearing the mobcap on his head. Before Maggie could protest, he clamped his hand over her mouth and dragged her inside a small brick building and down several wooden steps.

Pushing her against the closed door, he replaced his hand on her mouth with his mouth.

Maggie giggled as their lips met and their tongues mingled. He had brought her into the icehouse where ice was stored all summer insulated by thick brick walls and layers of sweet, clean straw.

"It's so cool in here," Maggie murmured, snuggling against his broad chest. "It feels good after the heat outside."

Grayson closed his arms around her, stroking her goose-pimpled arms. "When we were children we used to hide in here and pretend we were explorers in the mountains of Russia."

His warm breath tickled her ear. "Your mama obviously didn't give you enough work to do to leave you time for such foolishness."

He brought the back of his hand up against her cheek and stroked it. "We could pretend we're explorers," he teased, cupping her left breast. "What do you think?"

"Reagan's party—"

He touched her lower lip with the tip of his tongue. "We've been late before."

Maggie massaged the corded muscles of his neck. "She'll be upset with us."

"Can I help it if I find you irresistible?" He kissed the pulse at the base of her throat. "Can I help it if I can't get enough of you, Maggie mine?"

She slipped her hand through the keyhole neckline of his muslin shirt and rubbed her thumb against his nipple. "Always full of sweet words, aren't you, Captain?"

"Major," he told her as he lifted her into his arms. "I told you, I'm a major with our army."

She looped her arms around his neck and rested

her head on his shoulder. "And only a captain with the redcoats."

"Yeah, well, I've been promoted a few times, but then always demoted again."

"I know," she whispered, running her palm over his muscle-banded shoulder. "All for the sake of the part you played."

He knelt and lowered her into the thick straw that covered the floor of the icehouse. "You understand perfectly," he answered, a husky catch in his voice.

She strained in the darkness to see his blue eyes as he stared down at her. "I don't know if I can leave ye," she told him, her voice barely a whisper. "I thought I could, but I don't know now."

"Then don't," he pleaded. "Stay here at Thayer's Folly, and when my job is done in Yorktown I'll build you a house so big that you'll have to leave bread crumbs behind for me to find you inside it."

"You're not going back to Yorktown." She caught the bit of ribbon that held back his hair in the queue and tugged at the end. His hair fell across one shoulder, shiny and thick in the dim light of the slit windows cut into the roof of the icehouse. "You can't. You'd not make it out alive."

"So marry me before I go."

She sighed. "You don't understand. I've been married before. I don't want another husband."

He swept back her cascade of red hair with his hand, staring intensely into her eyes. "I wouldn't be 'another husband.' It would be different this time, Maggie, I swear it."

She rolled her head so she didn't have to look at

him. "I'll think about it," she heard herself say.

He tightened his arms around her. "That's all I'm asking, Maggie. Give it thought. I really do want to marry you before I go."

She turned back to him, bringing her knee up between his legs to feel the hard bulge of his loins. Straw crackled beneath them and the cold seeped up from the brick floor to envelope them. "I tell you, you're not goin' Captain-Major. Not if I have to tie ye to a bedpost."

"Oh, tie me, is it?" He brought his mouth down against hers as he lifted her arms over her head, pinning them. "Haven't tried that, have we?" he teased.

Maggie arched her back and lifted to meet him hungrily. Their tongues intertwined and she moved beneath him, wanting to feel his hard male body touch hers, limb for limb.

The bone-chilling cold of the icehouse mixed with the warmth of Grayson body sent shivers of exquisite desire through Maggie's veins. The bittersweet anguish of not knowing whether or not to accept Grayson's proposal made her cling to him, desperate to feel proof of his love.

"Ah, Maggie. Maggie," he whispered, unhooking the front of her gown. "You're so beautiful, so breathtakingly beautiful."

Maggie smiled, stroking the line of his jaw as he lowered his mouth to kiss the hollow between her breasts. The pleasure of the sensations he created made her sigh. No one had ever been this good to her. Why couldn't she believe Grayson when he said he would love her forever?

Grayson sat up and stripped off his shirt and then eased down the shoulders of her gown and chemise, all the while staring down at her with those soul-searching eyes of his. His nimble fingers found the laces of her boned corset and quickly he freed her breasts of the confines of her clothing.

"Oh, Maggie. I can't imagine another man touching you like this," he told her as he kissed his way to the dark circle of her aureola. "Don't leave me, sweet. Don't leave me for another."

"Another man." She laughed, drunk with the excitement he created with the tip of his tongue. "There could never be anyone else but you, Grayson."

"Marry me, carry me, he sang to the tune of an old ballad. "Far across the sea . . ."

"Hush your mouth," she whispered, twisting her fingers in his golden hair. "Hush and touch me. Touch me the way I like to be touched."

"Anything for you," he answered as he brought his mouth to her breast to suckle the rosy tip. "Just tell me what you want, Maggie."

She stroked his bare back, reveling in the feel of the strength of his corded muscles as a heavy-limbed aching filled her. *What I want?* she thought. *What I want you can't give me—not you, not anyone. I want guarantees. I want promises that there will be no pain. I want promises that I'll never feel about myself the way Noah made me feel.*

But instead of answering, she only took his hand and guided it beneath her skirts to the bed of curls between her thighs.

Grayson stroked her soft curves as he kissed the

arched mounds of her breasts and teased her nipples taut and peaked. Then, sitting up, he leaned back, and with an ice pick, he broke off several chunks of ice. Popping a chunk of ice into his mouth, he stretched out over Maggie and brought his lips to hers.

The hot and cold of his mouth made her writhe beneath him, her limbs trembling with sensation. Slowly Grayson kissed his way to her breasts and when he drew a piece of ice to her nipple she half sat up in surprise.

"Oh," she breathed, settling back into his arms in the bed of straw. "Oh, that's cold, Grayson."

"You want me to stop?" he whispered in her ear.

She shook her head.

Her nipples puckered in reaction to the cold of the ice, and then he touched them again with the tip of his tongue, making Maggie half wild with ecstasy.

Her breath came in short pants as her fingers found the waistband of his breeches. Once she had unhooked the buttons, she slipped her hand beneath the burgundy cotton and stroked his engorged shaft, sighing with pleasure.

"Now," she told him. "I need you now."

Stripping off his breeches, Grayson stretched out over her, pushing her mountains of skirts up around her waist. Using his hand as a guide, he slipped into her.

Maggie met his thrust halfway and moaned with satisfaction. When their lips met, she allowed him to slip the ice cube into her mouth. Water trickled down her chin and she laughed low and sensuously.

"Maggie, Maggie," he called as he moved faster inside her. "I can't live without you, Maggie. Marry me. Say you'll marry me."

It was on the tip of her tongue to say yes as she rose and fell with him. It would have been so easy to just say it. Yet she held back as her breath came quicker and she lifted again and again to meet each stroke. She was afraid, too afraid . . . so she said nothing. In another instant her cries of fullfillment mixed with Grayson's deeper ones, and together they climaxed in utter, glorious ecstasy. And when the waves of pleasure had subsided, Grayson slipped out of her and held her in his arms, kissing away the dots of perspiration above her lip and whispering tender promises.

Content in Grayson's arms, Maggie snuggled against his warm chest, pushing down her skirts to ward of the chill of the icehouse. Absently, she rubbed her wrist.

"I didn't hurt you, did I?" Grayson asked gently as he took arm.

She looked up into his deep-blue eyes. "No, of course not. It's just that my arm gets achy. Must be a big storm brewing."

"A storm?" He kissed her wrist. "The sun is shining; there's not a cloud in the sky."

She sat up and began to slip back into her clothing. "I know what I know, Grayson Thayer. When I was seven, I broke my arm jumpin' off the barn roof onto the back of Zeke's pony." She laughed. "We were playing Indian and he said it was the only way a proper redskin mounted. Well, I got a broken arm and he got his tail whipped."

Grayson lay with his hands tucked behind his head, a frown on his face. "So where's the storm come in?"

She shrugged and tossed him his breeches. "I didn't say it made sense. All I'm telling you is that when a big storm is brewing my wrist starts to hurt. My da had a great-grandfather whose missing leg always bothered him before a snow."

He came to his feet and slipped into his breeches. "That's absurd."

"Absurd or no, it's the truth." She picked a piece of straw out of his hair. "We'd best go. We both have to change for Reagan's party."

Grayson reached out and swept Maggie into his arms. "I'd rather stay here with you."

She rested her hands on his shoulders. "I almost think you mean that."

"Ah, Maggie, Maggie . . ." He pulled her against him and smoothed her tangled mass of fiery hair. "What did that man do to you to make you so distrustful?"

"It wasn't just Noah," she answered, her voice muffled by his chest. "It's the war, too. I've seen so much, Grayson. Too much to believe in anything or anyone."

He took her chin and lifted it until she was staring into his eyes. "I'd do anything to spare you of those memories. I'd do anything to take away the hurt."

She lifted on her toes and kissed him. "Let's go."

With a sigh, he finished dressing and, hand and hand, they left the icehouse in silence.

* * *

An hour later Maggie stood in one of the twin parlors of Thayer's Folly dressed in an elegant brocaded emerald gown. She was laughing at the tale being told to her of a woman who had smuggled a butchered pig through enemy lines into Valley Forge to feed the starving troops, in a coffin no less.

"When a patrol of redcoats stopped her on the road," the handsome patriot went on with his story, "she said she was Sarah Hogg and that it was the body of her husband John Hogg she transported."

"That can't be true!" Maggie protested, wiping at the corners of her eyes. She'd laughed so hard that tears ran down her cheeks.

"I assure you it is," he answered with a broad grin. "As God is my witness. A good friend, Forrest Irons, married her."

Maggie sipped a glass of Madeira a maid had offered. "Smart man."

A knock sounded at the front door and Maggie glanced up. Seeing no maids, she turned back to George Theis. "Excuse me, George. I don't see our hostess. I'd better get the door."

George bowed and stepped out of her way. Maggie smiled as she walked toward the door. It was nice, being treated like a lady. It made her feel good inside.

Reaching the door, she swung it open. "Yes?"

A young private dressed in the garb of the Virginia militia swept off his cap. "Good even to you, ma'am. I have message for Major Grayson Thayer."

She offered her hand. "I can give it to him."

The young man shifted his weight from one foot

to the other. "Actually, ma'am, Colonel Hastings ordered it be delivered to no one but the major."

Maggie paused a moment. "All right. Wait here and I'll find the major." This is it, she thought. Colonel Hastings had made his decision as to whether Grayson would return to Yorktown or be retired. She prayed it was the second option. Grayson had done far more than his duty and it was time he got out while his head was still attached to his shoulders.

Locating Grayson in the dining room, she took his arm and whispered into his ear.

"Excuse me, ladies," he said to the group of planters' wives who had gathered around him. "Duty." Then taking Maggie's hand in his, he led her through the rooms back toward the front door.

"This is it, Maggie," he told her, his voice nervous with excitement. "It's my orders."

"Sterling says Colonel Hastings is a reasonable man. He's not gonna let you go, Grayson. You're gettin' your hopes up for naught."

"The colonel can recognize an opportunity when he sees one. He and I, we think alike." They reached the door, and Grayson swung it open.

The young militiaman saluted. "Major Thayer, sir?"

"Yes, yes, of course. Just give me the message."

He handed it over to Grayson and made his retreat down the steps toward his waiting horse.

Grayson looked up at Maggie, hesitating before opening the message.

Maggie swallowed hard against the lump in her throat. She could feel her own heart pounding beneath the bodice of her new gown. "Ye can't change what it says by starin' at it, Grayson," she offered gently.

Looking back at the letter in his hand, Grayson took a deep breath and broke the seal.

Maggie held her breath. *Please God,* she prayed. *Don't send him back!*

Grayson gave a sudden hoot of excitement and Maggie's heart fell.

"I told you, Maggie! I told you Colonel Hastings would see it my way!" Grayson exclaimed, lifting her into his arms and twirling her around.

Maggie's face was grim. "You're going back to Yorktown?"

He released her, looking deep into her dark Indian eyes. "It's what I want," he said softly.

Afraid of the tears that threatened to overcome her, Maggie spun around. She walked into the house and straight up the grand staircase, ignoring Grayson's calls. Running down the hallway, her skirts balled in her fists, she fled for the safety of her bedchamber. Once inside, she slammed the door shut and leaned against it.

"Oh!"

"The sound of a familiar voice made Maggie look up. She wasn't alone. It was the maid, Inga.

The half-dressed girl backed up, obviously startled. She had been in Maggie's trunk. There were clothes strewn across the bed and the maid was wearing Maggie's favorite green-ribboned bonnet.

"What do you think you're doin' in my stuff?" Maggie demanded, coming toward the bed.

"Just tryin' it on," the girl answered haughtily. "I

wasn't gonna steal nuthin' if that's what you're thinkin'!"

"You've got no right Maggie exploded. "These things are mine. Grayson gave them to me. They were gifts!"

Inga scooped up her own maid's dress and slowly made her way toward the door. "Gifts, hah! These clothes were nothin' but payment for your whorin'," the maid spit venomously.

"Get out!" Maggie shouted. "Get out before I wring your scrawny neck."

"You think you're one of them, don't you? Well, you're not. You might wear them fancy dresses and say them fancy words, but you are no better than me, no better than the scullery maid!" She put her hand on the doorknob. "You won't never be one of them. Not as long as you've got that common blood running through your veins."

"Get out!" Maggie screamed as she lifted a pewter candlestick and hurled it toward the door.

Inga escaped the room just as the candlestick hit the door frame with a thud. Grayson came in as the maid went out.

"What the hell is going on in here?" he demanded.

Maggie turned her back to him. The truth of Inga's words had cut her deeply. She knew the maid was right. What was wrong with her to have ever thought she could marry Grayson and be one of the Thayers?

Maggie walked to the open window and Grayson came up behind her. The distant sound of thunder rumbled in the sky as dark clouds rolled in.

"A storm," Grayson conceded. "There's a storm coming fast."

She held herself stiff as he wrapped his arms around her waist and rested his chin on her shoulder.

"You have to understand how important it is that I go back to Yorktown, Maggie," he said softly.

"I understand."

"You do?"

"I understand." She turned in his arms until she could look up at his strikingly handsome face "Same as you have to understand. I'm going back with you . . ."

Chapter Nineteen

Grayson grabbed a black calfskin slipper off the bed and hurled it at the the wall. "Damnation, Maggie! I've no time to go round and round with you again. They're waiting for me downstairs. The exchange will take place in two days. You know I've got to go. Don't make me leave with things unsettled like this. Now, for once in your life, woman, be sensible!"

She went on with her packing, fighting back her tears. He was leaving. He was going back to Yorktown into a nest of redcoats and there was nothing she could do about it. "I'm a free woman, Grayson Thayer. So long as I'm not bound or *married,*" she said with emphasis, "I have the right to come and go as I please and it pleases me to go home to Yorktown."

"I'm not trying to imprison you here! You can go home after the fighting is over. I just want you to stay at Thayer's Folly for now. It's the only place where I know you'll be safe." He came around the bed, lowering his voice an octave. "We're going to beat them for good this time. With the money Rochambeau has offered from his own military chest, General Washington's been able to pay the troops. Admiral DeGrasse is safe in the Chesapeake with twenty-eight ships. Three thousand Frenchmen are ashore and headed this way to back up Lafayette and Wayne. No one will tell us for sure what's happening, but I'd bet my life Washington is headed for Yorktown. Cornwallis is cornered, don't you see? I tell you, Maggie, the cards are already falling. It won't be long before the war's over and I'm home. I swear it, sweetheart."

"Won't be for long. Ha! Seems I've heard that before." She folded a lacy chemise and laid it carefully in the trunk at the end of the bed. "Noah said those same words back in '76 when he walked off the farm leavin' me alone with a dying mother and crops to bring in. My *husband* wandered back one afternoon two years later with his feet rottin' in his boots and his breath smellin' of rum."

"You can't keep bringing Noah into every argument we have! I'm not Noah Myers!"

She looked up at Grayson, her eyes filled with tears. "You miss the point. The war's still goin' on, Grayson. Men are still dyin'. You're gonna walk out of here and I'm never gonna see you again if I don't go with you."

Grayson exhaled slowly, unable to tear his gaze from hers. *Christ, she really does love me, doesn't she?* he thought. Putting out his arms, he came to her and pulled her close. He smoothed her unruly bright hair and kissed the top of her head. "I'm not going to get killed. I've got too much to live for, now that I've got you, Maggie mine."

She sniffed and lifted her head from his shoulder to stare into his clear blue eyes. "Then stay," she urged. "Tell Colonel Hastings you've changed your mind." *Tell him you're going to marry and have a child,* she thought, but couldn't bring herself to say it. "Tell him anything, just don't go."

He glanced away, staring out at the open window. The first of September was nearly upon them, bringing with it the promise of fall on the wings of the morning breeze. Down below in the courtyard Sterling ran with his son, chasing after a leather ball. Grayson smiled a bittersweet smile, wondering if he would ever play in the same courtyard with his own son. He feared he wouldn't.

He looked down at Maggie, who clinged to him in desperation. "Maggie, how can I make you understand? I have to go back. I couldn't be the man I want to be for you if I don't redeem myself. I'm ashamed of the way I fouled things up back there. Don't you see I have no choice; I have to make it right."

She brushed the blond fringe at his forehead. "It wasn't your fault, what with all the demands put upon you."

His eyes narrowed; his face hardened. "You honestly believe that's an excuse for what I did, Maggie?"

There was a long pause as she searched her soul. "I . . ."

He took her hand and kissed her knuckles that

had been softened by sweet-smelling hand creams. "What if it was you, Maggie mine? You're as good a soldier as I've ever met. What if it was you that pulled that trick in Commegys' Ordinary a few weeks back? What would you do? Would you excuse yourself, take your pension, and live out your life knowing you failed . . . you failed yourself—your country." His voice caught in his throat—"Even your brother? Or would you go back? Would you right the wrongs or die trying?"

She hung her head, wanting to lie but knowing she couldn't. "I'd go back," she conceded finally, her voice barely audible.

"What did you say?" He took her chin and lifted it, forcing her to look him straight in the eyes.

Her own expression hardened to match his. "I said I'd have to go back," she answered more loudly.

"Ah hah."

She pushed his hand aside and walked away. "But that doesn't mean I have to like it."

"I'm not asking you to like it. All I'm asking is for you to accept it. Wait for me here at Thayer's Folly and I'll come back, I swear to God I will." He snatched a pair of cotton hose from her hands. "Better yet, marry me before I go. Be my wife."

"I've been a widow once." She calmly took back the hose and dropped them into the trunk. "I'll not be one again."

Grayson spun around, swearing foully. "It's like talking to a stone fence, talking to you. Maggie Myers! You're not hearing a word I say!"

"No. *You're* not hearing what *I'm* saying, Grayson. I'm saying if you have to go, I can't marry you, but I can go with you. I can be there to hold you in my arms on the battlefield when you die."

He grimaced. "A woman! No one's going to let you on a battlefield!"

She spun around in fury. She *knew* this would happen. She *knew* that if she ever became involved with another man, he would try to run her life. He would tell her when to come and go. Next he'd be telling her what to say. "What?" she shouted. "They're gonna put up fences? Now you listen and you listen well, mister rich Virginian planter. I'll go where I damn well please. Not you, not anyone is going to stop me!"

He threw up his hands. "I give up! I should have known a woman of your background could never make an intelligent decision!"

Stunned by Grayson's cruel words. Maggie watched him walk out of her bedchamber and slam the door. Tears rolled down her cheeks as she reached for his scarlet coat and hugged it to her chest.

The sound of chirping crickets and the whisper of the wind blowing through the pines eased the ache in Maggie's heart. Holy Mother Mary, but it was good to be home again! She climbed the back fence and left her hounds to watch her disappear over the hill. Once on the dusty road, she stepped aside, her hand falling to the pistol tucked in her skirt pocket as several greencoats galloped by.

She'd only been gone a few weeks, but in that short time, the war had taken a sharp turn. The British Navy was sealed in by the French, and Cornwallis and his troops were trapped on the York Peninsula. For the first time since '75 General Washington had a chance to take the offensive.

There was a strange electricity in the air in Yorktown. The British and their German counterparts were homesick and they were afraid. Maggie could hear the fear in their voices. Their movements were skittish. They were suddenly overly suspicious of every man, woman, and child who stepped foot in their camps. Redcoat and bluecoat alike seemed to be caught in a cauldron of simmering water knowing it was only a matter of time before it began to boil over.

As soon as she had arrived home this morning, Maggie had gone back into the camp peddling her wares and offering to make boot repairs in order to reestablish herself with the British Army. After all, who knew how she might be able to aid the patriot army that was closing in with each day? And then there was Grayson. She ran her hand over her belly. Even though Grayson and she had parted on ill terms, she still wanted to know when the prisoner exchange was made and that it had gone as it should. As far as she could gather, he'd not yet arrived in the camp.

With the Hessian horsemen gone, Maggie stepped back onto the road and quickened her pace, heading for Commegys' ordinary. Though she had sent a note to her sister letting her know she was safe, she was anxious to reassure her. And then there were the others. She'd gone to Zeke's house, but Mildred, after scolding Maggie for scaring her out of her wits disappearing like that, had said Zeke was gone but would be in the tavern tonight.

Maggie had fabricated a story to tell to those who would ask her where she'd been these past weeks and she'd been prepared to tell it to Mildred Barnes, but the old woman hadn't asked. Maggie didn't know if she knew the truth or not. Some things just seemed to be better left unsaid.

By the time Maggie reached the crossroad, dusk was settling in. The tavern was well lit, lanternlight spilling from every window in the two-story house. The haunting wail of bagpipes sounded from inside, along with the pounding of dancing feet. Smoke rose from the chimney and curled in the dying light rising heavenward, bringing with it the pungent smell of hickory and roast pork.

Maggie couldn't resist a smile. Home. It felt good to be home again among her own kind. What the serving wench, Inga, had said had cut her deeply. Logic told her the girl had spoken out of cruel jealousy, but Maggie's heart ached. Just when she had begun to hope, to dream, that she and Grayson just might have the barest sliver of a chance to live happily, the thoughtless chit had shattered that hope. And then what Grayson had said about a woman of her background . . . Even taking into consideration that he had reacted out of anger, Maggie feared he was right. It had been childish dreaming to think she could marry Grayson and raise her child at Thayer's Folly in happiness. This love she and Grayson felt for each other—it just seemed to be another casualty of this blasted war.

Maggie pushed open the door to the tavern and paused, waiting for her eyes to adjust to the lantern and candlelight. The public room was busting at its seams with red- and green-coated soldiers. Most of the townfolk who had frequented the tavern for years were visibly absent. With the threat of battle on the doorsteps, many had closed up their home and taken their families to safer ground in neighboring towns, praying they would still have a home to come to after the British and Colonists clashed. Sidestepping a Hessian's embrace, she made a beeline for the kitchen door.

"Oh, thank the Holy Virgin!" her sister Alice declared from across the room as she threw her arms into the air and clasped them as if in prayer.

Manny glanced up from where he crouched on his hands and knees attempting, with a scrap of meat, to bribe the spit dog out from under the table. "Good to see you, Sister."

Alice came around the table, her gait made awkward by her swollen abdomen. "I never thought I'd see you again, Maggie! I thought for sure someone had carried you off!"

Maggie hugged her sister. "Didn't you get my note? I said I was all right."

"I will set him in the safety he panteth for, did say the Lord," Manny quoted as he dove for the little spit dog and brought it up yiping. "Psalm, twelve." The spotted pup whined as it struggled to escape Manny's hold.

Maggie took the spit dog into her arms and smoothed its head, soothing it in a hushed voice. "I'm sorry I frightened you, Alice. I didn't mean to make you worry."

Alice wiped her drawn, perspiration-soaked face with the corner of her apron. "What happened to you? Where did you go?"

Maggie knelt on the hearth and the dog allowed her to hook him into his harness inside the wheel he turned, which rotated the spit over the open fire. She gave the dog one last pat and it began to walk; the ham on the spit began to spin slowly.

"I can't tell you where I've been," she answered finally.

Manny gave a snort as he lifted a pot of steaming turnips off the stove and set them down on the worktable in front of his wife. "I told you she'd not say." He handed Alice a wooden pestle. "Mash, wife. We've hungry men to feed."

Maggie picked up a carrot off the table and took a bite. "I'm a widow, Manny Commegys, I've got a right to come and go as I please."

"A widow too long, I say. An idle woman is the devil's work. My brother Lysias is looking for a new wife. Matilda was buried a good fortnight ago, God rest her soul." He crossed himself and then added, "The ague, they say. She wasn't sick but two days and then she was gone."

"Lysias's looking for a third wife? I wish him good luck." Maggie glanced across the table at her sister. "He's going to need it. The poor soul's got the face of a steer and the mind of a turnip."

Alice giggled and Manny gave her a pinch as he passed behind her. "Hush, wife. You encourage your sister's outrageous behavior."

The sisters looked at each other with an all-knowing glance and then both looked away for fear they'd burst into laughter. "I appreciate your concern for me, Manny," Maggie said, trying to soothe him. "Really I do. But I told you. I'm not looking for a husband."

Manny ran a carving knife over his sharpening stone, making a grinding sound. "Appreciate my concern, do you? Mighty fancy words you're carryin' these days, Maggie Myers. Someone been givin' you talkin' lessons or something?"

"You need help or don't you, Manny?" She dropped a hand to her worn homespun skirt. She'd been tempted to wear one of the day gowns Grayson had bought her, but of course she couldn't. Though she'd brought everything he'd bought her in her new trunks, they would have to remain stored until she went to New York. There would be too many questions if she appeared in a gown like the ones she'd grown fond of wearing at Thayer's Folly.

He tested his sharpened knife, seeming pleased when a drop of blood beaded on his thumb. "The greencoats under the south window, they'll be looking for their apple tarts."

Maggie gave a nod. "I vow I can handle that. Anything else?"

"That and check on that wench Lattice my wife

made me hire. Be certain she's servin' the ale and not drinkin' it."

Alice lifted her masher out of the turnips and shook it at her husband. "You can't expect to make money without spending some, Manuel Commegys!" She glanced back at Maggie, who couldn't hide her surprise at her sister's outburst. Alice went on to explain. "I stood there and I looked at Matilda Commegys bein' lowered into that cold ground in that pine coffin and I said to myself, Alice, that's gonna be you if things don't change. Manny's gonna be lowerin' you into your grave and then he'll be out lookin' for a new wife in a fortnight just like his brother!" She picked up her pestle and began to mash the turnips with a vengeance. "So I made Manny hire that girl. And I told him straight out, after this babe, I get two years' rest. If Father Rufus can vow a lifetime of celibacy for the Lord, Manny Commegys can certainly vow a year or two of celibacy for his wife!"

Maggie looked with round eyes toward Manny who was making an event of chopping carrots for stew. "I . . . I suppose I'll get to those tarts now," she said.

Still smiling at her sister's bold declaration. Maggie went to the pie safe and opened the punched-tin door. The spicy aroma of cinnamon and clove enveloped her as she removed half a dozen plump apple tarts from the dusty, floured shelves and closed the door again. Arranging the tarts on a pewter plate, she lifted it over her head and left the kitchen.

Maneuvering her way through the throng of boisterous enemy soldiers in the public room, Maggie's gaze wandered from face to face. Of course she knew Grayson wasn't here, but she couldn't help herself. Near the cold fireplace she spotted Zeke and the others. She gave a wave and pointed to the tarts, signaling that she'd be right with them.

"Aiee! Here iss the dessert," a round-bellied German soldier exclaimed. "The only question I haf iss, iss the dessert the tarts or the vench!"

Maggie made a face as she slid the plate onto the table. "Be there anything else I can get you?"

The greencoat that spoke English grasped her around the waist. "How about yourself, mine voman with hair of fire?"

When Maggie elbowed him sharply in the ribs, the German gave a grunt. "No? Then I'll be on my way." With a smug grin she turned away from the table and headed for Zeke's.

John slid in to make room for her, his grin broad against his sunburned face. "Christ but it's good to see you, Maggie."

Ed and Les both whipped off their battered felt hats. "We're real sorry 'bout what we did back a few weeks, Maggie. We just thought we was doin' what was right. We didn't know the major was one of us," Les said, lowering his voice, though he didn't have to lower it far. The Scot soldier had wound up his bagpipes again and the sound was nearly deafening.

Maggie offered a smile. "That's all right, boys, because I didn't know, either."

Zeke slid his hand across the table and laid it over Maggie's. "I'm sorry, Mags, for doubting your judgment," he murmured awkwardly, taking back his hand. "I'm just glad to see you safe."

Maggie leaned back against the wall and took a sip from John's leather ale jack. "It's so good to see you, all of you. I missed your ugly faces."

The two Bennett boys blushed and looked away.

"Has the exchange taken place yet?" John asked quietly.

She looked up. "You know about the exchange?"

"We were contacted by Colonel Hastings. He gave us the whole story."

"He's asked for our assistance," Zeke told her proudly.

Maggie folded her hands, choosing her words carefully. She didn't know what they knew of her relationship with Grayson, but it wasn't a matter she wanted to discuss, especially now that it suddenly seemed over. "I was in the camp this afternoon. I went by Gr—the major's tent. I saw Private Michaels who works for him, but I didn't speak. I thought I'd lay low and see what happens."

"Wise decision," John nibbled on a square of cornbread, "for all of us."

"Exactly what did Colonel Hastings say, as far as our involvement?"

"We're to be at the major's disposal. A new round of contacts are being set up."

"To replace Billy Faulkner," Maggie said, looking down at the table. The tune of the bagpipes playing in the background suddenly sounded like a funeral dirge.

John nodded solemnly and the group paused for a moment, as in memorial for the dead patriot. Finally, John spoke again. "Once the major is back in the Brit camp, we were told to contact him."

"How?" She crossed her arms over her chest. "The Brits have sentries around the perimeter of the entire camp. She's sealed up tight as a barrel."

It was Zeke's turn to speak. "We thought that was where you would come in if . . . if you were still willing to work with us after what we done."

"Me?"

"Well, we figured you can still get in and out with your bootmakin', and with you and the major . . ." His dark eyes met hers. "It's up to you, Mags."

She gave a nod, not wanting to go into what had happened between Grayson and her in front of the others. "We'll see, Zeke, once he's in safe."

When Maggie realized Zeke was looking past her as she spoke, she glanced over her shoulder to see who had caught his attention. It was Lyla. She was standing by the stairs, barefoot, dressed in a simple, clean sak dress of pale burgundy. Her gaze was locked with Zeke's.

" 'Scuse me, but I got to be goin'," Zeke said suddenly.

Les Bennett slid off the bench to let Zeke out. "Best watch yourself," he told his longtime friend as Zeke smoothed his queue. "That 'lady' spends more time in the Brit camp than the Brits do."

Zeke limped away, seeming not to hear.

John shook his head. "I don't like to tell a man what to do, but Zeke's playin' with fire."

Maggie glanced at John, not knowing what to say. She wanted to take up for Zeke, for his judgment; on the other hand, she knew about women like Lyla. If she was willing to sell her body to the enemy, wouldn't she be willing to sell secrets as well? Maggie reached for John's ale jack again. "He says we've got nothing to worry about."

Les pulled his three-cornered hat down over his ears. "Just hope the hell he's right," he commented gruffly.

"Maggie!" Manny called from the kitchen doorway, catching Maggie's attention. He had a keg tucked under one arm and a tray of dirty trechers under the other.

She slid off the bench and gave a wave. Coming, Manny." She turned back to the men at the table. "Promised Manny I'd help him and Alice out." She leaned over and whispered, "I figured it was a good way to hear what was happening inside the camp. Sometimes more's said here than there."

John nodded. "Well, go on with you then." He caught her hand and whispered, "We meet tomorrow night, midnight, the hangin' tree off Les and Ed's place."

She nodded and then turned back toward the kitchen, hurrying to help Manny with his burden.

Hours passed and Maggie grew fatigued as she served ale and trechers of food nonstop to the gluttonous soldiers. Her queasy stomach heaved and perspiration saturated her gown as she cleaned off table after table, only to reset them for another group of soldiers waiting outside.

Finally, near midnight, the public room began to thin out. The bagpiper fell unconscious in a drunken stupor and was carried out by several kilted soldiers. To Maggie's relief, the noise level in the public room immediately became more bearable.

"Barmaid," Maggie heard a voice call from behind. "Barmaid," he said a little louder.

Maggie froze in midmotion, her wet dishrag limp in her hand. "That voice . . . it still made her breath catch in her throat. He was safe! Thank the Virgin, he was safe!

"Barmaid! I've waiting nigh on twenty minutes. Have you something for a man with a fierce thirst?" Grayson demanded in his best captain's voice.

Slowly Maggie turned. There he was sitting behind her where he'd not been a moment before, his boots propped cockily on the table's edge. He wore his scarlet uniform all pressed and neat. His cap was tossed carelessly on the trestle table. On his face was the proud, insolent grin of a man who had fooled the enemy and was back in a seat of power.

Maggie came to his table. her dishrag still in hand. She leaned over and began to wipe tip the puddles of ale. "You're still all in one piece," she murmured, pushing his feet off the table. They hit the floor with a thump.

"Safe and sound." He slapped his chest.

When she said nothing, he laid his hand over

hers, to stop her from the motion of cleaning. "Maggie, sweet, I'm sorry for leaving like that."

She slipped her hand out from under his and began to stack several dirty plates and trechers onto a tray on the next table. "You hurt me, Grayson."

"I know." His eyes searched her flushed face as he tried to meet her eyes. "But I'm sorry. We can work this out, I know we can."

"Your idea of workin' it out is for me to go back to Williamsburg."

"I still think that's what's best."

"For who?" She turned to face him, not caring who saw them talking. "For you or for me?"

"For both of us."

She bit down on her lower lip. "The boys will be meeting tomorrow night at the old hanging tree southwest of my place. You know it?"

"Yes. Will you be there?" He tried to catch her around the waist, but she slipped away.

"Of course."

"I don't want you there."

"Of course you don't," she answered, her sarcasm thick.

"It's getting too dangerous."

"Is it that, or are you afraid a woman might show you up?"

"Maggie! What a terrible thing to say! You know better than that. I've already admitted to you that you're a better soldier than I am. But you're still—"

"A woman?"

"The woman I love. The woman I want to protect." He leaned on the table. "I was in a skirmish for the first time in several months yesterday and it scared me, Maggie."

"Sterling said you weren't ready to get back into the fighting."

He grabbed her hand, refusing to let go when she tried to twist away. "It didn't scare me because I was afraid to die," he said fiercely. "It scared me because I saw you. I saw you dying by a stray bullet, a crazed soldier with a bayonet."

"There's worse ways to die," she said, keeping her voice hard and emotionless.

"Ah, Christ, Maggie, listen to us." He kissed her work-worn knuckles. "Is this the way it's always to be?"

"We were raised on different sides of the cornfield," she said quietly. "It's not anyone's fault, it's just the way it is."

"But I don't want it to be that way!" Grayson came to his feet, placing her hand in his on his heart. "I want to fight for you, *and* for this country."

She gave a soft sigh of tentative surrender. "Wait for me outside, Grayson." She took away her hand and began to untie her apron.

He scooped up his grenadier cap.

His eyes searched hers. "Do you love me, Maggie Myers?" he asked.

"I love you," she whispered. Slowly she lowered her lashes and then in a hushed voice whispered, "Outside."

She waited until Grayson was gone and then she

headed for the kitchen. Manny was standing in the doorway.

Maggie handed him her apron. "I'm going home."

Manny eyed the doorway the dashingly handsome redcoat had just exited. "You're not done with the cleanin' up."

"You don't pay me, Manny. I come and go as I please."

"I offered to pay you a hundred times for all you've done for us!"

She smiled up at him, weary. "Why do you think I don't let you pay me." She turned away before he could speak again and gave a wave over her head.

He called after her. "I'm not a man to tell you what to do but—"

"Then don't!" she answered as she stepped out of the tavern and into the arms of her lover.

Chapter Twenty

John Logan raised his hands and a hush fell over the men who gathered beneath the twisted branches of the hangman's tree. A full, waxing moon cast an eerie light over the gathering. Long-fingered shadows thrown across the men's faces altered their features until Maggie wasn't quite certain who was who.

Except of course for Grayson.

She couldn't miss him standing at John's side, waiting in anxious anticipation, his fingers flexing at his sides.

Maggie couldn't help thinking of the way only an hour ago those fingers had played her body like a harp. Arm in arm, limb in limb, they had cried out in mutual pleasure and then Grayson had held her in his arms and again begged her to return to Williamsburg.

"Gentlemen, I'd like to introduce you to Major Grayson Thayer of the First Legionary Corps, but to you of course, he is *Captain* Grayson Thayer, king's soldier."

All eyes were fixed on Grayson. The Bennett boys

lifted their caps and crumbled them in their hands in reverence.

Grayson studied the group, taking note of their tattered clothing and haggard faces as his perceptive blue-eyed gaze moved from one man to the next. "Evening to you," he finally said.

"Evening," the group of a dozen patriots responded.

Maggie tightened the light shawl she wore around her shoulders. *Enough with the dramatics,* she thought. *Get on with it, Grayson.*

"A few of you already know me," Grayson said, allowing a grin to slip across his handsome face. "But I'm willing to forgive on that matter if you are."

Pete chuckled and several men joined in.

"What happened," Grayson went on, "was an unfortunate accident, one we'd all like to put behind us. I've been returned to my redcoat company. The trading of prisoners went off well, and there seem to be no suspicions. Just the same, I want to remind you men how vital it is that my identity remain a secret. You cannot tell wives, lovers, not even your best hunting hound."

Again there was a ripple of laughter. Grayson had put the rebel band at ease. Maggie could hear it in their voices. She could see it in their stances.

"It's my opinion that we're about to make history. We presently have the upper hand at sea and will soon have it on land. Right here on your doorsteps I surmise you'll see an end to this war."

"So what's our part?" Les asked.

Carter took a step forward. "How can we help?"

Grayson swept off his cocked hat. Though he was dressed in the same style as the other men, there was air about him that set him apart from the others. Maggie couldn't resist a proud smile. That man was the father of her unborn child.

"I can't say exactly how I can use you just yet. But I know I'll need you. I'll probably want messengers. And I'll need to know what you're seeing and hearing."

John stroked his chin. "With our men and the French closing in from Williamsburg, how much longer do you think you'll make it out of the camp without being scrutinized?"

"I can't honestly say. The Brits have pretty much taken over Commegys' ordinary. I imagine I'll still be able to get in and out of there for a while."

"Then what?" Chester Cage asked, his pipe bowl glowing in the semidarkness.

"Then I take over."

All heads turned to Maggie, who stood at the rear of the group.

She could see Grayson's jaw tighten. She ignored him. "I see no reason why I won't be able to walk in and out of the Brit camp, even once the shooting starts. I'll go with my boot repairs same as always. That way I can carry the captain-major's messages in and out without suspicion."

Pete hooked his thumbs into the waistband of his blue-striped tick breeches. "And you don't think no one will wonder what you're doin' spendin' so much time with the captain?"

"Before I left there were already rumors about me and Thayer."

Several men dropped their gazes guiltily.

"I just aim to play on those rumors," Maggie went on. "There are other women who seem to come and go without anyone questioning them."

"Never seen anyone stop Lyla," someone said.

Maggie had thought the same but hadn't wanted to say so in front of Zeke. She went on. "You see, the way I figure it, I go into his tent, stay a while, then walk right out with his message, written or otherwise." She finally lifted her gaze to meet Grayson's. He was seething inside; she could see it. But he had the sense to hold his tongue in front of her friends.

"Brave thing to do, Maggie," John said thoughtfully. "But there'll be a certain stigma that goes along with it. You certain you want to carry that burden on your shoulders?"

"Most of the people I care about are standing right here. The others in the town, what's left of them," she shrugged, "they can mind their own business."

"What about your sister and brother-in-law?" Zeke asked.

Maggie couldn't resist a smile. "I can handle Manny Commegys, I'll warrant you. My only problem with him is that he keeps tryin' to marry me off to that pig-snout brother of his."

The men laughed with good humor.

Grayson frowned. "It won't work," he stated flatly.

"Sure it will," she challenged, her eyes narrowing in defiance. "It'll work and you know it."

John looked from Maggie to Grayson and cleared

his throat. "Well, this can be worked out later, Captain. We can't stay here long. The Brits change their patrols nightly. There's just no predicting them anymore." He looked up at the small gathering. "Our next point of business is who's going to Head of Elk? We need a couple of warm bodies and any wagons you can beg, borrow, or steal."

"Head of Elk?" Maggie directed her questions to John. "What are you talking about? Who's going to Head of Elk?"

"Washington's marching his entire army down to Head of Elk, and from there they'll be taking anything that floats through the Chesapeake and down the James. We're getting a group together to transport food, medicine, some clothing. Anything to help. Some of those soldiers have walked hundreds of miles, Maggie. Besides being tired, they got to be hungry and in need of medical attention."

"In need of having their boots repaired I'd say," Maggie commented pragmatically. "I'll go." It was a split-second decision, but the moment the words came out of her mouth, Maggie knew it was the right thing to do.

Grayson shot her a threatening glare, shaking his head ever so slightly.

There he goes again, Maggie thought. *Thinking he can tell me what to do!*

John smiled. "Why did I know you'd be my first volunteer?"

She smiled back. "I've got a horse. My wagon's got a broken axle, but maybe—"

"We'll take care of that broken axle," Les offered. "Me and Ed."

"We leave tomorrow night after sunset. Those of you who are willing to go, I can provide you with the details."

Zeke pulled his pocket watch out of his vest and tapped the face. "Time, John. We'd best scoot."

John held up a hand. "All right, men. And lady," he amended. "The only other business we've got tonight is one I've mulled over several weeks before finally deciding to bring it up."

When there was a several second pause, Pete finally broke the silence. "Cat got your tongue, John? Get on with it."

John sighed, suddenly seeming older. "You're all aware that we've had a string of bad luck lately. The question is, is it luck we're dealing with here, or something else?"

"You sayin' we got a rat among us?" Les murmured, fingering the polished stock of his flintlock.

"No." John held up his palms in defense. "I'm not saying that. What I'm saying is we all need to watch what we talk about. I know it's hard keeping this all bottled up inside, not being able to share it with your wives or children. But it's *vital* that we keep silent. Even more vital now that the end is approaching."

"Loose tongue, you say?" Pete gazed at the men standing around him as he slowly sank his fist into his palm. "Guess I'd best not find out who it is."

"Now, Pete," John said. "I didn't tell you all this to cause unrest among us. I just wanted you to be aware of the situation. I want you to watch your tongues, and watch your backs. Now go on." He gave a wave. "Go home and get some sleep. I'll pass the word around tomorrow as to where we'll be gathering the supplies for Head of Elk and where we'll be leaving from."

The small crowd of men broke and scattered to the winds like the autumn leaves that would soon fall. Zeke came to Maggie. "You want me to walk you home, Mags? I know how you hate cuttin' through the Devil's Woodyard after the bewitchin' hour," he teased.

"No. That won't be necessary," Grayson said, stepping up to Maggie's side.

Maggie looked up into Zeke's face and impulsively reached up to stroke his hollow, beard-stumbled cheek. She hated to see him overwrought with worry like this. "I'll be all right," she murmured. "Go on home with you."

"You certain?" he whispered. Grayson stood behind him, towering over him, but Zeke stood his ground.

She forced a smile. "I'm certain."

Zeke gave a sigh, but stepped out of Grayson's way. Grayson waited to speak until the other men were out of earshot.

"What the hell are you talking about? You're going to Head of Elk?"

Maggie rolled her eyes heavenward and then spun around and started down a path toward him. Grayson strode directly behind her. "Well?"

"Well what? You've got soldiers who've been marching for weeks. Anybody with any sense would be able to figure out that those men are going to need their boots repaired. I've even got a few pairs started. If I could get to work, some poor soldier might get a new pair."

Angrily, Grayson grasped her arm and spun her around. "You can't go to Head of Elk, Maggie."

She pushed his hand aside. "I can go," she answered stubbornly. "I can go and I will go if that's where our men need me!"

Changing tactics, he softened his voice. "Look, sweetheart, I understand you want to do something for our men, but it's not safe. You could all be wiped out two miles from here."

"I'll take my chances just like you take yours."

He struck himself in the forehead with the heel of his hand. "What is it Maggie? What is it that makes you want to go out and get yourself killed? What are you running from? Me?"

It was her turn to grow angry. "Running? Who's running? I'm not running. I'm going to Head of Elk because they need me." She spun back around and stomped off down the moonlit game path.

"So maybe they do need you," he said, following in her footsteps. "But I still say you're running, you're running from me."

"That's ridiculous!"

"You're afraid."

"I'm not afraid."

"You're afraid to let me love you. You're afraid to let me take care of you the way you deserve to be taken care of."

"I'm my own woman," she countered. "I don't need you, I don't need anyone."

He stopped on the path. "Sure you do, Maggie. Everyone needs someone. It's taken me a long time to figure that out."

She stopped, her back still to him. There was a long pause filled with the night sounds of crickets chirping and rustling leaves before she finally turned to speak. "You don't understand."

He came to her, clasping her hands tight in his. "Make me understand!"

She shook her head, turning her face away. "We're fools to think this could ever work between us. We'd spend the rest of our lives butting heads!"

His eyes were riveted to hers. "So why'd you come back? Why didn't you run off to New York like you'd intended?"

She shook her head. *The baby,* she thought. *Because I wanted more for our baby. I told myself I was coming to see you before you were killed, but I was lying. I lied to you and to myself. I wanted to make it work between us, but I don't know how.*

"Maggie." He brushed a lock of hair off her cheek. "Don't you understand, I'm not trying to control you, only keep you safe so that when this blasted war is over, we can make a life together."

"You could have stayed in Williamsburg! I'd have stayed with you! I might even have married you right then and there!"

A lump rose in Grayson's throat until he could barely speak. "You know I had to come back." He draped his arm over her shoulder and they started down the dark path again. "You know why. I thought you understood."

"I do." She nodded. "So why can't you understand why I have to go to Head of Elk?"

Grayson looked away. "Ah, Christ, Maggie. Do

you feel like we're going round and round in circles?"

She had to laugh. "It seems like there's nothing right between us except beneath the sheets."

"No." He hugged her against him with the arm he left on her shoulder. "That's not true. I suppose we're just two strong people. I think I'm right, you think you're right."

"I *know* I'm right," she corrected.

Grayson brushed back a low-hanging branch off the side of the path. Behind it stood his horse, Giipa, waiting patiently. "Come back to camp with me tonight." He caught the horse's reins and stepped light into his saddle.

Maggie hugged her shawl. "I don't want to argue with you anymore. Not tonight, Grayson. I'm too worn."

He held his hand out to her. "So just come and lay with me. Let me hold you in my arms."

Maggie knew she should go home to her own bed, but the thought of spending another night with Grayson was too tempting. "You swear you won't say anything of Head of Elk, or going back to Williamsburg?"

He raised his right arm. "I swear."

With a sigh she slipped her foot into his stirrup and allowed him to help her into the saddle in front of him. Once settled, he backed Giipa out of the hedge and turned toward the British camp.

Cornwallis' camp, now perched on the York Peninsula, was well guarded this night. A sentry allowed Grayson to pass, making no comment on the woman who rode in his lap.

Reining in in front of his private tent, the young boy Michaels appeared sleepily at the tent flap. "Captain?"

Grayson jumped out of the saddle and helped Maggie down. "Take Giipa and see that he's watered," he said, tossing the private the reins.

"Yes, sir. Um . . . I've got some messages for you." He ground the toe of his polished boots into the dusty earth.

Grayson glanced at Maggie and then back to Michaels. "Well enough. Then I'll walk you over."

He caught Maggie's hand. "Go on in and pour us a glass of Madeira. I'll be back directly." He winked, a boyish grin on his face and then walked off, allowing Michaels to lead his horse.

But instead of going inside the tent, Maggie stood staring up at the heavenly canopy of stars that hung over the British camp. Tonight they seemed so close that she thought she might be able to stretch on her tiptoes and pluck one out of the sky. She wondered if the stars were shining down this brightly on the patriots at Head of Elk. Would God's grace be with the Colonists when they met the strongest army on earth? Or did God keep out of the business of war, ashamed by mankind's bitter struggles?

"A nice evening tonight," Maggie heard a man say.

She looked up to see Riker standing only a few feet from her, his ever-present smirk visible in the moonlight.

"A fine night indeed," she responded.

"So our Captain Thayer is safe in our bosom again, is he?"

"He arrived today."

Riker nodded. "Doing a little celebrating then, are we, Maggie the bootmaker?"

Maggie lifted her lashes, her gaze meeting his with icy insolence. "You've trouble with that, Lieutenant?"

He raised his index finger, the threat plain in his voice. "Watch your step, missy. I've eyes and ears everywhere. I don't know what game it is you and Thayer play, but I'm on to you."

"Why Grayson?" she asked. "You could ruin his career with the lies you pass around this camp."

Riker took two long strides, bringing his index finger firmly under her chin. "He made a fool of me in front of my uncle, the major, on more than one occasion. No one makes a fool of me and gets away with it."

Maggie slapped his hand away.

"Besides," he said with a shrug, "I'm merely keeping an eye on my fellow officers as we all must do."

Before Maggie could come up with a reasonable reply, Riker had disappeared into the shadows of the sleeping camp. A moment later Grayson returned. He put his arm around her and led her into his tent, lacing it up behind him.

"What's the matter, sweet? You look as if you've seen a ghost."

She glanced up at him, her eyes searching his. She just couldn't shake the chill of ominous fear that enveloped her. "Riker."

He scowled. That pettifogging cur. He's all bark."

"Please tell me you'll be careful, Grayson," she said desperately. She stroked his jaw with her fingertips. "Please . . ."

He took her into his arms, and held her tightly. His lips met hers in a soft, sensual caress and she squeezed her eyes shut against the fear that welled in her heart.

"It's going to be all right," he whispered. "Just trust me. I'm going to make it all right, Maggie mine."

The rain fell at a steady pace, casting a gray haze across the darkening sky. Rain was good on a night like this; it would aid the patriots in their escape from Yorktown. With rain falling and a chill in the air, sentries would be lax. Soldiers would be less likely to stop a passing farmer in a rickety wagon.

With her two-wheeled cart loaded and covered by a tarp and then horse dung to disguise its true contents, Maggie stepped back, giving herself a nod of approval. To a passing soldier, she would look like a woman hauling manure. A man would have to dig deep to find the squash and bags of grain she'd hidden in the bottom of the wagon.

Smiling to herself, she glanced up at the dark sky and lifted the hood of her old woolen cloak. It was time to meet the others. She crouched and gave a pat on the head to each of her dogs. "Good boy, Roy," she soothed. "Good three-legged dog!"

Honey whined and pushed her head under Maggie's hand. Maggie laughed. "Yes, and that's a good girl, Honey. Good Honey. Now you mind the place and keep the coons out of the kitchen. Zeke'll be over to feed you."

When she walked to the hitched wagon, the hounds followed. "No. Sit, Honey. Sit, Roy."

The dogs obeyed and Maggie hoisted herself up onto the narrow bench. As she lifted the reins, she took one last look at her clabbard farmhouse. She had thought Grayson would come to say good-bye. But when she'd left his tent early this morning, he'd said nothing of her traveling to Head of Elk, so she'd said nothing. She wondered, once her work was done at Head of Elk, if she should just keep moving north. Would it be better that way for both of them? She thought of her unborn child. All of them?

With a heavy sigh, Maggie clicked to her horse and rolled out of the drive and down the road.

Not half an hour later she met up with the others. John was there as well as Les and two other men she didn't recognize. John introduced them as farmers from the next county over and she nodded a greeting. John set the wet patriots to the task of taking an inventory of the supplies they would carry to the troops. They laughed at Maggie's clever manner of hiding her food and leather goods, thinking it a great joke on the English. As they counted the bags of flour and items of clothing, they found themselves pleased at the amount of food and medical supplies they had been able to acquire. The citizens of Yorktown and the surrounding areas had been generous. It seemed everyone had contributed something, no matter how poor they might have been. Women had gone into their cellars and dug out hidden baskets of potatoes and turnips meant for their own children and offered it freely. Men had taken the patched coat off their own backs in the hopes that one of Washington's brave soldiers might keep warm on a cold night.

John clapped his hand after he had tabulated the items in the four wagons. "If you're ready to go, I think it best we move on and cover as much distance as we can tonight," he told the huddled group. "The rain will cover our tracks and hopefully serve as a blanket to shield us from the enemy."

With a nod, the rebels climbed into their wagons. John took the lead on horseback. They were not half a mile away when they heard the sound of hoofbeats on the muddy path. With no place to pull off the road, the wagons came to a halt and everyone reached for the rifles beneath their seats. Maggie, who brought up the tail of the assemblage, stood and aimed her flintlock on the center of the narrow woods path. As the rider came into view, she cocked her hammer.

"Wait! Wait!" a familiar voice called.

Maggie immediately lowered her rifle. "Grayson?" She squinted. The rain came down in angular sheets making it difficult to see.

"Maggie! John!" the rider called. He was dressed in a black cloak with a large cocked hat pulled down over his head to conceal his face. "Wait! It's Grayson Thayer!"

John squeezed his horse by the wagons. "Thayer! What the hell are you doing out here? It's a hell of a night to be wishing a man good-bye."

Maggie could resist a smile as she lowered her rifle below the wagon seat where it would stay reasonable dry. Grayson had come to say good-bye to her!

Grayson rode up beside Maggie's two-wheeled cart, but spoke directly to John Logan. "Didn't come to wish you well; I came to offer my services as escort."

Maggie pushed back the hood of her cloak so that she could see Grayson better. "An escort? But how did you get out of the camp? You'll be named a deserter by morning!"

He shook his head, grinning. "No. It's Aunt Moriah. The woman who raised me. She's sick. Very sick. I have to get to New Castle, Delaware, right away."

Maggie flashed him a sassy smile. "You haven't got an Aunt Moriah!"

John chuckled as he offered his hand. "Glad to have you along," he said, clasping Grayson's gloved hand.

"Glad to be of service, sir," he told the older man respectfully.

Still shaking his head, John rode back to the front of the wagon train and waved them forward.

Grayson rode beside Maggie for several minutes in silence. First he looked at her and then looked away. Then she looked at him, turning her face before he looked back.

Suddenly both of them broke into laughter. "I can't believe the major let you just ride out!"

"Well, it seems the major's got family there." He patted his chest. "I've letters I'm supposed to deliver. I thought I'd just put them in a mailbag once we get to Head of Elk. Surely *someone* must be headed for New Castle."

She giggled. "Secrets in those letters, mayhap."

"I doubt it." He adjusted his hat so that the rain ran off it, keeping his face dry. "Most likely complaints of his gout and the poor food." He winked at her. "Just the same, I thought we'd best read them."

They laughed again, their voices mingling in the dark, wet night. Riding directly beside her, Grayson reached out and took her hand. "Ah, Maggie. Don't you see? I can't live without you. I'm mad in love with you."

She smiled, savoring the feel of her hand in his. "I'm glad you came," she whispered.

Chapter Twenty-one

In early September the columns of General Washington's rebel army reached Head of Elk, Maryland. Exhausted but in high spirits, the soldiers set up camp on the banks of the Chesapeake Bay and patiently waited their turn to board a vessel bound for Virginia.

Though there was an overwhelming shortage of boats, Washington was not to be beaten. He ordered his officers to round up every schooner, open barge, and dilapidated ferry they could find. The plan was to transport the army across the Chesapeake and down the James River. Boatload after boatload of soldiers, some who had walked half the continent to get to Head of Elk, boarded vessels and joined their fellow soldiers under Lafayette, Wayne, and St. Simon in the camps that surrounded Williamsburg. From Williamsburg, Washington intended to march his army southeast to Yorktown and defeat Cornwallis's army, trapped on the York peninsula.

The evening that Maggie rode into the patriot

camp she was immediately taken by the calm order of it all. There seemed to be a certain peacefulness that hung like a canopy over these weary soldiers.

As Maggie rolled past the neat lines of canvas tents she stared out at the men who moved about, cooking sparse evening meals over communal fires and making repairs to their weapons. Again and again, men nodded respectfully as she drove by in her two-wheeled cart.

She couldn't help making comparisons between the British camp in Yorktown and this patriot camp. The British encampment had become a quarrelsome place after weeks of idleness. These Colonials seemed thankful for a respite from the wages of war. Their camp was orderly, the men quiet, but not sullen. They were biding their time.

"Evening, ma'am," a boy of no more than fifteen called as he ladled gruel onto a wooden trencher and handed it to his companion.

"Pretty thing," a tall sergeant with "Freedom or Death" emblazoned across his brown-fringed tunic mused as Maggie passed.

"Holy Mary," Maggie sighed so that only Grayson, who rode beside her, could hear. "They're all so thin! They're starving to death, Grayson."

Grayson nodded a greeting to a soldier who squatted by his campfire. "Not starving, just lean," he told her. "Starvation won't come until winter." Still, it tugged at his heartstrings to see his fellow soldiers dressed in buckskin tunics, their moccasined feet bound in rags while he wore German boots and a clean muslin shirt. It had been too long since he last spent a night or two among his own kind. This trip would do him good to remind him of who he fought for, while living in the midst of the British army.

"Oh, Grayson," Maggie murmured as she pulled up the reins and her wagon rolled to a halt. "Go on ahead without me, I'll catch up," she called to John who was leading the train of wagons further into the camp where the headquarters were set up. She snapped back the brake and jumped to the ground. Grayson reined in his horse, his gaze following hers.

Stretched out in front of a tent was a red-haired man with a clipped red beard and mustache. Lying on his side, he cradled his head in his arm as another soldier unwrapped bloodied rags that bound his feet.

Maggie dug beneath her wagon seat and pulled out a canvas bag containing tins of homemade salve and rolls of bandages the women of Yorktown had sewn.

Grayson's eyes glimmered with pride as he watched Maggie approach the patriot soldiers and kneel.

"Let me look at that," she said softly, pushing aside the friend's hands.

"Ma'am?"

"I said, let me do it. But I'll need you to heat me some water, *clean* water."

The soldier crouched frozen for a moment, in disbelief. "Why, you're . . . you're a female woman!"

Maggie pushed her cloak off her shoulders, letting her bright-red hair fall in waves down her back as she tied it back with a green ribbon from her pocket. "That I am, soldier. Now fetch the water while I'll have a look at your friend's feet." That matter dealt with, she turned her attention back to the injured man. Her gaze met his; he had the clearest green eyes she'd ever seen.

"I dinna realize they were so puir till I came into camp this morning," he apologized, attempting to sit up.

She laid her hand on his arm. "Just lie back and let me have a look."

He eased back until his head rested on his arm again.

"So, where're you from, soldier?" She began to carefully unwrap the blood-encrusted bandages.

"Walked from somewhere in New York, but my home be down on the York River."

"You don't say!" She bit down on her lower lip as the ill smell of rotting flesh accosted her. She nearly had his left foot unwrapped. "I live in Yorktown! I have a brother-in-law that runs Commegys' Ordinary. You know it?"

"Ken it!" he swore excitedly. "I drank many a pint at Commegys' Ordinary a'fore this blasted war!"

"The name's Maggie Myers." She offered one hand and he clasped it warmly.

"Rob Campbell, ma'am, Lieutenant Rob Campbell."

She paused. "Rob Campbell?" The name rang in her ears. How did she know a Rob Campbell? Why was the name familiar? Suddenly it came to her, and she broke into a sly smile. "You wouldn't happen to know a lady by the name of Elizabeth, would you?"

His eye lit up. "My Liz? You know my bonny Liz?"

Trying not to cringe at the sight of Rob's swollen and bloody bare foot, she set aside the foul bandages and started on the other foot. "Know her! She lives not a mile from me! She loaned me a dress to wear to a bull roast this summer." Maggie's eyes suddenly went wide. "Rob, you've got to get home. Elizabeth's near her time."

He bolted up. "Her time?" His face lit up excitement. "The lass is with child!"

Maggie began to unwrap his right foot as quickly as she could. "Grayson," she called.

He walked over from the next campfire where he'd been speaking to several Virginians. "What do you need, Maggie?"

"You've got to get John here. This is Rob Campbell, Elizabeth's husband."

Rob offered his hand. "John's here?"

"We brought some food and medical supplies." Grayson clasped his hand in goodwill. "The name's Grayson Thayer."

Rob glanced up at him, taking in his neat appearance and shined boots. "You're nay a fighting mon?"

"It's a long story, Rob, but I'm a Virginian, same as you and one of Washington's army, same as you."

Rob gave a nod. "I dinna mean to offend. It's

just wi' my boy's wi' no decent coat wi' winter coming, I nay like to see a mon in fancy clothes."

Grayson looked at Rob's feet. "Where's your boots, Rob Campbell?"

The redheaded man grinned. "Left them in the Jerseys on some rutted road!" He laughed at his own joke and Grayson laughed with him.

"You're in luck, Rob, because I've got a lady here who just might be able to help you with that. What do you think, Maggie?"

"Got a pair of boots in my wagon. A few stitches here and there and you'll be in luck." She winked. "Just let me get these feet cleaned up."

Rob shook his head. "I juist canna believe my Liz is going to give me a bairn." His eyes teared. "The lass dinna say a word in the last letter I got back in July."

"I'm certain she didn't want to worry you," Maggie said as she tore a strip of clean bandage and dipped it into the hot water Rob's friend had brought. "Now this is gonna smart a bit, Rob, but I got to get the flesh clean else your feet are gonna fall off at your ankles."

"Just do it, lass. I maun speak to my commanding officer to see aboot leave if I'm to be there when my own bairn comes into this blessed world."

Grayson patted Rob on the shoulder. "I'll leave you in Maggie's capable hands and find John. I'm certain arrangements can be made to get you home ahead of the fighting if only for a day or two's time."

"I willna forget your kindness," Rob answered

solemnly. Just let me know if there's anything Rob Campbell can do for you."

Maggie dipped her clean rag into the hot water and applied it to the bottom of Rob's foot. "For now, friend, you can just lie back and hold still!"

The Scott laughed, but laid back, waving to Grayson as he walked away.

It was near midnight before Maggie finally settled down on a horse blanket in front of a blazing campfire. Grayson pushed a tin cup of coffee into her hand and hugged her against him. "You must be exhausted."

She nodded, taking note that he'd been drinking. She could smell the liquor on his breath. She sipped her coffee, wondering why it upset her to think that Grayson had shared a mug of grum—an awful homemade concoction—with another soldier. What man didn't partake on occasion? Still, it irritated her.

She took another sip of the weak, bitter coffee and rubbed the back of her neck to ease the tension. "I am tired, but it feels good to do something worthwhile," she said to Grayson, then pointed to a pile of boots just outside the circle of firelight. "And *see,* I told you our men would be in need of my services. There's not a decent boot in this camp."

John Logan entered the firelight and sat down across from Grayson and Maggie, reaching for the coffeepot. Les was right behind him. "I can't believe you found Rob! I thought there was one chance in a million of finding him among the thousands that are passing through here!"

"Is his commanding officer going to let him go home?" Maggie asked.

"He didn't take too readily to the idea. He was afraid every soldier in this camp would be wanting a few days' leave, but I think I convinced him this was a special situation. Rob Campbell's been a faithful soldier and a superior leader in his company. He's stayed in long after his enlistment was up. If I promise his major I can get Rob home and then back to his company by the time they make Yorktown, I think we've got ourselves a deal."

Maggie smiled, suddenly lost in her own thoughts. Rob was going to be home when Elizabeth's baby was born, or at least shortly after. Where would Grayson be when *their* child was born?

"Fine man, Rob Campbell" John remarked. "Did you know he came to us as a bondman? He was our overseer for years."

Grayson stirred the coals with a charred stick. "A bondman?"

"Seems he was a political prisoner in Scotland. When his service was up he stayed on with us. Married Elizabeth before he went off to New York to fight in '77."

Maggie leaned forward, hugging her knees. "Your sister married a bondman?"

"I said he wasn't bound when they married."

"You don't care that your sister married a man

who once worked your fields?" Maggie asked, scrutinizing John curiously.

"What mattered to me was the man. That's what this new country of ours is about, isn't it? Men and women being judged on their own merit? The social classes of Mother England are falling away before our very eyes."

Grayson took Maggie's hand, turning it in his. "We could be a part of that change if you married me, sweet Maggie."

She looked into his eyes. Was it Grayson who spoke, or the alcohol? His words always seemed to turn sweeter after a drink or two. She stood and said good night, then walked to where she'd laid out a blanket to sleep on. Several soldiers whose boots she'd repaired had offered her their tent, but she wanted to sleep here under the stars tonight.

Grayson said his good nights and followed her, stretching out on the blanket beside her. "What is it, Maggie?" he whispered. "Are you angry with me?"

She rolled onto her side, away from him. "Just tired," she murmured. "Go to sleep."

Grayson sighed, muttering something about feminine moods and then rolled into his blanket and closed his eyes.

When Grayson woke in the early morning, he saw that Maggie was gone. Spotting her near the fire that had been left to burn through the night, he got up and went to sit beside her.

She sat cross-legged on the cool ground, a boot in her lap as she attempted to thread a needle with coarse thread. It was still dark out, the purple shades of night just beginning to lighten as the September dawn began to break.

"What are you doing?" Grayson asked.

She didn't look up. She hadn't slept more than an hour or so last night. Her mind had just been too filled with thoughts to sleep. "I thought I'd get an early start," she answered him. "John said we can only stay another day and then we've got to be off if we're going to take one of the barges to Williamsburg with the men."

Grayson watched her for a moment and then took the boot from her. "Show me," he said.

She looked up. "What?"

"Show me, Maggie. Two can sew twice as many pairs of boots as one."

She couldn't resist a smile. "You're serious."

"Entirely. You're right. What these men need most is decent shoes and boots to carry them into battle. We've got food enough, and there's even a sufficient amount of black powder for once, but everyone's shoes are rotting off their feet."

She shrugged. "It's simple enough if you remember to keep the thread tight." She slipped the needle into his fingers and guided his hand. "I'm just repairing rotted seams so there's no need to punch new holes. It just in and out, in and out. You should knot between each stitch, but I'm afraid if I knot, there won't be enough thread to last."

Grayson sewed two more stitches on the side

seam and held it out to check his work. "I just might make a better bootmaker than you," he teased.

Maggie retrieved a pair of boots that were missing soles from her pile and sat down to cut out new ones. "No one's better than me, except my da, and he's dead."

Grayson lifted an eyebrow. "I have to say, you didn't do such a fine job on *my* boots, Maggie. You fixed the loose sole, but then the seam started rubbing my left heel. They wore such a blasted blister on my heel that I had to wear my old boots."

She lowered her head to trace a sole onto a square of the leather with a small knife. "Another blister? You don't say? Well, once we get back to Yorktown you'll have to let me get a look at it. You must have busted an inside seam."

Grayson was quiet for several minutes as he concentrated on sewing, but then he spoke again. "Maggie, did it ever bother you knowing that the English shoes and boots you sewed carried those soldiers into battle to kill our men? I mean, I understand you did it so that you could get into the camp, but—"

Maggie began to laugh.

"What's so funny?"

She looked up at him, an impish grin on her face. "Want to know a secret, Captain-Major?"

He narrowed his eyes, leaning toward her to steal a kiss. "Secrets are my business, love."

She kissed him and then pulled back, returning to her work. "Those boots I sewed for all of those men passing through Yorktown and then the ones in the camps . . ."

"Yes . . ."

"Well, I can't say I did my finest work on them."

"You didn't do you finest work? What are you saying, Maggie?"

She giggled. "What I'm saying is I didn't exactly *fix* their boots. I just made them *look* like they were fixed."

He stared at her incredulously. "You did what?"

She shrugged. "I sewed their blasted boots, but only so they could get on their merry way. I wager a week or so down the road there was more than one or two redcoats with blisters on their heels and loose soles."

Grayson burst into laughter, his rich tenor voice echoing in the chill morning air. "You sabotaged their boots. You're priceless, Maggie Myers. Priceless! Only a woman would be so ingenious!"

Maggie just smiled to herself and went on with her work, but secretly she was pleased that Grayson approved of what she'd done. She might not have been educated by fancy tutors, but she had a brain just the same as Grayson did, and damned if she couldn't use it when she wanted to!

All day and into the night Maggie and Grayson worked side by side repairing the seams and patching the soles of soldiers' boots. Word spread quickly that there was a real bootmaker with thread and needle among the ragtag army and soon the line of anxious men stretched beyond her vision through the rows of tents. Maggie was comfortable with the soldiers. She laughed and talked with them as she repaired their boots as best she could, making life more pleasant for the lonely soldiers, if only for a brief time. It was not until Grayson came for her near dawn the following day that she finally laid down her needle and thread.

"Maggie, the barge is loaded," Grayson told her gently. "We have to go if we're to get Rob back to Yorktown."

Maggie looked at Grayson and then at the seventeen-year-old, Joshua O'Banyon, from Massachusetts who stood beside her, holding a pile of rotten leather that had once been his shoes. She shook her head sadly. "There's nothin' I can do for you, Josh. I haven't got a scrap of leather left and . . . and there's nothing I can do with that." She indicated the sodden leathers in his hands.

Josh gave her a bright smile. "That's all right, ma'am. I'll just put 'em back on my feet and wrap 'em with a few strips of cloth. Be good as new. Honest."

Not knowing anything else to say, Maggie gave a nod and turned away. "Good night, Josh."

"Good night, ma'am. Safe journey."

Grayson took her arm and led her down toward the water's edge where the barge waited. "Cuts you in two to see boys like that, doesn't it?" he mused.

Maggie rested her head on his shoulder. "He looks too young to grow a beard stubble, but he's determined. They're all so determined. They think they can win, shoes on their feet or no. I only hope they're right."

Grayson came to a halt and pointed toward lanternlight that glimmered off the still water on the shore. "John and the others are waiting."

"Where're you going?" She laid a hand on his shoulder. "I thought you said the barge was about to push off."

"I'll be right back."

"Where you going?"

Grayson walked away, calling over his shoulder. "Just something I have to take care of, sweet. Don't worry. Get aboard and I'll catch up."

Still confused, Maggie made her way to the rickety barge that rested low in the water beneath the weight of soldiers and cannon and there she waited for Grayson. The mooring lines were just being lifted when she spotted him by the dim light of the glowing lanterns sprinting toward the barge. As burly sailors poled the vessel off the bank, Grayson leaped for the deck and in the pale, golden light Maggie saw that he was in his stocking feet.

Chapter Twenty-two

Zeke whistled between his teeth as he walked along the dirt road, his hands stuffed in his pockets. It was twilight, that strange time between day and night when dark shadows lengthened in the forest and strange sounds rose out of the mist that hovered above the humus ground. Zeke picked up his pace as he entered Devil's Woodyard. He'd certainly never heard the devil chopping his wood as he passed through this section of the forest as others had. Just the same, he whistled a little louder. Zeke wasn't a superstitious man, but he wasn't a fool who invited trouble, either.

Zeke checked his pocket watch as he rounded a bend in the road. It was seven-thirty. He had plenty of time to pass by Pete's blacksmith shop and still meet Lyla at eight-thirty in the churchyard. He smiled beneath his whiskers. She'd promised to pack a picnic supper. Wouldn't that be something to sit in the grass and eat with Miss Lyla! Zeke could barely contain his excitement. The longer he knew

Lyla, the more he liked her. Like . . . hell, it was more than that. He was downright in love with her. The thing was, Zeke didn't know just what he was going to do about the matter, but he was thinking hard on it.

Zeke came out of the woods and entered the crossroad at Commegys' Ordinary. He tipped his felt cocked hat in Mistress Wilberry's direction.

"A good evening to you, Zeke Barnes," the rotund, elderly woman called as she passed in her pony cart.

"A good even' to you, ma'am," he countered, veering left as the pony cart squeaked by.

Pete Clendaniels's smithy shop was located directly across from Commegys' Ordinary. Zeke walked up the slightly inclined driveway and waved to Mary Perkins, Carter's wife, who was just going up the steps to visit with Pete's wife. Zeke noticed Mary was heavy with child again and couldn't help wondering if he himself would ever father a son or daughter.

Mary stopped on the steps. "Good to see you, Zeke. It's been a while. Why haven't you been over for supper? The boys miss you."

Zeke swept off his battered hat, blushing slightly. Despite the hard life as a poor farmer's wife, Mary Perkins was still a pretty woman with a cap of dark curls and a comely face. When she smiled, her cheeks dimpled.

"Haven't been asked as of late," Zeke answered her honestly.

Mary scowled. "I don't know what's gotten into that husband of mine. He never invites anyone home these days. I have to practically boot him out the door to get him to go bring his father over for a decent meal!"

"How is Harry? I heard he was feelin' poorly with his gout."

"Pshaw!" Mary fluttered a small hand reddened by the strong lye soap she used to wash the laundry she brought in to make extra cash. "You know Harry. Nothin' keeps him down for long. He hobbled all the way up to our house two nights ago wantin' to know how I made a custard. Thought he'd try one himself."

Zeke gave a nod as he pushed his hat back on his head. "Harry's a tough bird, I'll give him that."

"Well, go on with you." Mary absently stroked her round belly. "The other men are already inside the barn. I don't want them sayin' an old hag kept you."

Zeke grinned, pulling his hat down over his head. "Wouldn't never say that, Mary." He touched his brim and turned away. "A good even' to you."

Mary laughed as she made her way across the porch to the front door. "Same to you, Zeke."

Zeke passed the glowing pit of coals Pete used to heat the iron he bent to his will to make horseshoes, wagon wheels, and the like. His young freckle-faced apprentice was busy putting away tools. Zeke walked into the open barn. Pete, Carter, and Edwin stood in a semicircle looking over a new cow Pete had purchased from a farming family fleeing Yorktown in anticipation of battle.

"Hey there!" Zeke called. "What you boys up to asides trouble?"

Pete grinned. He had discarded his blacksmith's leather apron, but his sleeves were still pushed up and a thin sheen of perspiration covered his face. He'd obviously just laid aside his blacksmith's tools, calling an end to the workday. "Hell's bells, Zeke! We been waitin' on you half an hour. Where you been?"

"Been!" Ed exclaimed. "I can tell you where he's been. I passed the river not more than an hour ago and there's Zeke, broad daylight, takin' a bath. Even had soap!"

Edwin chuckled. A tall, slender man with graying temples, he was the quieter of the two bachelor Bennett boys, but Zeke liked him just the same. "Sounds serious to me."

Pete patted the rump of his new spotted cow. "Bathin' and it not even' bein' a Saturday?" He gave a low whistle. "Sounds like Zeke's goin' prowlin' tonight. Gonna catch him a piece a tail, I'd surmise!"

The men snickered. Zeke's face reddened beneath his beard as he limped toward his friends, but he refused to let them bait him. What went on between him and Lyla was no one's business but his and Lyla's. The fact that he'd done nothing more than timidly hold her hand was beside the point. He wasn't discussing Lyla with these crude men and that was final. "We got business, or did you three hens just call me in for a peckin'?"

Pete gave Zeke a playful push in the shoulder. "Have we got business, you say? Damned straight we got business! Got better than business!" He broke into a wide-toothed grin. "We got ourselves a bag of Brit dispatches bound for New York. It seems our General Cornwallis is gettin' a little antsy stuck out on yonder peninsula. Seems he's lookin' for a little relief by way of the Chesapeake."

Zeke swore softly beneath his breath. "How the hell did you manage to capture dispatches?"

Pete hooked his thumb. "Would you believe Edwin here found the sack lyin' on the floor of the tavern?"

"Should have told 'em I killed a score and ten of greencoats for it," Ed said dryly. "Would've made a better tale."

Zeke crammed his hands into his pockets like he always did when he needed to think. "What makes you think some bloodyback didn't leave you those dispatches on purpose?"

"Because an hour later six soldiers come marchin' up the road lookin' for the bag. They turned over tables. Poured out a fresh-tapped keg of ale on the floor and threatened to cut off Manny's balls if he didn't tell them who had taken the bag," Pete answered for Ed.

"So where was Ed through all of this?"

"He brought the bag of dispatches to me and hiked back across to the tavern."

"Just pretended I was dead drunk, passed out," Ed said with a shrug.

"Didn't need to do much of an actin' job with that, did you?" Carter asked, sinking his elbow into Ed's side.

Ed pushed him away. "I wanted to see if anyone came back for 'em."

"Manny all right?" Zeke asked.

Pete nodded. "They didn't hurt him. Just shoved him around a little. You know Manny. He kept up a steady tongue quotin' the good Lord. Always got an answer for everything. I think the soldiers thought he was touched in the head. They left madder than hornets, threatenin' to put us all into the service of Georgie's navy. I stood right outside this door and watched 'em go."

Zeke ground his boot into the hard-packed dirt of the barn floor. "So what do we do with the dispatches? Wait for John and Major Thayer to get back from Head of Elk?"

"This information is too hot to wait on, I'd say. There's men in Williamsburg who need this information. I'd guess Washington'll be there soon." Pete rolled down his sleeves and pulled the drawstrings of his cuffs. "I think I can make arrangements to have a messenger pick up the dispatches by dawn."

Zeke glanced at Carter, who had a strange look on his face. "What do you think, friend?"

Carter spat a wad of tobacco on the ground. Pete glared at him. Most people had enough manners not to spit in a man's barn. "I . . . I think whatever you all think. Thinkin's not my business. I just do as I'm told."

Zeke gave a nod and turned back to Pete. "You're going to have the dispatches picked up here?"

"Nah. Too risky. Too many people come and go through this crossroad day and night these days. I thought maybe you could take 'em."

Zeke nodded. "Reckon I can."

Pete walked to the new cow's manger and dug into the fresh-cut grass, pulling out a feed sack. He tossed it to Zeke. "Dispatch bag is inside. Someone will come tonight for it. Pay no attention to whether he's male or female, old hag, or child. The code word will be," he paused, "boiled trout."

Zeke lifted a bushy eyebrow. "Boiled trout? That's a hell of a code word!"

"Won't have to worry about anyone comin' up with it on their own, will we then?"

Zeke laughed in agreement. "Well, guess I'll be goin' on my way."

"Go right home and wait," Pete instructed. "I don't know for sure when the messenger will be by."

Zeke's smile fell from his face. "Go home now?"

"That a problem?"

Zeke thought of Lyla and how long he'd waited for the opportunity to sit and talk with her. "It's just I got somewhere I got to be."

Pete frowned. "It's that whore, ain't it?" He shook a meaty finger. "I'm tellin' you, Zeke, you're headed for trouble with that wench."

Edwin walked up and took the sack from Zeke's hand. "Aw hell, Pete, let him be. I ain't got no woman to court. I'll go home and wait on the messenger. Good enough?"

"I suppose," Pete conceded.

Zeke looked up at Edwin, who was a good head taller than he was. The two men exchanged no words, but thanks were offered and accepted. With a farewell wave, Zeke went out of the barn and headed for the churchyard, whistling as he walked.

Zeke entered the grassy churchyard and walked around to the rear of the tiny log building the Methodists had built to hold their services in. Already there was a sprinkling of plain wooden crosses under the grandfather elm and ash trees. Soldiers who had come home to rest.

Zeke went on whistling. Faintly, he heard another voice join in. It was a sweet feminine trill that made Zeke's stomach go all soft and queasy. It was all he could do to keep up the tune.

When he slipped through the hedge he saw her and came to a halt. He could feel his palms growing cold and clammy. Lyla was dressed in a pale-blue sak gown that emphasized her petite but buxom figure. Her glossy honey-colored hair was pulled back with a thick blue ribbon the same hue as her dress. She was spreading out a wool blanket. To Zeke, by the light of the candle lantern she looked like an angel just spreading her wings.

He ended his tune; she finished just behind him. "You came," he said, an odd husky catch in his voice.

"Of course I came. And I brought supper." She indicated a woven basket covered by a napkin. "Nothing fancy like Maggie must feed you. Bread and cheese and apple tarts." She tucked her hands behind her. "I didn't make the apple tarts." Her face brightened. "My grandmam did, though."

"It don't matter what we have," Zeke said, coming to her. He felt awkward, so awkward that a part of him wanted to turn and run. But he didn't. "I'm just glad you came."

Lyla sat down and reached for the basket. "Oh, and I forgot, there's sweet cider. My sisters and I picked the apples."

"Your sisters?" Zeke eased himself down onto the

blanket wondering just where he should sit. "You didn't tell me you had sisters."

She shrugged. "I don't want to talk about me. Nothin' to tell." She handed him a thick slice of rye bread covered with a slab of white cheese. "Let's talk about you."

Zeke laughed as he accepted the bread. "Even less to tell about."

She took a bite of her bread, smiling over the cheese. "Guess we don't have to talk at all, do we, Ezekial?"

Her gentle gaze met his and the bread Zeke was trying to swallow caught in his throat. He reached for the mug of cider she'd poured and took a deep drink. He hoped none dribbled down his beard, but, good God, if he didn't get some air, he feared he'd start turning blue.

The bread finally went down and Zeke found his voice. "I don't know why you won't tell me anything about yourself. I don't care care where you live or *how* you live." He thought for a moment, an idea suddenly coming to him. His steely gray eyes crinkled at the corners. "You don't have husband, do you?"

She laughed, her voice sounding like churchbells in the still evening air. "God'a mercy, no. What made you ask?"

He shrugged, taking another bite of his bread, but this time making certain it was smaller. "Just wanted to make sure."

When they'd finished their bread and cheese, both ate a sweet, flaky apple tart and then licked their fingers like greedy schoolchildren. Lyla took a sip of the cider and offered the cup to Zeke.

She smiled at him as he drank and he lowered the cup. "What?" he asked. He wiped his beard with his hand. "Am I making a mess?"

She laughed. "No, 'course not. I'm just smilin' because I'm happy. I've known plenty of men in my time Zeke, but you beat all."

"What are you talkin' about?"

She shook her head. "You really don't care what I do for those soldiers, do you?"

He looked away, embarrassed by such talk. "I figure you got a reason," he mumbled. "Not any of my business."

"You don't care that other men touch me?"

He didn't say anything. Then to his surprise he felt her hand glide over his.

"I . . ." He cleared his throat and started again. "It ain't that I don't *care,* it's just . . . just that I don't think any less of you." He dared to look into her eyes.

She was smiling. She was smiling at him. "Bless you, Zeke. God bless you," she whispered.

Zeke wanted to kiss her, he wanted to kiss her so badly that he hurt for her. Slowly he leaned toward her. She didn't move.

His lips brushed hers and he heard her sigh. She rested her hand on his shoulder and kissed him back. It was Zeke's first kiss in well over ten years.

As he withdrew, she brushed his beard with her fingers. "Ah, Zeke. You're such a gentleman." She held him in the countenance of her smile for another moment and then began to pack away the leftovers. "I haven't long. I have to meet somebody," she said. "Let's make the most of the time we have left."

All Zeke could do was stare at her with big gray eyes.

Her airy laughter filled the churchyard. "So tell me, Zeke. Did you have a pleasant day?"

Ed Bennett drifted off to sleep in a comfortably lumpy chair in front of the fireplace. He had waited until midnight for the messenger who was supposed to come for the dispatches, but when no one showed up, he decided to take himself a little nap. He knew he would hear the knock when it came at the door; he was a light sleeper. He'd learned that the hard way back at Valley Forge when he'd fallen asleep in a perimeter camp and been hit over the head by a deserter. It had been Les who'd saved his neck that night.

Ed shifted, making himself cozy. He had a small fire burning on the hearth and a warm coon hound on his lap. What more could a man want, except maybe a little human companionship. And he expected Les within the next day or two.

Ed heard the latch on the cabin door lift, but by the time he straightened in the chair, reaching for his flintlock propped against the fireplace, the soldiers had burst through the door.

"Where are they?" an overweight redcoat demanded, bringing his rifle barrel down on Ed's fingers so hard that his hand went numb and the flintlock clattered to the floor.

"What? Where's what?" Ed asked, blinking away

the confusion of sleep. There were redcoats everywhere. Soldiers were ripping open goose-feather bed ticks and turning over tables. Feathers drifted through the air.

"Don't play stupid with me," Gordy bellowed. He lifted his bayoneted rifle, bringing its razor-sharp tip to Ed's throat.

Ed swallowed against the sickening fear in the pit of his stomach. The dispatches. The bastards were looking for the dispatches. How the hell had they known?

"I said, where the bloody hell are they?" Gordy repeated in a fury.

Ed made one swift movement, meaning to swipe the rifle from the fat lieutenant Gordy, but he wasn't fast enough. A soldier came from behind and dropped a rope over his neck, jerking it tight until Ed went down on his knees.

Ed heard an odd gurgle in his throat as he struggled to catch his breath. He felt light-headed, almost detached as two soldiers tied his hand behind his back and tied them to his bare feet.

"You can tell me now and make it easy," Gordy said. "Or you can tell me later." He picked up the fireplace poker and thrust it into the coals, watching it until it glowed red. "Your choice, Colonial clod."

"You've got to tell them," Ed heard someone beg in desperation. The voice was familiar. He opened his eyes and was shocked by the sight he saw. "Not you," he whispered in disbelief.

"Enough!" Gordy raised the red-hot fireplace poker up beneath Ed's nose so that he could smell the heat of it. "We've got no time for this!"

Ed closed his eyes. *Our Father who art in heaven* . . . The words tumbled through his mind as he gritted teeth in anticipation of the agony to come. But he'd not tell the pettifogging bastards the dispatches were down the well. Not with his last dying breath.

Suddenly Edwin heard a hair-raising scream. Then he realized it was his own.

Maggie slipped down off the wagon seat and massaged her achy lower back. Grayson dismounted and came to help her unhitch the horse. "You feeling all right, sweet?" he asked, concerned by the dark half circles beneath her eyes.

"Fine. Just dead tired." It had been a tiresome journey down the Chesapeake, then the James River to Williamsburg. Once in Williamsburg they'd set out immediately for Yorktown, riding to make it by morning.

Grayson rested his hand on her shoulder. "I'm proud of you, Maggie. I never heard a complaint on this whole trip."

She smiled up him. "Let's get my horse out to pasture and then let me make us some breakfast before you go back to camp."

He kissed her. "I really should go now."

She caught the stock of his shirt and pulled him to her. "Come on. Just a little breakfast." She lifted up on her toes and kissed his mouth. "Or maybe we could skip the corncakes and get on to dessert." Her laugh had a husky catch to it.

"Ah, Maggie. You'd tempt a saint," Grayson murmured as he encircled her waist with his arms.

Their lips met again, but the sound of a horse and rider broke them apart. Maggie shielded her eyes from the morning glare of the sun.

"Who is it?" Grayson asked.

She shook her head. "I don't know. Wait. It's the boy that works for Pete. His apprentice. I don't know his name."

The young apprentice astride his pony sailed over Maggie's fence and rode into the barnyard. "Miss Maggie?"

She came toward him. "Yes?"

"My master, Pete Clendaniels, says you have to come quick." He eyed Grayson.

Maggie waved her hand. "He's safe enough. "Go on."

"The Bennett boys' cabin, ma'am. Fast as you can get there." He wheeled his pony around and sunk his heels into its sides. "I've got to get Zeke, too."

Maggie stood stunned for a moment, then sprang into action. Her hands found the harness on her horse and she began to restrap it.

"Wait." Grayson rested his hand on hers. "The horse and cart will be too slow. Let me take you." He caught Giipa's reins and lifted easily into the saddle.

She looked up at him, her face etched with concern. "I don't know what the problem is. I'd best go alone."

He offered her his hand. "So I'll leave you in the woods near by where no one can see me."

Maggie took his hand and allowed him to lift her into the saddle. Seated straddled in his lap, she twisted her fingers in the gelding's mane and nodded. "Let's go!"

Giipa flew over the fence with the ease born of good breeding. The weight of an extra rider seemed not to hinder him as Grayson drove him hard across the field and into the woods.

"Which way?" Grayson asked.

"Left." A moment later Maggie pointed. "Right. Down the trail, than right again at the mullberry bush."

Too tense for conversation, they rode in silence. But even though Maggie didn't speak, she was comforted by Grayson's presence. He cared enough about her to be there when she needed him, even when she herself denied that need. Was that what love was? She only wished she knew.

"It's just through this hedge," Maggie murmured. "Let me down."

Grayson reined in Giipa and Maggie slipped to the ground. Without another word to Grayson she lifted her skirts and ran through the woods down the trail that led to the Bennett boys' cabin. The moment she came into the clearing, she spotted Pete at the door. There were no redcoats to be seen, only a few neighbors standing with their heads bowed, speaking in hushed tones.

"What is it? What's happened?" Maggie demanded, running across the grassy yard.

Pete's usually ruddy face was a pallored gray.

"What?" she repeated, coming to stop at the door. "Tell me!" She glanced through the doorway but could see nothing but the glare of morning sunlight.

He swallowed the bile that rose in his throat. "You don't want to go in there, Mags."

"Tell me!"

The blacksmith put his arm up to bar her entrance. "It's Ed. He's dead."

"Ed?" Her eyes searched his face for some explanation. "Redcoats?" she whispered.

He looked away. "He came by way of a dispatch bag yesterday. There were some important messages inside that we meant to send to Williamsburg."

With a sudden movement, Maggie ducked under Pete's arm. By the time he caught her she was halfway across the dimly lit log cabin. She came to an abrupt halt, her eyes cloudy with tears.

Over near the fireplace Les sat on the floor, Ed's mutilated body cradled in his arms. Les cried like no man Maggie had ever seen cry before. He rocked back and forth. "Why, why?" he demanded, the tears running down his stubbled cheeks. "Not my brother? Why my brother?"

Zeke suddenly appeared at Maggie's side. "Good God," he muttered as he turned his face away.

Instead of running, instead of turning away and being sick, Maggie forced herself forward. She went to Les and knelt beside him. "Let me take him, Les," she whispered. "Let me take him and clean him up right for buryin'."

"They kilt him, Maggie. They kilt my brother, Ed." He rocked back and forth, holding Ed's body against him.

"I know," she answered evenly. "I know what they

did and we're gonna get the bastards for it, but right now you got to get up off the floor and let me take him, Ed."

He shook his head. "Nobody's takin' my brother. Nobody's takin' Edwin and puttin' him in the cold ground."

Maggie stroked Les's graying head. "Now you know this isn't Ed here, this is just an old shell of a body. Ed's gone to heaven, Les. He's huntin' duck this very minute, I'll bet you."

Les sniffed. "Pete says they come for some dispatches Ed got a hold of. He died fightin' for us, didn't he, Mags?"

She rested her head on Les's shoulder, trying to ignore the stench of burnt human flesh that made her stomach heave. "He died a hero, I'd say."

Ed looked at her for the first time. "You think he deserves a commendation?"

"From Washington himself."

He smiled a sad smile. "You'll clean him up good?"

She smiled back. "Make him handsome, I will." She put out her arms.

Slowly Les lifted his brother's body and eased it onto the floor, allowing Maggie to take Ed's shoulders. Pete came to help Les off the floor.

Zeke knelt beside Maggie. "My God," he groaned. "This could have been me. It *should* have been."

Maggie looked up. "Don't say that . . . don't ever say that again, Ezekial Barnes."

"It's true. I was the one who was supposed to take the dispatches. Instead I met Lyla."

Maggie shook her head, looking back at Ed's face. "It was his time to go. God's will. Now hush your mouth about who this could have been or should have been. The truth is it could have been any of us." She paused. "Now go see what you can find out. We've got to carry on, Zeke. That was our agreement from the beginning. No matter what, we've got to carry on."

Knowing the truth of Maggie's words, Zeke slowly rose. Then, taking a deep breath, he went to Les's side. "I hate to ask," he told Les, gripping his friend's shoulder, "but do you know anyplace Ed might have hidden the dispatch bag? From the looks of this place and Ed's body, the bloody butchers didn't find what they were looking for. I just don't think Ed told 'em."

Les wiped his teary eyes with the back of his hand. "Hell no, he didn't tell them!" he answered gruffly. "I know just where the damned bag is!"

Zeke's compassionate gaze met Les's. "Can you show me, friend?"

Maggie watched Zeke, Pete, and Les go out the door and then she squeezed her eyes shut against the pain in her heart. She wanted to scream, to shout! There was no need for this man to die! No need for any of them to die! She felt the weight of Ed's body in her arms and she knew she had to get up from the floor. She knew she had a job to do.

"Maggie . . ." Grayson's voice penetrated her thoughts. "Maggie, let me help you."

She opened her eyes to see Grayson stooped in front of her, his hands extended. He took Ed's body from her, handling it as if it was spun glass and laid it gently on the floor. And then he took her into his arms and cried with her.

Chapter Twenty-three

Grayson came to a halt outside Major Lawrence's tent. Private Michaels paused beside him. "You want me to announce you, sir?"

Grayson adjusted his grenadier cap and looked down at the young man. He'd been seriously considering taking Michaels into his confidence. He'd grown so fond of him that he feared for the boy. What would happened to Michaels when the English were beaten here on the banks of the York River? Grayson had a mind to send him to Thayer's Folly where he'd be safe. There in Williamsburg he could build a new life for himself as an American. Grayson liked the idea of having the boy around after the war. "Have I got my breeches on backward, Michaels?"

Michaels broke into a grin. "No, sir."

"Then I suppose I'm ready."

Michaels ducked inside the tent and came out a moment later. "The major will see you in his inner tent," Michaels said. "You . . . you want me to wait here?"

"I swear by the king's bowels, son, you worry

over me like you were my wet nurse," Grayson chided. "Now go about your duties."

Michaels saluted and Grayson flipped back a playful salute. Yes, he decided, as he watched the boy walk away, he needed to figure out a way to get Michaels to Thayer's Folly before the real fighting began. Grayson knew he couldn't save the life of every fifteen-year-old boy on the battlefield, but damned if it wasn't in his power to save this one!

Taking a deep breath, Grayson walked into Major Lawrence's tent. He shifted his thoughts from Michaels to Lawrence. Each time Grayson was called in by the major, a part of him was afraid, afraid he'd been caught. But another part of him, the part he allowed to control him, was excited by the game. It was Grayson's wits against the major's, against the entire bloody British army's.

Grayson passed Major Lawrence's secretary seated at a small camp desk and walked into the inner tent. Grayson immediately came to attention and snapped a sharp salute, holding it.

"Yes, yes," Major Lawrence muttered, returning the salute. "Just get in here, Thayer. I called you a good forty-five minutes ago."

"I was bathing, sir," Grayson murmured apologetically. He didn't tell him he'd been bathing with Maggie.

Major Lawrence was seated in a chair allowing a young servant boy to fit an immense white wig over his head. Grayson was surprised to see that the major was entirely bald save for a sparse thatch of long white hair that stood up like a rooster's cock in the center of his head. It was all Grayson could do to keep from chuckling.

With the wig in place, the servant handed Major Lawrence a breathing cone and the major placed it over his face. Great billows of white hair powder filled the small sleeping tent as the servant proceeded to powder the officer's wig.

Grayson choked and turned away. Major Lawrence wheezed. The boy went on powdering, seemingly immune to the suffocating dust.

Finally, Major Lawrence lowered the cone and fanned it in the air. "Enough! That will be all, Gill."

The boy gathered his hair accoutrements and slipped out the tent flap, letting it fall behind him.

Major Lawrence gave a great sneeze, and then rubbed his nose. "Ah, much better." He blinked as if just remembering Grayson was there. "Thayer."

"Yes, sir." Grayson noticed that the usually thin man was now so underweight that he appeared emaciated. His cheeks were sunk into dark hollows and his eye seemed to bulge unnaturally. It was obvious the major was not sleeping well.

"Your aunt, Thayer?"

"Sir?"

"You aunt in New Castle. How does she fare?"

"Not well, sir. She's dead."

The major gave a sigh and pushed out of his chair, going to his desk. "Better off than the rest of us, I'll grant you." He nodded. "My condolences just the same."

"Thank you."

"And my letters, were they delivered?"

"Not by my own hands, I'm sorry to say," Grayson answered carefully. "I wasn't able to leave my aunt's side, but I had them delivered."

Major Lawrence nodded. "Good enough." Then there was a long, uncomfortable pause before he spoke again. "You know the Frenchman de Grasse engaged with our fleets under Hood and Graves yesterday."

"No, I didn't know. How did we do?"

The major lifted a sheet of paper and then let it glide back onto his desk. "Piss poor."

"I'm certain we'll whip their tails on the next engagement, sir."

"Christ a' mighty! Thayer, don't you see? Use your head, boy! They've taken control of the sea, Washington's in Williamsburg and we're caught on this bloody peninsula!"

"There's Gloucester Point, sir. Nothing but a few militia and farmers to defend her," Grayson said, offering information that was well known.

Major Lawrence shook his head. "It doesn't feel right, boy." He brought up his fist to the place on his chest over his heart. "I've just got this sick feeling in here." He looked up. "I'm thinking of sending my nephew to New York."

When Grayson said nothing, the major went on. "We'll be digging in here. There's going to be one hell of a battle no matter which side the coin turns on. I can smell the stench of death already."

"And you don't think Lieutenant Riker will want to be a part of that battle?"

"I understand that you and my nephew have not seen eye to eye, but he's my only living blood relative. I don't want to see him die."

Grayson cleared his throat. "Yes, sir, but what does this have to do with me?"

"I'll need you to double up on duties. I offered to General Cornwallis that I would take a fighting command. I'd like to start digging our first lines of defense today and I want you to be in charge of the work."

Grayson nodded. "Whatever it is you want, sir."

Major Lawrence lifted his head for an instant and Grayson saw fear in the older man's pale-gray eyes, primal fear. This was not the man Grayson had been wary of a few months ago when he'd come to Yorktown. That major who had fought beside Banastre Tarleton, the butcher, seemed gone. There's was nothing left but a tired old man.

"I'm asking as a personal favor to you that you not speak to my nephew on this matter," the major murmured. "I've no wish to argue with him. I believe I'll simply send him to Clinton in New York on some sort of business."

Just then the tent flap lifted and Riker came strutting in. "Uncle." He gave Grayson a nod. "Captain."

"I was just speaking to Thayer about beginning the digging on our outer lines. I have a special task for you as well."

"Oh?" Riker picked up an apple off a small table and took a bite. "What is it?"

"I need you to go to New York."

"New York!" Riker flashed Grayson a scowl. "Is this your idea, Thayer?"

Grayson lifted a taunting eyebrow. "I stand innocent. Surely you don't think I have anything to do with the major's decisions."

"I can't go to New York, Uncle. Not now! I'm this close," he brought his thumb and forefinger together, "to catching that entire band of filthy rebel troublemakers."

Riker's words immediately tapped Grayson's attention.

"I'm not certain how much longer they can do us harm," Major Lawrence answered, taking a seat on a campstool at his field desk.

"Can't do us any harm!" Riker exploded. "What of those dispatches they stole?"

The major sighed. "The bloody fools left the bag lying on the floor of the ale house! Those soldiers would have been court-martialed if they'd been my men. What did you expect the rebels to do? Return the dispatches unopened?"

"If we know who the traitors are, it's our duty as soldiers of the king to bring them to justice!"

Major Lawrence sighed. "Give your information to the captain. I have confidence that he can handle the matter."

Riker shook his head, his midnight hair brushing his shoulders. "Just a day or two, please, Uncle. I've found a Benedict Arnold among them. I'm certain I can bring the whole bloody nest of rebels down."

Grayson involuntarily flinched at Riker's words. His suspicions were finally confirmed. The information leaks that had been taking place had not been accidents as he had hoped, as they all had hoped. There *was* a traitor among them.

"A betrayer among them, is there?" Grayson smiled, his voice a smooth as liquid glass. "Damned Colonials, they've no honor!" He removed his grenadier cap and slipped it beneath his arm. "Give me the information and I'll take care of it, have no fear."

Riker's dark eyes narrowed venomously. "Oh, no you don't. I do the work and you take the glory?" He tossed his half-eaten apple, striking Grayson in the chest with it. "I've worked too damned long on this to let you bungle it like you bungle everything else!"

Major Lawrence dipped his quill into a inkwell and scrawled his signature on a report. "Listen to yourself. You sound obsessed, Nephew. Perhaps it was time you backed off. I keep telling you that you mustn't get emotionally involved in your duties. You have too many personal vendettas, including the one against Thayer, and I don't like it. It is unbecoming of a soldier."

Riker crossed the tent in three long strides. "A few days, Uncle," he pleaded. "A few days is all I need and I swear to God I'll hand you their heads on a platter. Then I'll do your bidding in New York. I swear it."

Major Lawrence shook his powdered head wearily. "I'm too easy on you. I've failed your father."

"Oh, you haven't, sir." He took the older man's gnarled hand. "I can catch these rebel devils. I can make you proud of me."

"All right, young man, a few more days, but then," the major held up a finger, "you go. It's important that I send a man I can trust. It's important I send you."

Riker spun around, offering Grayson a smug grin and then walked out of the tent.

Grayson shifted his weight from one polished boot to the other. "Will that be all, Major?"

"Yes. Take what men of mine you need." The

major returned to his stack of papers and Grayson was dismissed.

Once outside in the crisp autumn air, Grayson hurried toward his tent, his head bent in concentration. He didn't know who the traitor was among the Yorktown band, but if he didn't find out soon, they would all fall.

Beyond the point of caring about town gossip, Maggie walked into the midnight meeting on Grayson's arm. Once inside the high-ceilinged tobacco house, she and Grayson moved up to stand beside Zeke. One by one she stared at the faces of the men she had grown up with.

This morning she had heard the first guns of battle. Washington had begun troop movement toward Yorktown, and already skirmishes were taking place. As Maggie glanced from one man to the next, she couldn't help wondering who among them would die before the last cannon fire was volleyed here on the banks of the York River.

The faces of the men who gathered in John's barn were taut with worry. Their voices were hushed. Not only did they carry upon their shoulders the burden of coming battle, but also the burden of a friend turned foe. Each man seemed to look at the man beside him, wondering if *he* was the traitor among them.

When the last man had arrived and the door was closed, John cleared his throat. "Men," he said in a deep, resonant voice, "we've got trouble." His eyes scanned the small knot of men and the single woman who drew closer. "Major Thayer has learned that there is indeed a betrayer among us. He's somehow connected to Lieutenant Riker."

A murmur rippled through the men. A curse or two was heard in the semidarkness. Maggie glanced up high into the rafters of the barn, blinking away the tears that clouded her eyes. A pigeon roosting on a crossbeam fluttered its wings and flew a short distance to another beam. Maggie felt Grayson's hand tighten around hers.

"The suggestion has been made," John continued slowly, "that we simply disband."

"Disband, hell," Pete shouted. "I say we find the traitor and hang the bastard!"

"Our duty is coming to an end here. Most of us will be lifting arms to fight." John raised his palms as if in surrender. "I want no more lives lost."

"I can tell you one thing," Les said from far in the rear, his voice razor-edged. "I aim to find which one of you it is, and I aim to deal with it."

"Win or lose, how could we live in this town, knowing one of us betrayed the others," Harry offered. "We got no choice, boys. We have to find the rat among us."

"How?" someone asked.

"If we knew who it was, we'd have taken care of him long ago," someone else offered.

"Him or *her,*" Les muttered.

Maggie stiffened. "Now wait a minute, Les Bennett! You know better than that! If I was the traitor, don't you think I'd have made things a little easier on myself? You think I'd be dragging through the mud in the middle of the night carrying bags of Brit flour on my back?"

"Easy," Grayson soothed in her ear. "It's his grief talking."

Les chewed on his thumbnail. "Cool your petticoats, Mags. I weren't talkin 'bout you."

"Well, what other blasted woman is there among us?" Harry asked, striking his cane on the dirt floor.

Les turned toward Zeke. "I'm not sayin' this for a fact and I'm not sayin' it to hurt you, Zeke, but what of the whore."

"Yeah! What of Lyla," another men echoed.

"You know I wouldn't speak of what goes on here, not to anyone," Zeke said slowly.

"M-maybe it's not your fault," Carter piped in. "I . . . I mean what man's responsible for what he says when he's wrapped in a woman's web? Especially a woman of Lyla's talents?"

Zeke took a step back, his face awash with anger. "You got no right, Les, Carter—any of you."

Carter took a step toward him. "Les's brother's dead because of that bitch. You admitted yourself you went to meet her the night Ed was killed. She was the one who went runnin' to the Brits tellin' 'em about the dispatches."

Zeke shook his head, backing toward the door. "You accuse Lyla, you accuse me, friends." He lifted his head, his gray eyes meeting theirs defiantly. Then he turned and limped out the door.

Immediately all of the men began talking at once. Maggie hesitated for a moment and then leaned to whisper in Grayson's ear. "I'll meet you at home."

Grayson nodded.

Maggie turned and ran out of the barn, running

down the path in the darkness until she came upon Zeke. He didn't slow down for her.

"Zeke . . ."

"I didn't hear you speak up for me, Maggie. I didn't hear a word come out of your mouth. You think I told Lyla stuff, don't you?"

She walked beside him. "I don't know what I think, but I know you wouldn't do anything on purpose to jeopardize our lives. That I know, Ezekial Barnes."

He shook his head. "Ain't good enough. I'm tellin' you, Mags, she's innocent. She'd not say a word no matter what she knew, which is nuthin'."

Maggie drew her shawl tighter around her shoulders. "I'm going to ask you something, Zeke. You remember that time you asked me about Grayson before we knew the truth of who he was? You remember when I asked you if you would turn in someone you loved if you knew she was the enemy."

"I remember."

"I'm going to ask you again and then I'm going to take you on your word." She stopped him, her head reaching out to grasp his forearm. "Zeke . . . would you turn her in? Would you tell me if she told the Brits about the dispatches Ed was passing on?"

He swallowed against the lump in his throat, fighting the tears in his eyes as he met and held her gaze. "I'd turn her in without thinkin'."

Maggie nodded. "If you say she didn't do, then I believe you."

"You do?"

She nodded and then started down the path

again. "Besides, doesn't that sound too simple to you, Zeke? Too obvious?"

"I don't know what to think, Mags. I can't believe one of us could betray the others. I can't believe one of us would do that to Ed. We're like brothers, all of us."

"Wars a funny thing," she said as if she could console him. "We do things we thought we'd never do."

He nodded and then glanced sideways at her. "You gonna marry Major Thayer?"

She kept her gaze fixed on the path. "You going to marry Lyla?"

"Don't know," he answered.

"Don't know," she echoed.

The two walked in silence all the way to the edge of Maggie's property line and Zeke turned off. "I don't know what I'm gonna do, Maggie. Take off maybe . . . if she'll go with me."

"Sometimes takin' off is the answer," she said thoughtfully, her hand falling to her slightly rounded belly. "Sometimes it isn't."

He nodded again, and then headed for home. For a long time Maggie stood in the darkness wondering how this all was going to end.

At dawn Maggie walked out the front door toward the well to fetch water for breakfast. Grayson had spent the night, but he had to be back before Major Lawrence realized he was missing. With the first British lines of defense nearly complete, Grayson was finding it more and more difficult to get out of the camp without causing any suspicion.

Last night after he and Maggie had made love and he held her in his arms, he told her he thought this was the last time he could safely come to her.

As Maggie walked through the cold, wet morning dew, she listened to the quiet. By midmorning the sound of gunshot would be heard. Washington's army was advancing rapidly. Grayson said it would only be a matter of days before the British, lacking enough men to properly defend their outer works, would have to retreat farther out onto the York Peninsula. Cornwallis still held one supply and possible escape route through Gloucester Point across the river. Grayson surmised Washington was depending on the French navy to close that route.

Chilled by the brisk morning air, Maggie hurried to the well. The trees in her yard were turning breathtaking shades of orange and yellow as they shed their foliage for another winter. Maggie wondered how the sky could be so blue, the sun so bright, and men be dying only miles in the distance.

She lowered her bucket and brought it up filled with cold, fresh water. She would bake muffins this morning, using the last of her flour. She had purposefully used most of her supplies in the last few weeks, knowing the time would come when she would be forced to flee her home. With the patriot army marching on the British, she would be in the direct line of fire in a few days.

Halfway back across the lawn, Maggie came to an abrupt halt, mystified by the oddest sensation. Slowly she lowered her water bucket to the dry, brittle grass and pressed her hand to her stomach. There it was again! She smiled a bittersweet smile as she concentrated on the flutter she had felt. The babe. Grayson's child. It felt like the wings of a butterfly brushing against her insides. There it was again! Tears collected in the corners of her eyes as she savored the feel of her child's first movements.

"Maggie!"

She looked up to see Grayson standing on the front porch dressed in nothing but a pair of tight white breeches. The corded muscles of his chest rippled as he pulled a shirt over his head. "Maggie, you all right?"

She smiled up at him and leaned to catch the handle of the bucket. She had half a mind to walk right up those steps and ask Grayson to marry her. Today. Before the fighting started. But a part of her hesitated and the moment was lost. All of her insecurities came back, flooding her reason. What if what Inga had said was true. What if she *wasn't* worthy of him? What if Grayson turned to drink after the war. When moments were tense Grayson reached for a bottle of claret. She'd seen it herself. She could stand to lose another husband to drink. She'd be better to walk away now.

But what if he died on the battlefield? Would she regret the rest of her life not having married him and given her child a name. Yes.

Maggie groaned as she came toward the front porch where Grayson waited. "Holy Mother Mary," she murmured. "Why can't I make a decision?"

"What did you say?" Grayson asked as he took the bucket from her.

She flashed him a smile, brushing her fingertips against his cheek as she passed him. He caught her hand and kissed her. His face was cleanly shaven and he smelled of soap. It was moments like this that she wished could go on forever.

"How long before they get here?" she asked, going inside and heading for the kitchen.

"Days. It's time you packed up, sweet." He set the bucket down on her dry sink. "I could have you at Thayer's Folly in twenty-four hours."

She frowned. "Don't start that again or there'll be no breakfast for you. I'm not going to Williamsburg and I'm not going to talk about it with you. When the time comes for me to hightail it to higher ground I'll go to John's. Elizabeth and the baby will be glad enough to see me."

He sat down to roll on his stockings. "It may be time for me to make my move shortly, too. I sent a message to Colonel Hastings asking that I be permitted to join Washington when he arrives. My job is done among the Brits. I feel more of a hindrance these days than a help. No matter how much I stall, those trenches are still getting dug." He glanced up at her, a boyish grin on his face. "I do of course take care to always put the slowest-witted men on the job. Had one the other day that nearly buried another."

Maggie laughed, her voice filling the kitchen with sunshine. Grayson watched her as she prepared their morning meal. He liked to see her move across the kitchen, her skirts brushing the swept floor as she seemed to glide rather than walk. Her hair was brushed down her back in a thick curtain of curly waves, the color as breathtaking as the dawning of the sun they had watched together this morning from the bedroom window.

Pulling on one boot and then the other, Grayson rose and walked to where Maggie stood at the fireplace. He wrapped his arms around her, forcing her to turn and face him.

"Hey! Take care. Those muffins burn and there'll be no others," she scolded.

"You said last night you'd think about marrying me."

"So I'm thinking." She lifted her hands to rest them on his broad shoulders.

"And?"

"And I don't know."

"You don't know if you love me?" His blue eyes were riveted to hers making it impossible for her to look away.

"I love ye. I've loved ye since the cursed day I set eyes on ye."

"So why won't you marry me?"

"I told you, Grayson. It takes more than love to make a marriage."

He planted a kiss on the pale ivory skin of her neck. "Love conquers all, sweet. Marry me and I'll make you a happy woman."

"I *am* happy," she whispered. "Somehow in the midst of a war I'm happy." She made little laugh of disbelief. "How can anyone be happy at a time like this?"

"It's going to end soon and then I'm going to make you marry me."

"You can't *make* someone marry you!"

He kissed his way across her collarbone down to the swell of her breasts peeking above her thin bodice. "Ve haf vays of making vomen marry us," he told her in a poor Hessian accent. "Ve haf vays aff torture! Terrible torture."

She sighed, her eyes drifting shut as his warm lips

sent shivers of delight through her body. "You would torture me?" she whispered with a giggle.

"Yes I vould! Ve must use all methods at our disposal to best the enemy."

"You would torture me like this to make me marry you?"

"Yes!"

Her lips met his and she teased his upper lip with the tip of her tongue. "Perhaps this torture could work," she said in a silky voice.

His eyes narrowed as, with one sweep, he lifted her into his arms. "Could it?"

Their kiss deepened and Maggie strained against him, running her fingers through his golden hair. When she realized he had carried her down the hall and was taking her up the steps to the bedroom, she struggled in his arms. "My muffins! Grayson! The pan is already hot."

He nuzzled her neck. "Make *me* hot instead, Maggie mine."

Chapter Twenty-four

Maggie stood beside Zeke on the small bluff on the outskirts of Yorktown watching as the patriot army marched onto the peninsula. Tears brimmed in her eyes as she watched the ragtag army file by in columns, company after company, their new American flag held high, the sound of fife and drums in the distance.

Maggie's heart swelled with pride until she thought her chest would burst. She only wished Grayson could be here with her to see the sight, but he was stuck in the British camp overseeing the digging of trenches. Already the outer works had been abandoned by the British. They were backing onto the peninsula, caught between the bay and the advancing patriot army.

"Damned fine sight," Zeke murmured, embarrassed by the emotion evident in his voice. "After all these years, we've got 'em, haven't we, Mags? We've got the bloody redcoats."

She drew her woolen shawl over her head. There was a stiff breeze blowing in off the Chesapeake bay, sending dry, crumpled leaves scattering. A V of geese flew overhead, their calls melding as one with the haunting sounds of the fife and drums. "I don't know, Zeke. Grayson says it's too soon to tell. Cornwallis could still make it across the river to Gloucester Point. It depends on the weather, on the Brit fleet, on the French fleet, on our own ability to strike and strike hard."

"I don't care what the odds are. I feel a victory in my bones, Mags. Someday I'm going to sit a grandson on my knee and tell him of the great battle that took place here."

She glanced at him, smiling. "Grandchildren, is it? I haven't seen any children yet."

Zeke's cheeks colored. "I asked Lyla to go with me, but she said no. This here is home and she aims to stay. So I'm staying and I'm gonna prove that Lyla's not responsible for passing on information." He paused and then went on. "Did you know she's got three sisters to care for? I just found out a few days ago. That's why she does what she does, Mags. She don't have a trade like you. Her papa went off to war and her mama died of the pox in '77. She's been keepin' those girls safe in a cabin somewhere. Never brings 'em into town so they don't know what the rest of us knows about Lyla."

Maggie laid her hand on his arm. "I'm sorry for the things I said about Lyla, about you bein' too good for her. That was cruel. There's some that would say Grayson's too good for me."

"You don't believe it, do you?"

She looked down the hill to the passing soldiers. "I don't know, Zeke. We're so different. He went to school in London. He's so much smarter than me."

"It don't make him smarter just because he knows more."

She brushed back a lock of her strawberry-blond hair. "But what will we talk about across that big dining table? Will my children be ashamed of me?"

"Will my children be ashamed if they ever knew their mama had been a whore . . . for whatever reason." Zeke glanced at Maggie and then up into the clear blue sky. "I don't have the answers. Don't know that I'll ever have them."

Maggie suddenly took a deep breath. "Zeke . . ." She grasped his shoulder, trying to get a better look at the soldier passing. A space in the ranks had formed to make way for someone . . . a tall rider on a white horse.

"Zeke! Zeke! That's him!" She jumped up and down in excitement as she stared at the middle-aged gentleman dressed in blue and buff riding in the midst of an entourage. "It's General George Washington," she breathed.

Zeke swung off his hat in reverence. "Damn if it ain't. Who else could it be?"

Both watched in awe as Washington and his aides rode to the side and dismounted, allowing the troops to pass for the general's inspection.

"Hold this," Maggie murmured, whipping off her shawl, still staring wide-eyed at the general, who had dismounted.

Zeke grimaced as she shoved her wool shawl into his hands. "Mags, where are you going? You can't just walk up to the general of the Army and stick out your hand and say 'Pleased to meet you!' You're liable to be shot for the enemy!"

She shook her head, taking off down the hill, her fawn-colored skirts bunched in her fists. "I'll be right back," she shouted. "Wait for me!"

Maggie ran as hard a she could down the hill toward the commander of the patriot army. She didn't stop running until she was headed off by a tall, thin gentleman wearing the insignia of an aide-de-camp. "Whoa, whoa there, madame." He put out his arms to stop her. "I'm sorry, but you can't approach the general. He appreciates your kindness in wishing to greet him, but he's inspecting the troops at this moment."

Maggie shook her head, breathless. "I wouldn't think to disturb the general, sir. I only wanted to offer my house."

"Your house, madame?"

She nodded. "It's not but half a mile from the abandoned outer works. The general would be safe there, but close to the men. It's small, but the roof don't leak and it's out in the open so it could easily be guarded."

The aide stroked his chin thoughtfully and then held up a finger, telling her to wait a moment. He turned sharply and walked the few feet to where the general stood engrossed in conversation with one of his officers. The aide spoke in the general's ear, pointing at Maggie.

Upon hearing what the aide had to say, General Washington turned and smiled at her, giving her a most gracious nod. Then he turned back to his officer and went on with his conversation.

Maggie held her breath in awe. The commander of the entire Army had just smiled at her! The aide came back. "Yes? What did he say?" she asked excitedly.

"The general believes that your house may be of some use, perhaps as a hospital for the wounded, madame. He has instructed me to follow you home and see it for myself. Can we safely get there from here?"

"The Brits'll not bother us. It's noon. There'll be few patrols out." Maggie grinned. "You know how they like their biscuits."

The aide signaled for his horse, and a beautiful chestnut was brought around by a servant. The aide stepped easily into his saddle and took the reins. "You walked, madame?"

She nodded, turning away. "But it's not far."

"Come, come. Sit up with me. It will be faster."

Maggie stared at the aide's handsome face, hesitant. But then she thought, *why not?* It would be a hell of a story to tell Grayson.

Raising her hand to the aide, she allowed him to lift her. She settled side-saddle in front of him, her hands wrapped tightly around the horse's mane.

Riding up the bluff toward home, Maggie waved at a bewildered Zeke as she rode by on the aide-de-camp's horse.

"You're not eating, Carter," Mary, his wife, chided softly. She stared across the trestle table at him. Their four children had finished their meal and had been excused from the table to finish their chores before it grew dark. With the arrival of October, it seemed to Mary as if there was never enough daylight to get everything done on a small farm. "You're getting thinner by the day."

Carter stared at the plate of hearty venison stew he didn't have the appetite to eat. He pushed away the pewter plate. "Save it. I'll have it later when I'm hungry."

She scowled, but got up from her seat and took away the plate. Her small hand brushed over her protruding belly as she made her way to the side-table where the dirty dishes sat waiting for her daughter to scrape. "The babe's dropped. I'd say it's any day now and you'll be a papa again." When Carter made no response, she went on. "If we're going to lock up and move out of the line of fire, it will have to be tomorrow, Husband. Harry says we should have moved a fortnight ago. General Washington may need our house to put up some of his men. Could you imagine that Frenchman Lafayette sleeping on our goose tick?" She laughed, her soft voice filling the low-ceilinged kitchen.

When she turned around, dishrag in her hand, Carter was slumped over the table, his head cradled in his hands. "Ah, what is it, Carter? You been walkin' around like a ghost for weeks."

He shook his head.

"You can't tell me? You can't tell your own wife?"

A rap at the door startled them both. Her gaze met his. No one visited during the supper hour.

"I'll get it," she murmured.

"No." He leaped up out of his seat. "I'll get it."

Mary watched her husband cross the room and swing open the door. A black-haired redcoat walked inside, pressing Carter back.

Mary clamped her hand over her mouth.

"Carter Perkins?" Lieutenant Riker asked.

Carter nodded. "I . . . but, but you must be lookin' for someone else. There must be a mistake."

Riker looked over his shoulder. "Natty! This the man you've speaking with?"

Carter's eyes widened at the sight of Natty Watkins being dragged in by the collar of his coat by Lieutenant Gordy Moore.

"That . . . that's him all right, Lieutenant," the middle-aged, raggedly dressed man stammered. "That's him, I swear it."

"What's this about?" Mary demanded, coming across the kitchen. "Carter?"

"Mary, get out!" Carter snapped. "This is none of your affair!"

"None of my affair when redcoats break into my house? None of my affair!" She took her husband's arm. "Carter, what do these men want? What's he talkin' about? What would you be doin' talkin' to Natty Watkins? Everybody in the county knows he's an informant for the redcoats."

"Get Natty out of here," Riker commanded Gordy over his shoulder. "And you, woman," he pointed to Mary, "had best take yourself into another room. I've business with your husband."

"No one in this house has business with a redcoat!" Mary shouted. "Now, get out! Get out of my house before I put you out!"

Carter whipped his hand, striking Mary hard against the cheek. She cringed, more horrified than hurt as she slowly lifted her palm to the red mark on her cheek. "Now do as you're told, woman," Carter barked.

Mary's eyes brimmed with tears as she stared at the man she had loved for so many years, the man she thought she had known. "God save your soul, Carter Perkins," she whispered. Then she shifted her gaze to Riker, who stood impatiently by the door. "And may the devil take yours." After a moment of deadly silence, Mary squared her shoulders and walked out of the kitchen.

Carter licked his dry lips. "I'm tellin' you, Lieutenant, there must be some kind of mistake. I can't be the man you're lookin' for."

Riker walked over to the fireplace and lifted the lid on the Dutch oven that contained Mary's fresh stew. He dropped the lid with a bang. "Oh, no. I got the right man. Took some work, though. You see, Natty, he doesn't even report to me. Another man does." He shook a slender finger. "You were clever, Carter, to keep yourself so well hidden from all of us."

Carter shook his head emphatically, his entire body trembling with fear . . . with remorse. "I'm telling you, you got the wrong man."

Riker took two short strides and grasped Carter by a handful of shirt muslin. "We're past that, don't you see, Carter? Now stop wasting my time and let's get on with it." He brought his face inches from Carter's. "I want to know the names of the men who are riding around wearing those damned flour sacks and I want to know their names now!"

A tear slipped down Carter's cheek. *If only God would strike me dead at this very moment,* he thought. *It would be better for all of us.*

Carter had never meant to be a traitor to his country. It had been innocent enough to start with. He'd needed money, and the man, Natty, had offered him hard coin for useless tidbits of information. It was information everyone knew, so Carter hadn't figured he was doing any harm. But then Natty had begun to push him. He began to threaten to reveal his identity if Carter didn't come up with more pertinent information. By the time Carter wanted to back out, it was too late. His coat was lined with English coin; his soul was sold.

Riker tightened his grip on Carter's homespun shirt. "The names . . . I'm not a patient man," he growled.

Carter hung his head. "I can't," he whispered.

Riker shoved Carter down and brought his knee up sharply beneath his chin. Carter grunted in pain.

"Look, you can make this easy on yourself, or you can make it hard." Riker's steely gray eyes were fixed on Carter's ashen face. "What's it going to be, Colonial?"

Carter swallowed against his fear. Riker had been responsible for Billy Faulkner's torture and death and then Ed Bennett's. Torture was a slow way to die. He wondered if he had the strength to hold out.

A high-pitched scream startled Carter. Before the door even swung open and Gordy stepped in, Carter knew whose scream it had been. "Dear God, not my daughter!" he cried.

Six-year-old Lucy screamed and kicked, hammering Gordy in the back as the large redcoat carried the little dark-haired girl into the kitchen. "Right pretty thing," Gordy told Riker. "A hell of a fighter. Had to chase her halfway around the barn and clobber one of those brothers of hers to get a hold of her. Came after me with a hoe, he did."

At the sound of her daughter's screams, Mary came running, a fire poker in her hand. "You put down my Lucy this minute or you'll rue the day you ever set foot in my kitchen," she threatened Gordy in a low voice.

Gordy took a step back, chuckling as he looked to Riker.

"Quite a man you are," Riker commented dryly to Carter, "puttin' your family at risk like this over a few simple names."

Mary whipped around to face her husband. "There'll be no end to it, Carter. You speak and we'll be theirs the rest of our living days!"

Carter went down on his knees, tears streaming down his face. He clasped his hands as if in prayer. "If I tell you, if I tell everything I know, do you swear on your mother's grave you'll let me and my family go?"

Riker pulled out a chair, wood scraping wood as

he took his time in answering. "You tell me the right names. You give me some *good* information and perhaps that could be arranged . . ."

Carter lowered his face to his clasped hands. "I'll tell you," he declared. "I'll tell you anything you want to know."

"No!" Mary screamed. "No, Carter. They'll die. We'll all die!"

"I'll tell you what. You give us the name of the man in our camp who's a part of this masked rebel band and I believe I could even get you a commission in the king's army." Riker sat down in the chair and propped a booted foot on the corner of Mary's scarred kitchen table.

"Anything, anything," Carter sobbed.

"Mama! Mama!" little Lucy cried as she still struggled in the huge soldier's arms. "Mama, help me!" The faces of three other frightened children appeared in the doorway.

Raising the fire poker, Mary put out her hand for her daughter. Riker gave a slight nod and Gordy handed the child over to her mother.

"Clear the room," Riker commanded. "Gordy! Get the woman and children out and don't let them back in." He looked down at the pitiful sight of Carter kneeling at his feet. "Carter and I have a little talking to do."

Half an hour later, Riker and Gordy walked out of the Carter kitchen, mounted up, and rode away. Carter sat at the kitchen table, his head cradled in his arms.

When Mary was certain the redcoats were gone, she nodded to her eldest son, who immediately went out the front door to hitch the wagon. The other children gathered, packed bags, and followed their brother, their heads hung.

Mary walked into the kitchen, her progress made slow by her huge belly. She held her head high, her backbone straight. She retrieved two pots, several cooking utensils, and a sack of flour, and carried them to the kitchen door. On her second trip she took molasses, cornmeal, and the last grounds of coffee.

Carter finally lifted his head. "What are you doing?" he asked, his voice a ghostly whisper.

"You betrayed your friends, Carter Perkins! Your own father, for God's sake!"

He shook his head. "Not Papa."

Her eyes narrowed angrily. "I *heard* you. I heard the words come right out of your mouth!" She lowered her head. "I'm ashamed, ashamed to have ever known you!"

"I did it for you, for my family," he sobbed.

"You did it for yourself!"

"Where are you going?"

She turned away from the broken man who had been her husband but whom she considered her husband no longer. "I don't know. Away from here. I'm going to go pick up Harry if the redcoats haven't gotten to him first and then I'm leaving this town, I'm leaving this county, I'm leaving Virginia. I'm taking my children far from here where they'll never have to live with the stain of their father's betrayal."

Tears ran down Carter's face as he put out his hand to his wife. "You don't understand, Mary. I didn't do it on purpose. It just happened. You've got to believe me!" He touched her sleeve and she pulled back her arm as if she'd been burnt.

"You're a weak man, Carter Perkins, a weak, pitiful man!" With that, she snatched up the lantern and walked out the back door, leaving Carter in utter darkness.

Maggie lay stretched out on Grayson's cot repairing his boots. Grayson sat at his field desk sealing a message meant for Colonel Hastings, who had come to Yorktown and had been given a fighting command by General Washington. Once Grayson was relieved of his duties in the British camp, he would join Colonel Hastings as one of his staff officers on the battlefield.

A small stove in the center of the tent chased off the October chill making the tent a warm haven for Maggie and Grayson despite the occasional sound of gunfire in the distance. Skirmishes now took place daily, turning the entire peninsula into a battleground.

Just as Maggie had suspected, she was still being permitted to walk in and out of the British camp with little more than a nod from one of the sentries. Quite a few Tories had joined the British army once the patriots had moved on Yorktown, so Maggie wasn't the only civilian free to walk about the camp. Maggie had become such a familiar sight that it just didn't seem to occur to anyone that she could be any threat. So against Grayson's better judgment he allowed her to carry his messages out of the camp and into the waiting hands of the patriots.

Maggie was enjoying the game immensely. With General Washington using her home for a hospital, she stayed with Elizabeth at John's home at night and walked back and forth between camps during the day. On occasion she even convinced Grayson to allow her to spend the night in his tent. Tonight was one of those nights when he'd not sent her home at dark.

"Done?" she asked quietly.

He rolled the tiny strip of paper and inserted it into a quill. "Done. After he reads this, I imagine I'll be able to join him. I've had enough of this farce. I'm ready to fight. Just deliver the quill to Colonel Hastings, but mind you deliver it yourself."

She saluted, purposely using her left hand to aggravate him. "Yes, Captain. Right away, Captain."

He slipped the quill into her leather bag containing her bootmaking tools and came toward the bed in his stocking feet.

She couldn't resist a smile as she watched him cross the tent. He was dressed in his uniform breeches that hugged his thighs. His shirt was untied and left open down the center of his chest to reveal a sprinkling of golden curls. His hair had been freshly washed and swung at his shoulders in a golden curtain. In Maggie's wildest dreams she never imagined she would be in love with a man like Grayson Thayer. And the best part was he loved her, too.

"I shouldn't have let you stay the night," he told her, waggling his finger. "You'll be nothing but trouble."

She set aside his boot and moved over to make room for him on the narrow cot. "Too late. Not safe for me to travel to John's after dark. Soldiers everywhere."

"I fear it's the soldiers' safety I should be concerned with." He sat down, brushing her cheek with his fingertips.

She leaned to kiss him, hypnotized by the clear blue of his eyes.

When the tent flap lifted, Grayson turned around. "Michaels, I said that would be all for . . ." He left his sentence unfinished. There, standing just inside the tent, was Riker. Michaels stood between Grayson and the lieutenant.

Grayson rose. Maggie scooted to the edge of the bed. It was obvious there was something wrong. Instinctively her fingers found the knife she wore in her stocking.

"I told him he couldn't come in," Michaels apologized, obviously distraught. "I told him you had turned in for the night, but he came in anyway. I couldn't stop him."

Grayson nodded. "It's all right, Michaels. You can go."

"Sir?"

"Just step outside, boy." Grayson didn't like the wild-eyed smug look on Riker's face. If there was going to be trouble, he didn't want the boy in the center of it. Mentally, Grayson calculated how many steps it would take to get to the table where he kept his pistol.

Michaels backed out of the tent and let the canvas flap fall.

Riker smiled, nodding grandly in Maggie's direction. "I've found the two of you together . . . what a surprise! Who'd have thought I'd be responsible for such a romance."

"You've no right to burst in here like this, Riker," Grayson snapped in the voice Maggie had come to recognize as his cover, Captain Thayer. "I demand to know what is so deathly important that it cannot wait until roll call in the morning."

Riker lowered his hand and before Grayson could make a move, Riker drew his flintlock pistol from beneath his coat. "Why, I've come to arrest you, of course."

Grayson remained perfectly calm. "Arrest me? God's bowels, what are you talking about? I told you to ease up on that Colonial grum; it's making you slow-witted."

Riker brandished the pistol angrily. "Oh, no you don't. You're not going to talk your way out of this, Captain, or should I say, *Major?*"

Maggie's heart skipped a beat. He knew! Somehow Riker had found out who Grayson really was.

"I don't know what you're talking about. By whose authority have you come to arrest me? What are the charges?"

"I come by my own authority. I thought I'd surprise my uncle. He's been disappointed in me, you know. He meant to send me away because he thought me unworthy. But this will prove to him that I deserve his respect."

"You're rambling," Grayson said, still keeping the guise of innocence. He slid his foot to the right toward the table where he kept his pistol.

"Oh no you don't!" Riker took a step forward. "Stand right there. I don't want to kill you if I don't have to. I want to see you hang. I want to see you turn blue and kick your feet above the ground before you take your last breath."

Maggie started to rise up off the cot, but Riker turned his gaze on her. "You, too, Miss Bootmaker."

Maggie brought her hand to her breast. "Me?" she said innocently.

He grinned. "A woman riding with a band of men. I find it hard to believe."

"Look, Riker, I don't know where you got your information, but someone has taken your coin and is laughing his way to the tavern at this very minute."

He shook his head. "No. My information's good all right. The best. It took me months, but I finally found a man who'd talk."

Maggie lifted her head. "A man?"

Riker took another step toward Grayson, his pistol beaded in on Grayson's head. Maggie knew at that moment that Riker had reached the edge. If she or Grayson moved, Grayson was a dead man. "One of your own," Riker said with a funny laugh. "He turned easy if you're wondering."

"Who?" Maggie demanded. "Who did you talk to?"

Riker shrugged. "Guess there's no harm in sayin'

seeing as how I've got you both." His steely eyes met Maggie's. "A Colonial clod by the name of Carter, Carter Perkins."

The moment the words were out of Riker's mouth, Maggie knew it was true. Carter! She hung her head in pained frustration. How could he have done this to her? To them all?

Grayson threw a quick glance over his shoulder at Maggie. "I don't know what you're talking about here," he said, returning his gaze to Riker's taut face, "but I'm certain it can all be straightened out come morning."

"No, no, no, you don't understand, Thayer. You've been caught, you and the lady. The facts I have are true. You're not going to charm your way out of this one. You and this bootmaker are going to die." He looked at Maggie. "Now why don't you get up slowly so I can escort both of you to my uncle's tent. We want to catch him before he turns in for the night, don't we?"

When Maggie didn't move, he shook the pistol. "I said get up!" he shouted.

Maggie bounced up off the cot, fearing Riker would shoot Grayson before they ever made it out of the tent.

Riker began to back up. "Now come slowly this way the both of you, and I'm warning you, you make one bad move and I'll kill you right here, Thayer. You understand? Now get your hands up in the air where I can see them. Both of you!"

Slowly Grayson raised his hands. Maggie followed suit. Out of the corner of her eye, she thought she saw the tent flap move.

Suddenly Michaels appeared in the doorway, and before anyone could move, or even speak, the boy pulled the trigger of his flintlock rifle, shooting Riker in the back, point blank.

Chapter Twenty-five

For a sickening moment, Grayson and Maggie stood over Riker's body, staring in disbelief. He'd been dead before he hit the ground.

Grayson lifted his gaze to meet Michaels'. Tears ran unchecked down the boy's face. His discharged army-issue flintlock shook in his trembling hands.

"Good God, Michaels!" Grayson groaned. "You've killed him!"

Michaels nodded, his gaze fixed on the lieutenant's still body. "I couldn't let him take you to the major. I couldn't see you hang, sir." He looked up at Grayson, his lower lip trembling. For a moment he had been a man, but suddenly he was just a frightened boy again. "No matter who you are."

Maggie suddenly sprang into action. "Grayson! We've got to get out of here!" She threw his boots to him and grabbed his coat and bag of personal belongings he'd packed only this evening. "Where's your pistol?" she demanded. She knew they had to think and act quickly. If they didn't both get out of the British camp in a few moments' time, they might well hang as traitors to the Crown. There was no telling who Riker had spoken to before he'd come to the tent to make his arrests.

Both men stood staring at each other, dazed. "My pistol?" Grayson asked.

"Your pistol!"

"In the drawer."

Maggie grabbed the loaded pistol and swung around to face the rear of the tent. Cocking the hammer, she pulled the trigger and fired through the canvas wall.

"What are you doing?" Grayson cried.

"Michaels!" Maggie ordered. "Holler sniper."

The boy gulped. "Ma'am?"

"Holler *sniper!* There're rebel snipers firing on the camp! For God's sake, Michaels, don't you see? A sniper just killed the lieutenant!"

Michaels' eyes went wide with understanding. "Sniper," he squeaked.

"Louder!" Maggie ordered as she grabbed her bag of bootmaking tools and her wool cloak.

"Sniper!" Michaels shouted. "Sniper! Sniper!"

Maggie grabbed Grayson by the sleeve. He had by this time slipped into his boots and was reloading his pistol. "We've got to get out of here," she told him insistently. "We'll use the cover of the commotion." She turned back to Private Michaels. "Keep hollering! Get somebody in here!"

Michaels ducked outside the tent. Maggie could already hear soldiers running. Someone must have misfired because suddenly there was a spray of gunfire. Somewhere in the distance a cannon sounded. Whether it was English or American, she didn't know.

Maggie dragged Grayson out of the tent and into the darkness. She swung her cloak over her shoulders and lifted the hood to cover her face. She pushed Grayson's cocked hat onto his head, pulling it down low so that no one could recognize him easily in the darkness.

Half-dressed redcoats were running everywhere. Lanterns swung as soldiers hurried to their posts, hitching up their breeches as they ran. Men shouted and called to one another. A horse broke loose and hit a tent wire, bringing down a mess tent and adding to the general confusion.

"I think I see one!" a soldier shouted as he raced past Maggie. "There in the trees!" he called to his companion.

Rifles sounded again and again.

"Help! Help!" Michaels shouted. "A lieutenant's been shot!" Someone raced past Grayson and Maggie with a medic bag across his back and ducked inside Grayson's tent where Riker's body lay.

Grayson slipped into his coat and reached for Michaels, who was standing just outside the circle of light that poured from Grayson's open tent. "Michaels?"

The blond-haired boy looked up. "Sir?"

Maggie could hear the strain in Grayson's voice as he tried to find the right words. "Son, do what you have to with what you heard tonight, but I want you to remember . . ." He paused, glancing away before forcing himself to look into Michaels' teary eyes. "I want you to remember that no matter what happens, no matter what you think of me, I love you." Grayson threw his arms around the boy and hugged him tightly.

The private lowered his head to Grayson's shoulder, clenching him tightly.

"Grayson," Maggie said gently, tugging on his arm. "We got to get out of here before anyone realizes you're missing."

Giving Michaels a final pat on the back, Grayson took the canvas bag Maggie held out to him and together they slipped off into the night.

Grayson pounded on Zeke's back door with his fist. "Zeke!" he called. "Zeke, it's Grayson!"

Maggie hung behind him. "Something's not right," she murmured. "There's a light on inside. Zeke's never up this late."

Grayson banged again. "Zeke!"

Maggie heard the bolt slip on the door. Grayson pushed it open. "Get your rifle, Zeke," Grayson told him as he stepped inside, not taking the time to wait for an invitation.

"What is it? What's going on?" Zeke asked.

Maggie walked in behind Grayson. "It's Carter, Zeke. Carter's the traitor among us!"

Zeke's disbelieving eyes met Maggie's. "No . . ."

"Yes," Grayson said, taking Zeke's flintlock down from over the door and tossing it to him.

Zeke's hands instinctively went up and he caught the firearm. "How can that be? You have proof?"

"Maggie and I heard the truth of it with our own ears. Carter was Riker's informant. Riker's dead, but we've to get to Carter if we can."

Zeke swung the rifle over his shoulder by the leather strap and reached for his ammunition bag.

Maggie touched his arm. "Everything all right here?"

He shook his head as he reached for his buckskin tunic. "Mama's down bad. She's dying, Maggie."

"Can you leave her alone?"

"Lyla's here. They been gettin' on real good." He smiled grimly. "Mama likes her. Says her hands are warm."

"Can I see your mama?"

Zeke gave a nod. "She might still be awake."

"Maggie," Grayson said gently, "we've got to go. It's important that we get to Carter before anyone else does." He paused. "You could stay here if you'd rather," he offered hopefully.

"I'll be right back." She held up her finger. "Wait for me."

Slipping into the parlor, Maggie approached the bed Mildred was curled up in. A small figure sat in a straight-backed chair leaning over the old woman, offering her sips of tea.

At the sound of footsteps, Lyla turned.

"How is she?" Maggie slowly approached the bed. Mildred looked so small and lost in the mountain of quilts piled around her.

Lyla shrugged. "I don't know what's wrong with her except she's give out."

Maggie came to the bedside and took Mildred's wrinkled hand in hers. She was cool to the touch, despite the warmth of the room and the heavy quilts she lay beneath. "Mildred," she said softly. "Mildred, it's Maggie."

It seemed to take a great effort for the old woman to open her eyes. "Maggie?" Her voice was barely audible.

Maggie smiled, as she reached out to brush a lock of silvery white hair from Mildred's cheek. "Zeke says you're feelin' poorly."

Mildred smiled weakly. "Did he tell you I'm dyin'?"

Maggie forced a laugh. "No. Of course not."

"Well, I am."

"Oh, don't say that, Mildred. You're just tired. You'll be up and about in a few days."

"A few days and I'll be six feet under," Mildred declared, her constitution clearly a little stronger. "You met Lyla?"

Maggie glanced at the small blond-haired woman she knew Zeke loved. "I have."

"Nice girl. Make my Zeke a good wife. I only wish I was gonna live to see grandchildren."

Maggie patted her hand. "Of course you're going to see your grandchildren."

"Maggie," Zeke called from the doorway. "The major says we've got to move on. We have to get the others."

At the sound of Zeke's voice, Lyla immediately rose and went to him. He took her hand. "Is there trouble?" she asked.

He turned up her palm and kissed it. "Nothing we can't take care of. You sit here with Mama until I get back. You hear me? Any redcoats come to the door, you don't know where I am or when I'll get back. You're just here carin' for an old, sick woman."

She nodded. "I'll be right here waitin' on you, Zeke." She reached up with one hand to caress his straggly, bearded cheek. "But don't you go getting yourself killed on me." She smiled up at him. "Not when I was thinkin' of marrying you."

He grinned. "Wouldn't think of gettin' killed. I'm too ornery." He released her hand. "Maggie Mae!"

Maggie turned back to Mildred, touched by what had just taken place between Zeke and Lyla. They were so comfortable together. It was as if they had known each other a lifetime. Maggie couldn't help wondering how she and Grayson appeared to others. Did they look as if they belonged together as Lyla and Zeke so obviously did?

Maggie leaned over Mildred. "I'll be back later," she whispered.

"No need. I'll be dead."

Maggie kissed the old woman's cheek. Her skin felt paper-thin and fragile as a dry leaf against her lips. "Good-bye, Mildred."

"Bye, sweet." The old woman patted Maggie's cheek. "You've been a good friend to me and my son. You've done enough for others, Maggie girl, it's time you done something for yourself. You marry that good-lookin' man of yours if that's what you want. You let him buy you fancy gowns and silver teapots. I can't think of anyone in the world who deserves it more than you."

Maggie sighed as she watched Mildred draw her

withered hand beneath the quilt and close her eyes.

"Maggie!" Zeke called.

"I'm coming, I'm coming. Keep your breeches on!" She gave Mildred a final pat and then turned and followed Zeke out of the parlor and back into the kitchen. "I haven't got a weapon. You got something for me, Zeke?"

He reached into a rough-hewn cupboard and pulled out an old matchlock pistol. "She still shoots on the straight and narrow." He handed her a small leather pouch on a drawstring from a peg on the wall. "Let's go." He lifted his gaze to Grayson. "Major. You lead."

One by one the three filed out into the darkness, praying they reached Carter before the British did.

Maggie walked between Grayson and Zeke, trying to match her stride with theirs as Les led the way up the dark lane to Carter's house. Old Harry, Pete, and John brought up the rear on horseback.

Harry had been the first to know his son had betrayed them. After making arrangements to get his daughter-in-law, Mary, and his grandchildren safely out of Yorktown, he'd ridden straight for John Logan's. By chance Grayson and Maggie had come upon Harry and John as they all cut through the woods to Les Bennett's. John had then rode to the crossroad and retrieved Pete. Grayson and Zeke practically had to tie Les down to force him to wait until they were all gathered together before setting out after Carter.

"Harry, you don't have to do this," John murmured, riding beside the elderly gentleman. "We can do what's got to be done without you."

The old Virginia militiaman held his head high. "I been a part of this since the beginning," he said, trying to control the emotion in his voice. "My son betrayed me the same as he betrayed his friends and his country."

"But he's your son, for God's sake!" John laid his hand on Harry's.

Harry shook his head. "It's only right I be there."

John withdrew his hand. "I understand. I was just trying to save you the pain."

Harry glanced up at John, his pale-blue eyes filled with tears. "Too late. Nothin' left to do but sweep up the pieces and then move on. I'll be joining my daughter-in-law up Maryland way. I'm gonna live out what time I got left on this earth with my grandchildren."

John nodded. "I'm just sorry it had to happen this way, Harry. You're too good a man to have to live through this."

Harry shrugged beneath his moth-eaten cloak. "Many a thing has happened to me in the last seventy-odd years, son. Some of it good, some of it bad." His gaze met John's as he smiled a bittersweet smile. "But I have to tell you, I've had a good life along the way."

John smiled back at the old man and then urged his mount forward, swallowing against the lump that rose in his throat. He only hoped he could be as brave as Harry Perkins when it came to doing what he knew they had to do.

In silence, the rebel band rode up the wooded drive to Carter's house. Lamplight burned in the kitchen. *He's waiting for us,* Maggie thought with a stab of pain. Each of the men had tried to convince her to stay behind. Grayson said there was no need for her to come along, but she was one of them. She owed it to Carter to be there.

Just the same, it was hard for Maggie to walk into Carter's kitchen, the kitchen where in better days she'd sat around the table eating with his family, laughing about the good days before the war, the days when they'd been children growing up on the banks of the York River.

Carter was seated at the table. He just sat there with empty eyes as one by one his friends filed in. Harry entered the cold kitchen last. For an instant father and son locked gazes, but then Carter looked away, unable to hold up to his father's scrutiny.

"Tell me you didn't do it, Son," Harry said, leaning on his loaded flintlock. "Tell your papa you didn't betray him."

Carter hung his head. "You don't understand. I didn't do it on purpose. I never meant to hurt anyone."

"You just meant to turn a few coin," Les said bitterly. Harry had passed on to the others Mary's version of what Carter had done.

"I never meant to hurt any of you. I never meant for it to go so far!"

"My brother died because of you! They tortured him and they kilt him!" Les shouted coming after Carter, swinging his rifle butt.

Grayson dove to stop Les. Carter fell over his chair backward trying to get out of Les's way. Pete and Zeke hauled Carter to his feet, keeping him just out of Les's reach.

"You've got to tell us who else besides Riker knows our identities," John said quietly. "Major Thayer's especially."

Carter shook his head. "I don't know," he murmured. "It was only Riker I talked to." He lifted his head. "He was gonna hurt my little girl, John. I had to tell him!"

"You never should have gotten yourself into this predicament!" Les hollered, still struggling against Grayson's hold. "You never should have told nobody anything to start with!"

"I'm sorry! I'm sorry!" Carter declared through tears. "I'm so sorry, Les. I didn't know they were gonna kill Ed. He said they weren't gonna hurt him. He said as long as I told them what happened to the dispatches, no one was going to get hurt. Only Ed wouldn't give 'em up. I told Ed to tell 'em where the dispatches were," he sobbed.

"You were there, you bastard!" Les exploded, lunging for him again. Grayson held Les back, but it took effort.

"Whoa, whoa there, Les," John said, pressing his hand to Les's chest. "You said you could handle this. Now if you can't, you let the major escort you outside."

"He was there for God's sake! The bastard let them kill my brother!"

"I couldn't stop 'em," Carter sobbed. "I swear I couldn't!"

"Let's get back to Riker," John said, trying to maintain control of the situation. "Who did you talk to? It couldn't have been Riker from the beginning, else it wouldn't have taken him this long to catch us."

Carter allowed Zeke and Pete to drag him to the chair John had uprighted. "No, no, I never knew it was Riker who was getting the information, not until he came here tonight!"

"Who did you talk to before?"

"That Tory, Natty Watkins."

"But Riker didn't know where the information was coming from?"

Carter shook his head. "Mostly I just told Natty little stuff—"

"And warned them we were coming, like the time your gun 'misfired' the night we were looking for that mailbag and found the payroll," Maggie said from the doorway.

Carter looked up. "They wanted me to tell 'em where we were going to hit, Mags. I didn't do it, though. I saved you from an ambush."

"We could've just as easily been killed by those redcoats," John said.

"You don't understand," Carter mumbled. "You don't understand."

"We understand you sold your loyalty," Maggie said, her voice stark in the cold room. "We only lost Ed—"

"And Billy Faulkner and his family," Grayson amended. He looked at Carter, who seemed such a pathetic man to him. Just the same, he was angry, damned angry. The man who had claimed to be a friend to Maggie had put her life in jeopardy, and for that, he hated Carter. "Billy was my man, Perkins. He was working for me."

Maggie nodded. "All of us here tonight could have died if Riker hadn't come to Grayson's tent instead of going to Major Lawrence first."

When Carter said nothing in his own defense, John sighed. He was weary to the bone. "Is there anything else we should know, Carter? Was there anyone with Riker when he came here, anyone he might have told what you told him?"

"That Gordy fellow was with him, but he didn't let Gordy in when we were talkin'," Carter responded softly. "I got the idea Riker wanted to bring everyone in on his own so he could prove himself to his uncle." He looked up at the group. "Don't you understand? Riker was going to hurt my family if I didn't tell him."

"You're the one who hurt your family," Harry said. "The day you took the very first bloody cent." He looked to John. "Let's say we take care of this and get out. It turns my stomach sick just to look at him."

"Papa! You're . . . you're gonna turn me in?" Carter reached out toward his father, but Harry brushed him aside. "Please don't turn me in. They'll lock me up in the brig. They'll hang me!"

John gave a nod and Zeke and Pete lifted Carter out of his chair. "We're not going to let them hang you," John said solemnly. "We're going to do it ourselves."

Carter's face went ashen. "You . . . you wouldn't! Not your friend! Not your son, Papa!" He looked from one man to the next. "Mags?"

Maggie turned away and opened the door for Zeke and Pete, who began to lead Carter out. Carter made no attempt to fight them.

Outside, the stars hung low in the black sky. It was cold, but the night was clear. An owl hooted in a tree overhead, and then Maggie heard the sound of beating wings as the creature flew from the humans. Maggie felt Grayson's hand slip into hers and she was comforted.

"You don't have to stay," he whispered.

She looked up at him. "He was my friend, too. It's just fittin' that I be here for the end."

Grayson nodded. He understood all too well.

Zeke and Pete half carried Carter out into the yard. They tied his hands behind his back and lifted him onto John's horse. Zeke led the horse to the tree where Les was fixing a hanging knot.

"Make it tight," John ordered Les. "We don't want him suffering."

Carter shook with fear. "I can't believe you're gonna let 'em do this, Papa," he begged Harry. "I can't believe you'll let them hang me. I've been falsely accused! I didn't do it, Papa! Please don't let them hang me!"

"Let them!" Harry murmured. "Hell, I'm gonna do it myself."

John looked to Harry. "That's not necessary."

"Sure it is," Harry said with tears in his eyes. "I

brought this traitor into the world, caught him with my own hands." He held out his palms, staring at them as if in disbelief. "It's only right I take him out."

Maggie watched as Harry hobbled toward Carter who sat perfectly still on John's horse. Les lowered the noose over his head and tightened the knot.

"You got anything else to say?" John asked.

Carter squeezed his eyes shut. "No," he squeaked. "Nothin' except I'm sorry . . . so sorry."

Harry patted his son's thigh in one last compassionate gesture and then, drawing back his hand, he hit John's horse hard on the rump. The horse bolted and Maggie dropped her head onto Grayson's shoulder so that she wouldn't have to see Carter die.

Grayson led Maggie up the grand staircase of John's home and down the hall to the room Elizabeth had directed him to. Maggie walked like a sleepwalker, dazed by all that had happened in the last hours.

"Come on, sweet," he urged, his breath warm in her ear. "A little sleep and we'll both feel better." He pushed open the bedchamber door.

Maggie caught his hand. "You'll stay with me, won't you? You won't go yet?" She'd been strong when she had to be, but suddenly there seemed to be no fight left in her. Maggie was sick to death of the war and its destruction. All she wanted to do was be with Grayson, to be held by him.

He smiled down at her and leaned to kiss her

quivering lower lip. "I'm as tired as you. I thought if you didn't mind, I'd slide right into bed beside you and take a little nap."

She nodded. "I just don't want you to go. I know you have to join the others on the battlefield, but not yet."

"I think the war can do without me for a few hours," he teased as he draped his arm over her shoulder and ushered her into the bedchamber.

The drapes had been pulled against the morning sunlight and a small fire burned in the fireplace hearth. The room was dark and cozy.

Leading Maggie to the bed, he began to undress her. Her limbs felt as limp as a rag doll's. She just couldn't believe Carter had betrayed them. She couldn't believe he was dead.

Grayson pulled Maggie's shift over her head leaving her to stand naked and shivering as he tugged back the heavy quilt on the freshly made bed. "Climb in, love."

Maggie did as he told her, allowing him to pull the coverlet up to her chin. She reached out to him. "You're not leaving, are you?"

"No, no," he soothed, coming around the other side of the bed. "I'm just going to undress and then I'll snuggle in beside you."

Maggie watched as Grayson set his loaded pistol on the cherry candlestand and then stood on one foot, and then the other to tug off his boots. She watched him through the fringe of her lashes as he peeled off his tight white breeches and pulled his shirt over his head.

She sighed at the sight of his magnificent form

as she lifted the edge of the quilt so that he might slide in beside her.

"Ah, Maggie mine," he murmured in her ear, drawing her into his arms.

The warmth of his body blotted out all thoughts of Carter Perkins and the hanging. "Grayson," she whispered. "We came so close to losing each other last night."

"It's frightening, I know, but we're all right," he soothed, brushing his fingertips down her spine. "You were very brave tonight and I'm proud of you." He kissed her bare shoulder. "But you've been too brave too long. You've taken care of yourself too long. Why don't we start taking care of each other?"

She ran her fingers through his unbound hair, and guided his head until it rested on her breasts. "I'm not so certain we're going to make it, Grayson."

He lifted his head and stared into her dark Indian eyes. "We're both going to make it. I'm going to live to make you my wife," he slid his hand over her slightly rounded belly, *"and* give our son or daughter a name."

Maggie blinked. "Our . . . our . . ." She swallowed. She was too surprised to even try to deny her pregnancy. "H-how did you know?"

He rubbed his palm across her middle in a gentle circular motion. "How dumb do you think I am? I sleep with you most nights. You think I haven't noticed the changes in your body?"

She laid back on the goose-down pillow, not knowing what to say.

He stretched out beside her and stroked her head. "I was waiting for you to tell me, Maggie. When were you going to do it? When I could hear my child cry with my own ears?" He shook his head. "Why didn't you tell me?"

She looked up into his clear blue eyes. "Because it was my trouble, not yours."

"Trouble? We're talking about my flesh and blood, Maggie!"

She looked away. "I wanted you to love me for me, to want to marry me for me, not for a babe who needed a name. I didn't want you to think I was trying to trap you into marrying me."

"Trap me?" He laughed. "I was trapped the first moment I stepped into Commegys' Ordinary and saw you standing there among all of those men. I was trapped by my love for you—never the other way around." He squeezed his eyes shut. "I can see you as plain as day with your skirts hitched up, tossing the dice across the table. I can hear your laughter." He opened his eyes. "I can still taste our first kiss."

Tears clouded Maggie's eyes. "It's not that I don't want to marry you. It's just that I've been married before. Noah—"

"Damn it, Maggie, I don't want to hear about Noah, I want to hear about me. I know why you didn't want to be married to Noah. Tell me why you don't want to be married to me!" He cupped her chin, forcing her to look him straight in the eye. "Talk to me! Tell me what you're so afraid of."

"I'm not afraid!"

"You are. You're afraid I might really love you as much as I say I do."

She shook her head. "That's not it. You and I, we're so different. Your family and mine—"

"It doesn't matter. We're past this social-class claptrap. We've been through too much for you to use that as an excuse any longer."

She stared up at the white ceiling. "Your drinking. I don't like it. Noah—"

"So why didn't you tell me? Every man drinks, especially a man under the kind of pressure I've been under. But that doesn't make me a drunkard, Maggie. Noah was a drunkard. He couldn't stop himself. I could lay down a bottle and never pick it up again."

"You could? For me?"

He took her hand and kissed the tips of her fingers one by one. "Yes. I drank out of loneliness. I drank because I didn't have anyone to confide in. I'm not lonely anymore. I have you . . ."

A lump rose in Maggie's throat. "Oh, Grayson," she whispered as she threw her arms around him and hugged him. "I've been so afraid I couldn't hold on to you that I wasn't willing to try. I was so afraid it would hurt more to have you and lose you then to never really have you at all."

"You're not going to lose me. I'll follow you to the ends of the earth, if that's what it takes. I'm here," he assured her. "I'll always be here for you."

His mouth met hers and Maggie welcomed his kiss. Their tongues touched, retreated, then touched again. Her thoughts were in a jumble. Nothing made sense. Had she just agreed to marry him? She wasn't certain. But what she was certain of was the rising desire inside her for him. She lifted her hips instinctively, wanting to feel his hard, sleek body against her own soft curves.

Grayson's lips touched hers again and again until she was breathless. He kissed her cheeks, her eyelids, the tip of her nose, and then he lowered his head. He took her nipple between his lips and tugged gently.

Maggie moaned.

He stroked her silky thighs, his fingers glancing over her tight web of curls. She shuddered as his fingers stroked and probed, spreading a flaming heat that left her breathless, but still wanting more.

"Grayson," she murmured as she ran her hands over his muscular back, reveling in the feel of him over her.

"Ah, Maggie mine, I love you as the moon loves the stars, I love you as the dew loves the grass . . ."

She shared her husky laughter with no one but him. "A poet," she whispered.

"Marry me and I'll come to your window each night and sing of my love to you. Be my wife and I'll woo you until I'm too old to walk, too feeble to lift my voice."

She wound her fingers through his hair and parted her thighs. She could feel his hard shaft against her leg as she rose and fell beneath him. "It's tempting," she whispered. "I think I like this wooing."

He kissed the lobe of her ear, his hot breath

sending shivers of delight through her already quivering limbs. "I'll love you day and night, Maggie mine. I'll love you until death do us part and then on into eternity."

"Hush this foolish talk," she murmured. "Never trust a man with honeyed words, my mam always said. Deeds you can trust. No more words. I'm tired of words. Show me love."

Brushing her hair off her perspiration-dotted forehead, he lifted his hips and, guided by her hand, he slipped into her.

Maggie rose up with a gasp of relief . . .

With agonizing slowness, Grayson teased her with one thrust after another, letting the swollen tip of his engorged manhood caress her willing flesh until she thought she would scream for want of him.

A pounding, incandescent heat rose in Maggie's loins as she lifted again and again to meet Grayson halfway. She caressed his hard, sinewy buttocks with her hands, guiding him, pulling him deeper and deeper into her until together as one, they reached ultimate fulfilment.

Waves of spent passion washed over Maggie as she rested in the safety of Grayson's arms. He pulled her to him so that her cheek rested at the hollow of his shoulder and then he brought the quilt over them both, protecting them in a cocoon of warmth.

"Marry me, Maggie mine," Grayson urged in a half-whisper. "Say yes."

"Yes," she answered, still breathless from their lovemaking.

"When?"

"I don't know. Ask me tomorrow," she murmured drowsily as she rolled over onto her side and curled up into a ball, drifting off to sleep.

Chapter Twenty-six

"When, Maggie?" Grayson called to her as he watched her ladle out a serving of beans to a soldier who held out his wooden trecher.

"Soon," she answered as she moved on to the next hungry man.

She and Grayson had had a terrible fight when she had told him she was going to stick with him to the end of the battle. He insisted she go to Williamsburg, where she and his baby would be safe. She refused, telling him that if he wanted her for his wife, he had to take her as she was. It was important that she be at his side, doing what she could for him and the other men. He could accept it or not accept it, but she wasn't budging.

So Maggie moved through the earthen trenches the American army and their French allies had dug with a flintlock on her back doing whatever she could for the men. She cleansed wounds, fetched water, fed them what food could be scraped up, and patched leaky boots. She agreed to stay off the front lines, but that was her only concession. They were well into October now, and so far she'd still been able to remain at Grayson's side.

"How soon? How soon will you marry me, Maggie Mae?" Grayson smiled as he leaned his back against the earthen wall of the redoubt the British had abandoned in retreat. Ironically it was one of the redoubts Grayson had been forced to direct in its construction.

"Very soon!" she flipped curtly as she turned to Zeke and kicked him with the toe of her boot. "You know I always hated it when you called me that! Why did you have to tell *him* my middle name was Mae?"

"Ouch!" Zeke massaged his injured calf. "I wish you'd just marry him and get it over with." He held out his dinner plate and watched as she spooned out his ration of the hot beans. "We're sick to death of having to listen to the man's pitiful whining."

Maggie smiled at Zeke as she rubbed her wrist absentmindedly. Once he and Grayson had come to the conclusion that they need not volley for her attention, the two had gotten on well. The camaraderie was good for Zeke. The last two weeks had been hard on him, with Carter's betrayal and death and then his mother's death the very same night. To make matters worse, he hadn't been able to get away to see Lyla since his mother's funeral. He seemed to miss her tremendously.

Maggie reached Grayson, who held out his pewter plate as well. She passed by him and moved on to the next man.

"Hey!" he called after her. "What about me?"

She only laughed and moved on.

Grayson got up and came to her and she scooped out the last of the beans in the pot and placed them on the wooden trecher of a soldier who had one eye patched. He nodded his thanks.

Grayson laid his hand on Maggie's shoulder and looked into the pot. "You didn't save me a bite?" he asked, trying not to sound disappointed.

She grinned mischievously and hooked her finger, signaling him to follow her. Walking past Zeke, Maggie set the pot at his feet and followed the bend in the trench. Dim lanternlight guided her way. Hiking up her blue tick skirts, she climbed a dirt ladder.

"Hey! Where are you going? You can't go out there!" Grayson grabbed for her foot, but she slipped away with a giggle. He had no choice but to follow her.

"It's safe enough," Maggie whispered, taking his warm hand in hers. "It's dark out. Time for the Brits to have their palm toddies," she teased. "Besides, I need some fresh air or I'm going to fall over."

A shell exploded well in the distance, lighting up the sky.

Grayson squeezed her hand, but neither of them flinched. In last days both had gotten used to the nearly constant barrage of cannon and gunfire. "You look tired," he said. "I could get an escort for you to get you back to John's."

"Not on your life, my love." She spotted a sentry smoking a corncob pipe. "Even' to you, Lance," she greeted.

The bearded man gave a nod and went on puffing his pipe. It was his duty and that of many others to guard the men who were building and fortifying earthworks.

The night air was filled with the sound of men digging as their shovels scraped the soft earth. Another trench was being dug to link redoubts, drawing the American army even closer to the enemy lines.

Maggie walked a good twenty yards from the safety of the fortified redoubt before she came to a black cedar tree and slid to the cool grassy ground. Grayson sat beside her, laying his loaded rifle across his lap.

"I'm sorry I didn't save you any beans," she apologized. "Were you terribly hungry?"

He looked up into the dark-clouded sky. A British shell lit up the redoubt as it hit the grassy field, falling short of its mark. "Not so hungry."

She gave a sigh. "Well, that's too bad," she said, opening a canvas sack she carried on her shoulder, "because I've got all this bread and cheese and apples and no one to eat it!"

"Bread! Cheese! Where did you get it?"

She laughed. "Just eat and don't ask," she said, pushing the small feast into his hands.

"Ah, Maggie, what would I do without you?" He took a bite of the bread and then of the cheese, suddenly realizing how ravenous he was.

She bit into an apple. "You'd be better off than you are now, I'll warrant you."

"Don't say that. Don't ever say that." He kissed her lips, tasting apple on them.

Maggie looked out at the grassy battlefield stretching before them. In the distance she could see the light of the British campfires glowing in their redoubts. Bristling rows of sharpened logs jutted out of the earth protecting the British soldiers from easy attack.

If she squinted, she could even see the light from fires across the river at the British camp on Gloucester Point where she knew there was a log palisade and lines of white tents. To the right, the cloak of darkness obscured her view of the place where the river widened into the Chesapeake Bay where she knew French fleets kept the Brits bottled up.

"So why are we waiting?" she asked. "Why don't we take the full offensive and run them right off the end of the peninsula and into the water?"

He laughed. "You think yourself a general, do you?"

She grinned. "Maybe."

He laid back against the tree trunk so that he could see her face in the moonlight. "Would you tell your men to leap out of the safety of their trenches and fight hand to hand, bayonet to bayonet?"

"I don't think so. I think if I was in charge tonight, I'd be digging fast and hard straight for the enemy lines."

"Why, Madame General?"

She cut her eyes toward him. "Because they think they're going to be able to retreat tonight. Colonel Hastings himself said activity had been spotted down by the river at dusk. We've been waiting for them to attempt their retreat, and I'd bet you tonight is the night they think they're going to make it." She tucked her feet up beneath her dusty petticoats. "Only they're not."

"Why aren't they, Maggie?"

She rubbed her wrist. "There's a storm coming in."

He looked into the sky then back at Maggie, doubtful but not totally disbelieving. He remembered the time at Thayer's Folly when she'd predicted a storm and one had blown in within hours. "A storm?"

She took another bite of her apple, a smile turning up her lips. "I'd say with a little help from nature, and some strong arms to dig trenches tonight right to their back door, we'd have a surrender in our hands."

Grayson took her hand in his and rubbed her wrist thoughtfully. "A storm, you say?"

She nodded with a sigh and went back to her apple. "A pity I'm not commanding the Army, hmm?"

Grayson suddenly stood up, pulling her up with him.

"Where are you taking me?" she protested, dragging her feet. "I haven't finished with my supper!"

He swung his rifle over his shoulder and led her back toward the redoubt. "We're going to Colonel Hastings. I want you to tell him what you told me." He looked up into the sky. "He may want to pass the information on to General Washington."

Maggie stopped short, her eyes wide. "The general?"

He gave a curt nod and started for the redoubt again, Maggie in tow. "I'd say it's our duty, wouldn't you, soldier?"

A vicious squall swept down the York River from the west sometime near midnight. The British army kept up a steady shelling in an attempt to deceive the Americans as Cornwallis tried to make a retreat across the river to temporary safety on Gloucester Point. But luck was not with King George's army tonight. Pelting rain and sweeping water set the British smallboats off course, sinking some, marooning many on the north shore.

A glimmer of hope rose among the Americans in the early-morning hours before daybreak as word swept through the trenches that two boat loads of retreating English soldiers had been captured downstream. Cornwallis had sent a thousand men across the river in a first wave, including his infantry, most of the crack brigade guards, as well as several companies of the Twenty-third Regiment.

The Americans and the French dug all night in the driving rain, pushing closer to the enemy. The British could not understand why they fired their own cannon all night, with little response from the rebel army. When dawn came, spilling light onto the battlefield, the reason was all too evident. The American army had brought a trench and fourteen cannon so close to the British hornwork that the German and British soldiers could toss stones into it.

With the coming of dawn the American and

French again began to fire their guns. Sometime near midmorning, as Maggie fetched water for an injured soldier, Grayson came running to her, calling her name.

"Maggie!" he cried. "Maggie!" His clothing was covered in red dirt, his face and golden hair splattered with drying mud. But his face was lit up with the most beautiful smile.

Maggie grinned at him as he spun her around, spilling precious drinking water onto the muddy ground. "Come!" he shouted. "You have to come!"

"What? What is it?"

He tossed her waterskin to the nearest soldier and grabbed her hand, dragging her up onto a crude wooden platform so that she might be able to see the British lines.

The moment Maggie lifted her head above the earthen wall she clasped her hand over her mouth in joyous disbelief.

There, standing on a British parapet against the horizon, was a lone drummer boy beating out a steady roll on his battered drum. Fire slowly began to slacken around Maggie as she watched the small red-coated figure, wearing a bearskin cap, drum on, his haunting tune forever embedded in her mind.

Maggie clasped Grayson's hand, looking into his eyes, her own eyes filled with tears. "A parley," she whispered. "They ask for a parley?"

Grayson nodded, sweeping her into his arms and crushing his mouth against hers. "They're surrendering, Maggie mine. The war is over, my love."

* * *

Two days later General George Washington and his commander of the French troops, Rochambeau, led their armies into a field where the men fell into ranks, two files facing each other yards apart.

Maggie stood in the crowd of civilians who had come from miles around by carriage and on foot to see the surrender. Last night she had managed to make it back to John's, where she had bathed. This morning she had dressed in one of the gowns Grayson had bought her in Williamsburg. It was a simple forest-green sak gown, the bodice and sleeves edged in scalloped lace. Over her shoulders she wore a matching hooded cloak of forest-green wool, lined in apple-green watered silk. She had pulled back her strawberry-blond hair in a thick green velvet ribbon so that it tumbled down her back in a rich cascade of curls.

From Maggie's position, she could see Grayson's back as he stood tall in a blue coat he had borrowed from a private in the trenches. Though the coat was a little small and lacked the insignia of his rank, it was important to him that after all these years, he wear the colors of his newfound nation.

Bands played to pass the time as the ragtag American army and their smartly dressed French counterparts waited for the British. Finally, after what seemed an eternity, a roll of drums was heard and the enemy appeared, their flags furled as they marched to the melancholy tune of "The

World Turned Upside Down."

As the column moved toward Surrender Field, Maggie craned her neck to catch a glance of Cornwallis, but he was not to be seen. The British were being led instead by an odd man in outdated lavish clothing and great sausage curls hanging at his temples.

"General O'Hara," Maggie heard a man behind her say with a chuckle. "Could be no other in that garb!"

Maggie watched as O'Hara approached the Frenchman Rochambeau, who then directed him to General Washington across the way.

Words were exchanged as Maggie watched in fascination. Just beyond Washington and his staff was a field, where members of the light cavalry had sat their horses in a large circle. It was there that the British would surrender their arms.

Maggie stood proud as she watched the defeated army of some thirty-five hundred able-bodied soldiers pass by, some crying, others hanging their heads in shame. It seemed doubly hard for the English and Germans to surrender, knowing they, the greatest military power in the world, had been bested by farmers and shopkeepers. The American army remained solemn and respectful as the regiments marched by, though the joy of winning the Revolution at last was plain on their faces.

Out of the long column a single red-coated soldier strayed. Maggie tensed at the realization that the man leading a horse was headed straight for Grayson. Then she recognized the horse. It was Giipa! It was Grayson's horse he'd thought lost when he'd escaped the British camp. In the days before the surrender the British had slaughtered some one thousand horses and thrown them into the York River rather than letting them die of starvation. She and Grayson had thought for certain that Giipa had been one of those casualties.

But there he was, prancing across the grassy field led by Private Paul Michaels, who Maggie now recognized. An armed soldier stepped out to halt the boy, but Grayson stepped away from his regiment, waving back the soldier.

After a moment's hesitation, Maggie broke from the crowd of civilians and raced across the field through the line of Americans to Grayson accepting Giipa's reins from Paul.

"I . . . I kept him safe, sir," Michaels was saying as Maggie stepped up beside Grayson.

Grayson's gaze met Michaels. The boy's uniform was torn and soiled. He wore a bloodied bandage around one arm. A lump rose in Grayson's throat as he tried to find his voice.

"I'm sorry," he finally managed. "I'm sorry I had to deceive you, son."

Michaels squinted in the glare of the autumn sunlight. "You were good to me, sir, though I was your enemy. I want you to know how much I appreciate that," he said in a clear tenor voice that made him sound much older than his fifteen years.

Maggie watched as Michaels reached for the flintlock he wore on one shoulder. "For that kindness, I surrender to you." He laid down his weapon at Grayson's feet and straightened, standing at attention.

Grayson twisted Giipa's reins in his fingers. "Join me, son. Maggie and I are to be married. Come to Thayer's Folly and begin a new life."

Michaels bit down on his lower lip and dashed at his eyes with the back of a dirty hand. "No, sir. If I don't stick with this, I'll never stick with anything. I have to surrender with my fellow soldiers."

Grayson nodded. "I understand."

There was a moment of silence as the two regarded each other, neither wanting to say good-bye. Finally, Michaels lowered his gaze. "I understand I'll be made a prisoner and sent home to England eventually, but . . . but might I know where you live so I can look you up some day?" He offered the barest smile. "I've a mind to be a Virginian when I've seen this through."

Grayson reached out and squeezed his shoulder in a final gesture. "Come to Williamsburg and ask for me. Anyone can give you directions to my plantation."

Michaels nodded ever so slightly. "Then it's good-bye to you, sir, and to you, too, Miss Maggie."

"Good-bye, Paul," Maggie whispered, afraid she would break into tears.

Grayson took her hand and together they watched the boy join the ranks of the defeated army and walk off Surrender Field.

When Michaels was gone from sight, Grayson turned to her, his voice still filled with emotion. "When, Maggie. When will you marry me?" he asked.

She took Giipa's reins from him and began to lead the gelding off the field. "Today," she answered. "Today looks like a good day to me to be wed."

Lanterns swung, casting bright light in the darkness outside Commegys' Ordinary as Maggie stepped out the door, the bride of Major Grayson Thayer. A cheer rose among well-wishers as one of the sergeants in Grayson's regiment began a lively tune on an old fiddle.

Grayson followed behind Maggie, reaching to take her hand as his fellow soldiers crowded around to give their congratulations.

John had offered the use of his parlor for Maggie and Grayson to be married in, and though that might have been more elegant, the tavern where they'd met seemed far more fitting. The ceremony complete, the newlyweds had served their guests confiscated English wine and roasted boars Zeke and Les had rounded up in the woods. Well after midnight, Grayson and Maggie were finally taking their leave of the party to go to John's where they would spend the night.

Maggie accepted hand after hand and an occasional kiss on the cheek as the crowd of soldiers bade them farewell. Slowly they made their way to John's waiting carriage. Maggie laughed as she wrapped her arm around Grayson's waist and he brushed her lips against his.

"What's so funny?" he asked, still being jostled by the exuberant men.

"Nothing, I'm just happy," she answered, beaming. "Happy it's over with."

He laughed with her and pulled her against him, kissing her again, this time with such fervor that he brought a cheer from the soldiers.

"That's the way to see to it, Major!" a private shouted, raising a jack of ale.

"Just wish she'd married me instead of you," another hollered.

Maggie caught sight of Zeke, hanging back from the other men. She put out her hand and bashfully he came to her. She leaned to kiss him on his bearded cheek and he blushed.

"So where to now, Maggie girl?"

Maggie looked back to Grayson. "To Williamsburg. To Thayer's Folly."

Zeke nodded, scuffing his boot in the dirt.

"Where's Lyla?" Maggie asked.

He pointed behind him and Maggie followed with her eyes. There in the darkness of the tree was a small figure wrapped in a hooded cloak. Maggie lifted her forest-green skirts and pushed through the crowd of men, leaving Grayson behind. "Lyla?"

She stepped out from the tree. "Yes?"

Maggie offered her hands and took one of Lyla's. "You're going to marry Zeke, aren't you?"

She nodded. "He's a convincing man."

Maggie looked to Zeke and back at Lyla again. "So you'll live in Zeke's old house, I suppose. It's kind of small with just the three rooms and you with your sisters."

Zeke put his arm around Lyla's tiny waist.

"We'll get by."

"Well, seein' as how I won't be needing my house anymore, I thought you two might like the farm once the wounded men have been moved out."

"Your house," Zeke breathed. "There's no need to give us your farm!"

"I want you to take it. And I want you to take my da's tools. The town will be needing a good bootmaker." She winked at Zeke. "I'd say you know enough to get by."

"Someone say something about a decent bootmaker," Grayson called in a deep voice. He came up behind Maggie and wrapped his arms around her waist, nestling his face in her sweet-smelling hair. "I'm in need of a decent bootmaker." He lifted his foot to show half of the sole of his boot sagging. "I found myself a wench who claimed to be adequate, but I've had nothing but trouble since I first let her set her hands on them!"

Maggie began to giggle. Then Lyla, and finally Zeke joined in, his rich baritone voice filling the starlit night air.

"What's so funny?" Grayson asked, looking from one to the other. "What have I missed?"

Zeke shook his head as he dropped a kiss to Lyla's head. "What did you expect, you lettin' on like you were a bloody redcoat?"

Grayson looked at Maggie. "What's he talking about? What's my pretending to be a Brit got to do with my boots?"

Maggie covered her mouth with her palm, her laughter ringing out. Everything was going to be all right, wasn't it? He truly did love her and the baby she carried. It was going to be a fine life, being the wife of Grayson Thayer.

"What?" Grayson repeated, smiling down at her. Then his brow furrowed. "You didn't!"

She bit down on her lower lip a she took a step back. "It 'twasn't my fault. You were a Brit same as the rest of them!"

"You sabotaged my French boots!"

"It was months ago," she protested with laughter.

"How many times did I ask you to fix them?" he asked in disbelief.

Maggie couldn't get out a word for her laughter.

Grayson looked to Zeke who shrugged. "Guess she wanted to make certain you didn't get away, friend."

Grayson reached out to pull Maggie into his arms, his own laughter mingling with hers. "Ah, I love you, Maggie. I love you, Maggie mine."